M000251864

"So these guys are lugging in my supplies on their backs and on donkeys, and I didn't realize why I was tied up to the donkey. You know, led by a rope?" Deanna was regaling them with stories of her travels and they all smiled appreciatively at her description. "It was as I slipped off the narrow trail face first into the mud and started sliding down the steep slope, hitting tropical plants with my unmentionables, that I realized…that rope that kept me from falling down the mountainside. That was a good idea!"

They all started laughing, nearly choking on the beers they were sharing. "Oh, my gawd, Deanna! Did that really happen?" Magda wiped the tears away from the corner of her eye as she smiled at the story.

Deanna nodded. "Yeah, I've been to some pretty funky places. But you know what? It's one of the greatest things about what I do, seeing the sights. When they hauled my ass back up with that taut rope, I looked at that donkey and the phrase 'kiss my ass' had a whole new meaning."

They all collapsed into laughter again at her imagery.

A K'Anne Meinel Novel

Also by K'Anne Meinel:

In Paperback:

SHIPS *CompanionSHIP, FriendSHIP, RelationSHIP*
Long Distance Romance
Children of Another Mother
Erotica
The Claim
Bikini's Are Dangerous *The Complete Series*
Germanic
Malice Masterpieces *The First Five Books*
Represented
Timed Romance
Malice Masterpieces II *Books Six through Ten*
The Journey Home
Out at the Inn
Shorts
Anthology Volume 1
Lawyered
Malice Masterpieces III Books *Eleven through Fifteen*
Blown Away
Blown Away *The Alternate Cover*
Small Town Angel
Pirated Love

Pocket Paperbacks:

Mysterious Malice (Book 1)
Sapphic Surfer
Sapphic Cowgirl
Meticulous Malice (Book 2)
Mistaken Malice (Book 3)
Malicious Malice (Book 4)
Masterful Malice (Book 5)
Matrimonial Malice (Book 6)
Mourning Malice (Book 7)
Murderous Malice (Book 8)
Mental Malice (Book 9)
Menacing Malice (Book 10)
Marinating Malice (Book 17)

In E-Book Format:

Short Stories

Fantasy
Wet & Wet Again
Family Night
Quickie ~ Against the Car
Quickie ~ Against the Wall
Quickie ~ Over the Couch
Mile High Club
Quickie ~ Under the Pier
Heel or Heal
Kiss
Family Night 2
Beach Dreams
Internet Dreamers
Snoggered
The Rockhound
Stolen
Agitated
Love of my LIFE
Quickie in an Elevator, GOING DOWN?
Into the Garden
Menage a WHAT?
The Other Women

Novellas

Bikini's are Dangerous
Kept
Ghostly Love
Bikini's are Dangerous 2
On the Parkway
Stable Affair
Sapphic Surfer
Bikini's are Dangerous 3
Bikini's are Dangerous 4
Bikini's are Dangerous 5
Mysterious Malice (Book 1)
Meticulous Malice (Book 2)
Mistaken Malice (Book 3)
Malicious Malice (Book 4)
Masterful Malice (Book 5)
Matrimonial Malice (Book 6)
Mourning Malice (Book 7)
Murderous Malice (Book 8)
Sapphic Cowgirl
Sapphic Cowboi
Mental Malice (Book 9)
Menacing Malice (Book 10)
Charming Thief
~Snake Island~
Charming Thief
~Diamonds are a Girls Best Friend~
Minor Malice (Book 11)
Morally Malice (Book 12)
Morose Malice (Book 13)
Melancholy Malice (Book 14)
Mad Malice (Book 15)
Macabre Malice (Book 16)
Marinating Malice (Book 17)
Macerating Malice (Book 18)
Minacious Malice (Book 19)

E-Book Novels

SHIPS *CompanionSHIP, FriendSHIP, RelationSHIP*
Erotica Volume 1
Long Distance Romance
Bikini's Are Dangerous
The Complete Series
Malice Masterpieces
The First Five Books
To Love a Shooting Star
Children of Another Mother
Germanic
The Claim
Represented
Timed Romance
Malice Masterpieces II
Books Six through Ten
The Journey Home
Out at the Inn
Anthology Volume 1
Lawyered
Blown Away
Blown Away *The Alternate Cover*
Small Town Angel
Pirated Love

Videos

Biography of Books
Ships
Sapphic Surfer
Ghostly Love
Long Distance Romance
Germanic
Sensual Sapphic
Sapphic Cowgirl
Couples
Lie Next To Me
Sapphic Cowboi
Timed Romance
Readings (SHIPS)

K'ANNE MEINEL

Dear Deb -

Thanks for the editing!

K'Anne Meinel 6.1.16

DOCTORED

Publishing by Shadoe Publishing

DOCTORED

ISBN-13: 978-0692689998
ISBN-10: 0692689990

K'Anne Meinel is available for comments at
KAnneMeinel@aim.com
as well as on Facebook, Google +, or her blog @
http://kannemeinel.wordpress.com/
or on Twitter @ kannemeinelaim.com,
or on her website @
www.kannemeinel.com
if you would like to follow her to find out about stories and book's releases.

www.shadoepublishing.com

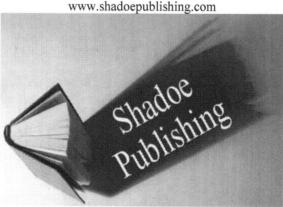

ShadoePublishing@gmail.com
Shadoe Publishing is a United States of America company

Edited by: Deb Amia
Cover by: K'Anne Meinel

PUBLISHER'S NOTE

This is a work of fiction. Names, characters, places, and incidents are the product of the author's imagination or are used fictitiously, and any resemblance to actual persons, living or dead, business establishments, events, or locales is entirely coincidental.

The publisher does not have any control over and does not assume any responsibility for author or third-party Web sites or their content.

CHAPTER ONE

"Hey! Where'd you get that huge bouquet from?" Bonnie asked her with a touch of innuendo and a sly grin.

"What? What bouquet?" Madison asked with a puzzled frown, looking around as though she could see them from her desk.

"The one at the nurses' station on the fourth. You didn't put them there deliberately?" she asked slyly, as though to get in on 'the secret.' She was actually hoping to ferret out more information.

"Why would I do that?" Madison stopped writing in the patient's chart and looked up.

"To show Tom that he isn't the only one interested? Payback for that bad date?"

Madison grinned ruefully at the ill-conceived idea of anyone being able to date Tom Masters. The arrogant asshole had told her equal rights meant he expected her to pay for her half of the expensive date he had taken her on. She shook her head. Had he sent flowers to make up for it? "I didn't see them," she told her friend, truthfully.

"Well, Sheila told me that they couldn't fit them on or in your locker so they decided everyone could enjoy them. There is no card though," Bonnie confided, and that confirmed that she had looked.

Madison rolled her eyes. Having friends among the staff could be a little bit of a pain in the ass. She had to be careful as she was their superior. She finished up the chart she was looking at, closed it, and filed it as she got up from the desk. "Guess I'll go have a look," she told her impatiently curious friend.

"Mind if I tag along?" Bonnie asked, falling into step beside her.

"Don't you have patients?" Madison asked, looking down at the shorter woman and stopping to give her a stern look. Friend or no friend, the patients came first.

Bonnie sighed and turned away, hoping that Madison would share who the flowers were from. She was certain they weren't from Tom—he was too self-absorbed to think of anyone…especially someone like Madison. She looked back to see Madison escaping into the stairwell instead of taking the elevator. She admired the clean lines of her nurse's uniform, the sterile whites instead of the scrubs that everyone else wore. It made her stand out, but then as a nursing supervisor she needed to. Her looks alone would have had her stand out. It wasn't that she was really that attractive, she just kind of grew on you. As you got to know her, you realized she was beautiful, but not in an obvious way. It was her personality that made her beautiful.

Madison went up to the fourth floor nurses' station and was astonished at the bouquet sitting there. Alyson assured her they were for her and she stared in consternation at the many Birds of Paradise along with the long grasses in the bouquet. It was simple and yet striking at the same time. The quantity of them was staggering.

"Ah, so who are these from?" Alyson asked, trying to dig for information. The other nurses and a few of the doctors were all gossiping. "Are they from Tom?" she slyly slipped in. Rumors and innuendo fueled the gossip mill, in between caring for patients.

Madison looked up from the massive bouquet and shook her head, first to clear it from her own surmising of who the bouquet was from, and second to refute the question. Tom wouldn't pay for something so outrageous. He'd make a penny scream before he let it go. "No, not from Tom," she assured the triage nurse.

"Oh, is there someone else…already?"

Madison looked at Alyson again. "No, there is no one else, but it's not from Tom," she said with absolute conviction. She also didn't want that guy getting credit where credit wasn't due, and Tom definitely didn't need the credit.

"Are you taking the bouquet now?"

"I'll come back after my shift for it." She was already wondering if it would fit in her Prius. Those stems were kind of long…perhaps on the floor. It was going to look gorgeous in her small living room on the dining room table.

She was asked about the flowers all during the rest of her shift, repeatedly denying they were from Tom. The fact that she didn't have anyone else to name and her answers being vague might have kept the gossip going. She wasn't happy when it spilled over into the operating room when she was trying to concentrate on her patients and her job.

"So, Madison. I saw that bush you got, sitting on the fourth floor nurses' station," Doctor Traff commented, smiling behind his mask to show he was teasing. The twinkle in his dark green eyes might have given it away too.

"Yesss," Madison said tightly from behind her own surgical mask, glancing up from the tray for only an instant.

"Clamp," he requested, and saw that she was right on the money, ready and waiting. She often anticipated what he needed and that made her a good nurse. She also followed up on the patients as much as any of the doctors. Many of the doctors liked working with her—she went above and beyond, and was extremely conscientious—and it was appreciated.

"So, who sent them?" he asked, making conversation as he worked.

Madison looked down into the gut briefly and returned her eyes to her tray. They didn't need more hands in there, much less eyes, and her job was to keep the tools of the trade available to the doctors. She just wanted the conversation to stop. Her nurses had been asking all day. "I don't know," she answered honestly. She was never so relieved as when the patient began to pump blood and the surgeon's idle conversation was cut off. He could now concentrate on saving a life instead of Madison's love life, or lack thereof.

"So, who do you think they are from?" Larry, another nurse, asked as they washed up after the surgery.

Madison rolled her eyes. The idle gossip wasn't going to stop. She was sick of it already and retreated into silence as she quickly changed. She glanced at the cleaning crew in the operating room and then checked off a few things on the chart before leaving.

Madison had a few more things to check, things she knew other nurses wouldn't check unless she followed up, but then she was thorough at her job. She changed into street clothes, not about to be seen in her nurse's uniform, and ended up on the fourth floor trying to carry the huge bouquet. There was no way she could easily walk it all the way down from the fourth floor, especially in the stairwell, so she pressed the button for the elevator. She saw many admiring glances and assumed they were for the enormous bouquet. It was really lovely, but she was embarrassed. Perhaps she should have left it at work, maybe divided it up and given it to a few patients. She wondered who it was from.

"Did you get in a fight?" Beth asked as she saw her maneuver onto the elevator with the bouquet, trying not to poke anyone in the eye with one of the sharp, pointy flowers or the long-bladed grasses.

"No," she replied simply, tired of the questions the flowers had engendered today.

"Are you seeing someone new?" Beth was determined to get more information.

"Nope," she grinned, hoping the doors would open again before further questions could occur to the woman.

The elevator stopped on the second level and a couple of people edged on, trying to fit in around the flowers. They eyed them warily…Bird of Paradise flowers could be used to maim, even unintentionally.

When Madison saw that one of the people who had gotten on the elevator was Tom, she seriously thought about using the flowers as a weapon. It would poke him quite nicely in the eye, one of which he was using to look at her suspiciously. She hadn't cheated. They had gone on one date only and that one had been a disaster. How dare he look at her like that! If she moved like so, it would accidentally poke him in the butt, but her humor wouldn't let her do the actual deed as the elevator settled on the first floor. He glanced at her and the flowers one more time before leaving the small box they were all in.

"You better go first," Beth offered generously. She had seen the look on Tom's face and couldn't wait to spread some rumors about it.

The flowers didn't fit well in her small Prius even if they were on the floor of the vehicle. They did, however, take up the whole dining room table and bring joy to her as she gazed at them over the wine she allowed herself after a full day's work. Who were they from though? That was the question she—and apparently many of the people she worked with—wanted answered. They were exotic and they were all over southern California, but this was a unique bouquet. Who had sent it to her?

Idly, she sat spinning the stem of her wine glass and gazing at the present she had received. She was trying not to read too much into it, but she couldn't help thinking about the who, the what, and the why. Her introspection was cut off as the children came into the house.

"Mom!" Chloe yelled with a smile. "Dad got us a puppy!" she said importantly as she came over for a hug.

Madison managed not to roll her eyes at Scott, taking her idea and going with it. It wasn't the first time…it wouldn't be the last.

"It's a shaggy beast," Conor said importantly, with all the dignity of an eight-year-old as he headed into the kitchen for a snack.

"A shaggy beast?" Madison nearly laughed as Scott came in and dropped off both children's backpacks.

"Hard day?" he asked as he saw her drain the remains of her wine. Then he saw the monstrous bouquet on her dining room table and turned to raise an eyebrow.

"No, not at all," she assured him, ignoring his questioning look. "A dog?"

"Yeah, we went to the pound after school. *Just* to look," he assured her. "Next thing I knew we had this shaggy, flea-bitten varmint."

She laughed, knowing the powers of persuasion her children possessed. "I'm sure you will adjust."

"It's going to cost me a fortune," he whined, trying to get her to see his side of things.

Madison was amused further. He had heard her suggestion that it was time for the children to have some responsibility and get a pet. He further wanted to be the hero and now had to deal with it.

"We went to Petco and apparently the dog needs one of everything," he lamented.

"Well, now you've done it," she assured him.

"Done what?" he asked, confused.

"You can't get rid of it now," she pointed out, knowing he wouldn't hesitate to take it back to the pound.

"Daddy, you won't get rid of Fluffy will you?" Chloe asked, sounding amazingly like her father with her whine.

"Of course not, honey," he assured her. "Now you go and play." He watched affectionately as she went off to the room that she shared with her brother in the tiny house.

Madison shook her head, knowing he'd backed himself into a corner and would expect her to get him out of it somehow. It really made more sense for her to have a dog in her small two-bedroom house with a yard than him in his small apartment, but she wouldn't rescue him, not this time. So many other times she had indeed gotten him out of his need to show off for the kids, but enough was enough.

"Here are your keys," he said as he handed over the keys to her minivan. She reluctantly handed him the keys to his Prius, preferring the smaller and more dependable vehicle to drive.

Madison was relieved when Scott left and she was alone with the kids. She needed her quiet time and sharing custody with him wasn't always easy. It was why she no longer wished to be married to him. He had needed so much of her time that it was like raising a third kid. She wanted a lover, not another responsibility. She wanted a partner, not someone who wanted to be taken care of, not someone who expected it. She sighed thinking about Scott and then her latest fiasco, Tom. Why the heck couldn't she meet someone nice who 'tripped her trigger' and could be a true partner? Someone who was adventurous and loving? Someone who didn't want something from her she wasn't prepared to give? She sighed again as she straightened one of the flowers and wondered who had sent her the absolutely outrageous bouquet.

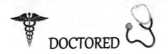

CHAPTER TWO

Madison had been working steadily for several weeks with just her normal Sunday and Monday days off. It meant that Scott took the kids every Saturday and she got to run errands and get things done on Monday when businesses were open and the kids weren't with her. She had every Sunday with the kids and they frequently went to the beach, hiking, or did something else together. They enjoyed each other and while they occasionally missed doing things as a family, at least Scott and she were cordial and could get along for the most part. He was still trying to puzzle out why she had divorced him last year. She just couldn't cope anymore, didn't want to try, and wasn't willing to put up with him anymore. She needed to be happy with herself and while she wasn't *yet*, at least she was happy with the kids.

She was working so much she hadn't caught up on the gossip of who was dating whom, the new arrivals, who was leaving the hospital to work elsewhere, and other happenings. She was, however, generating gossip because she had been getting a bouquet of some type every week. Every. Single. Week. This last week she had gotten six African violets of different types and varieties. She hadn't known there were different kinds. She'd seen them at the store, thought they were beautiful, but never purchased one for herself. Now she had six in her windows at home and she loved them. Whoever was sending these things had put a lot of thought into it and she wondered who it was. She was enjoying the mystery of it, but didn't like the gossip it generated.

This week it was a couple of Proteas. She had never even seen these flowers here. The last time she saw them was in…Africa. It was at that moment that she realized each of the bouquets, each of the plants she had received, all had Africa in common. Was someone playing some sort of trick on her? Few, if any, realized she had worked with the Red Cross in Africa a decade ago. Why would someone do something like this? Now she was feeling kind of uneasy.

Because she had been working so hard, she hadn't paid attention to the gossip, not that she normally did. Today she heard her coworkers at lunch talking about the new doctor, a Doctor Kearney who had been romanced into coming to work here at their hospital. Apparently he was hard to get hold of and had been highly sought after from various facilities all over the world. An infectious disease specialist, he had worked in the jungles. When someone mentioned Africa, Madison began to rack her brain trying to remember if she had met a Doctor Kearney there in her time, but couldn't recall anyone by that name. It was troubling to her.

"Apparently she told Doctor Stanoslovsky to get the *hell* out of *her* surgery," Bette was saying as she finished her yogurt at lunch.

Madison clued in as she had found herself daydreaming about Africa, something that seemed to be on her mind a lot recently. "Who told Stan-the-man that?" she asked, laughing. The man was a pompous know-it-all and they called him Stan-the-man behind his back as Stanoslovsky was such a mouthful.

"Doctor Kearney," she said exasperated. "Weren't you listening?"

The others chuckled at her and Madison flushed. "Yes, I was listening, but you said her…I thought Doctor Kearney was a man…."

Shaking her head, Bonnie chimed in. "No, no, no, Doctor Kearney is a *woman*," she clarified. "Pay attention," she teased.

Trying to catch up, Madison shook her head, her red curls bouncing, laughing at her friends and coworkers. "Okay, okay. I've been out of it," she admitted.

"Haven't you met Doctor Kearney yet?" Bette asked, curious.

She shook her head again as she grabbed a bite. Swallowing she answered, "No, haven't seen her," she admitted.

"Oh, she's nice. Very down to earth. She's been all over the world. Amazing!" Bette gushed.

"She's really attractive too, in a hard kind of way," Sheila piped up and then blushed. Everyone knew Sheila was bisexual.

A few felt the need to tease her about that and proceeded to do so for the next few minutes.

"How is she in surgery, and why did she kick Stan-the-man out of surgery?" Madison finally interrupted the teasing to ask.

"She's innovative, and that's what he got on his high horse about. Apparently her technique was something he hadn't seen before. When he kept trying to second-guess her, she kicked his arrogant ass out. Doctor Foster backed her up as it was her surgery and she was doing a terrific job." Bette was pleased as all get out that he had been put in his place. Some doctors treated the nurses horribly and he was one of them.

"Isn't that the patient who had gangrene or something?" someone else asked.

Bonnie nodded and put in, "Yeah, Doctor Kearney used maggots to clean out the wound before she would operate."

"Maggots?" Madison asked, a distasteful look on her face. Looking down at her meal, it suddenly didn't seem as tasty and she pushed it aside. She went to take a drink of her juice and looked at it suspiciously—as though it carried some of the disgusting slugs in it.

"Yeah, she got some sterilized maggots or something, and put them in the wound. They ate all the diseased flesh so she was able to operate and close up the healthy tissue," Bette explained and then laughed at Madison's expression. "Come on, you have to admit that's clever. They eat only the bad flesh, the corpulent stuff, and leave the healthy tissue."

"Yeah, but *maggots*," she sneered, her nose wrinkling at the thought.

"She explained to Doctor Foster that she had seen the technique used before and felt it was appropriate here as they didn't want to be cutting out all that flesh and get too much of the good stuff. This way, all that was left was to kill the maggots and clean the wound, stitching together the remaining healthy flesh."

"It's known as maggot debridement therapy," Bonnie explained

Madison was done with lunch and with the conversation. She got up to take her tray to the trash when Bonnie piped up with, "There she is," using her chin to point at the doctor who had just come into the cafeteria. She was surrounded by the crème de la crème of the doctors in their small-knit community, all vying for her attention.

Madison looked up to see high-top sneakers in rainbow colors. She had never seen any like that before. They were very colorful…and very bright. Her eyes followed the high-tops up the legs. Long slacks on a lean waist led up to a buxom figure that was very attractive. Her doctor's lab coat was a brilliant white, her name embroidered across the lapel in red versus the black that the rest of the doctors had. As Madison's gaze took in the woman she stared, wondering if she had met her before. She looked very familiar…and yet…not. She looked to be in her early twenties, but for all her experience, she had to be in her thirties or forties at least. Her hair was a deep brown and had shades of blonde and more red streaks in it. Madison couldn't tell if it was real, natural, or colored. She watched the woman for a moment, trying to figure out if she knew her and why she seemed so familiar. It was as the woman lifted her hand, the one with a large signet ring on the ring finger, and began rubbing her eyebrow thoughtfully with the tips of her fingers, that Madison realized she did indeed know the woman. The woman wasn't in her twenties after all, she was the same age as Madison's thirty-six years. The gesture so familiar, so endearing, she knew who that woman was in an instant. Just then the woman looked across the cafeteria to find Madison gazing at her and although at first startled, she smiled in delight. She said something to her companions and came across the lunchroom to meet her.

"Hello, Maddie, it's been a while," she greeted her familiarly.

All in an instant she recalled how she had met Doctor Kearney. She hadn't known her as Doctor Kearney…then. It had been a misunderstanding of gross proportions.

As Maddie and three other relief workers drove out to the site in East Africa to begin their tour of duty with UNICEF they were admiring the countryside…the hot, desolate countryside. It was dusty, it was barren, but it wasn't what any of them had expected. There were rolling hills covered in brown grasses, brush, even occasional trees.

"This is our dry season," the rich South African accent of their guide told them. He explained that the seasons consisted of the rainy season and the dry season, not much more than that. "It is hot even in our winter here," he rolled his 'Rs' richly and with relish.

Maddie decided she liked how he spoke and smiled whenever he looked her way, as if to encourage his explanations of what they were seeing and what he was telling. "Do you get floods?" she asked to get him to keep speaking.

"Yes, very badly," his own million-watt smile faded, the rich white teeth against his very black skin now hiding behind his grimace as he explained how dire the consequences of flooding could be to the people they would be helping. "It is very primitive," he explained as he gestured at the countryside, "like nothing you are used to." He went on to explain how they were teaching primitive people modern techniques to farm and use the land. "They don't listen," he said sadly. "They want to plow up everything and not save the land in spots to let the water run off safely, which leads to massive erosion. This is very bad."

The ride to their camp in Mamadu took three hours from the port on the Red Sea that they had flown into. Lamish was a coveted port and one of the many reasons for conflict in this part of Africa. By the time they arrived they were all covered in dust, half asleep, and very cranky. The two Americans—Maddie and a farmer from the Midwest who was going to help to teach new techniques—were acquainted since they had met on their plane from Paris to Africa. There were two others: one, a nurse like Maddie from Australia, and two, a bureaucrat from Switzerland. Maddie was certain the farmer wouldn't last long. He had ideas to help the natives, but didn't want to learn from them. The little she had surmised from him showed him to be narrow-minded. She had found you could learn a lot from people if you just listened. He was so certain he was going to change their world, he forgot they'd been husbanding this land for centuries.

"No doctor?" Lakesh had asked when he picked them up in the port. Their luggage was stacked high on the battered Rover he was driving and tied down to the roof.

The four of them exchanged looks and shrugged.

"None of you is Doctor Cooper?" he inquired. His intense black eyes looking out at them, a stark contrast to the whites of his eyes that were tinged with a little yellow. Maddie wondered about that yellow and if it could be jaundice.

They shook their heads and introduced themselves. Maddie was a nurse and Harlan a farmer. Leida was the other nurse from Australia, and the bureaucrat was Thomas, pronounced 'Toe-mass.' He made sure to pronounce it slowly, clearly and articulately so they all got it right. Maddie hid her amusement at his arrogance.

"Hmmm, they won't be happy without Doctor Cooper," he stated as he herded them into the Rover. Three sat in the back, Maddie, Leida, and Harlan, and Thomas took the front seat as though he belonged there.

Leida introduced herself to Maddie saying, "I guess us nurses will be working together, eh?"

"I'm sure we will," and they chatted a while with Harlan between them. He tried to contribute, but his opinions centered around what his farming techniques would do to enrich these poor underdeveloped countries' economics. Maddie and Leida had exchanged a look that showed they had a mutual understanding and opinion about that. Thomas ignored them all except to talk to Lakesh occasionally, usually to ask how much longer the trip would be.

"Doctors Without Borders, they fly in, they fly out," Lakesh explained, a quarter of the way into their long drive. "Doctor Cooper supposed to fly in, miss flight," he further explained. "Then to drive, but you no see." His pigeon English was endearing, at least to Maddie's ears. He didn't point it out, and Maddie wondered if she was the only one to realize there wouldn't have been room in the Rover for another person.

They were nearly to their destination when they saw another Rover on the side of the road. A shapely derriere was visible as someone leaned into the engine with the hood propped up. At the noise of their vehicle, the head popped up out of the engine. They were all surprised to see the grease-spattered face of a white woman. She made it worse by rubbing her nose on the back of her hand and trying to flag them down. Lakesh slowed their vehicle.

"You need help?" he said jovially in English.

"I'm headed for Mamadu. Am I on the right track?" a decidedly Bostonian accent greeted him with a smile.

"Yes, this is the road to Mamadu," he confirmed. "You a mechanic?" his voice sounded hopeful.

"Well," she said, spreading her arms and showing her greasy hands, "when I have to be."

"Ah, good. We need 'em mechanics," he assured her.

"Well, I'll catch up to you all later," she said dismissively since no one had offered to help. They all looked at her curiously. The deep browns and blondes of her hair couldn't hide the definitive red streaks in it. She was perspiring in the hot African sun, the grease and the sweat mingling on her face and dripping into a t-shirt that barely hid her assets. Maddie and the others smiled and nodded. They could get acquainted when they all met in Mamadu. Lakesh drove on and waved. If she had wanted help, he would have stopped, but she seemed to have it well in hand.

They arrived in the camp and were immediately surrounded by other relief workers. The Red Cross sign was prevalent on the buildings as well as the supplies they had brought with them. UNICEF and other organizations contributed to this ragtag collection of helpers. There were two full-time doctors, no nurses, and many assistants. Most of the assistants were black Africans whose tribes had been decimated by disease and war in this part of the continent. Trying to fight back against the diseases was the reason that Maddie and Leida were here. Trying to get the population back on its feet and feed itself was Harlan and others' jobs.

"Hi, I'm Richard Burton, not to be confused with the famous Richard Burton, but *Doctor* Burton and I run this little outpost of iniquity," he introduced himself with a self-deprecating smile. He was a tall, spare man, balding, with glasses and a French accent.

"I'm so happy you are both here," he said to Maddie and Leida. "We've been in need of nurses for months. I hope you will help train our assistants as your time is valuable and they learn fast."

"What happened to the other nurses you had?" Leida asked as she grabbed a box of supplies that Lakesh handed down, still sporting that jovial smile accentuating the startling contrast between his white teeth and black skin.

Doctor Burton looked uncomfortable. "You might as well know…they were killed in a small skirmish east of here. They were both male nurses and helping some of the villagers." He was reluctant to tell them any more so he quickly changed the subject. "This is Alex Whitley," he indicated another man who came up to grab a box. "He is in charge of the day to day," he explained. "Which one of you is Thomas?" he asked, using the American connotation of the name.

"I am Thomas," he said frostily, correcting the pronunciation to Toe-mass.

"Oh, excuse me," Burton said with a smile. "You will report to Alex there," he nodded towards another man as he took a box, then indicated the two women should follow him.

"Who do I report to?" Harlan asked as he took two boxes, showing off his bulging muscles.

"And who are you?" Burton asked, his French accent more pronounced.

"I'm Harlan Baker, I'm a farmer," he said proudly.

"Oh, I didn't know they had sent you. I was hoping you were Doctor Cooper," he said, almost insultingly. Recovering, he quickly added, "You'll meet one of the locals who will show you their farming techniques."

"Aren't I here to show them farming?" he asked, confirming his earlier conversations with the others.

"I'm sure you will learn from them as they learn from you," Burton replied confidently. He showed them where to store the supplies, some of the assistants quickly opening the boxes to see what they had received and then putting them away. Maddie found herself helping. She couldn't speak the language, neither could Leida, but they were having fun pantomiming with the assistants who smiled effusively as they showed the two of them where things went.

It was late when the two women were shown where they would be bunking. It was a large military style tent with a wood floor, six cots, and thick beams holding up the canvas. "You are here," one of the locals said in broken English, indicating two of the unused cots. There was a third, but it had a backpack on it. The others were obviously in use since the mattresses on them were made with sheets and blankets.

Maddie thanked the woman who had shown them to their tent and looked around. "Wow," she said as she realized how sparse it was.

"You weren't expecting a five-star hotel, were you?" Leida teased.

Maddie laughed and shook her head. "Nope, I expected to rough it."

"Bugger that for a game of soldiers."

"What the hell does that mean?"

"Rather you than me," she interpreted for her, laughing at the difference in English. It was the same language, but with so many different phrases.

"Is that an Australian colloquialism?" Maddie asked in laughter.

"British actually, but it certainly is rather colorful isn't it?"

"Oh, it's very colorful here, don't you think?" Maddie said wonderingly, looking forward to her work and more of the wonders she had already seen.

"Just look out for things that crawl and slither," another voice said from the tent flap doorway. The two nurses turned. A redhead stood there in khaki shorts and combat boots, her socks going halfway up her legs. Her shirt was ripped at the sleeves and sweat stains formed a V down the front and sides. "Hi. I'm Lenora, Lenny for short," she said as she came into the tent. "I'm one of the school teachers," she explained.

"I'm Maddie, and that is Leida," she said with smile as she shook Lenny's outstretched hand.

"Oh, you're American," she said with a returned smile. "I'm Canadian," she explained her own accent.

"I'm an Aussie," Leida shook the Canadian's hand as well. Her accent gave her away.

"Wow, we have all corners of the globe taken care of," Lenny joked. "I'm here to escort you two to the chow tent."

"I didn't know I was hungry until just this moment," Leida complained good-naturedly.

"Ah, the food isn't much, but there is plenty of it."

"I would love a shower at some point," Maddie sighed as she pulled the sticky shirt away from her sweating body.

"Now that is an interesting topic." Lenny explained that they got each other, or one of the locals who hung about, to pour water in a pan that filtered down and gave them a shower. It wasn't much, but they could get clean.

"How often do you shower?" Maddie asked. She'd known it was going to be rough before she joined up. It was a combined effort coming to these camps where the Peace Corps, the Red Cross, and UNICEF, as well as other charities and organizations like Doctors Without Borders or Medecins Sans Frontieres (MSF) helped out. This area of Africa had, up until a few years previously, been a battle zone. Now it was considered relatively safe.

"A couple of times a week. Don't worry, you'll get one," she assured the new nurse. She smiled. She'd already heard that they had dug in and started working immediately and that impressed people more than their cleanliness. They'd adjust. She showed them to the tent that housed their meals. Long tables consisting of plywood or planks made up the tables.

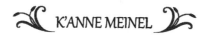

The food was hot…it wasn't tasty, but it was filling. The fruit mixed in with some of it was different than either of the women had tasted before, but at least their empty stomachs were filled. They both saw Harlan momentarily as he talked earnestly to someone on some subject and they met others they would be working with.

"No one has seen Doctor Cooper yet?" one of the other women asked Doctor Burton when he came by to greet them. She worked in the clinic keeping the beds clean. She wasn't a nurse or a medical person, but she was a hearty volunteer or relief worker and enjoyed what help she could give these people. She was from Switzerland, or so she said.

"Nope, I haven't seen him although we did get a bonus today. Some mechanic drove in," he indicated with his head the blonde/brunette they had seen on their drive in to Mamadu. She was talking animatedly with a couple of the locals, in French. She wasn't completely clean, but she looked even younger than they had thought earlier.

"Were you expecting a mechanic?" the Swiss woman, Magda, asked.

"Nope, but she's welcome," he assured her.

Magda immediately became suspicious as she looked at the woman across the tent who was obviously enjoying herself as she talked rapidly. Her hands were gesturing. The grease was gone, but still lined her fingernails. "You don't think it odd that a mechanic, which we desperately need, shows up? Especially a female one?"

Looking thoughtful, Burton glanced at the woman he had so readily let into their inner circle. When Lakesh had introduced her as a mechanic, he had just accepted it at face value. It didn't occur to him to question her too much. Magda had a point. He walked across the tent to Alex and murmured to him. The two of them got up and went over to ask the mechanic more about herself. The conversations began to quiet as others caught on to some sort of drama about to happen and wanted to hear.

"Excuse me," Burton interrupted the woman's conversation. His French was clear and precise.

"Yes?" she asked, flashing a smile of interest.

"You said you were a mechanic?" he asked, not sure how else to start this conversation.

She laughed, a hearty one at that, as though he had just told a joke that they were all sharing in. She shook her head to the negative. "I never said that, he did," she answered, pointing at Lakesh. Lakesh, understanding French, began to look alarmed. She wound down from her laugh and smiled again. "I am a mechanic of sorts," she said as she got up from the bench. Holding out her hand she said, "Allow me to introduce myself, I'm Deanna Cooper…*Doctor* Deanna Cooper," she stressed.

"From Doctors Without Borders?" he asked dumbly in return.

She chuckled as she nodded, almost hesitantly. "Yes, were you expecting another doctor?"

He smiled at the silly question. "No, but I was expecting a man."

She nodded again. "Yes, people are frequently expecting the D to stand for Dan and not Deanna." She was trying to let him off the hook easily, not to make a scene, but she was well aware that the tent had quieted as he confronted her.

"But you're so young!" he burst out, already feeling consternation at the grave mistake he had already made.

She nodded again, the look in her eye still one of amusement. "I know," she agreed. She said nothing further as she waited. She could hear several others around her shifting in their seats as they waited for him to make some sort of a decision.

"I wasn't expecting someone of your expertise to…" he realized how insulting he had just been and shut his mouth. Grabbing her still-outstretched hand, he shook it warmly. "I am sorry for the mix-up," he tried to apologize lamely.

"Don't think about it anymore," she advised. "Come, sit, eat," she invited, indicating a vacant seat at their table.

"I have several things to do," he hedged, still feeling foolish. "We will talk later?" he asked meaningfully. He meant to get to the bottom of things. This, this *woman*, this *child* was far too young to be a surgeon of some note. He had been promised a specialist. Doctor D. Cooper was an expert on tropical diseases and a surgeon to boot. He had expected the doctor to arrive by plane, but they had called and said the doctor had been delayed and would be arriving in Lamish. He had assumed that Lakesh would pick *him* up! Someone, somewhere, was pulling his leg and he intended to get to the truth!

She nodded and smiled again as he left, his face flaming. She continued her conversation with the locals as though it had never happened. The noise level of the tent slowly resumed.

Magda had whispered the translation from French to English so that the two nurses would be apprised of what had just happened. Maddie was grateful. Her student French wouldn't hold and she only caught a word here and there, but she hoped to improve it with practice. She looked at the young woman across the tent thoughtfully. The blonde was leaning on a hand, her fingertips rubbing along her brow absentmindedly, occasionally tugging at the hairs. Maddie didn't realize how long she stared and then blushed as the blonde suddenly looked up, directly at her. Flashing a friendly smile, she resumed her conversation.

Bonnie and Leida, along with Magda and Lenny, took a tour of the camp. There were brush huts that housed some of the local relief workers. Their various nationalities were a dizzying array of tribes from the African countries. So many were now homeless due to the wars in this part of the world. Mamadu was in what was now a relatively safe area after years of conflict between the various nations.

Some of the sturdier buildings housed the makeshift hospital, the school, and a meeting place of sorts. The village elders used it for meetings and in a pinch it could be used as an outreach of the hospital. They had been fortunate that only twice in the ten years since Mamadu came to be had they had to use it.

"Don't drink any water that has not been filtered," Magda advised.

"And don't sit down without looking first," Lenny added.

"Why is that?" Maddie asked.

It was Leida who answered instead of the other two who had been in country longer. "Snakes and bugs," she answered the second statement first. "I assume the water has been tainted somehow?"

"With all the mining and war, they have poisoned the water for human consumption. You'll get a case of dysentery that could kill you if you aren't careful," Magda answered.

Maddie had known that. The classes she had attended back in the States had prepared her for coming to Africa. She had been given shots, education, and a crash course in some medical training beyond her normal nursing duties. Being here, seeing it first-hand, was a lot different. She looked out at the countryside, seeing the beauty and wondering at the ugliness she had heard about including possible war, soldiers, and bandits. The locals she had met had all been pleasant and friendly and she felt comfortable around them.

"How big a snake are we talking here?" she asked to make a joke.

"They have all sorts here," Lenny smiled, seeing this nurse was made of sterner stuff. She went on to describe a few, but basically most of it was common sense. Don't sit under anything that had an overhanging branch. Don't kick at a log and cause it to roll, you didn't know what you might disturb. Don't drink the water. "You also don't want to go out unless you are in pairs," she advised. "The natives are friendly," she said smiling at some of the children who came to hang around them, "but you never know. Don't go too far without telling someone." She spoke rapidly to the children in a dialect that sounded pretty, but which the two newcomers had no hope of understanding. The children laughed and went running off.

The woman showed them the entire camp. It wasn't too large, but it wasn't small either. The natives that lived there were all smiling and inviting. They looked so different; not only from each other, but from what Maddie had previously seen. The beads and jewelry they wore was quite exotic. Leida, who had worked with Aborigines back in Australia, would later confide how much more exotic these people were from her natives back home.

As the sun set, they headed back to their tent together. The sixth bed was obviously to be occupied by this mysterious and young Doctor

Cooper. Maddie wondered at who occupied the fifth until Magda mentioned it was for one of the locals who felt she should be with the doctors and nurses. She was a magician among the tribes and insisted on this courtesy. She embraced everything that was white and this included a cot, a mattress, sheets, and a pillow. "Her name is Hamishish," she explained. The name sounded foreign and pretty to the American.

"Where is she now?" Maddie asked. They were gathering their bathing suits to wash up in. Magda had promised to pour water for the newbies and both Maddie and Leida had embraced the idea after their long, hot trip and the work they had already done.

"Oh, she comes and goes. If she doesn't get 'honored' into sleeping with some young buck, she'll be back," Magda told them airily. They exchanged looks, wondering what she meant by that.

She took them to the showers and dipped a bucket of water out of the large barrels. "Don't drink the water," she cautioned for the umpteenth time, "but you can bathe in this," she explained as she climbed the steps behind the shower and poured the first bucket into the trough that would allow it to shower down.

Maddie took the first 'shower.' She rinsed her body with the first bucketful. Quickly she lathered up with the soap she had been advised to bring. The next bucket allowed her to rinse that soap off.

"If you want to wash your hair, it will take two more buckets," Magda told her. The tone said she didn't want to keep lugging up the heavy buckets and there was still Leida's shower to arrange. Maddie took the hint and finished quickly, drying herself down briefly, but allowing the air to evaporate the moisture quickly. She wrapped the towel around her hips like a skirt.

"You may want to buy one of those," Magda told her as she indicated what the locals were wearing—colorful and beautiful clothing in this wilderness—the wrap around their bodies was like a sarong. The more colorful the better it seemed. It matched their jewelry and beads. The beads were carefully woven into their hair and in long necklaces around their necks as well as bracelets around their wrists, upper arms, and ankles.

Leida took the hint and only allowed Magda to pour two bucketsful for her shower too. They quickly returned to their tent.

Brushing out her hair, Maddie quickly felt the fatigue of the day, a full stomach, and the stress of travel envelop her. She finished brushing and put her things away in a footlocker next to her bed. She lay down for 'just a minute' and was soon asleep. Leida followed suit. They never heard the blonde known as Doctor Cooper come in. Later, much later, Hamishish returned and fell into her cot, snoring blissfully from her full day attending *her* people.

CHAPTER THREE

When Maddie woke the next day, she lay there a moment as she tried to orient herself. She listened to the unfamiliar sounds of the camp, to birds she had never heard before, and to the sounds of her tent mates. She heard the common, everyday sounds: a sigh, a snort, and even someone passing gas in their sleep. She smiled and laughed to herself. She was looking forward to this adventure. She'd signed up for six months and knew it would look good on her resume. She sat up and looked around, seeing that Leida was still asleep in the bunk next to hers and that Lenny was gone from her cot, as was Magda.

She saw the mechanic-turned-doctor sit up at about the same time she did.

"Good morning," the woman called solo voce so that they wouldn't wake the still-sleeping Leida.

"Good morning," Maddie returned with a smile. She wondered if the doctor had worked it all out with Doctor Burton. She had to agree, the woman looked entirely too young to be a doctor. Maddie reached down for her clothes at the end of her bed.

"Shake them out," the other woman hissed, still quietly so as not to awaken Leida.

Startled, Maddie looked at the woman and saw her exuberantly shaking out her own clothes before she unselfconsciously whipped off her shirt and pulled a bra on. Maddie hastily turned away to give her some privacy as she shook out her own bra and put it on under her nightshirt before pulling the shirt off and putting another on. By the time she managed to get dressed under her nightclothes for modesty's sake, the doctor was already pulling on her boots and tapping them on the floor to get her feet in them. As Maddie was reaching for her boots, she heard the doctor again.

"Tap them out, upside down," she called a little louder. Leida moved slightly as though she was beginning to awaken.

Annoyed at the commands to do things she should have done on her own, but had forgotten, Maddie turned first one boot, and then the other upside down and smacked them against the frame of her cot. She was glad she did. Some sort of insect fell out of the second boot and scurried away before she could see what it was exactly. If she had put her stocking-clad foot into her boot without checking, she might have gotten stung or bitten. Not knowing what it was that had taken refuge in her boot, she shuddered at the thought. Quickly, she put her boots on as the doctor remade her bed, her back to Maddie.

Maddie followed the doctor's lead, making her own bed.

"Would you like to go to breakfast together?" the perky voice was now at her side.

Maddie jumped, not expecting someone who was wearing boots to be that quiet on their wooden floor.

"Oh, gawd. I'm sorry," she tried to hide her amusement at startling Maddie, and failed.

"It's okay, I'm just jumpy," Maddie smiled in return as she finished making her bed. "And yes, I'd like to go to breakfast with you, but I have to stop at the…." She blushed at the need to use the facilities. Stupid, she knew, since she was in the medical field where being inconvenienced like that was part of the everyday scenario with patients.

"Yeah, me too," the doctor smiled in understanding.

"Hey, wait for me," a sleep-filled voice said from the bed next to Maddie's.

"You, sleepyhead," Maddie teased.

"It'll just take me a minute to get ready," Leida said and promptly got tangled in her bedclothes and fell to the floor.

"Are you all right?" the doctor asked, concerned, as she helped the Australian up from the floor.

"Just tired," she grouched as she thanked the woman and grabbed her clothes.

"Shake them out," the other two women said in unison and then, exchanging a look, laughed.

"While she is getting ready, will you help me bring in a few boxes?" the doctor inquired of Maddie.

"Sure," she answered as she followed the blonde out of the tent, giving Leida some privacy while she got ready.

The Rover the doctor had been fixing the previous day was parked not too far from their tent. The sides were all up now and it was also locked. "I don't know why I bother," the doctor muttered as she opened it and reached in the back.

"Why do you say that?" Maddie asked as she was handed two fairly light boxes to carry.

"Anyone with a knife can slit the sides," she was told.

Maddie had to agree, as the woman reached in the back for a couple more boxes of her own. Her shapely derriere looked nice in the khakis she had slid on. Her legs were very tanned from the edge of the shorts to the tops of the socks she was wearing above her boots that reached mid-calf. Maddie looked away and out at the camp, noticing the locals were very active.

"I'll help you with that," another voice could be heard as they turned to take the boxes into their tent. They both turned to see Doctor Burton hurrying up, hands upstretched.

"We got it," Doctor Cooper answered with a smile.

"Medical supplies are not to be stored in our tents," he said disapprovingly.

Maddie hesitated to go in, but Doctor Cooper bumped into her when she stopped. "Oh, these are my personal medical supplies," she answered as she encouraged Maddie to continue into their tent.

"Medical supplies are for the benefit of all," he continued to argue, reaching for one of the boxes that Doctor Cooper was carrying.

"Not these," she said shortly, in a no-nonsense voice. She turned her body so he couldn't get at the boxes she was carrying in, following the now-moving Maddie into their tent.

Doctor Burton wasn't about to let it go and followed them in.

"Crikey!" the half-dressed Leida shrieked, not expecting a man to enter their tent.

"Oh, I'm so sorry!" Doctor Burton turned around immediately. "Doctor Cooper, may I speak to you?" he asked in a stern voice, facing the entrance of the tent, his back to the room at large.

Maddie knew the sound of a doctor out of sorts. He was angry and embarrassed, and she could see that Doctor Cooper couldn't care a wit. She took her boxes to the doctor's cot and stood there as the blonde put hers on the cot, then slid them, one at a time, under her bed. She took the boxes from Maddie's arms with a smile and slid those under as well. "You certainly may," the blonde answered the doctor's demanding tone. With a wink, she hurried back to the entrance where he stood. Maddie went to help Leida make her bed, wanting to find something to do while the two doctors butted heads.

"All medical supplies are to be shared among our people," Doctor Burton began frostily as he indicated they should leave the tent with a nod of his head. It clearly stated, 'outside' without words.

Doctor Cooper smiled, showing she wasn't put off by his tone or demeanor. "I agree," she told him in a perky tone that she knew would irritate him. "That's why the rest of those boxes in the back of my Rover are for your clinic."

"But those," he began, his thumb pointing back at the four boxes that she and Maddie had taken into her tent.

"Are for me," she told him dismissively. "Give me a hand with these?" she indicated the boxes in the back of the Rover, effectively changing the subject.

Doctor Burton looked at the pile of boxes with the distinctive red cross on the side and read some of the labels. He practically salivated at some of what he read. If that was what was really in those boxes, they needed these things desperately here at the clinic. He called to a few people he recognized to help carry things over to the supply rooms, and the Rover was soon emptied. He had his concerns about this young doctor that looked like she should be in high school, but her folder showed her to be very competent. He wondered who she knew to get an assignment such as this. Her qualifications were even better than his and he resented that; he had so many more years of experience. This, this *cheerleader* wasn't going to show him up!

Doctor Cooper noticed that Doctor Burton had his dander up. She wasn't surprised. Those in authority frequently did when they met her. She also noticed he never thanked her for the supplies she had hauled in here for his little clinic. She knew that clinics like this were always short on things and she had brought everything she could fit in the back of her Rover that she knew would be beneficial to the clinic. From medicines to surgical gloves, she had brought a good quantity. A simple thank you wouldn't have hurt the man, but he was already angry about the mechanic mix-up. She had learned a long time ago that if she was going to work in the tropics, she needed to know how to be self-sufficient and fixing her own vehicle wasn't too much to ask.

"Hey, you two ready?" she asked the two nurses. She hadn't learned either of their names and set about remedying that as she saw that the Australian's bed was made and she was dressed. "Hi, I'm Doctor Cooper," she came forward with her hand out to be heartily shaken by the woman from down under. "It's Deanna to my friends," she promised with a smile, offering that friendship.

"I'm Leida Hanson," she smiled in return, appreciating the introduction.

"We didn't introduce ourselves earlier," Deanna said, turning to the other woman with her hand out.

"I'm Madison MacGregor, Maddie to my friends," she smiled.

"Maddie MacGregor, that has a ring to it," the Bostonian accent was apparent, and there was perhaps a little bit of the Irish.

"Yes, I've heard it all my life," she said with a long-suffering sigh.

"Oy, don't let it get to you," she said with a friendly pseudo-Irish brogue.

They all shared a laugh.

"Can we get this going? I'm floating," Leida complained good-naturedly and rocked from foot to foot for emphasis.

They all used the facilities, such as they were. A set of curtained-off areas with a hole in the ground, a bag of lime next to them, and a toilet seat on a frame, nothing special. At least it had a grass roof to ward off any rain, not that it would matter in the wet season.

"How long are you here for?" Maddie asked the doctor as they made their way to the meal tent.

"Not sure, depends a lot on how much I'm needed," Deanna answered.

"I'm sure as a doctor you are needed a lot," Leida put in.

"Yeah, unfortunately that is true," Deanna said in a tone that sounded sad. "And fortunately, I love what I do." Her tone had changed immediately to the chipper one that she had used earlier to annoy Doctor Burton.

"How long have you been working in Africa?" Maddie asked as they entered the food tent to get in line and get a tray.

"About a year with Doctors Without Borders. Before that I was in South America for a while."

They picked at their food. It wasn't great looking, but it was food. They had eggs and some sort of meat that looked like bacon but wasn't, as well as plenty of coffee and tea.

As they went to sit down at an empty bench, Leida was the one to bring up the elephant in the room. "You don't look old enough to have been a doctor that long," she hid her blush behind a napkin, realizing she had been impertinent.

But Deanna smiled. She knew others would be listening because the tent was full. They were speaking English, but the rumors—despite other languages being spoken here—would abound. "I was a child prodigy. I finished college at fourteen. I was a doctor by the time I was twenty-one, a surgeon actually," she clarified. "I've been working at this, infectious diseases and tropical diseases, for five years now." That put her at twenty-six, old enough to practice, but with a face of a sixteen-year-old.

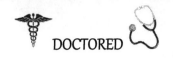

"Where did you do your residency?" Magda spoke up from a neighboring table proving that she, and others, had been listening in avidly.

"I was at Boston and then I went to Switzerland for infectious diseases so I could specialize," she explained, switching to French for the woman's benefit, but repeating it in English for the others who were listening.

"You've done a lot in your young life," Maddie commented, realizing they were letting their breakfasts get cold by all their questions, and finally digging in.

"Yeah, and I'm going to do a lot more," she commented wryly, digging in herself.

CHAPTER FOUR

Doctor Cooper indeed proved to be valuable. They found that she spoke German, French, a smattering of Italian and Spanish and Portuguese, as well as English. Using an interpreter to work with the patients, supervised at first by Doctor Burton and then later by Magda, she was soon learning the use of certain native words. It created humor between her and the patients they were treating. Some patients had a local virus that the staff had nicknamed the creeping crud. It was very similar to a modern day plague. Transmitted by the rats, it was also found in the local waters...another very important reason to drink only filtered water. One of the biggest reasons for the clinic was AIDS—Acquired Immune Deficiency Syndrome. It was at epidemic proportions in Africa at this point, attacking indiscriminately, poor and rich alike. It was rampant in the community and ignorance of the ways to prevent it allowed it to spread easily. Mothers transmitted it to their children through breastfeeding. Fathers, who frequently had several wives or even concubines if they could afford it, spread it between them. Sheer ignorance was what was killing these people.

Doctor Cooper, working with several of the local people, began a series of classes. Helped by Lenny, they soon devised a program of educating the young and the women. Using the balloons from her mysterious boxes that she kept in her tent, she got their attention; however, she knew explaining about condoms to the women was useless. The men governed this land and if their women didn't do as they were told, they were frequently beaten or traded. If the young ones were captured and raped they were useless to their families as a commodity and commonly abandoned. It was an uphill battle to educate.

Some of the locals understood what the clinic was trying to do. As a woman herself, they held Doctor Cooper in awe. Befriending Hamishish proved to be a bonus. As the local magician, she was held in high esteem. She delighted in the balloons and condoms alike, noting their similarity and used the humor to help Deanna educate. Deanna handed the balloons out to the children for deeds well done. Deanna frequently thought Hamishish must do the same with condoms with the many men she slept with. The doctor was amazed that Hamishish didn't have the diseases that were so rampant in this area. Later, Hamishish confided and showed a crude version of the condoms that they now gave out. It was more like a French Letter of old; reusable and washed thoroughly after use. Crude, but effective…mostly. The danger of catching AIDS was still there and the condoms brought an added measure of safety to this woman's world. Teaching the others might prevent more.

Maddie found Deanna a delight to work with. She was never arrogant or condescending like Doctor Burton, who still looked at the young woman with suspicion. Deanna taught not only the locals, but anyone who wanted to learn what she was doing and why. She even showed a couple of the helpers how to administer a shot, something that some of the locals had avoided since it not only hurt, but was mysterious to them.

"Education is the key," she kept repeating in her arguments to help the others.

Doctor Burton agreed with her, but hid behind his aura of mystery to keep his fragile grip on control of the clinic. It was hard enough to get supplies and keep their head above water with the many refugees who came through, but to let them understand what they were truly doing too, he didn't think that was a good idea. He felt helping them on many levels was to their benefit and, as a result, he befriended Harlan.

"Well, if we dig it all up, it's gonna be a helluva mess," Harlan was saying one night at dinner.

"Wouldn't it benefit the locals to learn to use the machinery?" Doctor Cooper asked as she pointed at him with her fork.

"Of course, but they don't have any idea of the value of it and think it's just for fun," he said disparagingly.

"What happens when you leave and they don't know how to use the tractor or the plow? They go back to their ancient methods that have worked for thousands of years?"

"Well, we have to get the crops in before the rainy season and I'll teach them later," he began.

"Aren't you only here for four months?"

"Yes, but that's plenty of time…."

"Then you should teach them at the same time so you know your work won't be going to waste after you leave," she looked back down at her food, missing the angry look that Harlan sent her.

Doctor Cooper seemed to know a lot about a wide range of subjects, and she didn't hesitate to offer suggestions. She wasn't hurt when they argued or didn't take her well-meaning advice. In the first few days there, she had asked Harlan questions, drawing him out, almost friendly, but after Harlan realized that Doctor Burton wasn't trusting of her, her suggestions fell on deaf ears.

"Does it ever bother you that they ignore you?" Lenny asked as four of them sat around drinking a locally brewed and bottled beer.

Maddie sat forward to hear better. After their long day of treating people, the noise from the children was a bit loud.

Leida was already on her second beer and feeling no pain. She claimed the beer was like water compared to Australian beers.

Deanna shrugged it off. "I'll get that for the next ten years or so," she commented, taking a drink and wrinkling her nose at the taste. Other than water—boiled of course—or coffee and tea, there weren't a lot of choices for beverages. "Then I'll just have to deal with the misogynists," she laughed.

They all shared a laugh, having dealt with the male superiority complexes that many men had, especially the natives. Strangely, it bothered them the most that the highly educated Doctor Burton and others like him, who knew better, followed his lead.

"Ah, all I have to do is my job and show them that I know what I'm doing," she shrugged again philosophically. "Doctors Without Borders knows that I'm qualified, and if I don't like this assignment I can leave any time I want. I really like these people though," she said emphatically, gesturing with her beer and nearly sloshing it out of the narrow neck in her exuberance. "Whoops," she said apologetically as she realized she had nearly doused Maddie. "They deserve so much more than they have or have gotten in the past," she said in reference to the many wars that had devastated this part of the continent.

"Some of their stories…" Magda shook her head sorrowfully.

"You can't think like that. It's the past. Learn from it. Move on. Keep it from happening again," Deanna preached. She was so exuberant in her need to teach, to educate, that it was no wonder she and Lenny got along so well. Teaching the children and the women whose modern husbands would allow them to be taught, that was her passion.

Conversations like this helped pass the time when they had a little downtime. Frequently they had full days at their little clinic. When emergencies came up, they sometimes spent eighteen hours on their feet, using what little resources they had to save these people, sometimes from themselves.

One night Maddie found herself taking a walk with Deanna. It was amazing that someone so young had accomplished so much. "I'm hoping someday to open my own clinic," she was telling the wide-eyed Maddie.

"Maybe I'll come and work for you," Maddie said, almost shyly. It was a little overwhelming to hear the young doctor expound on this subject sometimes. She had such enthusiasm for life. It was a little exhilarating and her can-do attitude could be infectious.

"You know, I'd like that," Deanna said quietly. The night was full of sounds. The sun hadn't quite set and it was light enough to walk toward the little stream that meandered through their camp. They had both been assured in the rainy season that it became a raging river, but right now it was small and simple. They could see signs of its violence in the high cuts in the banks beside it, as well as its distance from their camp. "What do you intend to do when you get back to the States?"

"I'm not sure. My folks want me to get married, but finding a husband with these hours is going to be difficult," she teased, their hours meant eighteen hour days.

"Is that all you want, a husband?" Deanna asked in a strange tone.

"It would be nice, and children. I want children someday. Don't you?"

"No, I don't think I do," she answered honestly. "I see so much here and elsewhere. These are my children," she said as she indicated the ones running about the camp, getting in some playtime before night tucked them back into their homes, the grass huts that abounded around the camp.

"That's too bad, really. You would make a great mother," Maddie said with conviction.

"How do you know that?" Deanna asked with an odd little smile.

"Because you are so good with them. You aren't just a doctor to any of the patients; you actually care. I know how much it annoys Doctor Burton that you take the time to talk to them…really talk *to* them. They appreciate it too. They love working with you much more than working with him."

"That's good to hear," she answered, smiling slightly. "I often wondered over the years if my youth was held against me. Hell, I'd have been a doctor at seventeen if they didn't require all those years as an intern, but specializing really helped me become the doctor I wanted to be. I'm still learning. It's why they call it practicing," she teased.

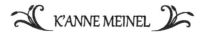

Maddie laughed. It was a common joke among the medical community that a doctor was only practicing. She really enjoyed talking to Deanna. Her intelligence shone through in her bright blue eyes; she got so enthusiastic they snapped. Her hair had bleached a very pale blonde from its darker browns and reds. She was what was commonly referred to as a dishwater blonde, the highlights in her hair changed from one sun-filled day to the next.

"Don't you want *more*?" she challenged.

Maddie thought about that question a lot in the coming days. Did she *just* want a husband and children? She was a nurse, a good one from what she was told by both Doctor Burton and Doctor Cooper. Being over here, helping out these poor, unfortunate people, that made her feel so good. But why was she here? Just to pad her resume? Sometimes that question 'Did she want more?' infuriated her. Doctor Cooper had a way of making people *think*.

CHAPTER FIVE

Doctor Wilson returned from his trip across to Lefeyette. He came with a large truck and many supplies, filling their shelves to capacity. He had been gone when Doctor Cooper, Thomas, Harlan, and Maddie had arrived. By the time he returned, they were settled in. He also brought glowing reviews of Doctor Cooper and the deeds she had done at other camps such as this one. He was definitely a fan and thrilled that she was in Mamadu.

"I'm a great admirer," he told her with a hand outstretched. He was a big, bluff man with a bushy beard. He reminded her of Mr. French from that childhood series she had watched, 'A Family Affair.'

"I'm thrilled to be working with you," she told him. He smiled, but didn't believe her. From the accolades she had gotten, he knew they were lucky to have her.

He put his arm across her shoulders as they watched the helpers unpack his large truck of supplies. "How are you getting on here? Can we entice you to stay longer?"

"Oh, I love it here. The work is very challenging," she hedged. She wasn't about to complain about any*thing*, or any*one*.

"This new serum from Harvard is supposed to be good," he commented, his arm falling from her shoulders. He changed the subject, sensing that something wasn't quite right. They were soon talking the benefits of the various medicines he had brought back with them. The guards around the truck attested to the importance of their supplies. They would stay at the compound, their automatic rifles necessary to keep the drugs safe so they could use them in the clinic and not have them stolen to be sold on the black market.

The two doctors talked as the goods were stowed and secured. Doctor Burton walked up, wiping his hands on a towel, obviously just come from washing up at the sinks. "Ah, you've met," he said with forced joviality.

Doctor Wilson immediately sensed the tension between the other two doctors. "Yes, I've heard her praises sung from Lefeyette to Mamadu," he smiled, showing brilliant white teeth against the black of his full beard.

"Ah, yes," Burton agreed, sounding unconvinced and then immediately talking about the supplies that Wilson had managed to get through. Deanna wandered away.

"You fool! Have you managed to insult her already?" Wilson asked, exasperated, as he waited for Cooper to get out of earshot.

"What? She may be brilliant, but she's young and inexperienced…" Burton blustered.

"You have no idea how brilliant she is…or how connected. How do you think I got all these supplies, or the guards?" he was furious and let it show.

"She arranged it?"

"Doctors Without Borders arranged it, on her recommendation. I was sitting in Lefeyette, trying to arrange one quarter of this amount when someone from that organization approached me. Apparently, Cooper got a message out and placed an order. They listen to that young and inexperienced doctor!" He had asked about the new doctor that he knew would be in Mamadu when and if he got back. The guards had made sure they got back across this violent land.

"So," he shrugged, unimpressed. "She has connections…."

"Yeah, and she used them despite your foolishness. Let her alone and let her do her job," he recommended heatedly. "You don't know who she knows or what she can do!" He had his suspicions, but he was going to keep them to himself unless he had them confirmed.

Over the following days, Doctor Burton kept a wary distance, allowing the young woman to do her job. He had to begrudgingly admit she knew what she was doing, did it well, and with enthusiasm. He was surprised that she didn't hesitate to operate when it was necessary. She knew techniques that he himself could learn from. One afternoon, he helped her perform a C-Section on a pregnant woman, only numbing her lower half.

She explained that by not putting the woman completely out, they not only saved on anesthesia which could be hard to get, but the mother would be less anxious to hold her newborn.

"Tell her we will have her baby out in five minutes," she said to the interpreter in French. The interpreter then spoke in the local dialect to the woman, explaining what the 'vroulike dokter' was saying. It wasn't the words that calmed the woman, it was Deanna's self-assurance and the calmness she maintained. Her sunny disposition frequently had flocks of locals around her, wanting to touch her and her now nearly white-blonde hair. She was special and they sensed that. Having Hamishish as a friend spoke volumes to the natives.

She lived up to what she said too, having explained to the mother that a normal birth wasn't possible since she had AIDS. By delivering this way, she could have more children and not infect this one with the dreaded disease. If they could only get her to feed the child formula instead of mother's milk, it would greatly increase this child's odds of never contracting the dreaded disease that was so prevalent in this part of Africa.

The women who had been given the life-saving formula, frequently sold it instead of using it. Breastfeeding was free, but it also passed the mother's bodily fluid to the child, who then could and would contract the deadly disease. Less and less babies survived to adulthood and these doctors were working against those odds. This village was increasing its odds, not at the hands of the doctors, but at the hands of their witch doctor. Hamishish, the magician, had told them that a great plague had come upon the land and that breastfeeding was no longer allowed, not for at least three generations. She explained that these white doctors had brought a powder that could save their babies. The women, superstitious to the core, believed her unfailingly. More than half of them used the formula that was given to them instead of selling it. Still, it took time.

In no time, a beautiful baby boy was born to this struggling woman. Deanna placed it on her chest, lightly wrapped in a beautiful birthing blanket the young woman had prepared for the child. Quickly, she cut the cord and stitched up the woman, using plenty of antibiotics to prevent a secondary infection. She was grateful for the recent shipment that Doctor Wilson had brought in that contained plenty of what they needed to be effective. It might only last a short time: some of it had an expiration date, some inevitably would spoil, be stolen, or used up, but for now they could save this one woman and her baby. She smiled as she finished cleaning up the woman who was smiling down in wonderment at the perfect baby she had just delivered.

She said something in her language and the interpreter laughed.

"What?" Deanna asked in French.

"She wants to know what your first name is, your Christian name. She would like to honor you and her baby by giving it a second name."

Deanna smiled, knowing this was indeed an honor. It denoted high status to have a child named after you in a lot of cultures. She knew of several babies in both Africa and in South America that had her name as their first or second. Sometimes they used Cooper, especially for boys when they learned that it was an acceptable male name, and sometimes they used Deanna, a hard name to get around some of their tongues. She told the interpreter and explained about the male surname. The translation made the new mother smile as she repeated the name Cooper back.

Deanna gave orders about their patient and the mother was soon installed in the hospital in a corner they called the maternity ward, away from the other patients. The cries of babies kept people up, but it was the infectious diseases that worried the doctors the most.

"We should use the meeting house for these cases," Deanna muttered to Maddie as she checked on her patients, the ones that weren't infectious.

"What about this building?" Maddie asked. She had heard Deanna state this before.

"It needs to be cleansed: the windows need to be opened and mosquito netting put on them, air out the place, and have the witch doctor do a cleansing," she ascertained.

"Surely you don't believe in all that?" she asked, wide-eyed.

"Medicine can prove a lot of that wrong, but I've seen some things that there is no scientific explanation for. People can believe and they can will themselves better sometimes. Having a blessing from the locals is all well and good, but, if you don't accept them and at least accommodate them, places like this will never work," she answered sadly as she finished.

She was as good as her word. Having thought about it, argued with Burton about it, she approached Wilson with her idea. She had the village elders come forward with Hamishish and with an interpreter, although she knew Hamishish and a few of the elders understood French. She formally asked them to bless the meeting house so they could turn it into a general ward. The more serious cases were left in the old clinic and were surprised to see Hamishish and others coming into the clinic in full dress, paint on their whole bodies, chanting and with smoke issuing from their smudges. The combination did more for the patients than any medicine.

Watching cynically, Doctor Burton and others shook their heads at the display, much less the waste of time and effort. By having two buildings instead of one, they now had to divide their time and efforts. Some simply didn't like change, others thought it all foolishness. Still, Doctor Wilson thought it had some merit and was amused to find an improvement on their never-ending stream of patients. Word of mouth told of the blessed clinics. A decrease in cases of death, whether a coincidence or not, helped immeasurably.

CHAPTER SIX

"**D**o you ever go into Lamish or one of the other smaller towns to get away?" Deanna asked Lakesh.

Leida perked up. They had been working non-stop for weeks. She needed some downtime, and while they had assigned days off, they rarely took them since there was really nothing else to do.

Three of them were sitting around the fire—Leida, Maddie, and the doctor—after a long day and a beautiful sunset. Deanna was poking the fire with a stick when Lakesh walked by.

"Yes, Missy, we go and get supplies," he answered automatically, and then realizing it was the doctor who had asked, corrected himself with a distinct twang of 'Doktor.'

"Would there be room for passengers?" she asked as she looked up and smiled at his mistake.

"Yes, Doktor," he bowed slightly out of respect to her profession. Having a female doctor was a novelty in this male-dominated country.

"I'd like to go with you next time you go," she stated to let him know there were no hard feelings and to make herself clear.

"I go tomorrow," he assured her.

"May I go?" Leida asked. She desperately wanted to get out of the village for some time away.

"Me too?" Maddie asked.

"We will have to ask Doctor Wilson and let Alex know we will be unavailable," Deanna answered.

In no time at all, Doctor Wilson gave them the well-deserved time off and Alex was informed in case anything else came up. The three women were scheduled to leave with Lakesh. He hadn't really planned to go the next day, but was accommodating them. Only Doctor Wilson and Alex knew that the guide hadn't originally planned to go the next day, but the three women were thrilled to be getting some well-deserved time off and to see some more of the country.

"How did you get involved with Doctors Without Borders?" Maddie asked Deanna over the noise of the engine.

"Ah, they held a seminar/recruitment off-campus at one of the libraries in Boston. I was curious so I went. I'd just come back from Switzerland and an intense course on tropical diseases. I wanted to be where the action was, not where they brought the patients. I felt I could help them more on site, you know?" she shouted. Leida, turning around to join in the conversation, nodded.

"How long did you sign up for?" the Australian asked and then hit her chin on the back of the seat from the uneven road. Rubbing it ruefully, she looked on inquiringly at the young doctor.

"At first they only let me sign up for six months. They sent me to the Amazon. God, I loved it despite the bugs, the heat, and the dysentery," she answered nostalgically. "I felt I was really doing something. It was such a challenge!"

"How long ago was that?" Maddie asked, fascinated by the enthusiastic doctor. She had such adventures to share. Getting time alone with her was becoming increasingly hard as everyone except for Harlan and Doctor Burton loved her.

"Over two years ago, I don't know. The time seems to blend after a while with all the work. I just want to make a difference, to help them," she said sadly, remembering the mass of humanity that came through these war-torn areas. One of the reasons she was heading into Lamish was to send a message herself asking why the other doctors from MSF hadn't arrived. She had been in Mamadu too long for them not to have come to get her and send her on to another location. She also wondered if her other messages had gone astray. "How about you?" she asked Maddie first and then glanced at Leida to include her in the question.

"I was in New York finishing up my nursing degree, but I wanted more. I knew that working in New York I'd see everything," she answered with a tone that implied that gunshots and other emergency calls were not what she wanted. "I think we probably had the same recruiter. I wanted to make a difference and learn triage in the field."

"You wanted to be a triage nurse?"

"Yes and no. I'm young enough that I have a lot to learn."

She was impressed with the nurse's dedication. "What about you?" she asked, including Leida once again.

"I needed to get away. I'd been in Sydney and they sent me to work in the bush. I liked it too much and I think they thought I was going off my head." She grinned ruefully at her confession. "I don't know if I was, but I'm damned good at what I do and I like helping. Some of this is a bit much," she gestured at the African countryside they were driving through, but they all knew she meant the people that came through their clinic. "Making a difference, that's what is important."

They all agreed on that and the conversation moved on to what Lenny was doing as a teacher. Fluent in both the local dialect as well as Afrikaans, French, and English, she was well-prepared to help out in the clinic as well as teach. She had worked hard with Deanna to educate on more than the three 'Rs', which would help both the next generation and those women who were attending her classes.

"What do you think of Alex?" Leida asked as she smiled shyly. It was obvious that the Australian had a crush on the administrator who would soon be leaving—once he had fully trained Thomas, who had a lot to learn.

They laughed and openly discussed Alex and Thomas and their potential as mates, even dates. Neither of the nurses realized that Deanna didn't participate in the conversation other than to smile and nod. She seemed to look at the scenery frequently as the two women laughed like school girls over the attributes of the two men.

"No, I wouldn't date him," Maddie disagreed with Leida about Thomas. She knew not to put Alex down as the other woman had staked an artificial claim to him, even if he wasn't aware of it.

"Why not? Have a fling while you are here," the Aussie encouraged. Even Lakesh smiled at that and laughed at the women. He had learned long ago that these Westerners were a lot different from the African people.

"I don't see anyone else having a fling except for Hamishish," she answered tartly.

At the mention of their friend, Deanna finally contributed. "For her, it's a duty," she commented.

"Isn't she more like a prostitute then?"

Deanna shook her head. "You need to open up your mind more. Stop thinking with your American values and morals. It's an *honor* to sleep with Hamishish," she tried explaining.

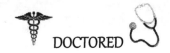

"But they give her things in exchange for her honors," she pointed out with a chuckle.

Deanna shook her head again. "You have to understand it from their point of view. She helps out with their spiritual well-being. She is almost as important, if not more so, than their elders or leaders of the tribe. All the different tribes that come through here," she indicated Lakesh, where they had come from, "have different ideals, and despite cultural differences, they understand a medicine woman such as she."

"I thought she was magic?" Leida asked.

"She is, but not in the way that a Western-raised person would think. Remember when I had the leaders and Hamishish clean out the wards?" As both of the women nodded, she continued, "The patients believed it was spiritually cleaned so they healed better, faster even, because it's in their mindset. If we didn't believe in ourselves or what we were raised to believe, we would lose more than our faith. It's in the body and mind that the healing begins."

Both women looked at the doctor thoughtfully. It was Maddie who asked, "Do you think you are a medicine woman? Do they?"

Deanna nodded. "Some do. I don't claim the title. If they choose to bestow it on me, who am I to argue if it helps them get better?"

The conversation continued until they arrived in Mamadu some two hours later. In rapid French, Deanna asked for directions to specific locations. "I'm going to be a couple of hours if you two want to explore. Stay together though, as you are Western women and white. Do not go anywhere alone," she warned.

"What about you?" Leida asked, curious as to why the doctor was ditching them. She already saw some open markets she wanted to explore and spend some money in.

"I'm taking Lakesh," she said brightly.

They agreed to check in two hours later at the Rover. Maddie saw Deanna talking to Lakesh and then they went their separate ways. She was suspicious, but had gone off willingly with Leida; she too wanted to see the markets. She wondered the whole two hours where the doctor had gone off to.

Deanna made her way first to a hotel where, for a fee, she was able to take a hot shower. She changed into clothes she had brought and for the first time in weeks felt clean from the dust and bugs that were a constant around Mamadu. No matter how many cold showers she took, a hot shower made all the difference. After a surgery, they washed with antiseptic. Unfortunately, that frequently dried out their skin. One of the things she bought in Lamish was, bottles of lotion without alcohol in them to soothe her skin. She made a few phone calls from the hotel room she had rented. It was a nice room, better than what the prostitutes rented by the hour. She had seen the look on the desk clerk's face when she asked about renting it for so short a time. The speculation had been immediate. Her money was taken easily enough, but she knew if they wanted they could throw her out and keep the funds. She went out to do some of her own shopping and easily met up with the others at the two-hour mark. All of them had many bags and boxes in their hands.

"Let's pack these in here," she suggested and then asked Lakesh to sit in the Rover to keep sticky hands from pilfering their purchases. "If you two want to take showers, I took a room upstairs," she indicated the hotel down the block. "I got a hot shower and can do some more shopping if you two want a turn."

A hot shower sounded good to the two of them. Leida reached back into one of the bags and took out a colorful dress to change into as Maddie was handed the key to the room. It was an old-fashioned iron key on a large fob so it was likely the original key to the door of the room and less likely to be stolen.

"You want me come with you?" Lakesh asked the doctor as the other two began to leave.

"No, please stay here and watch the Rover. We don't want things taken," she repeated, hoping her voice didn't sound exasperated at having to repeat herself to their guide. He was a nice guy, just tended to want to be a little too helpful now and then, forgetting what they had just said. He ran errands all over the camp and probably made a trip into the port at least once or twice a week to fetch packages or supplies. He also had a nice little side business on the black market he thought no one in camp knew about. All the doctors and nurses knew and kept him away from their supplies, just in case. He did, however, find them some rare medicines and supplies from time to time.

He watched as the doctor went into another alleyway and almost got out to warn her not to go in there, but she obviously knew where she was going. She didn't notice that Maddie was watching where she went too. They all returned to the Rover some time later and waited for the good doctor to show up. She returned with some more bags and boxes and took the key back to the hotel to check out, not saying a word about where she had been. Maddie, who had showered first and come back downstairs, had seen her in the market—an arm around a woman, talking earnestly to her—but she had disappeared in the crowds of shoppers down one of the aisles and Maddie hadn't wanted to follow. She wondered about it though.

As they drove slowly back towards Mamadu they resumed their conversation about dating and Harlan's name came up. "He's a nice enough bloke if you don't mind never expressing your own opinion," Leida commented and the women laughed.

"What about Lenny?" Maddie asked thoughtfully.

"Lenny and Harlan?"

"No, I mean, who would you see her paired off with?"

"I'd say Hamishish, but I don't think Hamishish is into gals," Leida said with a grin.

"You mean Lenny is..." gasped the redhead.

"Well, there are certain signs," the Aussie replied.

Imperceptibly, Deanna stiffened in the front seat. She had been listening in case she wanted to turn around and contribute, but the turn the conversation had taken meant she was staring out the cracked and spider-webbed windshield firmly.

"You really think she's into...?" Maddie asked, not sounding as shocked as she had the moment before.

"Well, you know...I just sense she isn't into guys," her voice lowered conspiratorially.

The two of them continued their conversation, never noticing that Deanna didn't join in from the front seat. Later as the ebb and flow of it continued, Maddie noticed that Deanna must have fallen asleep in the front seat; her eyes were closed and she seemed relaxed.

They arrived back in Mamadu to find the place in an uproar with new patients arriving. Apparently some skirmish or another had broken out west of the camp and they were bringing the casualties here into their village and camp. Word of mouth had spread and the three doctors were needed and so were the nurses. Lakesh promised to unload the Rover into their tent while the three medical personnel hurried off into the clinic to help.

Later, much later, a blood-spattered and sweating Deanna made her way back to the tent to find all the boxes and bags stacked neatly inside the door. She was grateful that Lakesh had done what he promised. She pretended not to notice that one or two boxes of what she had purchased had gone missing. She separated her purchases from Maddie's and Leida's.

"You okay?" Maddie asked from the doorway as Deanna finished straightening up her things.

"Yeah," she sighed gustily. "I just need a shower. You pour, I pour?" she asked with a grin. It was a common enough practice that two would go to the showers and pour for the other.

Maddie nodded with a grin as she went to get some clean clothes.

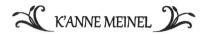

CHAPTER SEVEN

Some of the boxes that Deanna had brought back contained athletic shoes. She gifted them to specific people within the tribe. A luxury that few, if any, had seen. She'd been appalled to see them wearing plastic bottles on their feet to protect them from the rocks and thorns that abounded throughout the landscape. Guessing at sizes, she'd been pretty fortunate that most of the shoes she had bought fit those she bestowed them on. It was a matter of prestige to ceremoniously give away their footwear to others who used the plastic bottles tied to their feet as foot coverings. The athletic shoes were a novelty. They might not last, but for now it made those wearing them look impressive.

It was as she distributed the shoes that others realized that Christmas was not too far away. It was hot and sweltering and those from northern climes were used to having snow. It was Deanna who had the idea of showing the school children the Christian practice of having a Christmas tree. Since pine trees were non-existent on these plains, she made one out of surgical gloves. Getting others to help her blow up the gloves, they attached them to a short pole. The fingers pointing out provided great 'branches' to hang ornaments from. They weren't exactly ornaments like you would find on a Christmas tree, but the students enthusiastically helped with the idea, using their imagination and the pictures in Lenny's books, which showed snow and decorated pine trees. A bit of cotton around the base provided the snow. They laughed together when the gloves slowly lost air and deflated. It was a challenge to keep it looking 'Christmassy.'

"Doctor Cooper, I think that is a terrible waste of resources," Doctor Burton censured her, making sure there were witnesses to make the impact of his message more humiliating.

Deanna had been prepared for this ever since she had made a point of giving gifts to the village elders and notables and incorporating western culture into the festivities. "Yes, I'd agree, if they were your resources," she nodded sympathetically.

"These aren't from our supplies?" he asked, confused.

"Nope, part of my private stock," she assured him with a friendly smile. "But don't worry, I'm almost out, so you can find something then." With that she walked away, leaving him blushing and gasping at her audacity. She had no respect for his authority! He went to Alex to have him inventory their gloves and provide him with proof that she had used the clinic's stores.

"God, that man!" she sputtered as she entered their tent that evening.

"Have a wee bit of problem with the good Doctor Burton?" Lenny asked astutely from her cot where she was playing solitaire with a deck of cards.

"How'd you guess?" she fumed as she walked over to her cot and sat down angrily.

"He's been jonesing for you since you got here," she commented astutely.

"Yeah, he hasn't liked you since day one," Magda added. She was already under her blanket, trying to doze off, unsuccessfully, but she wasn't tired enough, not yet, and joined in the conversation.

"It's not my fault he didn't know who I was," she answered as she unlaced her high boots and pulled her sweaty feet from one and then the other. Slowly she peeled the socks off, noting she couldn't wear them a second day in this heat.

"It was pretty funny that he accepted you as a mechanic, but not as a doctor," Magda laughed as she remembered his face that first day.

"Maybe he has a crush on you," Leida put in. She was dressed in pajamas for bed, but lying on top of the blankets.

"Gawd," Deanna shuddered at the thought.

"Yeah," Lenny agreed, laughing, as she faked a dramatic shudder.

This got Deanna laughing as she smiled at her friends. Laughing at irritations was the best way to struggle through them. At least Doctor Wilson believed in her and liked her ideas. He allowed her to do her work without interference, but if Doctor Burton had had his way, she would have been packed off already. She had received a letter forwarded from France asking if she would stay longer at Mamadu. The next plane of Doctors Without Borders that could come in, would come in. She had taken her own Rover off for a ride to the next village and worked all day alone, much to the anger of Alex who kept track of such things for their clinic. It further angered Wilson when she couldn't be found and he lectured her on going off by herself.

Deanna knew the work in Mamadu was enough for any one doctor, much less three. She shouldn't go off in search of more—she didn't need to as so many came through their clinic. The supplies that Doctor Wilson had brought in were rapidly depleted. The war-torn country was home to a lot of refugees trying to escape the conflicts. They were all grateful it was no longer an issue in this area; this was considered a 'safe' zone.

"Harlan found another unexploded land mine today. Fortunately, he saw it before he plowed it up," Maddie put in to change the subject. No one liked working with Doctor Burton these days. He definitely had an attitude that was not conducive to harmony in the ranks.

"One of these days we are going to be bringing that guy in on a stretcher," Leida contributed.

"At least he is teaching the locals how to use the equipment now," Maddie answered. She averted her eyes as she saw Deanna changing for bed, but she noticed that Lenny didn't bother looking away. She watched the physically fit doctor, who had a penchant for nice underwear, change into a t-shirt and shorts, taking her bra off under the t-shirt. Maddie wondered once again if the rumors were true that Lenny liked women.

"Yeah, but that was due to Wilson's suggestion, not Deanna's," Lenny added. She turned away from the show of the fit doctor changing for bed.

"I kinda want to smack his head to get him to see sense sometimes," Deanna put in.

"Which one, Harlan or Burton?" Lenny said with a smile.

They all started to laugh at that. Two hard-headed men in camp were two too many!

"Would you like to go for a walk?" Deanna asked Maddie a few nights later when the rush of their daily work was over.

"I'd like that," Maddie said from where she was reading a book on her cot. She quickly smacked her boots together upside down and put them on, tying up the laces.

"Today wasn't so bad was it?" Deanna asked as they walked along the path toward the river.

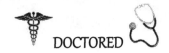

"No, not really. Not that much different than any other day," the shorter redhead added.

"Getting bored with it all?"

"No, I find it fascinating. I wish I could learn the languages," she lamented. Maddie held Deanna in awe. She was picking up words very quickly and could, in a way, speak with the locals. She wasn't completely accurate, but she already knew enough that they were pleased to help her.

They chatted easily, as friends were apt to do. A little gossip, a little teasing, and a lot of fun as they walked along before the sun set completely and they had to be back in camp.

Maddie liked that Deanna challenged her way of thinking. They were of a similar age, but Deanna had done so much more, had a head start in life, and very definite ideas of where she was going. She loved working with these people, found it challenging, and was looking forward to her next assignment. "I got stuck in the Amazon four more months than they planned because of a typo on some paperwork; they lost me!" she explained in one of her stories, telling about how much she learned by having that extra time with the tribe she had been working with. "They were fascinating people!"

"Weren't you scared that you would never get out?"

She shrugged philosophically. "I was willing to stay another year if I had to. I think I may go back someday. There was so much to learn from them. There is so much to learn in a tropical rain forest, and so much to learn from the locals. They know so much, but they have to trust you before they will impart it." She smiled in remembrance of other times, pleasant, happy times that she had actually enjoyed.

"Someday you might get married and have to settle down," Maddie teased, knowing her friend wasn't there yet, might never be there. She was young and smart and adventurous. It was amazing to see the dynamo that was Doctor Cooper.

"I don't think that will ever happen," Deanna said sadly.

Maddie wondered at the sad note in her voice. "Did you have someone back home?"

"Once I thought I did, but it didn't work out," she explained without giving particulars.

"Well, we have all loved and lost," she answered philosophically and then felt like an ass for saying it.

Deanna laughed instead. "Yeah, I guess we have to date a few before we find our one."

"I'll find my Prince Charming," Maddie assured her.

"No thanks."

"What! You don't want a Prince Charming?" the teasing was back.

"Oh, hell no. He would probably leave you in that castle. Maybe up in one of those turrets, scrubbing the floor for his lazy ass," she elaborated and they both started laughing at the image she created.

"But he could ride in on his noble steed and sweep me off my feet," she countered.

"Or, as he is sweeping you up, his horse sidesteps and you end up in the mud."

They both laughed harder at the imagery and the sarcasm that Deanna shared. It was silly and fun.

"Oh, gawd. My side is aching," Maddie leaned over slightly as she tried to get her breath back.

"You okay?" Deanna gasped, also trying to get enough oxygen into her lungs from laughing so hard. She put her hand on Maddie's lower back to comfort her.

"You are hilarious," she added as she slowly straightened up and Deanna's hand fell off her. "You don't want to ever get married?"

"Oh, I'd like to, but it's frowned on," she confided and then thought perhaps she should have kept that to herself. She glanced at Maddie who was looking at her with questions in her eyes.

"Your family doesn't want you to marry?"

"They'd love me to. I just don't like their choices," she answered, perhaps with a trace of bitterness in her voice.

"Are your parents alive?"

Nodding Deanna continued on this safer subject as they turned to head back to camp. The sun was setting and they wanted to be back before dark. "Yes, my father runs a firm and my mother spends the money it makes," she laughed.

"Do you have any sisters or brothers, or are you an only child?"

"I've got an older sister. I was an accident. I think my parents ran out of TV to watch one night and oops, I was conceived. Since I was such a surprise and so late in their life, I think God made me a child prodigy in order to hurry up my development. When they realized what they had, they threw everything they had at me to challenge me. I rose to all of them." She smiled in memory at her childhood, which had been very, very short. "I loved all the knowledge I could gain; I absorbed books. I finished high school in two years and only because they tried to hold me back. I was done with college by fourteen, medical school and my internship by the time I was twenty-one."

This confirmed some of the other stories that Deanna had told them so Maddie knew that she wasn't lying. It still amazed her. It almost made the rest of them feel so...inadequate. "You seem *normal*," she muttered.

"Oh, yes, my parents made sure of that. I had regular sessions with therapists, psychologists, psychotherapists…anyone with a pysch in their degree examined, poked, and prodded my brain. I'm a freak. I know it, I relish it."

"But you were in college when most of us were just getting pimples," she stated, remembering her own awkward teenage years.

"Yes, but I was also in private schools and being challenged. I didn't realize I was missing anything. To me, that was *normal*," she explained.

"You make it sound so simple. I can't imagine."

"Well, it wasn't like my hormones had kicked in then. Yeah, I had pimples, but they showed up when I was like nineteen. I already looked like a kid. Can you imagine your doctor having pimples?" she laughed and Maddie shared in the laughter at that thought. "Seriously, I'm grateful my parents had the money to send me to the schools that I was able to attend. I graduated debt-free and, while they didn't approve of my specialties, they allowed me to indulge. There was a time they had tried to get me to go into business or law," she shuddered for dramatic affect and they shared a chuckle as they walked along.

"I can't imagine you in business or law," she snickered a little at the thought. "What does your sister do?"

"She went into the family business with Dad. She had to do something. She's ten years older than I am, but I caught up and surpassed her. She was pretty resentful until she found her groove."

"That's good. I guess it wasn't easy having a super smart sister."

"And a teenage one at that." She chuckled again. "God, I was such a smart ass. We're good now, but I had to mature, and fast. Dealing with adults who weren't about to put up with a smart-aleck kid, I learned."

Maddie could only imagine. This woman had such an amazing life, she really respected her. She was so...normal to talk to.

Their walk took them back to their tent. It wasn't the first time they had gone off alone together and it wouldn't be the last. The women often went off in twos and threes to get to know each other better. A couple of times the men went with them. Occasionally a man and a woman would pair off.

Everyone noted when Lenny began walking out with one of the elder's daughters more and more. At first it was supposedly so the woman could learn English better, but as it became more frequent, rumors began.

"Do you think she is really...?" whispered Leida to Maddie.

Deanna overheard, and remembering the conversation in the Rover, she stiffened up. This time, Maddie noticed and just shook her head at Leida to quiet her and the gossip. It was inevitable in a community as small as theirs that this type of behavior was noted. She thought perhaps that Deanna just didn't approve of the gossip. She asked her about it the next time they took a walk.

"You don't like gossip do you?"

Deanna already sensed this was about Lenny. She thought the two of them made a fine couple, but it was no one's business but the women involved. "I don't encourage it, if that's what you mean," she answered carefully.

"So, what do you think about Lenny?"

"I think what she does is her concern," she answered in a no-argument tone.

"You don't approve?"

"Actually, I do."

"You do?"

"Yes, if what they are saying is true. Love is hard enough to find. It shouldn't matter who it's with."

"But they are..." she trailed off, not able to say the word.

"Lesbians?" Deanna finished for her and looked down at her judgmental friend. They had stopped walking and hadn't noticed the clouds moving in from the west. The sun was fading faster than normal. They were due for some storms and the dry season would officially be over. The villagers had feared grass fires and Harlan had fretted that the crops he was planting would shrivel and die.

"Y..ye..yes," she stuttered at the word.

"What's wrong with that?" she challenged.

"It's immoral, it's...."

"Different?" she finished for her again. She was getting angry. She knew why, but it didn't stop her. "Why is it that anyone who is different than what people consider their norm is wrong or not allowed?" she asked, her voice becoming stern.

It was then that Maddie realized where Deanna was coming from, or thought she did. She'd always been different, the outsider, too young to fit in with her contemporaries, too smart for her own age group. "I'm sorry. I didn't mean anything by it. I was just surprised that it would be allowed."

"Are you aware that some cultures readily accept homosexuality? Even some species? It's only humans that don't. Hell, the American Natives accepted it hundreds of years before the Europeans even landed in the Americas! They called it Twin-Spirits. They understood that a male essence can live in a female's body or vice versa." She realized she was lecturing and stopped herself. Glancing around, she became aware that the birds had stopped chirping. She looked up and saw the oncoming clouds. "Come on, we better be getting back."

Maddie looked up too, realizing the danger of being caught out. While it hadn't rained the entire time they had been here so far, they had heard stories of flash floods and worse. They hurried back. They were the first in their tent, and none too soon as the rain that had waited months to come back, came down in droves. "Hey, I'm sorry back there. I didn't mean anything by it..." she began as they both watched through the open doorway at how quickly it got dark and the rain began pouring down.

"Think nothing of it," Deanna said back. Her sunny disposition was apparent as she quickly forgave the words between them.

Maddie wondered at how tolerant Deanna was. Was it because of her higher education or perhaps because she more intelligent than the rest of them? The woman was fascinating on so many levels and could converse on almost any subject.

Suddenly Magda ran in. She had a towel over her head, but she was soaked to the skin. They both saw her at the last instant before she collided with them and stepped back to let her into the tent. "Is Lenny here?" she asked breathlessly in French.

"No, we just got back before the rain started. No one is here," Deanna answered. She reached for the wet towel, but Magda pulled back. "Is something wrong?"

"The villagers are looking for Emmanulla and she was last seen with Lenny. I was hoping she was here so that they wouldn't find..." she stopped when she realized what she was saying aloud.

Deanna understood her concern immediately. She bit her lip, thinking. There was nothing they could do at the moment but wait until they were found, or until they returned.

Magda dripped there a moment before heading to her bunk to open her footlocker and get some dry clothes. The other two turned to look outside as Maddie asked Deanna to clarify what Magda had said…her French wasn't as good as the others.

"What happens if they are discovered together?" she asked in English once Deanna explained.

"I don't know. The elders know they walk out together," she answered worriedly.

"But what if they are, you know, *together*?" she wondered aloud.

Deanna wanted to snap at her friend, but she had wondered that too and just hadn't verbalized it. She knew it was dangerous what Lenny might be doing. It depended on the culture and what they would accept. Lenny was white, Emmanulla was black, and they were both women. She was pretty certain, but she didn't *know*, if that was acceptable among *any* of these African cultures or tribes. She hoped if they were found, it was in an acceptable situation and not what was being implied here. She shrugged in answer to Maddie's statement. Turning, she went to her cot and began to change for bed. It wasn't quite bedtime, but she couldn't imagine going out in the deluge outside the tent.

Maddie looked at Deanna and then gazed outside for a moment, wondering what it would be like to kiss a woman instead of a man. Deanna had given her food for thought. She wondered if she was just intolerant because of how she was raised. Just because others believed it, didn't make it right or wrong. As Deanna had said, it was accepted in some cultures, and it was certainly accepted in some species—she knew that from biology. She had a lot to think about as she got herself ready for bed.

It was still raining the next morning when they all got up. It was decidedly cooler and no one was wearing shorts as they pulled on jeans, pants, and then slickers to keep the rain off. After a mad dash to the latrines and then the food tent, they were soaked through. The rain seemed to leap up off the ground. The dirt didn't absorb the water and the splashes from the rain drops came back up off the ground to get them wet a second time.

It made for a wet and miserable time in the wards as the doctors and nurses and their helpers attended to their patients. Everyone seemed to be on edge. Some of the crew were aware that Lenny was missing. Some even knew that the Chief's daughter Emmanulla apparently was missing *with* her. Twice Deanna stopped gossip about Lenny's sexual orientation, snapping at the people who were discussing her like an object. Maddie knew enough about Deanna's feelings on the subject to stop from discussing it at all even though Leida and a couple of others attempted to draw her into conversation. For some reason, after several talks with Deanna, she felt it demeaned her somehow to engage in such gossip. She avoided it like the plague they were dealing with in their patients.

"Doctor Cooper?" she addressed Deanna formally in front of the ward as it made the patients respect them more. Only when they were all alone and kicking back was she addressed as Deanna.

As Deanna looked up, her familiar chirpy smile was in place. For the first time, Maddie realized her light blue eyes also lit up when she answered her. "Yes?"

"The patient in bed nine is complaining of abdominal pain. Can we increase some of the medication?" she asked as she handed her the chart.

The number of patients hadn't lessoned because of the weather. In fact, there was already a small increase in the numbers. Weather-related accidents were already occurring. There were no signs of a let-up in the rain either. Doctor Burton had already warned their people to stay well away from the river and not to leave camp unless in pairs, if at all.

Deanna looked at the chart, finishing up with the patient she was attending and walking with Maddie over to bed nine. Her interpreter followed in their wake, but she knew she might not be needed as Deanna had picked up quite a bit of their language. She discovered the patient was a child, his mother was sitting anxiously next to the cot where he lay moaning from the pain and thrashing about a little. She examined him and noted his sweat despite the coolness from the rain. She listened to his heart with her stethoscope, checked his stomach, and examined the whites of his eyes, the color of his nails, and poked and prodded at him as she talked a little with him and his mother. She used a combination of their language—the words that she knew—and French, which her interpreter effortlessly translated for her. This relaxed the mother and even the boy, who was obviously in pain.

"Prepare him for surgery," she ordered Maddie. "He's got appendicitis. Wish we had a way to run cultures faster or an X-ray machine," she said under her breath to the nurse. It was the only thing she did complain about, that in this modern world things such as that took days, sometimes weeks, and by then patients could easily die.

"Are we going to be able to keep the generators going?" Maddie reminded her of the sporadic electrical outages that they had to deal with. Losing lights during such an operation could prove fatal.

"I'll inform Doctor Burton," Deanna said with a grimace. "Get the boy ready."

Maddie nodded as she watched Deanna walk off to the doctors' office. Deanna was rarely in it, preferring to write her notes in her charts among the patients, chatting with them, making them laugh at her attempts to speak their languages, socializing with them all. It put them at ease and she had earned the respect she now commanded of them. Word spread that she was competent and friendly. It made women want to listen to her, learn from her, and it was why some of her classes with Lenny were more enjoyable.

Deanna knocked on the office door before opening it. "Doctor Burton?" she called cheerfully. He wasn't in the office, but Doctor Wilson was. "Oh, Doctor Wilson, do you know where Burton is?"

"I believe he is handling something in the village." Deanna wondered briefly if it had anything to do with Lenny and Emmanulla, but then focused on the matter at hand. "Will I do?" he asked with a grin.

She smiled, showing she was actually a very attractive young woman. "I have a boy with an appendicitis and I'm going to need the surgical booth," she told him. "I just want to be sure we have the generator as backup in case of an outage."

"That's a good idea to check," he answered thoughtfully. "Have you checked his white count?" he asked.

"No, I was just about to do that. I won't open him up until I do," she promised. "I just wanted to prepare the surgery while I do that."

He nodded. She was most efficient, setting things in motion on several fronts so that she could multi-task. He knew it drove Burton crazy that this young thing was so good at what she did. He would be sorry to see her go; she was good at this. He'd been prepared to be impressed based on what people had told him about her, but the reality was, she was even more impressive in person. He could only imagine what she would be like in ten years. Hell, in five years she could run a clinic like this. She probably could now, but he knew they wouldn't give such a responsibility to a twenty-six-year-old woman. "Do you need help?" he asked helpfully.

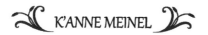

Deanna smiled. She knew Burton wouldn't have offered. He would have tried to take it over, treating her like a nurse or a messenger. "Thank you, I'll let you know." She also knew that Wilson had many of his own patients to take care of as well as any that would come in while she was in surgery. She left him to go take blood from her patient and look at it under a microscope. It would tell if all the signs that pointed to an appendicitis were accurate. Blood didn't lie. She explained to the mother and the boy what she was doing and why.

The boy wanted to know if she would see all the bugs, since the direct translation from French didn't really explain micro-organisms or white count. She assured him that the microscope would indeed show her what she needed to know. He bravely allowed her to take a blood sample. She smiled and ruffled his hair as she got up and Maddie quickly put a bandage on the small spot that was oozing a little blood.

Deanna put a drop on a glass and put it under the microscope. It was teeming with white blood cells, which told her there was an infection in the small boy's body. As all the other signs pointed to the appendix, her mind was made up and she nodded at Maddie. She sought out their anesthesiologist. He was new, but competent, and kept Deanna and the other doctors from having to do more than one job for their surgeries.

In a short period of time the surgery was prepared—the boy was put under and Deanna had scrubbed herself at the sink. It wasn't as sterile as the hospitals she had worked at in the States or in Europe, but they did what they could to ward off infection. Many times it was a secondary infection that killed their patients, not the initial surgery or illness. She knew by keeping things as clean as they possibly could they would have to make do on the rest. She herself had boiled the instruments she was now using. She wished she had a tray of scalpels, instead of the few she used. She could feel the slight tug against the tissue as they dulled. She tried to use each one sparingly as she looked for and found the sharp edges to cut open her patient. She could hear her own breathing behind the mask as she peered into the boy's abdomen when she had cut him. She found a greatly distorted appendix, like an engorged worm or tic. It was full of putrefying puss. She tied off each end twice and then she gingerly cut off both ends that fed the little monster, careful not to nick it and get the contents in the cavity. Slowly she exorcised it from the wound, putting a spit tray below it quickly before cutting beyond her sutures at both ends. The little blob of flesh soon began to pump its poison into the tray, but it was okay, it wasn't in her patient anymore. She whisked it away and handed it to Maddie.

Maddie watched as Deanna made it all look so easy. She knew it couldn't possibly be as easy as the young woman made it seem. She didn't seem to hesitate...ever. Her confidence was a wonder to watch. She knew her stuff, that was obvious. Maddie enjoyed working with her. She could only hope to measure up as her nurse and do the best she could for this amazing young doctor.

Quickly she cleaned the incision and then sewed it up, taking pains to make the sutures small so that it would heal without too much scarring. She wasn't sure of this tribe's beliefs. Some tribes thought scars were a sign of strength, but she erred on the side of caution.

It was less than an hour later that she herself was helping to clean up the surgery. She never put on airs, expecting others to clean up after her. Many doctors felt their work was done when the surgery was done, but Deanna chipped in. Maddie had returned to help her along with the anesthesiologist and a couple of helpers. Keeping their surgery as clean as possible was very important. They couldn't keep it germ-free. That was impossible in this area, but they tried. All they could do was try.

"He comfortable?" Deanna asked conversationally to Maddie.

"Yes, his mother wanted to know when he would awaken?"

Deanna smiled. It was a common enough occurrence and parents were the same worldwide. She finished her section of cleaning, put away her supplies, and washed her hands once again before going to her patient to check on him and reassure the worried mother.

CHAPTER EIGHT

Lenny and Emmanulla were discovered the next day when the rains stopped almost as abruptly as they had arrived. They were cold, they were tired, but they explained they had been caught out by the sudden storm. They hadn't seen the clouds rolling in and fortunately they had found a crude rock shelter in a hill, high enough from the waters churning through this section of the large valley. The river was running full. Because of the way the river wound through, it nearly circled back on itself in an oxbow. They had to walk wide around its dangerous waters to make it back to the village. They were believed for the sake of propriety and the chief made a great show of thanking the school teacher for keeping his daughter safe. Deanna and Lenny exchanged a look that promised a conversation later, but other than that, the two of them were brought back safely and welcomed.

"You think she stooped the chief's daughter?" Thomas said crudely to Harlan and they both sniggered like schoolboys.

Walking up behind them, Deanna frostily replied, "If you can't remain professional, I suggest the two of you go back to your tent where you can't be overheard. They may not speak English, but if they do, the villagers would be grossly offended by your conversation."

"It's really none of your business what we say, now is it?" Harlan defended himself and his companion.

"What if people were talking about the two of you the way you are talking about others?" she asked, arching a brow as though to judge them.

"What do you mean?" Harlan asked, genuinely puzzled.

"That you two were going at it," she replied succinctly.

"That's disgusting," Thomas put in angrily.

"Yes, and so is the subject of your conversation," she pointed out.

They realized what she was trying to say and quieted as they turned away and got their meals. Deanna put food on her tray too, but she wasn't hungry. The constant speculation as to Lenny's sexual orientation was upsetting her. She was sick of the gossip.

"What did the frat boys have to say?" Leida asked with a grin to cheer up Deanna. She was rewarded by the doctor with a small smile.

"They need to grow up," she answered, taking a bite of the bread she was tearing apart.

"Boys will be boys," she responded as she dug into the food. They had recently gotten a shipment with plenty of canned fruit and she relished the change. "You have to try this," she advised as she pointed out the offerings to Deanna.

"Boys may be boys, but that is no excuse for these supposed men," she answered angrily. She looked at the fruit, decided it did look good, and got up to get herself some. Her tray was still fairly full and she didn't realize anyone was behind her. Much to her mortification, she bumped into Maddie with the tray and it poured the contents down the redhead's front. "Oh, I am *so* sorry," she said apologetically.

"Oh man, I just managed to get a shower after all this mud," Maddie said mournfully in response as she looked down, horrified at the mess on her clothes.

"Looks like you are going to need another," Leida answered as she tried unsuccessfully not to laugh.

"And I will gladly pour it for you," Deanna promised. "I am very sorry," she repeated, looking genuinely contrite.

Leida's laughter got a glare and then Maddie realized it really was an accident and laughed herself. "I guess dinner is on me this time," she teased.

That drew a laugh out of the blonde. "I'll pay your cleaning bill," she offered. They all chuckled. They were fortunate that some of the locals, for a small fee, washed their clothing for them. They did a good job too. "Let me help you clean that up," she offered, but as her napkin came up Maddie took it from her, suddenly flushing in embarrassment.

"I got it." She wouldn't let Deanna help and shooed her away.

Deanna went to fill her tray again, this time with foods she knew she would eat including the delicious-looking fruit that Leida had on her own tray. By the time she returned to her spot, Maddie was sitting down eating her own food and chatting with Leida. Magda had joined them as well as Alex, and they were all discussing supplies and when the next truck would be due.

"What were you thinking?" Deanna hissed at Lenny. They were in the classroom talking, the only private place they had been able to find in the days since the two women had disappeared together.

"I was thinking I wanted to be alone with Emmanulla. We didn't see the storm coming on and when we did, we thought we could make it back!" she defended herself hotly.

"You almost got caught," she warned, keeping her voice low. One never knew who spoke what language or was listening. They couldn't walk out in the village as it was too muddy.

"I know and I'm sorry. I hope Emmanulla didn't get into too much trouble with her father."

"Do you think he knows? Do you think he disapproves?"

"He wants to marry her off," she said bitterly. "Emmanulla doesn't like any of the men her father has found for her."

"He's got to be suspicious!"

Lenny nodded miserably. "I've made a real mess of this. Maybe we should go away, but how am I going to get her back to the States? It takes years to get a passport here!"

"You can't possibly take her back to the States. They won't let her in and what are you going to say? She's your student? She's a little old for that! Your servant? They won't let her in!"

"I know," she moaned, "but what am I going to do? I love her!"

"Dammit, you shouldn't have fallen in love with her!"

"I know, I know!" she repeated.

"Shit!" Deanna ejaculated under her breath, still whispering. It wasn't a good situation and she felt bad for her friend, but there was nothing they could do. If they were exposed, they would both be disgraced: Emmanulla would be married off to the first man that her father could find, and Lenny would be shipped back to Canada. Lenny would never be allowed another post like this. If she was exposed as a homosexual, they would label her as unfit. If they heard it was with the chief's daughter she would be labeled as the perpetrator on that 'innocent' child. Deanna had another thought. "You didn't..." she began.

Lenny looked up. "We've...well, you know..." she began, whispering louder.

"Shhh," Deanna warned. "No, I don't know. Spell it out."

"I didn't do anything she didn't want to do," she defended herself.

"Oh shit, did you take her virginity?" Deanna asked, horrified at the possible consequences.

"No, there are other things you can do for pleasure," Lenny blushed. "Oh, God! What am I going to do?" she started to cry into her hands.

Deanna went to take her friend in her arms, but hearing a noise outside she hesitated and decided not to. "You are going to have to stop seeing her," she advised.

"No! I love her!" she protested, looking up, her eyes awash in her grief.

CHAPTER NINE

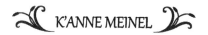

"So these guys are lugging in my supplies on their backs and on donkeys, and I didn't realize why I was tied up to the donkey. You know, led by a rope?" Deanna was regaling them with stories of her travels and they all smiled appreciatively at her description. "It was as I slipped off the narrow trail face first into the mud and started sliding down the steep slope, hitting tropical plants with my unmentionables, that I realized…that rope that kept me from falling down the mountainside. That was a good idea!"

They all started laughing, nearly choking on the beers they were sharing. "Oh, my gawd, Deanna! Did that really happen?" Magda wiped the tears away from the corner of her eye as she smiled at the story.

Deanna nodded. "Yeah, I've been to some pretty funky places. But you know what? It's one of the greatest things about what I do, seeing the sights. When they hauled my ass back up with that taut rope, I looked at that donkey and the phrase 'kiss my ass' had a whole new meaning."

They all collapsed into laughter again at her imagery.

Nights like this made the women close. Using a combination of English and French, they regaled each other with stories about their lives.

It wasn't often they were all there at the same time, but it was nice when they were able to share like that.

The rainy season provided plenty of time for introspection. No one wanted to be caught away from camp, not after Lenny had disappeared. She was quieter since she had been found, watchful. She still talked occasionally with Emmanulla, but they were unable to walk out together anymore. It seemed to be creating a tension. The others noticed their friend's agitation and came up with their own conclusions as to why she was like that. Although Deanna knew the real reason, the others could only speculate.

"Hey, I bet we can walk to the river in ten minutes and back, before the next rain shower," Deanna challenged Maddie.

Maddie laughed. "That's only because the river is so far over its banks we don't dare get any closer."

"That's why I said ten minutes," she repeated dryly. They shared a smile.

"Sure, I'll go. I'm starting to get cabin fever." They started walking through the camp as they bantered.

"Why cabin fever?"

"Well, I go from our tent, to the food tent, to the clinic, and if I'm lucky I get a shower in there at some point."

"Yeah, I feel wet all the time and slightly muddy," she agreed. Then she grinned as she realized something and then proceeded to share, "You do get time in the latrine too? You can't discount that."

"Of course I get time in the latrine," she sputtered in laughter at the incongruity of that. "You're silly."

"Of course I am, that's why they adore me," she spread out her hands indicating the children that would have followed them if their parents hadn't been calling them in for the evening. The rain clouds were already boiling up over the plains.

"They adore you because you tease them and give them balloons. That was really clever of you to bring in such a supply."

"Yeah, I realized our technology and advances meant nothing if you couldn't relate to them on simple things."

"Why do you always gather up the popped ones so carefully?"

"I don't want that rubber getting into the environment. It doesn't break down and recycle," she explained.

Maddie nodded. "That makes sense."

They chatted as they made their way to the roiling and dangerous river's edge. Seeing it in person was impressive. It carried away massive amounts of water. "This is gonna piss off Harlan," Deanna commented wryly.

"Yeah, but it should bring a lot of mud down from those," she indicated the hills that the water drained off from.

"Won't that make a mess?" she commented.

"And bring nutrients to the soil."

"Yeah," she agreed. She hadn't been thinking of that. "That's probably why the jungles get so rich with all that mulch and greenery."

"So this desert isn't to your liking?" she asked, curious about her friend.

"Oh, each has its pluses and minuses. I love where I am at the moment. I'm sure they are getting antsy to have me go soon," she confided.

"I'll miss you when you go."

Deanna looked at Maddie and smiled. Glancing at the clouds rolling in, she unconsciously turned them to walk back to the village. "I'll miss you too, but we can be lifelong friends can't we?"

"Absolutely!" she assured her.

"What are you going to do when your tour here is over?"

"Probably go back to the States and settle down in a hospital. I like the hustle and bustle here at the clinic. I can imagine some of it will translate and yet some of it will be so different."

"You don't have someone waiting for you back home?"

Maddie looked up at the taller woman and shook her head. "No, I wanted to see something of the world, so I didn't allow anyone to get that close. Besides, I wasn't ready. How about you?"

"Well, there was someone once. They didn't understand why I wanted to see these places." She gestured once again towards the village and smiled at a child shyly peeking out of her hut at them. "I can do more here than I could in the States, and I learn so much."

"You already know so much," Maddie said in awe. She really enjoyed working with her.

"Yes, but it can be lonely when you don't have someone."

"I hear you."

"So, what happened?" she asked, curious.

"With what?" Deanna asked, confused. Her mind had moved on to something else already as she looked up at the clinic, thinking about patients.

"Your *someone*," she smiled at how absentminded the blonde could be. She knew she was probably already working out some problem that had come up recently.

Deanna glanced over at the smaller but sturdier redhead and invited her to sit on the clinic steps. Not many people were out and about as they took shelter in anticipation of the expected showers rolling in. It was a fine spot to watch the clouds as they brought the rain. As they sat down she asked, "Do you really want to know?"

"Of course I want to know. Hell, we all talk about everything here," Maddie gestured to their tent and the campfire circle where the women spent time swapping stories, sometimes personal stuff that they would take to their graves. It was a nice bonding moment for them all.

Deanna considered for a moment, wondering if she should share or not. Shrugging internally, she figured, why the hell not? "It was when I was an intern. I fell for someone unexpectedly. She wasn't my first, but I did fall hard. She taught me a lot," she smiled nostalgically.

"She?" Maddie caught on quick. Her eyebrows rose in surprise.

Deanna nodded, staring intently into the redhead's eyes. "Yes, *she*," she said quietly.

"Oh, so you're...?" she wasn't sure quite how to finish that question.

"Gay?" Deanna supplied her with the word.

Maddie nodded and then quickly asked, "Or were you experimenting?" She figured that made a whole lot more sense for the intelligent, young woman.

"Yeah, I think I am," she answered philosophically. "I mean, I enjoy men. I like them. They look good, like a sculpture or a work of art, but, they don't *do* anything for me. I haven't been attracted to them sexually since I started practicing kissing one in college."

"Did you go all the way with him?"

"Oh no, that wouldn't have been allowed," she laughed as she watched the lightning streak across the darkening sky. It was going to be a pretty dramatic storm from what they were seeing. "I was in my early teens and he was seventeen, a freshman at college."

Maddie had forgotten that this woman, this accomplished woman who was of a similar age to her own, had graduated college at fourteen. She shook her head. "So you've never actually been with a man sexually?"

Deanna shook her head. "I may have kissed a couple, heavy petting even, but no sex. None. Heck, I wasn't even brave enough to sleep with a woman until I was nineteen," she confided with a grin. "She was special. She was a good first." The grin turned to a nostalgic smile.

"But are you sure that's what you want?" she asked, curious, wondering if it was a phase.

Deanna nodded. "Yeah, I'm just not attracted to a guy or his anatomy." She grinned at how clinical that sounded. "I think if I was, it would have changed how I went about pursuing my career."

"How so?"

"Well, that whole male superiority crap. My father would have wanted me to stay around, maybe marry someone who was like him and could go work for him. Who knows? My sister, fortunately, wants to be just like him, so he has someone to leave it all to."

"Leave it all?"

Deanna snorted slightly at what she had almost revealed. It came out almost as derision and Maddie took it to be an inside joke. "Yeah, since I was this Brainiac, my sister Doreen had to excel at something. She can have it."

Maddie nodded. Sibling rivalry was something she had seen and understood. "But how do you know you won't change your mind?" She shifted from sitting on the hard wood of the steps, glancing around to see if they were being listened to. The conversation was interesting, but she didn't want anything being misunderstood.

"I *know*," she said with conviction.

Maddie was surprised that someone so young, that someone who knew so much, could have such absolute certainty about something like that. She wasn't so sure that Deanna wasn't delusional.

"How about you?" Deanna turned it on her red-haired friend.

"How about me, what?"

"Are you so sure you are straight?"

"Absolutely," she answered automatically, but something about her voice lacked conviction.

"How can you be sure?" she challenged.

"Because I want children," she answered as though that explained everything.

"Just because I don't want children and I'm gay, doesn't mean I couldn't have them if I wanted them," she pointed out gently, smiling at her friend to get her point across.

Sighing slightly, she nodded to concede the point to her. "Yes, I understand that. But all my life I've had this picture in my head of the white picket fence, children running around the yard, and a dog maybe. My husband would come home after a hard day's work and we would work together to make dinner...."

"Are you sure he wouldn't put his feet up and expect *you* to make the dinner?" Deanna interrupted with a grin.

Maddie grinned at the teasing tone of her friend. "Yeah, knowing my luck he would. That's just what I need, someone like that. I'd work all day long and he'd expect to come home and relax." She shook her head at the stereotypes she had just spouted.

"Is that what you really want? Or is that just the dream you always had?"

Maddie wasn't used to someone always challenging her or what she said, but Deanna did have a point. She'd think about that a lot in the coming days.

The rain that had been rolling in decided to come down with a bolt of lightning that lit up the plains and their little community. The answering crash of thunder had them both running for their tent and shelter. They made it with a few moments to spare before the rain began to come down in earnest. “Whoa, that’s a gully washer,” Leida said in greeting as they ran in.

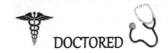

“It’s beautiful,” Deanna agreed as they turned to watch it from the doorway.

“Is there nothing you see that you don’t find beauty in?” the Aussie asked her with a smile. This young doctor was so pleasant to work with, always positive.

Deanna considered for about ten seconds. “No, I always try to find something positive in any situation.”

“Even if you have a sarcastic comeback,” Maddie said as she contributed to their conversation with a grin.

The three of them laughed together as they lit a couple of lanterns to ward off the darkness that accompanied the storm. It was starting to blow too, as the winds caught up with the storm.

“Whew, that’s something,” Magda said as she came into the tent. She was drenched from the downpour.

“Here,” Deanna threw her a towel to dry off.

Maddie was thrilled that her student French was improving. She had understood everything the two of them had said. The four of them had a pleasant time once Magda dried off, playing cards to pass the time. Lenny joined them an hour or so later, looking guilty. No one asked her where she had been.

CHAPTER TEN

"You know, for a fairly new used vehicle, this Rover sucks," Deanna said succinctly as she bent over fixing a flat.

Both Leida and Deanna had to agree with her. It was the second flat she had fixed that day. They had dropped Harlan off at one of the many fields he was propagating. They had dropped Hamishish off at the neighboring village after she directed them to the sick woman they had come to see. They also vaccinated those children that she directed them to. While there, a woman had gone into labor and Deanna had delivered a fine, healthy baby boy. It had meant they had a late start heading back to their own village and the clinic. This flat tire was another inconvenience.

"Why did you buy your own?" Leida asked conversationally as she held the spare tire. There were extra tires on the roof of the Rover since a flat could happen at any time.

"Well, they dropped me off in Lamish to catch up with you all when you came in…they didn't want to fly out here for just little ole me. I had enough supplies that I knew it would get crowded if they didn't bring a bus or two," she teased at the mode of transportation they had taken to come out to Mamadu. "But I wanted it for myself. When I leave, they can keep it," she said as she kicked the flat tire she had just fixed on the vehicle.

"Are you serious? Wouldn't that be an expensive gift?" Maddie asked as she took the flat tire and began to lift it onto the Rover. Leida rushed to help lift it. They weren't overly heavy, but they were awkward and dirty. They were both filthy with dust and the grime unique to tires made of rubber.

"Yeah, but the camp could use it, much more so than where I might go next. Besides, with the supplies I'm able to get in Lamish, they can continue doing that after I'm gone."

"Not if Lakesh does the transporting," Leida said succinctly. They all knew he was into the black market and things had a habit of disappearing all the time on the rides to and from the port city, not to mention around camp.

"Yeah, something is going to have to be done about him eventually," Deanna replied as she attached the lug nuts, first by spinning them on, and then by tightening them with the lug wrench. In no time at all the tire was changed and Maddie brought down the jack. "There we go. Let's get out of here," Deanna said as she glanced at the near dark they would have to drive in on their way home.

"Afraid of the boogie monster?" Leida asked as she got in the back and Maddie got in the front.

As they drove off, Deanna denied it, "No, more likely lions or something else."

"Come on, that was an isolated incident," Leida referred to a villager in the next village over who had been brought to their clinic after being attacked in the field by a lion.

"They still travel," Deanna pointed out.

Conversations such as these helped pass the time as they headed back to their own clinic. They didn't go far afield since there was the real threat of being attacked…not by animals, but by humans. By traveling in numbers, and especially with Hamishish along for the ride, they had thought themselves safe, but they hadn't anticipated being out after dark. They arrived safely and parked the Rover, returning the extra supplies they had packed to the supply hut. Carefully they put them away and put them back into inventory.

"*Doctor* Cooper," a frosty voice greeted them at the door as they finished up.

Deanna looked up at Doctor Burton and her smile of greeting faded. "Yes, Doctor Burton. What can I do for you?" she asked in reply, sounding professional.

"Would you be so kind as to join me in the office?" he requested. There was a gleam of satisfaction in his eye that the others saw there.

"Of course," she said as she looked at the other two in the light of the bare bulb in the hut. They nodded, showing they would finish up the work and lock up. She followed him as he abruptly turned away, marching towards the administrative office that Thomas now worked in alone since Alex had finally taught him the system and moved on.

"What can I do for you, Doctor Burton?" she asked, trying to sound cheerful. She hated these meetings. He frequently requested them and she dodged them whenever possible. She wondered where Doctor Wilson was this evening.

"Thomas," he barked, making sure he pronounced it Tomas, as the man had frequently requested. Everyone, at one time or another, had gotten it wrong. "Would you give us a moment?" he asked, but there was really no question in the sound of his wording. It was a command.

"Yesss," replied the man as he finished scratching in a ledger and looked up at the same time. Seeing the look in the doctor's eye, he hastily gathered up his books, put them in the desk, locked it, and got out of his way. He looked curiously at the blonde-haired woman doctor, wondering what she had done, before he left the room and closed the door behind him.

Doctor Burton went to sit in the vacated chair and indicated one of the two that were across the desk from him for Doctor Cooper. As she sat down, she realized with some trepidation this reminded her of the many meetings she had had over the years with her superiors, instructors, supervisors, and counselors. People still had a hard time understanding her mind and constantly questioned her. She still hated the feeling it gave her in the pit of her stomach.

"Doctor Cooper," he started, there was almost a hesitation over the name 'Cooper.' "Do you think of yourself as an honest person?" he asked.

Deanna was a bit surprised by the line of questioning and a puzzled look appeared on her face. "I am," she confirmed, wondering what this was about.

"So you believe that you always tell the truth?" he asked, almost as though anticipating an untruthful reply.

"I do," she confirmed again. This didn't bode well. The man was practically gleaming.

"Then can you tell me why Doctors Without Borders has no record of a Doctor Cooper on its rolls?" he asked with relish.

So, that was it? She nearly smiled. "Oh, there is a Doctor Cooper, and it is me," she assured him. She knew that any humor or happiness at this moment would be a bad idea, further irritating the man. "It is, however, on a need-to-know basis."

"I assure you, I have it on the utmost authority that there is NO Doctor Cooper in Doctors Without Borders. I want you to know I intend to get to the bottom of this and have you arrested for practicing without a license," he told her, clearly incensed at her audacity and lies.

"I don't know who you got your information from–" she began, but he cut her off.

"I'm not without resources," he assured her with relish.

She continued as though he had never interrupted, "but if you check with Doctor Wilson, he has and knows my credentials."

"I don't know who you bribed or what you are holding over them, but I assure you, you won't get away with this!" his voice was rising along with his temper.

"I'm not bribing anyone or holding anything over anyone," she tried reasoning with him, keeping her voice level and trying not to let her temper get the best of her.

"Then explain why you don't exist?" He had her and he was going to make sure she paid. He was going to love seeing her in handcuffs. How dare she impersonate being a doctor, a most noble profession! What they did here was important. He didn't care how smart she thought she was…she wasn't getting away with this! He'd make sure of it!

Doctor Cooper was alarmed, not at the information that Doctor Burton supposedly had, but at his demeanor. If he didn't calm down, he was going to have a heart attack. "I assure you, it really is none of your business. Doctor Wilson is satisfied with my credentials–" she began, only to be interrupted again.

"Doctor Wilson be damned!" he practically shouted, slamming a hand down on the desk. They both jumped from the noise.

Doctor Cooper assessed the man across the desk from her. Clearly, he was incensed. There was no reasoning with such a man. She sat back coolly in the chair and viewed him, not unlike how she viewed the insects she watched from a chair when she relaxed.

It was obvious the woman wasn't going to deny the accusations in a manner that he had expected. He was ready to get up and call one of the soldiers in to arrest her for impersonating a doctor. It was then that they both heard the rushing of feet and Doctor Wilson opened the door.

"What the hell is going on in here?" he asked, alarmed. The walls of these places were not that thick. He could hear the raised voice of Doctor Burton from a good distance away.

"I would like to inform you, *Doctor* Wilson, that this woman is a fake, a fraud," he said, pointing his index finger at her.

Deanna nearly smiled again. The man was very upset, and for all the wrong reasons. She sat there quietly, watching him, not answering his charges.

Doctor Wilson relaxed a little. He had thought something dire had been happening in here. "Is that all?' he said in his relief.

"Is that *all*?" Burton nearly screamed. "I'll have you know she has fooled–" he began, a little spittle flicking out as he ranted.

"DOCTOR BURTON!" Wilson raised his voice to drown out the other doctor and to calm him a little. "I assure you, I have it on good authority and my own investigations that Doctor Cooper is who she says she is."

"Oh no, not this time, Emeril," Burton said triumphantly. Deanna had to wonder…*this* time? There were others? "You have been duped, I'm sorry to say. I have it here," he showed a folder he had been carrying, something Deanna hadn't even noticed, "that there is NO Doctor Cooper in the MSF!"

"Yes, I know," Doctor Wilson agreed and watched as the man deflated.

"What? You knew?" He couldn't believe what he was hearing. Wilson was in on this?

"Doctor Cooper is a doctor, and yes she is in the MSF. Doctors Without Borders is a small organization. Do you really think she could get away with faking this?" he tried to reason.

"She has! And you were in on it!"

Wilson nodded. "Yes, I know who she is, and I know why you didn't find what you thought you would. However, I assure you, that her credentials check out. If you spent more time looking after your patients instead of on this..." he spread his hands in helplessness, "...witch-hunt, you'd get a helluva lot more work done." His voice was stern and it was obvious he was angry too.

Deanna studiously examined her hand, deciding to trim her nails again that night. It was important to keep her nails short for her patients, so she didn't accidentally scratch them. Her other hand came up and her fingers began to play with her eyebrow distractedly, pulling slightly at the short hairs.

"And I assure you, that you are mistaken," he began again, trying to inflate with his anger.

"DOCTOR BURTON, if you don't stand down NOW, I'm going to have to have you relieved," he promised him.

"But I have–"

"No, you have nothing," he promised him as he held out his hand for the file.

"But..."

"No buts. You *drop* this and you drop it *now*."

Burton debated whether arguing would be worth it. He determined that it would not be. He slapped the file into the outstretched hand and left the room, nearly knocking Wilson aside in his anger and haste. Burton slammed the door on his way out.

Quietly, Wilson counted to ten to give Burton a chance to walk away from the office. He went to sit on the corner of the desk. Looking down at the blonde doctor he was amused to see her examining her hands, something he caught himself doing from time to time. "Well, what do you have to say for yourself?" he asked sternly.

Deanna looked up and caught a glimmer of amusement in the older doctor's eyes. She grinned a little as she replied, "Nuttin'," in the slang of the day. "I don't got nuttin' to say."

He grinned. "Troublemaker," he mumbled ruefully. "You know he won't let it go?"

She nodded. "I'm staying though."

He nodded gratefully. She was worth two Doctor Burtons, who, while a fine surgeon, was terribly narrow-minded. He couldn't get past the little hurts. He still thought the woman was a fine...mechanic. He'd heard that one from the good doctor more than once. "Then that's it," he finished.

"Don't you want to see what's in that?" she gestured curiously at the file.

He shook his head. "I'm not even going to look," he told her. "Want to start a fire?" he asked, offering it to her.

"Nope," she answered as she stood up. "I got work to do."

"See ya," he said and watched as she walked out the door. He smiled. She was such a good doctor. People couldn't understand a brain like hers. He was glad he knew who and what she was. If he had a dozen doctors like her in Africa, they could take on the world…she was that good. He sighed gustily as he looked down at the file. Despite assuring her he wouldn't look, he did. He sighed at the contents. Doctor Burton, while a sexist moron, had been thorough and had letters from key people. He pulled a few of them out and pocketed them. Then he carried the file and made a show of throwing it on the nearest bonfire. He was pleased to see that Doctor Burton was peering from the clinic and saw the papers burn.

CHAPTER ELEVEN

"I'm so sick of this rain!" Leida complained good-naturedly as she helped clean out the mud that was endlessly tracked into the clinic.

They all enjoyed the rain after the hot, dry summer. The dust was an endless plague, along with the flies and other vermin. The fans in the rafters of the huts couldn't drive away enough of the bugs in the hot season. The rain was a cool, refreshing change...except for the mud. There was always something. They learned to live through it and already there were signs of it waning. They didn't get as much in the 'rainy season' here as they should, that was part of the reason people were starving to death.

"I won't be able to plant my crops!" Harlan complained. He understood about the river bringing rich soil to his fields, but he couldn't plow while they were under water! He couldn't plant or it would all be washed away. He hoped for a lessening of the deluge that had hit them. Meanwhile, he helped with manual labor around the clinic and village—the villagers appreciated his great strength and willingness to help repair their homes.

Deanna watched as the rain came down in a steady downpour. It was relaxing, but she too was sick of it. It had gone on too long and she was getting antsy to get out, a kind of cabin fever that she recognized. They couldn't go anywhere in this weather, and when they did, they got soaked. It made for miserable living conditions. She remembered living in the rain forest. It rained there almost every day, sometimes for weeks on end. This felt similar, but at the same time, any rain forest that had existed here was long gone as the desert tried to claim the continent. These beautiful plains were fairly parched. She was certain that men like Harlan would probably fail at what they were attempting. It wasn't her lookout though. She was here to help save lives in a different way.

"Penny for your thoughts?" Maddie asked from behind her.

Deanna turned and smiled at her friend. "Nah, they aren't even worth that."

"Are you bored?" her friend grinned teasingly. There was always something to do at the clinic.

"Nope, just taking a break," she turned back to watch the rain. The water running in rivulets across what had been hard-packed earth was now muddy and little streams of it, all rushing away towards the river that ran through the valley. Since the roof of the clinic was made of tin, it was a loud noise and they had to speak up to be heard over it. "Come on, I'm going to see if there is any coffee left," she encouraged.

"You'll get soaked!" Maddie promised, but she followed the taller woman as she ran down the steps and out into the rain. Quickly they splashed through the deluge towards the food tent. She was right, they were wet through and through within moments. Neither minded, it was a constant state of affairs these days. They just had to remember to stay warm or they'd all come down with colds or worse.

They were the only ones in the food tent, the first time that had ever happened. They helped themselves to the ever-present coffee and nibbled on some crackers that were left out. Crackers were something that couldn't go bad in the African air. No other food was out yet, but there was at least another hour before it was dinnertime. They sat down at one of the benches, facing the doorway so they could watch the rain.

"Mmmm, that smells heavenly," Deanna said as she inhaled the aroma.

"Tastes even better," Maddie quipped before taking a slurp and burning her tongue. "Ouch," she swore under her breath.

"Now, now, didn't your mother teach you better?" Deanna teased as she sipped hesitantly.

Maddie chuckled knowing that Deanna had been known to swear up a blue streak now and again. She thought for a moment and when an odd look came over her face she looked away, but not before Deanna saw it.

"What?" the astute doctor asked.

"What, what?"

"C'mon, I saw you had a question or something."

"Jeez, there is no getting by you is there?"

She shook her head. "Nope, so don't even try."

She chuckled as she took another hesitant sip of her hot coffee.

"C'mon, I'm waiting," she started tapping her free hand on the table in time with the drips outside the door.

"Alright already," she sighed. Taking a deep breath, she glanced at her friend and then looked down into her coffee cup before asking in a rush, "What's it like to kiss a woman?"

Deanna's eyebrows raised in surprise on her pretty face. Of all the things her friend had asked her over the months they had worked here, that would not have been the question she would have guessed she would ask her. She hesitated for a moment, almost gasping for air as her mouth opened and closed and she thought up a reply. Finally, she answered. "I guess it's no different than kissing a man..." she began. Shaking her head to the negative she quickly added, "No, that's not true. It's totally different than kissing a man." She looked out at the rain as she thought back. "It's more...sensual. It's softer. Depending on who you kiss of course, and how good they are," she grinned. It told a lot more than what she was saying as she remembered her own shared kisses. "It's beautiful with the right person."

Maddie hadn't known what to expect in response, but Deanna made it sound wonderful. She didn't know where she had gotten up the nerve to ask, but she knew since their last talk she'd been thinking about it a lot. She'd guessed that Lenny was gay too. In fact, she wondered if Lenny would get in trouble if someone found out she was involved with Emmanulla. She dismissed that thought as they had been carrying on for months and no one had caught them. Her thoughts returned to Deanna and what she had told her. Biting her lip, she hesitated to ask further and then figured, why not? "When is the last time you kissed a woman?"

Deanna met the redhead's eyes. Blue eyes bored into dark green eyes and she searched for the questions that Maddie hadn't had the guts to ask yet. She carefully considered what really was being asked here. "It's been a while," she said quietly, grateful that the canvas roof of the tent made it easier to talk in here than in the clinic. They would never have been able to have this conversation otherwise. "Why are you asking, Maddie?" she asked softly, putting down her coffee cup to give the redhead her full attention.

Maddie shook her head. "I don't know." She looked out at the rain to avoid Deanna's eyes. They were too blue and saw too much. Her mind didn't work like the rest of them. It saw too much, ascertained too much, processed things far too quickly. Sometimes it was like she read their minds, she was that quick.

Deanna picked up her coffee cup again to take a sip. "You let me know when you do know, okay?" she advised in a carefully controlled, friendly tone. She didn't let on that she thought she knew the reason. Maddie would have to come to that conclusion herself. Everyone had to make these decisions themselves.

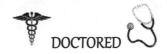

They were silent as they listened and watched the rain come down. It was a companionable silence and both were lost in their own thoughts.

It was after midnight that same night when they were woken out of their sleep by calls. "Everyone UP!" they could hear both Burton and Wilson yelling. The women got up and lanterns were lit. They were surprised to see Hamishish there as well. She'd been absent a lot lately. Quickly, the women changed from their night attire to pants or shorts, and shirts. Eyes were averted to allow for privacy. Jamming their stocking-clad feet into hastily shaken boots, they hurried outside in the rain.

"A bus has overturned at Zalick," they were told. The next village down the way was about a thirty-minute drive in good weather. "It's gone into the river and they are bringing us casualties. Everyone UP and get prepared for them!"

Everyone ran to the clinic or the supply hut to do what they could do for this mass casualty situation. It wasn't long before they began to arrive. Some, while not hurt, had come with information. They were shaken up as they told that the bus had been fired upon. The driver had done well to avoid the shooters, but it was a long bus and it was inevitable that they would be hit, that someone would be hit. The flames were instantaneous when their gas tank had been struck. The bus driver had swerved to avoid something and slipped off into a culvert. The culvert, overflowing with water, had led to the river. They were pulling those they could find out of the river. It wasn't easy as they weren't sure who had fired on the bus or why.

"Let's get these ready here," Burton called his medical staff to the various tables they had to ready to deal with the more serious injuries. He might not believe in Doctor Cooper, but he would use her and her abilities.

They were well ready by the time the more serious casualties came in. The bus had been jammed, even some on the roof apparently. Those on the roof had been the first into the water and were swept away by the current. Some of their bodies would never be found. The ones that were coming in now, more than half of them were already dead. Others that they were able to help were banged up badly, most were suffering from exposure to the cold rain.

It was a horrible night. As the rain tapered off and the sun finally shone through the clouds, they didn't even notice when the assistants began to turn off the lanterns.

"Jeezus Christus," Deanna swore as she straightened up from her fortieth patient. She hadn't meant to keep track, but she had, unconsciously. Some she had saved—most that could be saved—but it had been terrible to have to let some of them go. There was nothing she could do for some of them. Mothers cried over their babies, children cried for their parents, trying to match up families was terrible.

"You okay?" Lenny asked as she put her hand on the doctor's shoulder. She'd been pressed into service to help carry the wounded and sick. The floors of both the meeting hall and the clinic were full of people.

"Yeah, my spine could use a crack," she mentioned as she rubbed her forehead with the back of her hand. She removed her rubber gloves and tossed them out. She couldn't remember how many pairs she had gone through this night. Her fingertips removed dust from her eyelashes...dust that wasn't there, as she pulled lightly on the hairs.

"Yeah? You got a chiropractor out here?" she asked, as though Deanna kept one in her pocket. She removed her hand from her friend's shoulder. It didn't pay to be too friendly these days. She knew there were rumors aplenty going around.

Deanna smiled, as she was expected to, and stretched a little more. She looked out where the sun was already drying up the mud. It was a mess. Old cars, jeeps, horses, and any animal they could find had been pressed into service to deliver the casualties here. She was depressed at the numbers of people who had died although there was simply nothing they could do. It was a primitive place. They did what they could do, comforting the living and providing healthcare where they could. It wasn't an easy job and it was at times like this she wondered why she had gone into this career. "Look at that," she pointed with her chin, nodding towards the beauty that was outside the clinic: on the plains, the savannah, the flowers that always bloomed quickly after a rain. "How can anything that beautiful hide so many deadly things?" she asked of no one in particular. Deanna sensed, rather than heard, others coming up behind her on the porch to see what she was seeing. The sun looked gorgeous and was welcome after so many days of rain. She looked out at the brush beyond the edge of the camp, which was green and already beginning to grow lush. In a few days the grasses would almost paint a sweeping path across the plains providing nourishment to the huge herds of grass eaters. Following those herds would be the meat eaters. They would all have to be a little more vigilant, already there were rumors of lions.

Deanna was one of the last to head to her bed, after checking on her patients one more time. It was frustrating how limited she was in what she could do for them. Still, it was gratifying that she could use her skills to help some of them.

"You should get some sleep," Maddie came up after changing a dressing on a patient.

"I could say the same of you," Deanna turned and smiled down at her.

"I am going to go take a shower," she informed her.

"Yeah? Found someone to pour for you?" she asked, interested, as they began to walk through the ward together.

"Not only that," she bragged, "but it's *warm* water."

"Really?" she asked, actually interested in the way the conversation had gone. "How'd you manage that?"

"Hamishish arranged it for me. Come and I'll share the showers with you," then she blushed deeply as she realized how that sounded. "I mean...I didn't mean..." she stammered.

Deanna chuckled and said, "Don't sweat it." They both laughed at that turn of phrase. Already the sun was hot and drying up the place. There were actually several places they could walk now without encountering the mud.

They made their way to their tent, got clean clothes to change into, and then went to the showers where a small fire had been lit to warm the water for them.

"You sure they won't mind pouring for me too?" Deanna asked, worriedly. She hadn't thought of bribing someone to do this and wondered why Hamishish had offered to the nurse.

"Naw, I told you, they owe me," she assured her as she went into the curtained-off area and quickly stripped out of her dirty clothes. She hung up the ones she intended to change into and carefully pushed the other curtain across to keep them dry as she saw the women carrying up the heavy buckets of warm water.

Carefully they poured half the bucket of hot water into an empty bucket and added a little of the cooler water until the water wasn't so hot. They poured this into the shower receptacle and this sprinkled down on the two women. They quickly utilized the warm water and shampooed their hair and scrubbed their sweaty bodies with soap. The water got progressively warmer as the carriers tired of hauling bucket after bucket up the platform, but finally they were done. Both women relished the feeling of the hot shower they had received and dressed in their clean clothing.

"Oh, my gawd, that was great," Deanna gushed as she used a towel on her short, blonde hair. The hot African sun had been bleaching it whiter, removing the various browns and reds.

"I thought so too," the nurse answered as she gathered her dirty clothes in a ball.

"Have you eaten?"

"No, have you?"

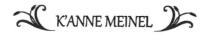

"No, and I'm starving, but I'm going to have to eat, walk it off a little, and then collapse for a few hours," she explained her itinerary.

"Sounds good to me," and there was a note of absolute exhaustion in the redhead's voice too.

They did exactly that, hurrying to shovel down the food, ignoring all attempts by their associates to converse as they wished to finish their meal in a hurry. Taking a walk on the now drying paths, they still couldn't go far as the river hadn't receded enough; it was too soon after the inundation they had received.

"Would you look at that!" Deanna exclaimed as she pointed out an animal.

"What is that? A cheetah?" The alarm in her voice was obvious.

"No, I think it's a serval or what they call a bush cat," the blonde told her excitedly.

"A serval? I don't think I've heard of that..." she began as she peered at the spotted cat.

"It's Portuguese for wolf-deer," the brilliant doctor informed her. The tone of her voice told how excited she was to see one in the wild and not too far from their home. "They also call them a giraffe-cat, but I can see why you thought that was a cheetah. They once thought they were just a smaller cheetah." There was no hint of superiority in her tone as she explained what she knew about the cat. She was just sharing it with her friend. "The ancient Egyptians used to worship them for their grace and power. I'm not surprised that we're seeing them here on the plains. I've even read that they are called the 'Savannah Stalker' because they hunt on these plains."

Just when she thought she couldn't be more impressed by Deanna and her brilliance, she still surprised her. "Look at those ears," she gasped. They were huge! The animal itself was long and sleek, not as big as the lions she had seen in the zoo, but still, definitely a big cat. It sat on an outcropping, just above the grass, sunning itself.

"You know, there are people that have them as pets," the doctor said with a tone that implied she wouldn't mind having one for herself.

"Well, you go catch one," she teased.

"Maybe I will," she laughed with her friend. The cat heard her laughter from far away. It looked at them momentarily before slipping off the rock and disappearing into the long grasses. "Oh, too bad," she lamented.

"Ah well, you'll just have to try again next time," she teased some more. Maddie smiled up at the blonde, noticing how white her hair had become in the African sun. The roots were definitely darker where they were growing in. "You need a haircut," she said when she noticed, and without thinking, her hand came up to run her fingers through the spikey locks.

Deanna froze where she stood as she looked down at the redhead. The feel of her fingers through her hair felt wonderful. She forgot to breathe for a moment and they locked eyes.

Maddie realized her mistake as soon as their eyes met. In that moment it was just the two of them out on the plain, within sight of the village, but far enough away that they couldn't be seen clearly. She took a step forward, hesitated for a brief moment, thought about stepping back, and then leaned up for a kiss.

Deanna wasn't sure she should, but at the same time she knew she had been attracted to the redhead for quite some time. It wasn't that she was attracted to all women, but Maddie and she had spent a lot of time together and she considered her a friend, a good friend. To take this step might ruin their friendship, but, she hadn't been the one to take it. She leaned down to allow Maddie's lips to capture her own.

The first thought Maddie had was that Deanna's lips were softer than any man's she had kissed. Deanna had been right about that. They were warm, supple, and slightly moist. They invited her to taste further and her tongue hesitantly snaked out.

Deanna didn't want to scare the smaller, robust woman off, but she so badly wanted to pull her against her own body and feel it full length, to enthrall all the senses. As she explored her lips, inhaled her essence, and her tongue began to taste, it was a near thing.

The kiss went on for a while and finally Maddie pulled back, looking up at the blonde for reassurance. Quietly, she asked, "Was that alright?"

Not trusting herself to speak, Deanna nodded. Her eyes glimmered. Her face was deadpan, showing no emotion. She didn't want to encourage Maddie, but she didn't want to discourage her either. It had to be the redhead's decision.

"Maybe I shouldn't have," she began and her body started to pull back.

'The hell with it,' Deanna thought and her hands quickly snaked around Maddie's shoulders. "It's okay," she breathed, leaning down with her forehead touching the other woman's. Her lips hovered above Maddie's. "I've been wondering what you tasted like too," she admitted.

Maddie pulled back marginally, but only so she could look into the blue eyes of the doctor. "You have?" At Deanna's nod she asked, "Why didn't you say anything?"

Deanna grinned ruefully. "I didn't want you thinking just because I'm attracted to women, that I hit on *all* women."

"But, you are attracted to me?" There was an almost hopeful note in the nurse's voice.

Deanna nodded. "So, why did you kiss me?" she whispered, her lips hovering again.

"I was curious," she admitted. "I wanted to know what it was like."

"And now?"

"I want to know more," she said as she pulled Deanna in and kissed her again, harder.

They explored each other's lips. Deanna got her wish as she pulled Maddie's body into her own, wrapping herself around the shorter woman. Maddie was surprised at how different and how right Deanna's body felt against her own. The kisses, the tongue, and even the nibbling went on for a while. Their hands began to soothe, caress, and wander. It began to become heated and finally Deanna sensed that Maddie was becoming overwhelmed and calmed herself to reluctantly pull away. "Are you okay?"

Maddie nodded, bemused. "I didn't know. I didn't know it could be like that."

"Like what?" she asked, pulling back far enough to hold Maddie in place, but not far enough to let her completely go.

"Like a romance novel," she responded inadequately. She felt shy now that she had admitted her attraction to the doctor, had felt her mutual attraction, and knew that she was interested. Her body spoke to her and she hadn't even known it could feel like that.

"Not all romance novels have a happily ever after," Deanna warned.

Maddie smiled, showing off the dimples that rarely appeared on her face. "No, they don't," she shook her head, "but I'm willing to turn a few pages and find out."

Deanna smiled in response. She liked the dimples. They added an almost fairly-like quality to the redhead's pointed face. "Let's just take it slow and easy," she promised. What she wanted to do was take the redhead right there on the wet ground. Her body had been a long time without the touch of another human being and she knew she wanted Maddie's touch.

"What now?" Maddie asked, unsure.

"We see if this is really what you want to pursue."

"What *I* want?"

Nodding, Deanna smiled slightly. "I've been here before. I think I know what I want."

"Do you want me?" Her shyness and indecision was endearing.

Deanna heard a sound from camp and let her hands fall from the now steady Maddie. Turning slightly, she glanced to see others taking advantage of the sunny evening and taking a walk. She tried to make it look natural as she turned Maddie so they could walk back to the camp. "Yes, I want you, but, Maddie, this is a big decision for you. I don't want you to get hurt. I don't want to get hurt. If you are just curious...."

"Yes, I was curious, but, it was like it made so much sense once we kissed," she explained, her hands emphasizing what she was trying to say.

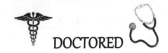

Deanna nodded. It had been that way for her too at one point as she realized her attraction to women. It just...fit. It just...felt right for her. No one could have told her that, she had to find out for herself. Maddie had to find it out for herself. "Think about it. Do you really want to get involved like this?" her voice lowered as they walked by others making their way towards the river. "Good evening," Deanna said cordially and smiled.

"Is it wetter over there?" one of the relief workers asked.

"No wetter than camp, and it's drying out fast," she answered as they continued walking. Once out of earshot she turned to Maddie again. "Think about it," she repeated.

"I will," the redhead promised.

They returned to their tent. Not another word was spoken, but both had a lot on their minds. Each changed clothes and got ready for bed. Each took a lot longer than she should have to fall asleep despite their fatigue.

CHAPTER TWELVE

"Lenny is gone," the whispers abounded.

One of the camp cars was missing, and so was the chief's daughter, Emmanulla. When it was discovered that Lenny and her things were gone as well, people put two and two together.

Doctor Wilson had no choice but to send out inquiries. He didn't want to, but with Burton watching him and conspiring behind his back, he had to. He took the time to write to the people who had supported Burton in the past, explaining the doctor's paranoia, and his own position regarding the Doctor Cooper situation. He didn't reveal what he knew about the brilliant young specialist, but he made it clear that she had been highly vetted and recommended by Doctors Without Borders and it was no one's business but theirs about their personnel. He was not happy with the Lenny situation. They were now without a teacher. Worse, the chief was angry about his daughter's defection. This was incontrovertible proof of their liaison. He couldn't deny it any longer. He was embarrassed and had lost face.

The car that Lenny had stolen was eventually found in Lamish. One of Lakesh's contacts had found it for him, stripped and gutted. However, a letter addressed to Doctor Wilson and left at the hotel, told how she had left it at the hotel for him to reclaim. It must have been stolen from there. Wilson had his own opinions of Lakesh and his friends and didn't doubt that the car had been taken from the hotel. Lenny had tried to make good on a bad situation and simply left. Taking the chief's daughter had been only logical on her part. The aftermath was nothing she could have foreseen.

"You think that dyke sold the parts for money to finance her flight?" Harlan was overheard saying with relish to one of the relief workers. He was very busy these days, teaching the locals to use the equipment that he farmed with. A new tractor had been donated and between that and the other equipment, they were plowing fields on the plains for food. He only had another month to teach them in Mamadu before he rotated out and another farmer came to replace him.

Deanna overheard the ignorant redneck and wanted to defend her friend Lenny, but knew it would be a mistake. Her own burgeoning relationship with Maddie was too new and too raw to allow something like rumors to destroy it.

They were taking their time. They were 'dating' such as it were…taking walks along the now normal river that had subsided considerably from its flood stage. They looked at the fields that Harlan and the tribe members were plowing and planting, discussing it in great depth, and enjoying spending time together. And the kisses…they spent plenty of time exploring those. Deanna could sense the frustration in Maddie that they weren't taking it further, faster. She didn't want this to be a quick romance. She wanted more. It was a natural progression to her that someone she had so much in common with might be her soulmate. They were both in the medical field. They both enjoyed helping people. They both wanted to see more of the world. It was obvious they were meant for each other…at least to Deanna.

"Why are you *here*?"

Deanna looked at Maddie from where they were sitting in chairs, looking up at the stars. They were alone around the fire, having outlasted the others. They were all tired from a full day in the clinic. Lakesh had come back that day from Lamish with a Rover full of supplies and Doctor Wilson was pissed because half of them were 'missing.' They had to make do with what they had left. They had been sitting around the fire discussing the current lack of supplies and the possibility that Lakesh had been robbing them blind. "Here?" she asked as her foot snaked out and gently rubbed along the back of Maddie's leg.

Maddie was enjoying the buildup. She was so curious about what came next that Deanna distracted her admirably. Knowing that she wanted sex so badly with this woman wasn't easy. She'd felt conflicted for days, and frustrated. Her mind couldn't stop thinking it all over, analyzing how she felt, and why. She tried to focus. "I meant *here*, in Africa. You've spoken about the Amazon and South America before. Why did you leave?"

Deanna turned from looking at Maddie to looking into the fire as she contemplated how to answer. "It was time to move on," she said musingly as she shrugged. "I felt I was needed elsewhere."

"Africa's a vast continent. Doctors Without Borders works all over. How'd you end up *here*?"

Deanna looked up from the fire, blinked a few times to clear the glare of the fire from her eyes, and answered. "I let them choose. I'm at their disposal, but it was nice to feel needed again."

"Again?" she probed, sensing a story.

The doctor swallowed, deciding what she could share and what she shouldn't share. She'd not been this close to a woman in so long. She had to roll the dice and see if this relationship was going to go anywhere. "I'd outlived my usefulness in the Amazon, at least in that section."

"You? I can't imagine your skills wouldn't be in demand..." she objected.

"It wasn't my skills that had been used up," she sounded bitter.

"Then what?" she asked softly, sensing it hurt.

Deanna was looking down at the dirt so as not to have any more night blindness from the fire's glow. Glancing up, she sighed and began to share. "I loved it there," she answered nostalgically. "Everything about it was fascinating, even the animals and the bugs," she smiled wryly. "You can't imagine how much is hidden in the jungle. Turn over a leaf and you stumble upon a new discovery. They know more in that jungle than we have learned in four thousand years."

Maddie watched as Deanna enthused about the place she had lived. She'd seen this enthusiasm before when she talked about South America.

"I was so young and naïve when I went there. I thought I'd find something to cure the ills of the modern world."

"And did you?"

Deanna smiled at her potential lover. She shook her head. "There is so much to be learned there. So much that we are too blind to see. The people who have lived there all their lives have it as common knowledge. We Westerners are stupid."

"You are *not* stupid," she pointed out.

The doctor shook her head. "No, I'm not stupid, but I *was* young, immature."

"What happened?"

"I was fortunate. The tribe we were studying with had a witch doctor."

"Like Hamishish?"

Deanna nodded. "And yet, not like her," she grinned wryly. "It's different with each culture."

"No wonder you made friends with her so quickly."

She nodded again. "Yes, that friendship with the shaman proved to be an invaluable tool." She glanced at the fire and for a second her eyes were drawn to the flames again before she blinked and looked away. "She taught me so much."

"Did you speak her language?"

"No, but pantomime and time cured that as she seemed fascinated with a *female* doctor. All the researchers who had come before were men. White men. She had never seen a white female doctor before. She took me under her wing and began to teach me. Really teach me."

"That must have been fascinating," Maddie commented knowing how much Deanna loved to be challenged and learn new things.

She nodded and then looked sad.

"What happened?"

Deanna looked up at her, trying to see her eyes through the darkness. In the flickering light of the fire she didn't see condemnation, merely curiosity. "I fell in love."

"With the shaman?"

Deanna shook her head. "No, that would have been acceptable. Two medical mystics coming together. It wasn't with her and that almost insulted her. What really pissed her off though, was that I fell in love with her daughter."

"How old was her daughter?" she asked, intrigued, wondering at this faceless person and how she had fallen for this brilliant young doctor.

"Eighteen summers," she answered and leaned down to pick up a stick to throw on the fire.

"How old were you?"

She leaned back and looked again at Maddie. "I was twenty."

"How long did it last?"

"One year," she said bitterly.

"Were you discovered?"

"Oh yeah...." She grimaced ruefully. "We were discovered, exposed, and eviscerated before the entire tribe."

"Do they not accept," her voice lowered to a whisper, "*homosexuality*?"

Deanna nearly laughed aloud at the tone, as though it were a forbidden subject. Given that they were contemplating entering into a relationship themselves, it was hilarious. "Many tribes accept that there are people within their society that like the same sex," she responded almost prudishly to Maddie's question. "No, it wasn't that," she continued. "It was the fact that she was married," she almost stopped telling her tale at Maddie's gasp, "to the chief's son," she finished.

"You dated a *married* woman?" she asked, shocked at the thought.

"Well, I didn't *know* she was married until much later," she defended herself. "It's not like the language barrier and different cultures didn't enter into the equation."

"So, what happened?" she asked, curious despite herself.

Deanna looked sad for a moment. "I was upset when I found out that she was married. It was a tribal thing and when they found out about us," she almost shuddered at the embarrassment, "I was asked to leave."

"Why would you ever consider going back there?"

"Because it's a magical part of the world and it's a huge continent. I don't have to go back to the same place I was," she explained. "There is so much more to learn."

"That's why you came to Africa?"

"It's even bigger here. I can learn anywhere."

"What have you learned here?"

Deanna went on about what Hamishish had taught her. When they went to the other villages, despite the language barrier, she was shown things that helped her do her job. Using modern medicines, she could help the locals. Learning local medicines and techniques, she was accepted easier. It was part of why she was drawn to Hamishish. She knew a lot of Western people wouldn't accept the woman, equating her to a whore, but she really was knowledgeable and who she chose to share her body with, was her choice.

"Is that why you and Lenny hit it off so quickly?"

Deanna was brought back to the present. She nodded. "That and my gaydar went off."

"Your what?" She had never heard the term before.

"My gaydar. It's when you can sense that someone else is gay too," she explained.

"Do you have to become gay to feel it?" she asked, worried.

The blonde chuckled and shook her head. "No, it's more like knowing if someone likes you or if someone has certain mannerisms. Sometimes you are right when you guess that they are gay, you can be equally wrong."

"Have you ever been wrong?" She was curious again.

Smiling she answered, "Occasionally."

"What about me? Would you have guessed I was gay?"

"You aren't, are you?" she pointed out.

"Not for lack of trying," she admitted ruefully.

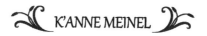

CHAPTER THIRTEEN

"**H**ey, I'm going into Lamish for supplies on my next days off. I'm going to stay overnight." Doctor Cooper informed Doctor Wilson.

"Oh good, maybe we'll get what we ordered in full for a change," he said with a remorseful grin.

"Why don't you get rid of Lakesh if you think he's stealing so much?"

"Because I don't have any proof, and who else is going to drive?"

"I'm sure there are a half a dozen of the relief workers who would be glad to, given a chance. You have to start asking," she pointed out.

He sighed gustily. "I have a letter I'd like you to post, if you would."

"Sure, why didn't you send it with the regular mail?" Lakesh took their mail in at least once a week for them.

"I have, but I'm not certain it hasn't been subverted," he confided. They exchanged a look.

Nodding, she agreed, and they spoke of a few supplies she could pick up for him as well as the clinic.

"Do you mind if I ask Maddie to go along?" she tried to sound innocent as she asked.

He shook his head. "No, I don't mind. Does she want to go?"

"No idea. I thought I'd ask you if she could have the same days off before I asked her if she wanted to go along. That's such a long and dry, dusty drive."

He nodded. The road had gotten worse since the rainy season and it wasn't like anyone would be repairing it. "Make sure you get your tires fixed while you're in town."

They finished up their list of things he would like and then he promised, "I'll have that letter, maybe letters for you before you leave in the morning."

She nodded as she turned to leave, nearly bumping into Doctor Burton as he entered the office. "Oh, excuse me," she said politely.

He looked at her coldly and sidestepped so she could leave, never saying a word. She left, shaking her head at his rudeness.

"Hey, you," she greeted Maddie, who was bandaging an arm. "Can I give you a hand?" she asked with a grin to show she was joking. After all, Maddie was holding the hand of the boy in one hand and bandaging with the other. The only way to keep him from moving as he wouldn't hold it still.

Maddie sighed in relief. This was one time the language barrier was not a good thing. The little boy would not sit still because of the pain, and he needed the wound to be covered. She had cleaned it, which caused him pain and now he wouldn't sit still, making it difficult to wrap the wound. Furthermore, his mother refused to keep him calm or even talk to him. Without being able to say a word to each other, the pantomime wasn't working well. "Oh, thank you," she said with genuine appreciation for Deanna showing up. "This little wiggle worm needs this bandaged properly and he won't sit still."

Deanna fixed a stern look on her face and said a couple of words she had picked up of the local dialect. The boy looked at the female doctor in awe and sat completely still as she took his hand from Maddie's and held it. Quickly, Maddie was able to wrap the arm.

"Jeez, that was a lot easier," she complained good-naturedly. "What did you say to him?" she asked, curious.

"I told him that this witch doctor," she pointed with her thumb at herself, looking proud, "was not pleased with him bouncing around when the good nurse was just trying to help me."

"You said all that with a few words?" she looked up from where she was putting away her materials to see Deanna grinning with a twinkle in her blue eyes. "You did not!" she accused.

"No, I just told him to sit still," she admitted.

"Oh, you," Maddie flirted as she pushed the bandage roll at her. Unfortunately, she didn't completely let it go and it rolled at Deanna and over her shoulder. They both ended up laughing over the mishap.

"Hey, what are you doing on your next day off?" she asked, picking up the roll off her shoulder where it had unrolled and beginning to roll it again.

"I have no idea when I get another day off," she said wearily.

"Well, on your next day off, would you like to go into Lamish with me?"

Maddie stopped dead where she was walking and looked at Deanna to see what she meant by that. "For the day?" she clarified.

"Overnight," she answered meaningfully, looking intently down at the roll she was making. She glanced up quickly to meet Maddie's eyes.

Swallowing, she realized the time had finally come. They were going to consummate this relationship. Not that they couldn't have, half a dozen times, but Deanna wanted it to be right, because it would be Maddie's first time. "I'd like that," she said shyly.

"Good, because Doctor Wilson said you could have the next two days off," she informed her and waited for her reaction.

At first Maddie was taken aback. Then she was kind of angry that Deanna had assumed....

"So, if you would like...I'd like you to come with me...but if you don't want to..." she teased as she saw the storm building in the green-eyed redhead. She grinned, hoping that Maddie wasn't truly angry.

"You told him why we were going?" she gasped, thinking about what the doctor would think about her after the hoopla over Lenny's defection.

Deanna chuckled as she shook her head and put the rolled up bandage on a tray. "I told him I was going to get supplies and asked if it was alright for you to go along with me."

Maddie relaxed a little at that news. Then she tensed, realizing that this was the moment. They could actually be...together. She looked around to see if anyone could overhear them and whispered, "But what if I can't...I mean...what if...you know?"

Deanna smiled down at the woman. "It's okay. Let's go and get out of here for a few days and enjoy each other's company," she said, equally as quiet. "If it happens, it happens. If it doesn't, it doesn't."

Maddie nodded and before she could ask any more questions or comment, Deanna was called away to attend to a patient.

"So you are going into Lamish? With Doctor Cooper?" Leida asked as she looked through a magazine.

Maddie looked over at her to see if she meant anything by the seemingly innocent questions. If there was an innuendo in it, she couldn't detect it. She shrugged nonchalantly and said, "Yeah, she asked. God knows I need some time off from this place," she gestured around the tent from where she was packing a small bag. She had wondered if she should even bother packing her pajamas. She didn't want to assume anything... She glanced again at Leida to answer her, the woman was reclining on her cot. She didn't seem to be paying any particular attention to Maddie.

"I hear you. I could use some time off myself."

Not sure whether she should say anything, she ventured on the hazardous side and asked, "Why don't you come with us?" She was pretty certain that Leida wouldn't be able to get time off at the same time. The previous time they went into Lamish together had been a fluke.

"Nah, I got things to do," she answered airily as she continued to page through the magazine.

Maddie heard a noise by the entrance to the tent and saw Deanna turn and leave. She must have heard her invite Leida. She dropped what she was doing and rushed after her. "Deanna, wait up," she called.

Deanna never even paused as she headed determinedly towards the clinic.

"Deanna, wait up," she tried again, trying not to raise her voice too loud as others might be watching and she certainly didn't want to create a scene.

Deanna quickly got to the steps of the clinic and turned to look down at the nurse. Her face registered anger that Maddie had rarely seen. Usually it only came up when something stupid or preventable came through the clinic. "If you didn't want to go, you could have just said," she said in a low voice. People were coming and going from the clinic.

"Would you let me explain?" she asked sotto voce, trying to pull Deanna aside on the porch.

Shrugging, the doctor answered, "What's there to explain?"

"I just offered because I knew she couldn't or wouldn't go. I didn't want her to think there was anything special about this trip." She could have kicked herself for phrasing it that way as she saw Deanna's face change from one of anger, to one of hurt, to one of fury. "I mean, if I offered and she said no, at least I offered," she said lamely. "I wanted the trip to seem innocent," she hissed in her attempt to keep their argument low.

Deanna considered what she had said and decided she was being entirely too sensitive about it. "Have you changed your mind?" she asked to be certain.

"No, I'm...looking forward to it," she said sincerely.

Deanna decided not to let it bother her, but she had her own reservations about this little trip. "Okay, then be ready to go first thing in the morning," she answered in a tone that had no emotion. She turned away and went into the clinic so there could be no further discussion.

Maddie went to go after her, reconsidered, and returned to her tent to finish her packing. It had been a relatively slow day at the clinic so she wasn't really needed. The fact that Leida was in the tent too, proved her point. She knew she had probably hurt Deanna's feelings and she hoped she could make it up to her on the trip so they could resume the easygoing friendship they had always enjoyed. She had been the one to pursue Deanna, it was up to her to make it better.

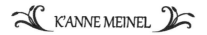

CHAPTER FOURTEEN

The drive itself was the same. Looking out at the savannah and the surrounding plains was no different, except for the changing scenery. It still took the same amount of hours. Deanna kept it interesting as she shared stories with Maddie, some of them she had heard already, but they were always fascinating.

"I've got some things I have to do to legitimize this trip. Would you check us into the hotel?" Deanna asked as she dropped Maddie and their luggage at the front door.

"One or two rooms?" she asked hesitantly, feeling foolish. They both knew why they were here.

"It's cheaper for one, but ask if they have two beds." She shrugged realizing that Maddie would have to get over some of her inhibitions. "If there is only one bed we can share," she said as though they were 'just friends.'

Maddie worried that she had unintentionally insulted Deanna again somehow. She felt so unsure of herself as she asked at the desk for a room in her halting student French. They didn't have one with two beds available and asked if she would take their best suite. She did. Their best suite turned out to be merely larger than the last time she had stayed here, maybe a little cleaner, but the bathtub was definitely appreciated. She didn't hesitate to unpack and get in the deep tub to luxuriate not only in the cleanliness of the water, but also the heat of it. She was pruney before she got out and pampered herself, cleaning up for Deanna who seemed to be a long time coming.

Deanna had taken the Rover to a repair shop to get all the tires looked at, including the four spares on her roof, several that were in need of repair. She had them change the oil and the air filter too, watching as they worked effortlessly. She could have done these thing herself, but didn't think Maddie would appreciate her showing up back at the hotel with oil around her fingers and nails. She thought about why she was really here in town…to make love to Maddie for the first time. Would she like it? Would she want to continue after her curiosity was assuaged? Was she the one? Deanna worried that she would prove an adequate lover to the untutored Maddie, but then the woman had nothing for comparison, so would that matter?

Deanna picked up a few things that weren't on her list at the open air market. She stopped to post letters for poor Doctor Wilson who was caught between a rock and a hard place due to Doctor Burton's vengeful nature. She wondered if these letters would stop the witch-hunt the man was perpetuating. She wondered if these letters would make it to their destination this time. She remembered that Doctor Wilson had said he thought they were being subverted.

Deanna arranged to pick up their other supplies tomorrow when she was ready to leave. It wouldn't make sense to pick them up now and put them in the Rover where they could possibly be stolen. Not everyone was a thief, but why tempt anyone that might recognize the vehicle. Deanna knew that if she really wanted, with the amount of time they had and how early they had come to town, she could have returned to the clinic. She didn't want to return to the clinic. She wanted to go to Maddie, and in the time she wasted on the necessary and even the unnecessary errands, she was impatient to get to the hotel. Finally, she was finished and heading to the hotel. The clerk informed her of the room number, gave her a key, and watched as she lugged her bag up towards the stairs of the hotel.

She knocked before using the old-fashioned key in the lock. She heard Maddie call, "Come in," as she turned the key in the lock.

"Hi there," she called as she put her bag down near the door and looked around the room. It was nicer than the others she had stayed in, bigger. She saw Maddie with a robe on, sitting and looking out the window. "You okay?" she asked.

Maddie had turned excitedly when she heard the knock on the door, but then turned determinedly to look outside—trying to behave nonchalant about the imminent lovemaking they were planning. She wanted the much more sophisticated and knowing Deanna to think she was cool. She turned back, smiling tremulously. "I'm fine. I took a hot bath," she said quickly, showing her nerves with how fast she was talking. "You might enjoy one," she said as quickly, then felt foolish as though hinting that Deanna *needed* a bath. "I mean..." she began, showing her nervousness.

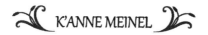

"It's okay, a hot bath sounds wonderful," Deanna assured her. She was feeling nervous herself and hoped it didn't show. She picked up her bag again and opened it on the bed to look for her bag of toiletries including shampoo and toothpaste. She'd have to remember to replace some of it while they were in town and made a mental note to that effect. She smiled at the awkward-looking Maddie, sitting there in her robe. Grabbing her own robe from the bag, she headed for the bathroom.

"I got the tires all taken care of," she called as she turned on the faucets. She put her bag of toiletries on the counter within reach of the tub and hung up her robe. She wasn't sure if she should close the bathroom door completely or if she wanted to continue the conversation with Maddie.

"That's good. How bad were they?" Maddie grasped at the conversation opener. At least if they were talking about inconsequential things, they were talking.

"Holes galore," she reported, still debating on the door. She compromised, leaving it ajar as she began to disrobe. She cursed the clunky boots she wore, a necessity here in Africa. She wanted to be wearing something sexy, something seductive, but had nothing like that with her. This was when she missed living back in the States. Sigh, she would have to make do.

"Yeah, they do get more than their fair share," she answered inadequately over the noise of the water echoing in the bathroom. She felt stupid. Talking about tires with her potential lover.

Their conversation veered from the tires to the supplies that Deanna expected to pick up. "Don't let me forget to buy more shampoo," she called as she soaped her dirty hair, not once, but twice in the luxury of the bath. She watched as the suds spread out on the water and reminded herself to shave her underarms and legs as she pulled the plug.

Their inane conversation continued as Deanna rinsed out the tub, brushed her teeth, and finger-combed her unruly hair. She liked its length and yet couldn't spike it up as much as she normally did. She shrugged, there was nothing for it at this point, she didn't even have gel. She put on antiperspirant and used the hairdryer to dry under her arms. She also used it to dry the junction between her legs, wondering if she should have shaved there, or at least trimmed. Finally, she used the hairdryer on her head hair. She looked at herself in the mirror and wondered what Maddie was attracted to. Her eyebrows were too thin, her eyelashes stubbly, and she made faces at herself in the mirror. Finally, she bravely put on her robe, gathered up her dirty clothes and hung them up, then opened the door fully to find Maddie sitting in the same chair.

She could see that the nurse was uncomfortable. After all, they had come here to pursue her curiosity. No love had been spoken between them. They were just indulging in healthy sex, at least that's what Deanna told herself clinically. The conversation had died with the hairdryer. She walked slowly over towards the window to see if there was anything to see. The balcony blocked most of the view and she wondered what Maddie had been looking at. The woman had stood up to look out the window when she heard Deanna come out of the bathroom.

Deanna went to put her arms around Maddie and just then there was a determined knock on the door. Glancing at Maddie, exchanging a look of concern with the redhead, she headed for the door.

"Fire, fire," the man on the other side of the door called in French. She nodded that she understood and quickly closed the door. She was reaching for her bag as she translated for Maddie, but she had already understood.

"Of all the timing," the redhead muttered.

Deanna grinned understandingly as she turned to give the nurse privacy as they both quickly changed into something more appropriate, hoping they had time as they heard the banging on other doors. They were both dressed and in their boots in no time, carrying their room keys as they followed others down the steps and out into the streets.

"Do they know what happened?" Deanna asked some of the onlookers. Everyone was looking at the hotel, smoke billowing out the back of it.

"Fire," she was told time and again, not really telling her anything. She thought it a bit ironic.

"That man there said it was something in the kitchen," Maddie had overheard and told her.

They watched as the fire brigade put out the fire quickly. It was a while, a long while, before they called that the guests could safely return to the hotel. Deanna wondered if it had been some sort of ruse to get the hotel guests out of their rooms so they could be rifled and then cursed herself for being such a cynic. Theft was a way of life here for some, but there were still good people and she refused to forget that. As she walked up the stairs to their room behind Maddie, she admired the redhead's curves in the jeans she was wearing, wondering how the buttocks would look naked and hoping that this little incident wouldn't ruin things for them. They were both on edge and she didn't want to lose the opportunity to be with Maddie. It had been building for too long.

Maddie wondered if she smelled like smoke now…or worse, perspiration. She was nervous, excited, and overanalyzing every little thing. What if she was inadequate as a lover and Deanna didn't really want her? What if this turned out to be a colossal mistake? Was she just curious? Did she really want to be with a woman? Was this just because she was out of her normal element and Deanna had been kind? Deanna...she was so kind, and patient...and yes, she wanted her. She turned in the room and asked, "Do you think there will be any more fires?"

"Nope, I think this was a one-fire deal," she teased as she watched Maddie nervously walk over to the window, this time leaning out to look up and down the darkening street. Deanna's hand went up to her eyebrow and began touching the hairs. She walked determinedly over to Maddie, coming up behind her.

As Deanna leaned up behind her Maddie gasped. "Are you okay?" Deanna asked concerned.

"Yes," she whispered, feeling very shy.

Deanna slipped her hands slowly around Maddie, feeling every curve, every line through her clothes, pulling her body against her own. She could feel the redhead tremble slightly. "Are you sure?" she asked softly, her lips a breath away from Maddie's ear, her breath caressing it.

Maddie thought for a second, her eyes closing at the soft caress, imagining what it would feel like if Deanna's lips touched there, or on her neck, perhaps her tongue as well.... She wanted to shudder at the tightening of her body—it was that erotic as her mind took leaps. "Yes, I'm sure," she breathed softly, not wanting to talk, wanting to go wherever this was going to take them, but unsure of how to proceed. "Are you? Have you changed your mind?" She sensed a hesitancy in Deanna. This confident and knowing doctor, who bravely cut into a body to repair it, who she had admired from the first moment she met her, she seemed...almost afraid to take charge.

Deanna smiled at the answer and wanted to laugh at the questions. Instead, she unknowingly obliged Maddie's unspoken fantasies. Her lips touched softly on the shell of Maddie's ear, her tongue darted out to taste the skin. Gently, she licked down around the curve of her ear, then tasted her neck, her lips touching here, then there. "Yes, I'm sure," she echoed Maddie's statement. "No, I haven't changed my mind." Her hands began to unbutton the shirt that Maddie was wearing, effortlessly opening the buttons that hid her skin from Deanna's agile fingertips.

Maddie wanted to lay her head back on Deanna's shoulder, she wanted to just say "take me," but instead she sighed into the feelings that the doctor was invoking within her body. She loved how Deanna's hips felt against her buttocks. She wondered if Deanna realized they were ever so slightly dancing against her, rubbing a musical rhythm that only the two of them could hear.

Deanna finally had the shirt open. She pulled it off Maddie's shoulders slowly, her lips following along the material's line as it fell down to Maddie's elbows.

Maddie straightened her arms so that the shirt could fall to the floor, but it didn't. Their hips were glued together, Maddie's buttocks to Deanna's pelvic bones. Neither woman noticed. Deanna's hands had immediately moved to touch all that bared skin, her fingers caressing the naked expanse. When they encountered the bra holding Maddie's breasts up, she reached inside. At the first touch of her fingers on Maddie's nipples, Maddie gasped and arched into the hands holding her. Maddie's own hands had curved around behind her to hold Deanna to her, to clasp Deanna's curvaceous ass, grinding suggestively against her pelvis.

Deanna spun Maddie around in her arms, reaching for the clasp that held her bra together and effortlessly releasing it as she leaned in for a kiss. The shirt fell to the floor, neither noticed. Maddie obliged her as she opened her mouth to breathe, instead finding her breath captured in a titillating kiss that had her further gasping for air. Deanna reached once again for the breasts that were now surging against her own shirt-clad breasts, aching to be touched.

"No fair. You're still dressed," Maddie complained between kisses as her own fingers grasped Deanna's ass firmly so that she could rub her center against Deanna's.

Deanna was the one to gasp now, she was so aroused she could have come right then and there. She wanted to take it slow, for Maddie's sake. She wanted to make their first time together memorable…to make Maddie's first time with a woman something she would never forget…to make love to her so that she would love her forever....

Slowly, between the two of them, they removed the rest of their clothes. As they stood there naked, breast to breast, pelvic bone to pelvic bone, mons to mons, leg to leg, Deanna smiled dreamily at Maddie. Maddie had closed her eyes, not ashamed at her nakedness, not ashamed at seeing another woman naked. As a medical professional she had seen patients in various stages of nudity over the years, but this was Deanna, this was the woman she was about to have sex with. No, not sex. She was about to make love with this wonderful, brilliant, caring woman. She knew she loved Deanna, had not only fallen in love with the idea of making love to a woman, but had fallen in love with the woman herself before she even knew that it would be possible. She hadn't wanted to ruin the moment from her fantasies with the reality, but already it was better than the fantasy. She peeked with one eye squinting, saw Deanna smiling at her, and was brave enough to open both of her eyes. Deanna smiled even more as she saw the amazing green eyes in the redhead looking back at her.

"Get on the bed," she requested as she began to gently push, using her entire body to maneuver Maddie to the bed.

Maddie felt the mattress behind her knees and nearly fell ungracefully. Quickly she caught herself on her hands, letting go of Deanna's delicious body, but only for a moment because the other woman was lowering herself onto Maddie. In that brief moment, with the glimpse she got of the physically fit doctor, she felt inadequate. Her own body, while not fat, and on the 'barely edible' diet they had both been on, still felt a bit like an ox in comparison to Deanna.

Deanna obviously didn't notice as she wanted to feel Maddie under her. Her skin against her own. She immediately resumed making love to the nurse.

Maddie forgot her insecurities as Deanna kissed her, the warm body above her own feeling so sweet, so welcome, and so good. She invited Deanna in, her own hands caressing down her lover's back, her nails one way, her soft fingers the other, up and down until she got bold enough, once again, to cup Deanna's buttocks and press her own pelvis upward while pulling Deanna down, their middles gyrating slightly as they ground suggestively.

Deanna kissed her way down to those pointed tips on Maddie's breasts, feeling the arousal under her lips. Gently she tongued first one and then the other, blowing air on the one, making it harden more, if that were possible. She was rewarded with an intake of air that she was sure Maddie wasn't aware she was making. She could scent Maddie's arousal in the air and desperately wanted to taste her. Not this time though, she didn't want to scare her. Instead, her hand slipped between them, gently caressing skin, until Maddie unconsciously shifted towards the hand. Deanna wanted to smile, to gloat a little at the telltale signs Maddie was giving off, of her need to be touched so intimately.

Maddie was on fire. She had felt arousal before. She had daringly, one night, even relieved herself among the snores and snufflings of her tent mates. Tonight though, she needed, she *wanted*, Deanna to touch her there...and now! Her hands caressed and rubbed Deanna a little more frantically than she realized when Deanna began to touch her skin towards her center. She wanted her so much! She wanted to experience it all and she was impatient.

"Easy, baby, easy," Deanna soothed her. Her fingers never stopped their descent though. She moved unerringly down Maddie's body, feeling the dimpling of her curves, the lines of her amazing body, and then the soft pelt that was her pubic hair. Deanna was relieved that Maddie wasn't one of those women who shaved. She had experienced that in a past partner and didn't like it at all. It reminded her of making love to a child—not that she had ever done that—but no hair to her meant a child. She wanted a woman, and in her arms right now was a woman! A curvaceous and real woman! Her fingers found the slit that was hiding the jewel she was looking for. She could scent Maddie's arousal earlier and now she could feel it. The folds were slick with it. She could feel the viscous fluid on her fingers, wondered at the quantity of it, longed to taste it with her tongue. She played with it, her hand cupping the redhead's mons and squeezing slightly. Maddie gasped with delight at the sensation.

Those endlessly fascinating fingers of Deanna's were going to be her undoing and she relished the prospect of it. As they touched her intimately, she shifted over so that they would have full access, her legs spreading a little and Deanna's leg fell between them.

Gently Deanna raised her leg, her thigh hitting the back of her hand, she began to thrust her leg up, her hand curving into Maddie's body. With two fingers inside and her thumb on the small appendage that thrust up, wanting attention, it was a definite pleasure to hear the gasp Maddie let out at the sensation. She began to thrust suggestively with first one and then two fingers. Her tongue moved back up Maddie's inflamed body, entering her mouth and fencing with Maddie's own tongue.

Maddie wrapped her arms around Deanna, her fingers plunging into the blonde's hair, pulling at it, encouraging her without even knowing it. She wanted it all, and she wanted it now.

"Easy, baby, easy," Deanna murmured comfortingly, sensing her lover's increasing frustration. She was thrusting in and out and knew she had to increase the pace. She wanted Maddie so aroused that when she did come, she would do so memorably. She didn't have long to wait though. She knew that a lot of what Maddie had been feeling, a lot of what had built up, was in her head. She just stroked it out physically and smiled in her kiss as she felt the other woman stiffening as she began to come. She caught Maddie's cries of release in her mouth in a searing kiss. She continued to thrust and play with the wetness, hoping to bring out a second orgasm from Maddie and wasn't disappointed as it built up once again.

Finally, Maddie pushed at her arm, mutely begging her to stop. Reluctantly, Deanna ceased and pulled her fingers from Maddie's overheated body. Slowly, she moved to Maddie's side, removing her weight and enjoying watching the woman regain her equilibrium. She caressed the expanse of skin she could reach, calming the redhead and enjoying the skin she could see in the fading light. She finally just held the woman close to her.

Maddie lay with her head on Deanna, deeply contemplating what they had just done. She thought there would be more, and yet she was satisfied. Then she realized that Deanna hadn't had satisfaction and she began to feel guilty. It was only fair that Deanna enjoy herself too. Yet when Maddie began to caress Deanna, the blonde grabbed her hand and held it close. She was still breathing hard, but didn't seem to want to continue.

"Is something wrong?" Maddie asked, unsure if she had done something she shouldn't have.

"No, not at all," she answered, pulling herself in.

Maddie lifted herself onto her elbow, pulling slightly away from Deanna to look down on her. She saw something there she couldn't quite fathom. "You don't want me to make love to you?" she asked, feeling hurt for some reason.

Deanna looked deeply into Maddie's eyes. How could she tell her how disappointed she felt in the experience? That she hadn't taken her pleasure because she lost all desire for it. She didn't want to ruin the experience for Maddie. They'd built up such expectations for it all. "It's okay, I'm fine," she found herself saying and then mentally groaned. Fortunately, Maddie didn't know the universal woman's call for 'everything is not okay, definitely *not* fine.' Maddie wasn't experienced enough and Deanna certainly wasn't going to enlighten her.

"But what about...?" Maddie asked, confused.

"You don't need to cum each and every time," she hedged, not telling the whole truth. While it was true that cumming was the ultimate pleasure, it was the lead up to it that was truly the best part. The actual act of cumming was merely the culmination of that lead up. Deanna hadn't felt it and her analytical mind was picking it apart already.

"But..." she began again.

"Shhh," Deanna said and pulled Maddie's head against her chest, hoping to be left to her thoughts so she could slowly decipher why she hadn't felt what she should have. Her first conclusion was that Maddie didn't do it for her, and she knew that was false. Maybe she had just put too much emphasis on this encounter, this *first* time.

Maddie might not be as experienced as Deanna, but she wasn't stupid. She knew instinctually that *something* was wrong, but she couldn't figure out *what*. And she would not turn this into an argument, not now. She chose to retreat and to enjoy the aftermath of her own experience as she thought over every moment, reliving it in her mind.

Deanna heard Maddie's breathing slow, indicating she was falling asleep, and she was relieved as her mind needed time to go over the whole experience. Why hadn't she felt the need for her own body's relief? Why had it stopped when it should have been brought to its own natural conclusion? She felt something was missing, and not just the orgasm she should have pulled out of her own body even if Maddie didn't know how. She could have ground down on Maddie, getting her own enjoyment. Her body told her that now it was possible, but she wasn't happy at all with how this had concluded. It took her a long time to fall to sleep as she analyzed, no, she *over*analyzed the situation.

Because Deanna had fallen to sleep so late, it was no wonder she overslept the next morning. Maddie woke well before her, watched her sleep for a while, and laughed at the fact that she was snoring slightly and drooling. She carefully extracted herself from Deanna's arms, wondering that she had slept within them the entire night. That had never happened to her before. She went to the bathroom, washed herself, and thought about the previous night. She was no longer certain that Deanna's explanation was correct. In her mind, Deanna should have cum too, an expression of her body's release to Maddie, just as she had cum for Deanna. She didn't know why Deanna hadn't cum too, but she felt vaguely dissatisfied about the situation. Something felt wrong. While she knew not everyone needed that release, she was certain someone of Deanna's passionate nature would need that. She sat naked in the chair by the window and watched Deanna sleep. She'd turned since Maddie's body heat wasn't there to draw her in, and had flung her leg outside the blankets and left herself exposed. Maddie looked at the doctor's firm, young body for a long time before an idea came to her. Gently, she slid in next to Deanna and began to caress her, touching everywhere she dared, arousing her in her sleep.

Deanna was enjoying the nicest dream…butterflies were giving her sun kisses. Her body was warm in the sunlight. She didn't realize it was Maddie kissing where her caresses had been placed previously. The warm morning sun was streaming through the window onto her naked body. Maddie's hair was feathery soft as it brushed against her skin. "Oh, yes," she murmured dreamily, not waking up to the soft caresses, simply indulging in the arousal of her dream.

Maddie smiled. This was what she had thought she would be doing the previous evening—giving pleasure to her lover, as she had done for her. She could feel herself becoming aroused at what she was doing, at her daring. She glanced repeatedly at the juncture of Deanna's legs, wondering if she dared to go down there, to explore…to taste? She kept thinking to herself that if she didn't do that, she wouldn't be a lesbian. She wasn't sure she wanted to *be* a lesbian. There was such a stigma attached to it, she knew there was—she herself had thought it wrong not so very long ago. The attraction to this woman was undeniable though, and she wanted to explore these feelings, this body, which was responding to her ministrations, responding to what she was doing with her fingers and mouth. The first taste of Deanna's erect, little nipples surprised her at her daring. Deanna was nearly flat chested, her breasts small, yet fully-formed. It reminded Maddie of when she had been a teen and her breasts and nipples had popped—not very big, but there none the less.

Deanna shifted, her legs rubbing together as she turned into Maddie's warmth and caresses in her sleep. "Mmm," she murmured at the sensations being drawn from her sleeping body. The dream was so delicious.

Maddie was enjoying touching Deanna, her skin was so soft, much softer than she would have thought possible. She wasn't hairy like a man.

In fact, the more she caressed all over, the more she enjoyed the sensation and the novelty of it. She began to become aware of the scent of Deanna's arousal. It intrigued her and she wanted to touch it. She wondered if she would ever be daring enough to actually taste it…no, she wouldn't be a lesbian if she didn't go down on a woman, right? Her hand drifted to the curls between Deanna's legs, strangely darker than the blonde hair on her head. Then she remembered that when Deanna had arrived her hair was a lot darker, various shades of brown and red, and now the sun had bleached it. These curls were softer than expected. She had thought they would be wiry and stiff. They nestled there and her fingers entwined in them, brushing Deanna's clit unintentionally.

At the sensation, Deanna hissed, or rather sucked in a great quantity of air in her sleep. She woke up coughing, trying to get her equilibrium back. She froze when she realized Maddie's hand was between her legs and her mouth was fastened to her nipple. She went to push the other woman away, but Maddie looked up at her cough, releasing the nipple and smiling up at the other woman. The weight of her body held Deanna down and then she moved up to kiss her. "Wait, what…?" Deanna began as she tried to avoid Maddie's kiss.

"I think that should be obvious." Maddie smiled and laughed at her friend's expense, her fingers curling reflexively.

"But I don't…" she began again, but was silenced as Maddie kissed her again. Her tongue began to creep into Deanna's mouth. Her last coherent thought was that she probably had morning breath and should have brushed her teeth, but her body was not cooperating. It had already been aroused by this untutored woman's caresses and Deanna felt very vulnerable at the moment. She thought of pushing her away, but she wanted…no *needed* release. She spread her legs, throwing one of them over Maddie's hip as she ground into the accommodating hand.

Maddie was pleasantly surprised as Deanna began to respond. She was awake now, and while she was unsure exactly what to do to Deanna, she continued on with her explorations, hoping that would be adequate.

"Fingers, inside," Deanna ground out, her body trying to help by thrusting against the hand, but it was obvious Maddie didn't know what she was doing.

Remembering how good it had made her feel, Maddie curled her fingers and found the wetness she had smelled earlier. Her fingers sought for the source and began to follow it inside, first one, then a second, and amazingly a third curled inside. She found she had more control with just two and began to thrust. She loved the gasp of surprise that Deanna released when she unexpectedly hit a certain spot within.

Deanna thrust against the fingers inside, gasping when Maddie hit her g-spot. The incredible sensation that went through her made her go weak for a moment; she didn't care how vulnerable it made her. She needed this release now that Maddie had started it. As Maddie thrust within, Deanna's hips thrust against the fingers. Between the two of them, the feelings began to spread across her body. The blood began to drain from Deanna's lips, a sure sign she was about to cum. Her toes began to tingle as the blood ran from them. She stretched, arching her breasts into Maddie's warm body, her hands falling limply behind her own head before coming back to grasp at Maddie, hard.

"Oh, oh, ohhhh," she moaned as she came. Her body convulsed as she went through a series of orgasms.

Maddie was fascinated. She had never seen another human being orgasm. She'd always kept her eyes tightly closed when any man she had been with had cum over her. Something about them in the throes just never appealed to her. This however, was glorious because she had caused it in Deanna's body. It was fascinating. She didn't stop what she was doing until she began to sense that Deanna was coming down from the mountain she had just climbed. She pulled her fingers from Deanna's body and discreetly wiped them on the sheets as she held the doctor's body to her own. Her smile of contentment over what she had caused was hidden over Deanna's shoulder as she held her close.

Deanna was amazed that this unschooled woman had managed to draw that from her body, but she was pleased too. Whatever hang-ups she had the previous night that she hadn't been able to cum, that she had lost her arousal, were long gone at this point. She wanted more though, and began to kiss the skin presented to her in the form of Maddie's naked shoulder. Her hands began caressing down the back, feeling how cool her skin had become in the exposure to the air. Gently she turned their wrapped bodies so she was on top and could move down Maddie's body. She stopped to kiss her passionately on the mouth, her tongue probing deep to convey her feelings for the other woman before moving on to her jaw, her cheek, her neck.

Maddie couldn't help but respond. Her body had become inflamed at what she had caused in the doctor's body and seeing what she had done. It was empowering to know she could make this confident and brilliant woman come undone. *'Oh, gawd, how good she made her feel,'* she thought as her own arms wrapped around Deanna to encourage her to continue. Her kisses were delicious.

She stopped to tongue both nipples fiercely, unknowingly sending a bolt of electricity between those lapping caresses and her lover's center. She began to head further south this time. She didn't care whether Maddie had bathed or not, she wanted, she *needed* to taste her. The fingers that wound through her hair unknowingly encouraged her as she continued. She stopped to kiss around the belly button and then continued on between Maddie's legs. Deanna's shoulder shoved between Maddie's legs, spreading them as her face caressed along the silky red hairs. Her first taste was worth the wait. She gently probed between the folds with her tongue, relishing the gasp of surprised delight she heard from Maddie, the gentle arching into her as Maddie realized her intent.

Maddie wasn't certain what Deanna was doing to her other than making love so thoroughly to her body, but she didn't mind. She was enjoying every moment, every caress, every kiss. She couldn't hope to imagine the immense pleasure when Deanna continued on to the juncture between her legs. She didn't know the nerve endings would be quite so…sensitive. She arched slightly, almost afraid that Deanna would stop. Fortunately for her…she didn't. She gasped as the woman's mouth enfolded her center with a warmth she couldn't have imagined.

Deanna smiled triumphantly as she tasted a new wetness; Maddie was gushing as she aroused her. She brought her fingers into play, encouraging the wetness to come out so that she could drink greedily. When the hard, little nub rose up to demand attention, she licked at it with her tongue, twirling it around, making sure to clean off every drop of moisture and to leave only her own saliva. Gently she blew on it, noting Maddie's reaction as she arched at the sensation. She buried her face into the curls, her nose deep as she licked at every fold, her fingers thrusting as they had the previous night. She lifted Maddie's legs over her shoulders so she could go deeper, her tongue plunging inside.

Maddie hadn't known it could be like this. She wondered if she could cause the same sensations in Deanna and then didn't think any more about anything but her own pleasure. Such pleasure as she had never received before was sweeping over her. She was almost disappointed when the convulsions began. Her mouth opened to scream out her frustration that it might end, and ended up grabbing a pillow to scream into as they didn't end…they continued on and on until Deanna had wrung out every bit of pleasure from her body. Maddie was left in liquid heat, her body useless and cold. Deanna covered her with her own overheated body, pulling up the sheets that had been kicked to the bottom of their shared bed and holding her close and comforting her as she came down from the most incredible high she had ever experienced.

Deanna was pleased with herself. Not only had she experienced a set of incredible orgasms herself, but she had caused them in Maddie. She glanced at the clock on the side table and knew they would have to get going soon or arrive back in Lamish very late. At the moment, she didn't care.

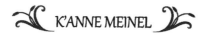

CHAPTER FIFTEEN

She watched the rain come down, knowing it was welcomed by the farmers of the tribe. These weren't the torrential rains of the rainy season, just a stray shower that came down out of the mountains and across the plains. She knew Harlan would be thrilled. He was trying to cram as much knowledge as he could share with the locals through his interpreter. They were grateful, and cynical. It was a frustrating experience for the young farmer.

"You look like a hound dog doing that," Maddie commented as she handed her a coffee. She had watched the doctor raise her face to the rain. She took a sip of her own hot chocolate.

"Maybe, I'm scenting my prey," she laughed as she accepted the coffee mug and lowered her nose to its fragrance. She grinned at her girlfriend with a knowing smile.

Maddie blushed and grinned back. "Do you miss being in the jungle?"

She nodded. "Sometimes. I loved it there in South America. They have them here too of course. I've worked in a couple of camps here. It's the same, and yet the people are so vastly different. The many personalities, the traditions, it all fascinates me." She glanced at the slight chocolate mustache that was on Maddie's lips, longing to lick it off. "Do you know how they collect the cocoa beans to make that?" she asked, and when Maddie confided that she didn't, she explained. She seemed to really know the process too.

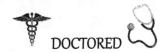

"Have you been there when they harvested?" Maddie asked, fascinated.

Deanna nodded. "Yeah, the hooks and blades they use to pull down the high pods can really cause a nasty cut. Sometimes they have amputated their own fingers or toes!" She went on to explain a few of the procedures she had performed in an attempt to save their appendages, talk that only medical people would understand, or so they thought.

"We no grow that here," Hamishish said as she walked by them near the door, proving she had been listening to their conversation.

"No, it doesn't grow everywhere," Deanna admitted. She almost laughed as Hamishish continued on, no longer interested. Something people found rude about her, but Deanna understood.

"Seems like a lot of work for that small bean pod," Maddie commented, watching the witch doctor walk away in the rain as though it didn't bother her. The rain had plastered her hair to her head already.

"It is," Deanna agreed, smiling at Maddie and her interest in the many stories she had to tell. "After they have the pods, it takes about ten days before they remove the bean. They use these wooden clubs which makes it easier to extract the beans. All of this by hand. If they can't get them open with the club, they use a machete. The accidents," she shook her head in remembrance, "are legendary."

"Can't they do it by machine?"

"Some of the bigger plantations are now, but the smallholders do it all by hand. Then after they extract the bean from the pod they have to wait for the beans to undergo a fermentation and then a drying process before they bag them and send them off."

"Wow, I guess I never realized how hard it was to get a cup a cocoa!"

"Then there are the many different kinds of chocolate bars," she finished with a smile.

They smiled a lot, happy with each other, enjoying their many conversations and exchanges. Few, if any, realized how much time they were alone. Many just thought they had become very good friends.

"Happy to see me?" Deanna asked as she leaned Maddie against their favorite meeting place, a rock around the curve of the river, out of sight of the camp, but near enough that they felt safe.

"Shut up and kiss me," Maddie demanded, anxious to feel Deanna's touch.

Deanna obliged her, kissing her deeply, her tongue playing with Maddie's, then groaning when Maddie sucked delicately on the appendage. "Gawd, I've wanted you all day," she whispered in the redhead's ear.

Maddie's hands were roaming, feeling the firm body against her own. At the words, her hands began to wander into the waistline of the doctor's pants, seeking and finding her underwear. Today she wondered if Deanna was wearing one of the sexier lingerie she had seen back in Lamish. She didn't really care as she sought for and found Deanna's clit; it was aroused, hard, and wet. "What have you been thinking about," she murmured, her lips tightly against Deanna's skin between her breasts, nuzzling aside the clothing with her nose.

"You, only you," she breathed, feeling the touch of Maddie's fingers on her most intimate spots. Her body arched harder against Maddie, almost trapping her hands, causing her to pull back so that she could be touched in the way she needed, craved really.

"I think you've been naughty," she teased as she sought and found Deanna's nipple. It was a hard, little bead and she remembered the beautiful pink areola that circled it.

"Oh, yes, very," the doctor agreed, her body curving to accommodate Maddie's fingers between her legs. "Ugh," she grunted as the fingers went up and in, a slight squishing sound that only they could hear between them.

"Oh, yes," Maddie murmured, knowing she was driving the woman crazy, her hand was swamped in wetness, making it easier to thrust inside. Her thumb rhythmically rubbed at the same tempo, her body thrust into it.

"Oh," Deanna whimpered joyfully. "Don't stop, please don't stop."

"Come for me, baby," she pleaded, knowing that the blonde was near to going over the edge. A gush of wetness greeted her hand, telling her that Deanna was cumming. Gently, she sucked harder on the nipple she was worrying.

"Oh, Oh, OH," Deanna smothered her little cries into the redhead's neck as her body began to spasm. Her one leg came up, clasping Maddie's body to her own, over her hip, her body wobbling on the sole leg left, trying to maintain her balance against the woman.

"Deanna? Maddie? Are you out here?" a voice called.

Both of them froze for a moment before they each pulled back guiltily. Deanna quickly adjusted her clothes, trying to get them in order, grateful she hadn't undressed, although being naked against Maddie was something she craved. Maddie hadn't lost any time in straightening up and walking around the corner of the rock. She just had time to glance back at the good doctor and lick her fingers suggestively before Leida came towards them from the village.

"Hey, what are you two doing?" she asked curiously. She was carrying a lantern.

"Oh, we were watching the river and it got dark before we realized…" Maddie said, but it sounded lame. It was already getting dark when both of them left the compound, trying not to be noticed.

"Well, you better head back with me," she said.

"Good idea," Deanna answered, having recovered sufficiently. She had wanted to scream out her rage at being interrupted, but these little interludes were becoming harder and harder. She wanted another weekend away with Maddie, but knew they couldn't ask too often or there would be suspicion cast on them.

"Hey, Deanna. Could you drive me to Lamish next week?" Leida asked as they walked along

"Sure, what's up?" Deanna answered, trying to sound calm. Her legs felt a little wobbly and she could feel the gushing feeling between her legs. She longed to pull her underwear away from her overheated body.

"I've finished my rotation. I'm heading home, remember?" she asked curiously. She'd talked of nothing else.

"Oh, I thought you might sign on again for a spell," she covered. She had known, but when she had heard, she had worried more that Maddie might be going soon too. After all, the two women had arrived at the same time. So far, she hadn't worked up the nerve to even ask her. Her own rotation had been extended more than once, but no one had commented on it.

"Wonder if we can manage to get me some time off too so I can come and wish you goodbye," Maddie asked, innocently. Her glance over at Deanna spoke volumes.

"Maybe," Leida answered.

CHAPTER SIXTEEN

"I'm going to miss you, Leida. You be sure to write me back in the States," Maddie hugged her as they stood in front of the station.

"I'm going to miss you too. This has been quite the adventure," she assured her.

"I'm surprised you aren't signing on for more," Deanna teased as she too got a hug.

"Ah, remember, I was at the other camp. I've done my duty. I kinda want to see what I can do back home now," she answered, her Australian accent never sounding more clear. She would travel by train from the port to one of the major airport hubs. She wasn't going to take one of the smaller planes, although that would have been more efficient. There had been a crash a couple weeks ago, so she altered her plans.

It worked out well for Maddie and Deanna as they could spend the night in Lamish and head back the next day and no one would be the wiser.

"Ms. Cooper?" a voice called and Deanna looked up in surprise.

"I'm Doctor Cooper," she corrected, a habit of a lifetime. After all, no one believed someone that looked as young as she did was a doctor.

"Message for you, ma'am," the porter told her with a pull on his cap and a not-so-subtle hand held out for a tip.

Deanna gave him a tip and opened the unsealed message. It was from Doctor Burton, asking her to stay an extra day to pick up two replacements that were coming out to the camp. He must have radioed it in after they left the camp.

"What is it?" Maddie asked, worried. She was always so sure that something bad came with a message like that. She was sure they were expected to come back to the camp immediately.

"Apparently we are getting a nurse and someone else, it doesn't say, but Doctor Burton asks that we stay an extra day to wait for their arrival," she explained with a meaningful look meant only for Maddie.

Maddie tried not to show the absolute joy on her face at this news. They had an extra night in town together.

"They didn't waste any time replacing me, did they?" Leida asked with a hint of self-mockery. They had known for a while that her time was up and she wasn't continuing on.

"Now, you know you are irreplaceable," Deanna teased.

"Well, not to Doctor Burton," she pointed out realistically. "That man is positively on a witch-hunt," she warned, knowing Deanna would catch the meaning.

"Yes, he is, isn't he?" she answered sardonically. Just then the whistle sounded and Deanna caught up her bag and handed it to Leida as she mounted the steps.

"Goodbye, goodbye," she called as she waved.

"Don't forget to write," Maddie reminded her.

They waited a moment for the train to pull out of the station and for Leida to be out of sight before turning and walking back to the Rover.

"Now, what would you like to do for the rest of the afternoon?" Deanna asked teasingly.

"Well, I could use a shower. Maybe we should go check in at the hotel?" Maddie answered in the same tone.

"And then what?"

"I'm sure we will think of something to while away the hours."

They barely made it through the door of their hotel room, shutting it firmly behind them, dropping their bags and falling into each other's arms, tearing at their clothes in their haste to get naked.

Maddie was finally able to go down on Deanna, something she had wished she had done the first time they were together. She had fantasized about it ever since. Knowing the extreme pleasure Deanna had given her this way, she wanted to return the favor. The results were even better than she had hoped, giving her confidence to make love to Deanna repeatedly through the night. Neither one of them got much sleep that night, but neither of them really minded. The time they waited to be together like this again had been spent experimenting, wishing, and dreaming…Now they could fulfill those dreams and make them a reality.

Much to Maddie's surprise, Deanna managed to make love to her in the shower, nearly drowning as she kneeled and took Maddie's sex in her mouth, making her cum. Maddie hadn't thought it possible, and she was thrilled to realize there was so much more she could learn from this incredible woman. "I love you," she screamed as she was in the throes.

Deanna smiled, her lips still busy as she heard her girlfriend's cry.

"Why do you do that?" Maddie asked Deanna as she saw her once again absentmindedly playing with her eyebrows and eyelashes. Occasionally, one would come out and she'd bring it to the tip of her lip as she poked it and feathered it across the skin there.

"Do what?" Deanna asked, surprised, dropping whatever she had been holding and sitting up.

"You pull at your eyebrows, sometimes your eyelashes," Maddie pointed out, explaining further the things she had observed.

Deanna sighed wearily. She shook her head. "It's a nervous disorder. I try to keep it under control, but frequently I don't even know I'm doing it," she explained. "It's call Trichotillomania or trichotillosis. It's a hair-pulling disorder."

"You can't stop it?"

"I try, and most of the time I'm successful, but I don't know I'm doing it half the time."

"It's not contagious is it?" she teased, knowing a nervous disorder wasn't contagious.

Deanna smiled ruefully. "I'm lucky. I don't eat the hairs," she pointed out, explaining that some sufferers of the nervous order did that, even ending up with hairballs. She sighed again. "I do wish I'd stop it though. Sometimes I end up with no eyelashes or holes in my eyebrows."

"It's that bad?"

"It's a compulsion, usually brought on by nerves."

"When did you start?"

"When I went to high school. Being nine and in high school was very stressful," she confessed. "I started with my eyelashes, then moved on to my eyebrows. At least I don't pull my hair," she indicated the mop on her head that had been bleached a bit more by the hot African sun, the roots still quite dark. "Some even pull nose hairs," she grinned and wrinkled her nose at the thought. "Or even," she leaned down and tugged the pubic hairs between them.

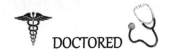

"Ouch," Maddie said reflexively. She had wondered about that, but having it confirmed was a bit odd. "Must be a bit embarrassing now and then."

Deanna nodded. "Yeah, and as a doctor, I *should* know better. Having holes in my eyebrows *is* embarrassing." She looked ashamed.

"Is there anything I can do?" she asked softly.

Shrugging, she answered, "Just let me know when I'm doing it. Not obvious or anything, so I'm not embarrassed, but if you could grab my hand maybe?"

Maddie imagined holding down Deanna's hand, those amazing hands that gave her so much pleasure and could handle a scalpel as an extension of those magical fingers.... "I'll do what I can," she promised. "Isn't there anything a doctor can do?"

"It's hard to treat. It's chronic and," she shrugged, "a behavior disorder...it's mental." She soon changed the subject as it obviously made her uncomfortable.

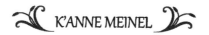

CHAPTER SEVENTEEN

Two days later they were sated, and still hadn't had enough of the other. They were young, enjoying themselves, learning each other in ways that were intimate to lovers around the world.

"I can't believe I can derive so much pleasure from a woman," Maddie had stupidly remarked.

"What?" Deanna asked, feeling curiously hurt over her statement.

"I mean, I love what you do to me, to my body, but I had never thought a woman could please me like a man."

"But it's not like a man..." Deanna began, only to be interrupted.

"No, it's not, it's better," she was assured and then Maddie kissed her, trying to soothe away the hurt she heard in the young doctor's voice. "I love you," she added quietly.

Deanna pulled back at the words. It was the first time Maddie had ever said them when not in the throes. Deanna had said them many times in her head, but she wouldn't say them until Maddie did. Something had told her that if she did, Maddie might pull away. She looked back and forth between the redhead's green eyes, looking deeply to see if she was sure, if she was teasing, if....

Maddie nodded, knowing Deanna's indecision and sorry for it. "I do love you, you know?" she asked softly.

Deanna smiled, then rather than answer, she leaned back in for a kiss. That led to other amusing pursuits—touching her lover in intimate ways that told her physically rather than verbally how much she loved her in return.

"It's your fault we're late," Deanna assured Maddie as they hurried through the train station.

"*My* fault? You were the one that wanted to try..." Maddie began in response, but stopped as she realized they were in a public place and anyone could hear them.

Deanna smirked, knowing she had gotten Maddie's goat and loving it. She saw Maddie begin to blush and laughed. Redheads did not blush well.

"Oh, you…" Maddie admonished as they came through the doors to the platform and began to look for the two people they were to pick up.

They weren't hard to spot. They looked out of place standing there and gawking at the colorful people that stood on the platform waiting for a train or for people getting off of them. The different African modes of dress were exotic to say the least, but after months of seeing them, the doctor and nurse were used to them.

"Hello. Are you going to Mamadu?" Deanna asked by way of introduction. They were the only white people on the platform and it was kind of obvious they were out of their element.

"Yes. Were you sent to pick us up?" the woman asked, holding out her hand. "I'm Kimberly Applewood," she stated as she shook Deanna's hand.

"Deanna," she responded to the woman, wondering at her profession. Was she a nurse or a volunteer? She knew they weren't expecting any more doctors and was sorry for that, but at the same time, not sorry in the least because it meant they needed her and she could stay on.

"I'm Shawn Jackson," the man introduced himself. "Aren't you Doctor Kearn…" he began, only to be interrupted by Deanna.

"Cooper, I'm Doctor Deanna *Cooper*," she said meaningfully.

"Ah, yes, my mistake," he apologized. "I saw you in Bambini," he explained. "Someone pointed you out."

"Yes, I was there for a while," she said dismissively, her eyes ablaze in warning and anger.

"Is this all you have?" Maddie asked, not to be excluded.

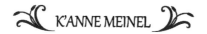

"This is Maddie. Maddie MacGregor. She is a nurse at the clinic," Deanna introduced her, feeling ashamed that in her anger, she had forgotten she was there for an instant.

"Shawn Jackson," he introduced himself again to shake Maddie's hand.

"Kimberly Applewood," another hand was held out to be shaken. "Yes, this is all we brought. I was told to pack lightly," she explained her lack of baggage.

"That's a good idea out here," Maddie confided. "What do you do?" she asked as she began to walk with the woman who had scooped up her bag.

"I'm a nurse. This is my second rotation," she assured her, to establish that she wasn't a newbie.

"How about you?" Deanna asked Shawn.

"I'm a nurse too, but I'm on my third rotation. I can't seem to get enough of these places," he laughed at himself as he tried to figure them out, the dynamics of new people.

"Doctor Cooper, Doctor Cooper," a voice called singsong as they approached the Rover.

Deanna turned at the voice and saw a line of men, boys really, carrying boxes. "Yes?" she asked, confused. She hadn't been expecting anything. She saw on the sides of the boxes stamped very clearly, "Pharmaceuticals," the other name on each of the boxes had been smudged out, *deliberately,* she thought and wondered at that.

"These came for you on the train," the man told her. He knew her from the many trips she had made into town. He also remembered that she tipped well.

"Ah, I wonder if we are going to have enough room," she mused as she looked at the amount of supplies and the lot of them.

They managed, with the help of the carriers. They stacked many of the boxes up on top of the Rover and tied it all down. It looked ungainly and like it might fall down in an instant. The back of the Rover was also filled. The passengers in the back seat, Kimberly and Shawn, had their bags on their knees, with boxes on the seat between them. Deanna tipped the man and each of the carriers. This was not normal, but she knew if she didn't pay each of them, the leader might not pay the boys for their hard work and the boxes had been heavy.

"Did you order all this?" Maddie asked as she looked at the height of the load above the Rover. It looked very unsteady.

Deanna shrugged. "I wonder how much of this Lakesh would have brought to camp if I hadn't been here to pick it up?" she asked meaningfully and Maddie nodded.

They carefully turned the Rover around through the throngs of people and Kimberly remarked as she fanned her face, "It's rather crowded here, isn't it?"

"That's because Lamish is a port. With the ships that come in and the train, it gets pretty busy," Deanna explained as she drove cautiously.

As they made their way out of town and prepared for the long drive, Deanna took on the role of guide—she explained what they were seeing and how far they had to go. Maddie looked on regretfully, hating that these outsiders had cut into her time alone with Deanna. She tried to be pleasant to the two nurses, knowing they were needed desperately, but she still resented that they were here when she could have had the entire ride back to Mamadu alone with Deanna. Deanna didn't seem to mind. She entertained their new arrivals with stories the entire ride back.

"You brought more in that one shipment than we've been able to get in here in months," Doctor Wilson told her in awe of the amount of supplies he saw taken off her Rover.

"Well I didn't expect it, and I'm sure that had Lakesh arranged it he wouldn't have told us about it. I think it's time you replaced him," Deanna advised.

He nodded reluctantly. She was right. It had been going on too long and too much had disappeared. To run the clinic effectively, he needed those supplies. He'd had to replace one of their guards just the other day because he caught him going in the supply hut to take things that he knew would sell well on the black market.

"Who do I know that I can trust?" he asked, exasperated.

"Ask Hamishish for someone from the village. She can make it a matter of honor," she advised.

Nodding thoughtfully, he smiled. "You're right. Good idea."

Kimberly was assigned to Leida's old and barely cold cot. She fit in the rhythm of Mamadu effortlessly, proving she had done this before. She was, however, a gossip. Ferreting out the most salacious news that she could find, she frequently could be found wide-eyed either sharing something she had learned or having some past indiscretions shared with her by others of her ilk.

"What is up with that?" Deanna asked Maddie one day as she saw Kimberly avidly talking with one of the volunteers.

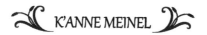

"She found out about Lenny," Maddie said dryly in a disgusted sounding voice.

"Shit," Deanna muttered under her breath as she administered a shot. "That's it," she said kindly to the beautiful African woman who rubbed her arm. "You come and see me for that, okay?" she further asked, pointing at the woman's distended belly. Her interpreter laughed as she translated.

"What? What's so funny?" Deanna asked. It wouldn't be the first time she was the butt of some joke between her interpreter and a patient.

"You said that to her the last time she was here," her interpreter explained.

"I did?" she asked in surprise, looking at the patient again and not recalling her at all.

"Last year," it was explained.

Deanna realized how long she had really been here; she knew it had been too long. Doctors Without Borders only stayed a few months and she hoped that no one had noticed. She did, however, wish to get to know Maddie better and see if this could work out to being a relationship. She smiled at the patient and assured her she would be happy to help her. She turned to the next patient and was unhappy that she had to work with Kimberly on this one.

Working quickly, she saw that there was a bacterial fungus on the skin of this man. After asking many questions, she determined that she would have to ask Hamishish for some input on this one.

"Can't we just put an ointment on it for eczema?" Kimberly asked her.

"Are you questioning my professional opinion?" Deanna countered, looking at the woman. She didn't like her on principle. She sensed the woman didn't think her too competent, due entirely to her age.

"I just thought…" she began, but Deanna dismissed whatever explanation she had been about to make.

Waving her hand dismissively she interrupted with, "When you are here longer, you will understand that including the local witch doctor is not only wise, but prudent. She not only knows the people she sometimes has a local cure that we in the west would be wise to learn from." She could see that Kimberly wanted to argue with her, but wisely kept her mouth shut.

That day, Deanna was called to the village to deliver not one, but two babies. It was a successful delivery for both mothers and she was in a good mood as she returned to the clinic.

Shawn had been assigned to the men's tent. He fit in well with all the doctors as well as the nurses. He got along well with the volunteers and seemed to actually try to learn the local dialect, which endeared him to the villagers. He could frequently be found down in the village taking lessons.

Deanna found him there one evening when she was called to attend to a cat. As a doctor, the villagers felt she could be a good veterinarian as well as a witch doctor.

"I'm sorry. I tried to attend to it myself, but there was nothing that they would let me do, or rather that Hamishish would let me do," Shawn told her apologetically.

"Don't worry about it, I enjoy these different calls," she laughed it off. She wasn't laughing too much when she realized it was a very pregnant caracal that someone had brought to the village. "Is this a pet?" she asked Hamishish, alarmed.

"No, but pelt worth lots. Children want kits," she said bluntly and watched expectantly.

"Someone watch those teeth, wouldja?" Deanna asked nervously.

Shawn grinned and sat down on the head, keeping the wild cat down. She was pretty far gone though and unable to fight, which was a good thing Deanna thought when she got a good look at the claws on it.

Deanna examined her patient quickly and efficiently. There were at least two kittens in there and they were still active. She looked at the mother cat knowing that there wasn't anything she could do for her—she had been shot and was fading fast. Without hesitating, Deanna performed a cesarean section on the cat, popping out two healthy and active kits.

The chief reached for them and handed them to one of his wives, who began to wipe at them with a towel. The gaspy mews of the newborn kits were barely heard. A bottle was procured, the type that the clinic had been trying to give out to pregnant mothers with AIDS, and they attempted to give formula, meant for human babies, to the newborn kits.

Deanna watched and then shrugged. It wasn't her concern. The kits sure were cute, but she watched as the mother died before her. There was a grunt behind her and an interpreter explained, "You cut as well as our best hunter." Deanna smiled, knowing they meant it as a compliment that she hadn't ruined the valuable pelt. Her job here was done and she took her leave, Shawn walking alongside her.

"Now you can't say you would find that variety in the emergency rooms of America," he laughed pointing backwards with his thumb at the hut they had just left.

"No," Deanna laughed with him. "Definitely a variety out here."

"You think those kits will survive?" he asked wonderingly.

She shrugged. "They can only try. I'm surprised that the tribe will try though, they barely have enough to eat themselves. Maybe they will turn the kits into hunters."

"That would be so cool," Shawn enthused.

Deanna loved his enthusiasm, it was so positive and non-destructive. She definitely felt he was an asset to the clinic. She saw Kimberly eyeing them as they returned, walking together. She supposed she would be the subject of her gossipy tongue tomorrow for being seen with the male nurse.

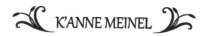

CHAPTER EIGHTEEN

Deanna found herself called upon for the kittens more than once. They weren't strong without a healthy dose of mother's milk and were foundering. One day Maddie went along with her and suggested that another cat or something be found to nurse the little cats. Amazingly, one of the villagers had a lactating dog so they tried her. The bitch, an amiable thing, immediately sensed how helpless the kittens were and her mothering instincts took over. She began to nuzzle them and lick them, pulling them close to find her teats with her half-grown pups nearby. The pups sniffed the new additions and she growled to warn them. All the human adults looking on got a good smile from that. It was a satisfactory beginning to the tale.

"Wasn't that beautiful?" Maddie enthused, totally enamored of the kittens that looked so cute.

"Those babies are going to grow up very large!" Deanna warned, reminding her of the wild ones they had seen in the past.

"But they are so cute now," she said in a girlish voice. "I love babies!"

"Yeah, but babies grow up," the blonde laughed at her girlfriend, wishing she could easily put her arm around her as they walked back towards the clinic.

"Don't you like babies?" she asked playfully. She had seen Deanna deliver several and saw how kind and sweet she was to the children. She'd get down on their level and despite the language barrier, either through an interpreter or through pantomime, she'd make the children laugh in delight. Her balloons were always a big hit. Nothing was sweeter than the sound of children's laughter.

"Of course I do, I just don't want any of my own!" she said emphatically, still laughing at her girlfriend's enthusiasm over the kittens.

Maddie stopped and looked at the young doctor. "Are you serious?" she asked calmly, the laughter fading from her voice.

Deanna nodded. "With all this," her hand encompassed the clinic, the village, and all of Africa. "Why would I want to bring another life into it?"

"To have one of your own, to pass on your genes, to pass on what you know?"

"I can do that by teaching," she answered reasonably, not understanding why Maddie was so still. This was an odd conversation to be having.

"You really don't want children of your own? You are one of the most brilliant women I have ever met, you could pass on those genes to children. They would be so lucky to have you as their mother."

"I know I'm an anomaly. Look at my sister, she didn't get this *brilliant*," she made quote marks in the air, "gene at all, and yet she's smart in her own way. There is no guarantee if I had a child that it would inherit my genes."

"So you don't ever want children of your own?"

Deanna shook her head realizing that Maddie was making some sort of point. She followed, wondering what was going on as Maddie turned to walk the rest of the way back to their tent. "Do you want children?" it suddenly occurred to her to ask.

"Of course. Don't all Irish families want big families? Lots of kids?" she asked sarcastically, clearly hurt.

"Hey," Deanna stopped her from going into the tent, her hand on the redhead's shoulder. "Did I say something to piss you off?"

Maddie shrugged off the hand as she entered the tent, coming face to face with Kimberly.

"You two go on a walk?" she asked, her voice held a hint of innuendo. She saw the anger on Maddie's face and her own lit up in wonderment and curiosity. "Are you okay?" she asked right away.

Deanna wanted to tell the woman to mind her own business, but knew that antagonizing a gossip was not necessarily a good thing. She let Maddie go and went to her own bed to change her clothes and get ready for bed.

Kimberly wasn't done and tried to engage Maddie in conversation. "So this Lenny, she was a..." her voice lowered in a conspiratorial whisper, "*homosexual*?"

Maddie almost answered, but glanced towards Deanna, who was sitting on her cot. Her back had stiffened up at the word, clearly able to hear Kimberly despite the whisper. She knew Kimberly was trying to verify something she had heard the other day, to get concrete and reliable words from someone in-the-know. She shrugged. "She was a nice woman and a good teacher," was all she would give the woman.

"But she left with the chief's daughter?" she continued on eagerly.

Maddie glanced at the woman. She was clearly enjoying the gist of the conversation. She wondered how she would fare if this woman found out about her and Deanna. "That's what they say," she shrugged. "I wouldn't believe everything I heard though. She did her job well."

"Well, I heard..." she began again and kept going until Deanna turned and said, "I'll have you know that more than half of that bullshit you just spouted is untrue. Lenny was everyone's friend here, and anyone who says something bad about her will have to answer to me. I considered her a good woman and despite what they may 'say' about her, I think it's terrible to keep talking about it."

Surprised at the doctor's defense of this unknown woman, Kimberly looked at her contemplatively. "Were you one of her special friends?"

"Oh, for Christ's sake, you're disgusting. Just because someone is friends with someone else of the same sex doesn't mean there is something going on. What about you? Is that why Lenny's story intrigues you so much? You are looking for *special* friends?"

"Well, why, I never...."

"Maybe you should," Deanna muttered, too low for the nasty woman to hear. Louder, so that Kimberly could hear her, she said, "You didn't know her so why don't you just let the stories die down. She didn't deserve this and you won't get anywhere repeating what you have heard."

"Well, I just wanted to know...."

"Then you should ask her, and as she isn't likely to make another appearance here, you'll have to let it go."

Sensing she wasn't going to win this argument with the young doctor, she went to attack, but Magda walked in at that moment. Kimberly liked and respected Magda and didn't want her to think badly of her so she shut her mouth with an almost audible snap.

"Everyone ready for bed?" the Swiss woman asked politely.

"Yes, we just came from the village," Deanna told her, to change the subject. She glanced at Kimberly who deliberately turned her back to change for bed. Her glance took in Maddie, who rolled her eyes, her own back firmly to the other nurse.

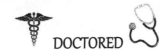

"Oh that's nice. I hear you delivered kittens," the woman teased with a delighted smile.

"Yes, I did and Maddie had the wonderful idea of putting her on another cat. We found a dog willing to take them."

"Did you say a dog?" she asked, wondering if the difference from English to French was causing her to misunderstand.

Deanna chuckled and nodded, finishing up her clothes change. "Yes, it's the darnedest thing, but the bitch is feeding them. Apparently the formula we tried to feed them wasn't suiting their delicate palettes."

"Oh, I must see them! May I go with you next time?" she asked, delighted.

Deanna promised and soon found a regular rotation of people coming with her to see the kittens being fed by the bitch. The bitch didn't like all the additional visitors, but since Deanna was a regular she accepted her.

Deanna found herself watching the kittens' growth, enjoying their exuberance as they grew rapidly.

"I thought you were a human doctor?" Burton sneered at her a few days later in the chow tent.

"Oh, come on, Richard. We're all one procedure away from being horse doctors," Wilson teased him. His eyes laughed at Deanna, who grinned in return. She knew anything she did would annoy Burton these days since he hadn't managed to have her replaced or dismissed despite his letter writing campaign. "It's a matter of goodwill. You make the villagers happy and they spread the word that we are good doctors. Hell, Deanna is regarded as a witch doctor…now that is an achievement," he shared, with a genuine laugh of admiration.

"Yes, well, I won't be wearing the costume," Deanna said wryly and they all shared a laugh, all except Burton who was certain the young doctor was making fun of him somehow.

Deanna really enjoyed the time with the villagers over the kittens. It also allowed her to find places and time with Maddie. She'd been a little distant lately and all she could attribute it to was a letter she had gotten and not shared.

"What is it?" she asked, exasperated. She'd had a hard day in the clinic and had desperately been looking forward to some time alone with Maddie.

"It's nothing," she shrugged.

"You won't tell me? Then there is nothing for us to talk about," she got up to go back to the camp. She was too tired to try to pry it out of her.

"Wait, don't go," the redhead pleaded prettily.

"Look, I'm tired. You've been annoyed with me for days and won't tell me what it's about…" she began.

"I got my letter. I either have to re-up or go home," she explained.

"Is that what this is about? Why you've been so upset lately?"

Maddie's face gave her away. There was more, but she wasn't going to share it, obviously. "I don't know if I want to re-up, but I know I don't want to stay here forever." She'd known the letter would come eventually, but seeing it had surprised her. After all, Leida had left a while back and they'd arrived at the same time.

"Then come with me. They've been after me to move on for months," Deanna told her earnestly. "We can go as a team. I'll write a couple of letters and get you put on..." she trailed off as she saw Maddie's face. "What is it?"

"I don't know that I want people to know that we are a *team*," she put a bit of emphasis on that final word, giving it more than one meaning.

"Are you afraid people will find out about us?" she asked, worriedly, wondering if Maddie was having second thoughts.

"I don't want anyone to *know*…people like Kimberly especially," she sneered at their local gossip. "She's so nasty...."

"Yes, she is; however, I want you to go with me. Are you thinking of going back to the States?"

"I did promise only one rotation to my folks," she explained and, looking at Deanna, she thought she would promise her anything.

"What about me?" she asked softly, feeling like they were on the edge of a very important step in their relationship. Maybe she had expected too much from Maddie. Maybe she didn't really want this.

"I love you," she assured her earnestly. Even though Deanna had never told her the same words, she thought she felt the same. "I just have a lot to think about," she told her honestly.

"Well, you know where I stand. I want you with me," she told her, but she wanted to plead with her not to leave, not to leave her. Her heart was squeezing painfully in her chest. Her hand came up unconsciously to rub her eyebrow.

"Stop that," Maddie said as Deanna's fingers grasped at the short hairs worriedly and Maddie leaned in and kissed Deanna, her soft lips feeling so familiar and still she couldn't get enough of them. She loved kissing this woman. She was so special, so incredible. She never made Maddie feel like a second class citizen, unlike many in the medical profession who felt nurses were just servants with medical knowledge. Deanna treated her as an equal and still managed to maintain her doctor status, more knowledgeable, personable, and yet, brilliant. As a lover, Maddie had never had someone as caring, someone who actually thought of her first.

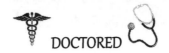

"I can't do this," she told her a week later as they met by their rock.

"What do you mean?" Deanna looked intently into Maddie's eyes.

"I…just…can't…do…this," she gestured with her hands helplessly. Indicating them, everything around them. "I can't…do….us," she finished lamely. They had finally managed a couple of hours away alone and had hidden from the village and camp to spend them together, but Maddie had resisted Deanna's attempts to make love to her.

"Don't say that. Don't give up," Deanna felt herself pleading as she realized the enormity of what Maddie was saying.

Shaking her head, Maddie backed away slightly. "I want…I wanted…" but she shook her head harder as she began to cry.

"We can do this, we can *try*," Deanna tried to reason. The tears were hitting her soul like a hammer on an anvil.

"Don't you see…don't you see?" she shook her head again, the tears rolling down her cheeks. "We will never be accepted. We can't have this." Her hands gestured helplessly again.

"We can make it what we want. We can do this," Deanna stated firmly, willing it to happen. "Don't do this! Don't doubt us. We can do this." She tried to take Maddie's hands in hers, to compel her to change her mind.

Shaking her head, Maddie backed up and put her hands childishly behind her back. "No, it was a fling. That's all," she said dismissively, minimalizing it.

"We both know it was more than that," she said sadly as Maddie's words began to tear her heart from her chest.

"You can't give me what I need…what I want!" she continued as though Deanna hadn't stated the truth.

"What do you need? What do you want?" Deanna asked quietly. She felt the need to cry too.

"I want children and you can never give me that," she grasped at the one thing she knew would hurt Deanna the most. She watched as the pretty doctor's face crumbled before her.

"I'm too young to make a decision about having children," Deanna pointed out.

"You tell me you don't want children of your own…" she recalled a previous conversation.

Deanna nodded in agreement. "I don't want children of my own. It makes no sense with all these children," she indicated the ones in the village, "that I would procreate and bring more into an already over-populated world."

"But don't you see, I want to have children. I want to procreate. I want the joy of giving birth, even the heartache that family and children cause. I want that. You can't give me that. You don't *want* to give me that."

Deanna shook her head. "No, I can't give you children. We could adopt," she pointed out. She gestured towards the village again and Maddie knew she meant the countless orphans they saw all the time.

Maddie shook her head. "No, I want my own. I want…" she didn't go on as she watched Deanna realize the futility of arguing with her.

Deanna looked at her sadly. How could she argue with her? She couldn't give her what she wanted. She couldn't give her something so simple. She had to try though. "We could find someone who would want to give you a child, for us, for…" she tapered off what she was going to say as she saw the horrified look that came over the other woman's face at her suggestion, at what it would mean. She shook her head sadly. "You don't want that do you? You don't want a family with me?"

Maddie looked down quickly so that Deanna wouldn't see the truth in her face. "No, I don't want you," she confirmed, twisting Deanna's words, deliberately, cuttingly. "How could I let someone…" she left off when she saw the hope spring in Deanna's eyes, she looked down again before she changed her mind. "I can't do that," she finished.

"Don't say that. We can work it out…." Deanna wanted to plead, to argue, to get her to capitulate to her plan. She wanted them to walk off hand in hand into the sunset…together. She wanted them to leave here, to go to other camps, maybe other countries…as a couple. She'd had their future planned out…together.

"No! I can't do this! I won't!" she argued fiercely. She wouldn't let Deanna talk her into it. She didn't want this. She didn't want her, she lied to herself. She knew she was afraid of what people would think of her if she became a lesbian. As she walked back alone, she glanced up and recognized Kimberly from afar. People like *that*…

CHAPTER NINETEEN

A film crew drove into Mamadu the week before Maddie was officially due to leave. They asked that the doctors each give a plug about the work they had been doing. Maddie, along with the others, watched as Deanna spoke clearly and succinctly:

"Every year over three thousand field staff in Doctors Without Borders help in over sixty countries worldwide to provide medical treatment and assistance to those who would otherwise have no access to healthcare of any kind. With the outbreak of hostilities and humanitarian crises all over our planet, this means we need help in many areas of field work. We are recruiting you," with that Deanna pointed into the camera. "We need technical people, doctors, surgeons, anesthesiologists, nurses, plastic surgeons, and administrators, even farmers and other volunteers. If you don't think you can help, you are probably wrong. Please check with your local recruiter to see if you can help. If you can't help physically, your money will go a long way to supplying these people," her hand swept to the ward of sick and dying people, "with medicines and help." She finished the taping and then they filmed her again, this time in French. Instead of saying Doctors Without Borders, this time she said Médecins Sans Frontières. Her rich voice was pleading without begging, assertive without being belligerent, and the film crew chief was certain it would go well in the series she was filming for the association. They needed to recruit as many people as they could, and they needed money. Doctors like Deanna Cooper were a godsend. She was pretty, which was a bonus, she was young—they dirtied her up some so she didn't look quite so young—and she was earnest. They needed to make some posters with her face on them.

"Good job," Wilson complimented her when she finished the French version.

Deanna shrugged. "If it helps," she said dismissively. She was trying to maintain the facade that she was okay, but she was really hurting. Maddie wouldn't discuss their breakup with her. She had, in fact, been avoiding her. They both knew she was leaving the following week and Deanna was heartbroken.

"Will we be losing you soon too?" he asked quietly so that the others wouldn't hear.

She looked up. "Is it that obvious?"

He nodded. "I know you stayed on longer to get to know her."

She looked up, not surprised that he had known. She nodded in agreement. "Well, I stayed on eons longer that would normally be allowed, but it's time...."

"Do you know where you will go?"

"I heard there are cholera outbreaks. I'm needed..." her voice trailed off as she watched Maddie walk determinedly across the compound. She stopped to chat with the affable Shawn, and Deanna saw him put his arm around her as they shared a laugh. Her heart twisted, right across to her stomach. Shawn was the kind of man who would give the redhead the children she so desired. Deanna shook her head to clear her mind and wandered off, not finishing her conversation with Wilson. He watched her head for the village, sure she would be playing with the kittens that were growing so quickly.

Wilson was right. She spent many pleasurable hours playing with the caracal kittens. They were boisterous and yet, being socialized with the tribe, they were treated as the dogs that were kept as pets. They still answered to their foster mother, the bitch who had taken them in and fed them. Her pups were now grown and given away, traded, or sold. The kittens still minded their 'mother,' their capacity for human interaction was amazing. They were smarter than any other kitten she had seen—some of it instinctive, some if it learned. It was fascinating to the doctor. It also provided her with an escape from Maddie and her change of heart.

"Doctor Cooper. Wakey," an insistent voice near her ear made her want to swat it. "DOCTOR!" the voice persisted, like a mosquito in the tent. Deanna reached up to swat it. She had gotten in late from the village and was tired.

"Deanna!" another voice called and she sat up a little dreamily.

"Whaaa?" she asked through a yawn, using the backs of her knuckles to wipe away the sleep in her eyes.

"There's been an outbreak of fighting and they overran the lines. We're expecting mass casualties," Maddie told her. "They are talking about evacuating us," she explained as she dressed.

"How do you know so much?" Deanna asked, trying to get her sleepy brain working as she automatically started to dress, shaking out her clothes.

"I woke up when they came in to tell us," she indicated the worker who had come to rouse the women.

"I do hope we have enough supplies," Kimberly said, a hysterical note in her voice, but also a lot of excitement.

"We will make do otherwise," Magda answered as she buttoned her pants.

Deanna turned her back to pull her own pajama bottoms down and pull on some jeans. She sat down to pull her socks on, shaking them out before pulling them on. She clapped her boots together upside down. She watched something scurrying away as it fell from one of them, before stomping her feet into them. The others were ready and out before she was finished. She went out into a madhouse.

The casualties were already there and kept coming. The doctors were overwhelmed, the nurses as well. Triage consisted of making instant decisions by lamplight in the area in front of the clinic. The men involved, from both sides, were stacked there, ten men deep. Some tried to keep fighting, killing their 'enemy' if they happened to notice the wrong color uniform or tribe marking. Some of the volunteers ended up policing them, taking away weapons that would be used otherwise. The doctors took turns doing the first assessments as each were elbow deep in surgeries. And still the casualties came.

Deanna looked up after her first twenty-four hours of surgery. She was subsisting on hot chocolate and crackers that the nurses fed her. She was beyond exhausted and there was no end in sight. The blood and gore and stupidity of it seemed unceasing.

"You need to take a four-hour nap," Burton ordered as he came on.

"What about you?" she asked saucily, not so inclined to take his advice at the moment. She had just had to send a man to his death. The procedure he required would have meant the death of several others due to the length of time it would have taken to do his.

"I just came back on. When you wake up, tell Wilson, so he can take a break," he told her as he glanced at her appearance. She looked terrible, with blood on her operating costume. They'd run out of new or clean outfits after the first twelve hours.

Deanna wasn't going to argue. She went through the triage before she headed for the showers, sending a few critical cases on to Burton and Wilson before she stood under the shower heads, two buckets of water poured over her to wash away the blood. She went back to her tent and collapsed in her robe, remembering to pull the blanket over her head before she fell soundly asleep.

"Deanna, it's four hours," Maddie woke her, handing her a coffee.

"No hot chocolate?" she asked, trying to force her eyes open. She'd just shut them, she was sure.

"I wasn't sure which you wanted and brought both," Maddie told her, handing her another cup, as she looked at her. They both looked a sight, exhausted.

"Has it let up?" she asked as she burnt her tongue on the hot chocolate.

She shook her head. "The women and children are being evacuated," she informed her, getting up from the bed. She couldn't stand to be next to Deanna anymore. She wanted her, she wanted to comfort her, she wanted to be comforted herself, but she stuck by her resolve. A lesbian relationship was not what she wanted…or needed.

"What about the staff?" she asked as she put on her jeans again, the smocks had bled through and the jeans were stained and stiff with blood. She shrugged and put them on anyway.

"We're next," she told her and looked out the tent. People were shouting and occasionally screaming in pain.

"How stupid this is," she muttered angrily, sipping at the hot chocolate. "Do I have time to eat?" she asked at Maddie's back.

Maddie didn't turn, she just nodded. "They still have the kitchen going, but not for long."

She nodded, but knew Maddie wouldn't turn and look at her. "Okay, I'm ready," she said instead, officiously. Maddie wanted nothing more from her, she would give her nothing.

She was able to get two sandwiches down. She washed them down with a second lukewarm cup of hot chocolate before she plunged into the fray again, relieving Wilson who was looking every bit his age.

"Thanks," he said wearily when Deanna relieved him.

She didn't look up again for the next twelve hours. By then the women and children of the village were gone, their meager possessions held in their arms. They disappeared into the savannah, away from the war, away from the conflict. The men of the village followed soon afterwards. It was that or be conscripted into an army they had no business in. It wasn't as if they would have a choice either.

All that was left were the volunteers, the doctors, and the nurses. There were a few Africans who stayed on to interpret, help, or assist where they could, but many were frightened.

Doctor Wilson ordered all non-essential personnel to be evacuated. The women, the nurses, and the volunteers were the first to go. He tried to order Deanna to go, but she laughed at him and he knew she wouldn't leave. The last Deanna saw of Maddie, she was getting into Deanna's Rover, which she had given to the cause, along with Kimberly and Magda…a relieved Alex Whitley was behind the wheel. They headed for Lamish, hoping the conflict wouldn't circle around and cut off their flight.

Maddie took one more look at Deanna, not realizing the doctor had been staring at her. The last she saw of Deanna, she was bending over a patient, working busily. With the nurses and others leaving, they would be terribly short-handed.

CHAPTER TWENTY

Madison looked up to see high-top sneakers in rainbow colors. She had never seen any like that before. They were very colorful…and very bright. Long slacks on a lean waist led up to a buxom figure that was very attractive. Her doctor's lab coat was a brilliant white, her name embroidered across the lapel in red—versus the black that the rest of the doctors had. As Madison's gaze took in the woman, she stared, wondering if she had met her before. She looked very familiar…and yet…not. She looked to be in her early twenties, but based on all the experience she had heard the woman had, she had to be in her thirties or forties at least. Her hair was a deep brown and had shades of blonde and more red streaks in it. Madison couldn't tell if it was natural, or colored. She watched the woman for a moment, trying to figure out if she knew her and why she seemed so familiar. It was as the woman lifted her hand, one with a large signet ring on the ring finger, and began rubbing her eyebrow that Madison realized she did indeed know the woman. The gesture was so familiar, so endearing, she knew who that woman was in an instant. Just then the woman looked across the cafeteria to find Madison gazing at her and, at first startled, she smiled in delight. She said something to her companions and came across the lunchroom to greet her.

"Hello, Maddie. It's been a while," she greeted her familiarly. She was unsure if she should hug her or shake her hand. She hesitated for a moment before enveloping the other woman in a hug.

Madison was surprised…and relieved to find herself in a great bear hug. She had been unsure how to greet Deanna. She smelled…differently. Her scent was the familiar scent of antiseptic so prevalent in the hospital, but underlying it was a perfume, nothing she had ever smelled on her that she could recall. But before she pulled away, she indulged herself with a quick nose in the shoulder and could smell the scent that was purely Deanna. She recognized it instantly, even after all these years…her body recognized it too. "It's Madison now. It's good to see you," she said formally, almost stiffly.

"I saw you a few weeks ago, but didn't get a chance to say hello," Deanna said as she pulled back and put a little distance between them. They were being watched and she knew the gossip would be around the hospital in a matter of hours, good or bad.

"So that was you?" she flung her hand so her finger ended up pointing upside down at Deanna, "with the flowers?"

Deanna's eyebrows beetled together. "Yes, didn't you get the cards?" she asked, concerned. At the other woman's shake of the head, she laughed as though she had just told a joke and shook her head. "That's because I didn't send any."

Madison laughed with her, but felt distinctly uncomfortable.

Deanna looked over her shoulder at someone calling to her and looked back at Maddie. "I've got to go. We should get together…catch up?"

Madison nodded and watched as the doctor walked away. She stood there bemusedly for a moment. Deanna had aged. She now had a nose stud in the left side of her nostril. She was also wearing jewelry. She had a ring on her ring finger, which looked bulky and heavy and she had piercings in her ears—not just one, but two on each side and another in the upper cartilage of her left ear. It must be terrible to keep track of all that jewelry when she was in surgery.

"Madison, you okay?" Bonnie came up to empty her own tray.

She nodded and woke up from her thoughts. "Yes, I'm fine. Why?"

"I thought you said you didn't know Doctor Kearney?"

"Well, when I knew her she was Doctor Cooper," she answered truthfully as they began to wander off towards the exits.

Deanna watched Maddie from the corner of her eye as she talked with her colleagues. They were fascinating men and women, but she found some of them terribly stuffy and boring. She didn't know how long she could stand to be in this atmosphere, but she had agreed to a six-month stint and she'd honor that. They were grateful to have her. She was surprised to find her past here.

What was Deanna doing here? Of all the hospitals in the country, how had she wound up in Los Angeles? It was a long way from Boston where she had grown up and gone to college, much less the world where she studied people and diseases from all over. It was especially a long way from Africa where she had last seen her. How had she come to be in the same hospital that Madison was in?

Madison kept thinking and rethinking all during her afternoon shift. She caught herself daydreaming, remembering when she last saw Deanna in Africa. She'd thought about her a lot over the years, even during her courtship with Scott and eventual marriage. She knew in her Catholic mind it was a sin to think about her, but she had loved her once. It had been her first love. How could she ever forget Deanna? Now she was here a decade later. Why?

Madison wasn't surprised to 'run into' Doctor Kearney that night after work. She wondered if Deanna had married and taken his name. It was obvious Deanna was waiting for her.

"Would you like to go to dinner, maybe get a drink?" Deanna asked her.

"I have to get home to my kids," Madison told her.

"Ah, so you had them after all. I wondered."

"Yeah, I got the white picket fence I wanted," she said wryly. She wondered if she should tell her about the divorce too.

Deanna laughed as expected. "I'm happy to hear that," she told her truthfully as she walked with the nurse towards her vehicle. She wasn't surprised to see it was a minivan. "I've wondered about you over the years."

"I've wondered about you too," Madison was truthful. She glanced at Deanna speculatively for a moment and then asked, "What are you doing here?"

Deanna had known that question would come up, but was surprised Maddie, now Madison, had been brave enough to voice it so quickly. "I agreed to come as a favor to the board. It's only for six months, but I didn't know you were here. I saw you a few weeks back and I wasn't sure how you would feel…." She had seen her from afar and thought the bouquets a nice way to break the ice. They had, after all, seen many of those flowers in their natural habitat, although some of them were derived from the original species and looked nothing like them anymore.

Madison unlocked the door to her vehicle with the key. "I was surprised," she admitted, looking at the doctor. The high-tops were funny and funky, a far cry from the boots she had worn in Africa, a necessary evil. They suited Deanna, made her appear cool and hip. She wondered if anyone on the board or the stuffy doctors had said anything about them. She could well imagine Deanna telling them to stuff it. "We will have to get together and catch up," she promised.

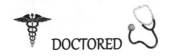

"Tomorrow?" Deanna asked persistently.

"I'll get a sitter," Madison agreed and got in her vehicle. She waved in response to Deanna's wave, wondering what tomorrow would bring.

"Hey, ready to go?" Deanna called, hurrying up as she saw Madison waiting near the entrance that they all used.

Madison had waited all day for this meeting, a bit on pins and needles. She wasn't hungry, but at the same time she was starved. She couldn't inquire at the hospital as the gossips would have a field day. Her divorce alone had provided food for fodder, but she wouldn't explain the reasons she had decided to file. It was no one's business but hers and Scott's. She didn't need anyone to speculate on her relationship, past or present, with Deanna.

She saw that Deanna was wearing different shoes, black with rainbow laces. It amused her as she knew that the doctors must be disapproving of so blatant a display. The kids the doctor dealt with must love it—Deanna looked hip and cool. Their parents probably realized that it was a subtle way to affirm her sexuality, but Maddie wondered at that. Why the name change? Had Deanna married? Had she given up being a lesbian?

"You want to go in separate cars or…" Deanna gave her the option.

"Let's take separate cars so we can drive home from wherever…" she responded, startled out of her surmising.

"I thought we'd go over to the steakhouse," she pointed down the street from the hospital.

Knowing how tight her budget was since the divorce, Madison hesitated. She hadn't wanted a fast food restaurant, but…

"Hey, I invited you out, remember?" Deanna reminded her, seeing the hesitation. "I'll meet you there," she finished, not giving her a choice, and walking away before Madison could argue. She seemed to recall money had been an issue back in Lamish ever so long ago.

Madison watched from her own vehicle as Deanna walked over to the doctor's parking lot. She was amused to see her get into a Rover. After ten years she couldn't drive a different vehicle? She made her way out of the general employee lot and turned onto the busy roadway towards the steakhouse. She was there only a moment when Deanna pulled in beside

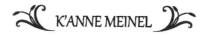

her. Still amused by the Rover, she greeted Deanna with a smile plastered to her face.

Seeing the amusement in the redhead's still amazing blue eyes she asked, "What?"

"Not much for variety?" she tilted her head towards the Rover to indicate what she was talking about.

Deanna caught on immediately. "Yeah, I guess I don't like some changes." She turned to walk into the restaurant.

"Ah, Doctor Kearney," the greeter said with obvious familiarity. "We have your usual table..." she said, cutting off when she saw Madison was with the doctor. She didn't look too happy about it either.

"There will be two of us this evening, Lauren," Deanna answered easily.

They began to follow the greeter and Madison asked to Deanna's back, "Come here often?"

Deanna turned back to address her, "Every night practically. It beats cooking."

Madison had to agree with her. They were seated in a booth built for two, maybe three people if someone sat at the back of the curve.

"Do you need menus or the usual?" the greeter asked, looking only at Deanna.

"I think tonight we will need menus," Deanna said easily, deflecting the rudeness of Lauren.

The greeter handed them both a nice embossed menu and asked, "Drinks?"

"I'll take whatever is on tap," Deanna answered and then looked at Madison.

"I'll have the same," she answered, feeling foolish. She didn't go out often and hadn't been out in a long time, except perhaps the fast food restaurants and through the drive-thru for the kids. She quickly opened her menu, knowing Deanna was looking at her and feeling…inadequate.

Deanna already knew the menu by heart, but wanted to make Madison feel comfortable. She was relieved when Lauren left to get them their beers. She glanced away and looked around the restaurant to see if there was anyone from the hospital that she knew. The furnishings were deep, rich, and polished woods. She was glad there were no animal heads on the walls, but it was a near thing with the rest of the furnishings encouraging deer hunting and big game. The beautiful pictures of the animals in their wild settings were much more preferable than the actual trophies, at least to Deanna's way of thinking. She saw one of the board members, and at their acknowledgement she nodded her head, smiling in that fake way that you often did when you saw someone you didn't particularly care to see. She knew at some point that person would come over to say hello. She didn't wish to be disturbed, but there was nothing for it. She looked back at Madison to see her finishing the menu.

"Find something you like?" she asked.

"It's kind of pricey, isn't it?" the nurse responded warily.

"I told you, I got this," she promised. "Don't worry about the prices. Order whatever you want."

Lauren returned with their beers and smiled, a fake little smile that she saved for customers. Deanna saw it and was amused. She watched as the woman left and wondered if she had some sort of crush on her…Deanna hadn't encouraged her in any way. She'd been coming here regularly for a while, but only because she liked at least one hot meal a day that she didn't have to cook. The cafeteria at the hospital wasn't the best place to get a real meal, although the food was healthier there than in other hospitals she had visited.

A man hurried up. "Oh, hello, Doctor Kearney. Would you two like to hear the specials?" he asked courteously.

"I don't need to hear them. How about you?" Deanna asked Madison, looking at her curiously. "Do you know what you would like?"

"The stuffed pork chops sound good," she answered.

"Would you like green beans or asparagus with that?" he asked, scribbling.

In no time he had both their orders and Deanna reached for her beer to take a sip. "Ah, that hits the spot," she said with a sigh.

"It does," Madison agreed, not knowing how to start talking to the woman she remembered from so long ago. She looked different. She was definitely more mature, but still had that youthful look about her that belied her age. She knew that Deanna was the same age as her, but she certainly did not look it at all. Madison had spread out a bit and hated that her hips had the middle-age spread from having given birth. Deanna was still thin, her breasts a bit fuller, but maybe that was how she had aged. She was wearing a white blouse…was it silk or satin? Madison wouldn't know. She couldn't have afforded to even look at that on her salary. Deanna carried it fine, with a nice blazer over the ensemble. She had definitely gotten better with age.

"So…what have you been up to for the past ten years?" Deanna began with a smirk, laughing at the incongruity of the question.

"Well," Madison started laughing, "I've been married, I have two kids...and I'm divorced."

"Oh, I'm sorry. Didn't it work out?" she sounded genuinely compassionate and Madison hated her for it, momentarily.

"It just didn't feel like it was right," she admitted honestly. "He didn't meet my needs, I guess."

Deanna wanted to ask more in-depth questions, but didn't feel it was her place. She didn't know Maddie, *this* Madison, like she had so long ago.

"What about you? What's with the name change? Did you get married?" Madison asked her.

"Well, I've always been Doctor Kearney, but I wanted my anonymity in Africa, no special privileges. Fortunately, Doctor Wilson understood that. Doctor Burton, not so much," she admitted wryly as she remembered how hard he had made things. It didn't have to be that way.

"Ah, so you were Doctor Kearney all along? Why didn't you tell me?"

Deanna shrugged as she looked at Madison. "I guess it didn't really matter to me at the time. It matters more to others. I prefer to get by on my own merit. What about you? Why Madison now? What happened to Maddie?"

"Oh, that was a child's name. I found I was taken more seriously when I went by my full name," she dismissed.

Deanna nodded understandingly. "Do you have pictures of your children?" she asked kindly, genuinely interested, wondering if she had some of her husband too. Who had she procreated with? She remembered that male nurse Shawn from so long ago.

Madison pulled up pictures on her phone and, sliding around the curve of the booth slightly, began to show Deanna pictures of two children who were absolutely precious. Chloe was about eight and Conor about seven. Both had Madison's red hair, but it was obvious that Conor would take after his father, a robust and hearty man from the picture of the four of them that Madison shared.

"They are beautiful," Deanna told her and meant it. Chloe looked like Madison so much that Deanna was certain that was how she had looked as a child. They both scooted back to their sides of the table as their food was brought up.

"This looks delicious," Madison commented before digging in to her pork chops.

"Is there anything else I can get you?" their waiter came back to ask.

"I'll take another one of these?" Deanna tapped her fork on the glass of her draft beer.

A persistent noise went off and Maddie looked at Deanna wondering why she didn't take care of it. It was after the third time that she asked, "Are you going to answer that?"

"Answer what?" Deanna asked in return, genuinely confused.

"Your phone?"

Deanna looked at her for a moment and then began to fish around in her pockets for the device. Pulling it out, she kept pushing buttons on the side until a screen lit up. "Well, what do you know?" she murmured. She looked up at Madison and said, "It was easier when they had beepers.

Excuse me for a minute, will you?" She got up and walked away, an amused Madison watching as she tried to make the phone work for her. It was obvious she wasn't familiar with the technology.

When she returned to the table, they both finished their meals, chatting easily, but really not telling each other much of anything.

"Doctor Kearney?" a voice asked as they were chatting. Deanna looked up, went to get up, but the man addressing her quickly motioned her to sit. "Sit, sit. I didn't want to interrupt, but I wanted to introduce my wife before we left," he said. "Audrey."

The woman had a pinched face that looked like she had been drinking straight lemon juice.

"Hello," Deanna said, holding out her hand to be shaken. The woman's grip was limp and too effeminate for a real handshake. Something must be wrong with her arm as it went up and down oddly, the woman must have thought it was effusive.

"This is Deanna Kearney of Kearney Pharmaceuticals," he explained to his wife. "We're hoping to get her on the board and…" he would have gone on to explain more, but Deanna interrupted, distinctly uncomfortable.

"I've explained it would be a conflict of interest and not compatible with our dealings. As a doctor I can practice without entering into the dealings with my family's holdings." Her voice sounded pained as she glanced at Madison to see if she had caught on to what the man had just disclosed.

"You don't even run the…" he began to argue, trying to persuade her.

"This isn't the type of conversation we should be having here," she warned him with a charming smile.

He got the hint and, not wishing to offend the valuable doctor, he soon made his exit, trying to be charming…and failing.

Deanna waited until they were both out of the restaurant before remarking, "Money, brains, and no class." She sighed, wondering when the questions would begin. She wasn't disappointed as Madison asked one right away.

"Pharmaceuticals?" she asked, puzzled, trying to put the pieces together.

Deanna sighed again. She had hoped to keep her anonymity as long as possible, but it was impossible with people like the one that had just left. They considered her a feather in their cap and they would use her and her name to the hospital's benefit if they could. She began to tell Madison the truth. "My family name is Kearney. They own Kearney Pharmaceuticals." She heard the intake of breath from Madison and knew the reason for it. The company was huge, well-known, and meant a lot of money. "When I decided to work overseas, I asked to use my mother's family name of Cooper. It was less likely people would put two and two together. It worked fine for the most part, and those who knew who I really was agreed to keep the secret."

"Like Doctor Wilson?" she asked astutely, remembering some of the halted conversations.

Deanna nodded. "Doctor Burton found out there was no Doctor Cooper in Doctors Without Borders and went on a witch-hunt." She grinned in remembrance at the double meaning of that.

Madison chuckled. Deanna had been respectfully called a witch doctor, and with Hamishish to back it up, she had been well-liked. Doctor Burton hadn't seemed to like her youth, her sex, or the fact that the villagers accepted her so willingly.

"It was the pharmaceuticals that I was able to ask for and obtain that really bothered him though. He was somehow getting kickbacks from Lakesh, I found out later. That's how Lakesh always knew what and where to steal, shipment-wise," she explained. "When I would go into Lamish myself to bring the supplies to Mamadu, it often screwed up their availability and they had to steal from the inventoried supplies. It was easier to steal before they were in the camp."

Madison remembered one trip that they had the boxes stacked pretty high on Deanna's Rover from Lamish to Mamadu; it had been a memorable trip. She blushed, hoping Deanna wouldn't notice.

Deanna noticed, but ignored it. "When I left Africa, the support died down from Kearney Pharmaceuticals until they were able to figure out some ways to combat the black market trade. Hamishish helped put a few of them away; they targeted her for a while."

"What happened after I left?" Madison asked. She had always wondered.

"With the camp or…?"

"Both?" she asked, finishing her meal. She signaled for an ice water to settle the meal and dilute the two beers she had drunk. She would have to drive home after all.

"We were overrun a few days after you left. For a while we were a mobile unit. Our Red Cross status didn't seem to keep the armies from coming at us." A look passed over her face, but it was so brief that Madison would have missed it if she hadn't been watching the woman tell her tale.

"How long did you stay?"

"Another three months and then I needed to move on," she explained without giving the reasons. "When I got home, my father was ill and dying. I stayed on during his illness. He had a touch of dementia, but by then my sister Doreen had the company well in hand. I was looking forward to her running things indefinitely for the family. A year after I got back," she deliberately skipped over that time, "she was hit by a speeding car in a crosswalk in front of one of our office buildings. She was killed outright."

"I'm sorry," Madison stated sincerely, almost reaching out to comfort Deanna, but pulling her hand back before she could complete the gesture. Deanna noticed it, but chose to ignore it.

"Yeah, my mom was pretty upset…first dad and then Doreen. Doreen's husband wanted to take over the company, but she left no will and he wasn't qualified. It got pretty contentious. He began to drink and let their kids run wild, so my mom got a conservatorship and is raising them. They are pretty unruly teens. They seem to live for their trust funds and nothing more. Selfish brats," she commented bitterly.

"Is your mother running the company too?" she asked, concerned for this woman she knew nothing about. It was obvious that Madison had some affection for the woman by the way her voice changed.

"No, my mother couldn't be that brutal if she had to. I'm technically the CEO, but I have a small group of people running it for me so I don't have to be there in the day-to-day bullshit," she put in succinctly. "I hate the politics of it all. I was advised to sell, or sell stocks, but my family owns it outright and I'll be damned if all that hard work will benefit the sycophants like my brother-in-law who has done nothing to earn it." She sounded a little bitter.

"Nor should they," Madison consoled. "So you've been working there ever since?" she asked, curious.

Deanna shook her head. "No, once it was set up to my satisfaction, I got the hell out of Dodge and back in the field. I had to make adjustments of course." She didn't illuminate just what adjustments, but Madison made assumptions regarding the running of an international pharmaceutical company, and Deanna didn't correct those assumptions. "I only came back last year when Mom asked me to," she explained.

"Did she need help with your sister's children?" She was really interested in this side of Deanna. She hadn't spoken often about her family and now she realized why.

Deanna shook her head. "No, I think my mom finally realized I would have stayed in the jungles forever…" she began, but Madison interrupted.

"You went back to South America, the Amazon?"

Deanna nodded. "For a while, but wherever I went, nothing was the same. I learned so much though," she shook her head as the memories of the last years assailed her. Some of it was too much to relate in one sitting. She knew she couldn't have explained the beauty of what she had seen, not adequately, or the healing that she had needed. "I did, however, make an incredible discovery," she bragged with a bit of pride.

"What did you discover?" Madison smiled at her.

"You know what an aloe vera plant is, right?"

Madison nodded, wondering at the turn the conversation had taken.

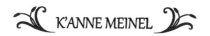

She was more interested to know if Deanna had found that woman she had been in love with back in the Amazon. Her heart twisted a little knowing there had to be others who had known this incredible woman. She'd let her go long ago, knowing she couldn't have her. She'd given up that right.

"Well, it's a succulent and it helps with burns," she explained. She went on further to explain how many species of it were found all over and they had discovered that certain types went beyond helping with burns. "It also creates a second skin. It works with the body's own natural ability to grow skin. The platelets that form from a scab, along with these specific aloe vera plants, combine to help heal and regrow skin."

"Wait, are you talking about the Cooper-Aloe procedure?" she asked. She had heard about this and she began to realize why Deanna had brought this up, and the correlation of the name.

Deanna nodded. "Yes, I figured it out. We can propagate these wild aloes, but in the fifth generation it deteriorates for some reason and we need to get the wild species back in and start over." She sounded disgusted at her own human frailties. "We found that the best of the wild species are in the Amazon. God, that place hides more in its lush foliage than we have found. Logging and forestry have really made a dent in the jungle. We had to buy so much land to keep it in its original state. We worked with the natives to ensure that no one trespasses. It's been a nightmare as we try to keep the land in its natural state and the loggers salivate after the trees and woods that make them so much money. I bought enough land that they can't get to the deep reaches. They can't come on privately owned land, but still they try; it's a constant war. The aloe plant is the least of it. The way of life of those natives will be preserved as long as I can manage it!" Her fist thumped on the table and it was obvious she was passionate about this.

Madison had no idea that Deanna could look so impassioned. It was rather...arousing and she wasn't immune to it. It was also fascinating. Deanna had made a separate fortune from the Cooper-Aloe procedure in burn products. It was all under Kearney Pharmaceuticals, but she was rich in her own right, much less her family fortune. It was obvious it hadn't affected her in the least. She was still brilliant, still down-to-earth and charming. Madison resented some of that, wanted to dislike her. "No wonder they want you on the board," she commented.

Deanna nodded. "I won't though. I hate being in boardrooms," she said adamantly. "I want the freedom to treat people, to actually help them. Do you know, when I requested to work in the emergency room they wanted to deny it to me because I was more 'useful' elsewhere? I disabused them of that notion pretty damn quick."

Madison didn't doubt it. With that much power behind her, the hospital should be grateful for her presence and probably were afraid she would walk. That reminded her of the funky shoes that Deanna wore. As they chatted on, she mentioned them.

Deanna held one out beyond the table, nearly tripping someone who was walking by. "Oh, excuse me," she apologized profusely. Laughing, she turned back to Madison. "I have a bunch of these in different styles. They are so much more comfortable than the patent leather they would like us doctors to wear. We are on our feet most of the day. I'll be damned if I'll wear something uncomfortable like that!"

"You don't think that gives you away?"

"What? That I love sports shoes?"

"No, that you are…into women?" She felt uncomfortable bringing that up and wondered if Deanna was still gay, maybe bringing it up was wrong...

Deanna shrugged. "It's Los Angeles for Christ's sake. If they have a problem with my sexuality that is their problem, not mine. If I can survive my mother and her disapproval over that, I can survive anything."

"She accepts it now?"

"Let's just say she values her only surviving daughter being in her life *now and then* enough to keep it under wraps. Her grandchildren aren't what she thought she would get and she thinks there might still be hope for me," she shook her head and grinned unrepentedly. "I live my life as I see fit and I will continue to do so. What's the point of living in someone else's world by someone else's standards?"

Madison wondered if that was a dig at her and her decision to break up with Deanna so long ago. She had wanted children and couldn't see how they could have them at the time. This was before in vitro-fertilization had become so common. She'd thought of all of this over the years. She still couldn't get past the gossip and stigma of being a lesbian. What people would say and think still bothered her. She could see that with Deanna, it wasn't an issue and never had been. "Not all of us have that luxury," she said coldly.

Deanna was surprised at the tone and didn't really understand it. Before she could ask, the bill came. She pulled out a credit card and handed it to their server. Madison didn't seem to want to talk anymore as she gathered her things and said she had to get home to her children.

"I'm hoping we can be friends while I'm here," Deanna held out the olive branch hopefully as they waited for her credit card to be returned. She signed the slip and left a generous twenty-percent tip without really looking at the total.

Madison saw the total and realized how many groceries that type of meal would have bought for her small family. No, Deanna had no clue of the realities of someone in her position. She did, however, have no problem being friends with her. It couldn't hurt. They had, at one point, loved each other, or, at least she had loved Deanna. She had wondered about that years ago. Deanna had never actually said the words. What Madison had assumed hadn't been said to her…ever. She wanted to ask about it now, but felt it inappropriate. Perhaps dragging up the past wasn't a good idea.

CHAPTER TWENTY-ONE

Deanna was explaining the Cooper-Aloe product to a group of doctors involved with burn victims. "It helps burn victims up to 80% more often than previous therapies."

"And you profit, right, Doctor Cooper? Oh yeah, it's Kearney of Kearney Pharmaceuticals, right? They, or rather *you,* make money off of this product you're pushing?" someone called out viciously.

Deanna nodded. "Yes, I've never hidden that I discovered it after the locals in Mário Terezena taught me. They benefit as well as the rest of their tribe. They have a stake in this, it is not just me. I simply had access to the company to commercialize it," she admitted defensively. She shrugged. "Don't use it if you don't see an improvement, but don't let your attitude towards me personally or Kearney influence you. The product itself should sell you on its viability. With laser surgery later on, the scars that develop from this procedure are less noticeable. They are less likely to die from the scar tissue that used to build up in the victims."

Madison was watching from the balcony, hidden in the dark. She should really be on rounds with the other doctors' patients she had worked on, but she was fascinated to see how Deanna was contending with those who thought her an elitist. She had heard the rumors around the hospital.

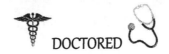

While most liked her, there were some who were jealous of her brilliance and her money, or suspicious of her genuine need to help victims of so many things. The burn unit was the least of the areas where her knowledge of other procedures was questioned. She watched as Deanna convinced some of her sincerity, her slides and other visual aids assisting her in persuading some to at least give it a try.

"I swear! They gather the beans after the cats poop them out," she was enthralling her audience with the gross tale about how the coffee beans for one of the most expensive coffees in the world were gathered.

"C'mon, that's too gross to be true," someone objected, laughing at Deanna's tale.

Madison, listening at another table, knew it was probably true. Deanna wasn't one to spread a story like that unless it was true. She had a full table enthralled. People loved the doctor's personality and she always had a new story to share.

"I tell you, look it up. Kopi Luwak is like thirty-five to a hundred bucks a cup."

"Have you had some?"

"Hell, no! Do I want to drink coffee that is also known as cat poop coffee? They get the cats, these civets, to eat these beans. The beans go through them, they collect feces, and sell it as Kopi Luwak," she explained. Those who didn't want to believe her would be looking it up later. Others were amused by the story.

"Why would their poop...?" began someone trying to trip up the brilliant young woman.

"Some sort of fermentation goes on as it goes through their digestive juices," she explained in anticipation of the question.

Madison, listening in, was amused. It was probably all true too...she Googled it later only to find out it was.

"Look, I was brought in on this...this is what I *do*. Use me, use my expertise! Don't dismiss it because of your prejudices..."

Bonnie was hearing yet another confrontation between Doctor Kearney and another, more senior doctor. The hospital was rife with stories about this doctor who had come in and shaken up the establishment. She was well-liked by the staff and patients, but not so much by older doctors who felt she didn't have the experience that she so obviously did. She still looked too young, had started too early. They felt she was confrontational, but Doctor Kearney wasn't afraid to take them on. Later, Bonnie would relate the story in the nurses' lounge and Madison, who had heard this sort of thing time and again, shook her head, wondering if Deanna would stay. For all the accolades they wanted from this highly sought-after doctor, the headaches might outweigh her highfalutin connections and name.

"But the insurance only covers so much pain medication," a younger doctor was clarifying to Deanna as though she wasn't bright and needed to have it explained to her.

"So we should let them cry in pain when we have the means to alleviate it?" Deanna shook her head at the stupidity of it.

Madison, coming across the after-surgical follow-up, watched as Deanna gave the medication she felt the patient should have, insurance be damned. She was amused. Today, Deanna was wearing sneakers that lit up like a child's when the heel of them came in contact with the floor.

"Where in the world did you get those?" Madison asked her when they had a chance to chat alone, the only time she would be familiar with Deanna.

Deanna looked down at the high-tops in surprise, forgetting what she had been wearing. "Oh, these old things?" she said turning her feet sideways and back to front. "I had them specially made. Why should kids get all the fun?"

"Maybe you should have them made and market them," Madison teased. She wouldn't mind such shoes herself, but knew she wouldn't be able to get away with it. Other doctors, much less nurses and staff, had tried and been admonished for copying this doctor. Deanna was a bad influence.

"I have," Deanna said with a smirk and moved off to help another patient in the emergency room.

Later, looking for Deanna to update her on a case they had shared, Madison found her sewing up a little old lady, something any intern could have done, but Deanna was doing it herself.

"Mrs. Gabriola," she rolled her Rs causing the delighted lady to laugh, "I'd prescribe laughter because it is the best medicine." The patient and doctor shared a conspiratorial laugh together.

Madison couldn't help but smile. Deanna was terrific with everyone it seemed. Her mastery of several languages had helped time and again with patients that came in from all over. Her general surgery skills allowed her to take on a variety of cases that kept her interested, and her specialty of tropical diseases made her skillset unique.

After an unusually bad day, Madison came upon Deanna looking at babies in the maternity ward.

"Are you lost, Doctor Cooper?" Madison asked with a tinge of bitterness. "Oh wait, that's Doctor Kearney now isn't it?"

Deanna ignored Maddie's sarcasm as she answered, "You know, I've delivered dozens of babies over my career. The miracle of life still amazes me. Babies struggle and survive in the most…unlikely of places."

She couldn't believe what she was hearing. Was this the same woman who had vehemently stated she didn't want children…*ever*? "Maybe you should have had one of your own," she jibed.

Doctor Kearney turned to look at her with a strange look. "Maybe I did," she said quietly as she turned and walked away, leaving Madison gaping after her.

Deanna was talking about a case and the intern she was talking to referenced a popular TV show. "You got that off of GSP," she stated, disbelieving.

"GSP?"

"General Surgical Procedures."

"What is General Surgical Procedures?" Deanna asked, curious.

"It's a TV show…" she began.

Deanna shrugged, blowing it off. "I don't watch TV much…."

Several people who knew Deanna's propensity for stories had found them all to be true. They believed her, and yet the intern wanted to argue that Deanna couldn't possibly know this information herself.

"Doctor Campa, if you spent more time reading up on procedures and less time watching the boob tube, you would know that this is true. It is not off some drama on that idiot box," Deanna finally finished irritably.

Later, Madison ran into her once again. "Bad day?" she asked seeing Deanna's face.

"This place is too structured," she said, annoyed. "How can anyone get anything done if you have to fill out insurance papers or get an opinion from an idiot or, or, or…" she ran her fingers through her hair. She had cut it in a style that allowed her to have it stand on end in an attractive feathered look. It was cut above her ears, showing off the double piercings in both lobes and today, instead of the stud at the top of ear, she was wearing an ear cuff with a chain down to one of the piercings. She looked hip, stylish, and an antithesis of the other doctors in the hospital.

"Are they pressuring you to get out?" Madison wondered.

Deanna look at her. "No, I am."

Madison looked worried. She had only just begun to get to know her again and if she left, maybe to go back to Boston to her family's holdings, there was no way they could remain friends. They would both be too busy.

Later Madison texted her, a common form of communication between them with their busy schedules.

'How was the rest of your day?'

'You wouldn't believe the day I had.'

'What hap?'

'I devoured a baby.'

'Damn phone...delivered.'

'Good, because otherwise...gross.' She waited a moment and then sent, *'Boy or Girl?'*

'Gorilla.'

'That was either hysterically funny or extremely racist.'

The phone rang then and Madison picked it up, "Hello?"

"They call these *smart* phones?"

Madison couldn't help but snort-laugh through her nose. "It's technology," she tried to console her.

"I can't believe that people put up with these things. I wanted to throw it!"

"Uh oh, sounds like phone rage!"

"Phone rage? Is that a *real* thing?"

"You're the doctor, you tell me?" Madison could almost hear Deanna shaking her head.

"Why does anyone use these things? It doesn't matter whether I type it or speak it, it gets it wrong!"

"Convenience?"

"Embarrassing!"

"You know, there is a way to turn off some of those features."

"You better show me the next time I see you," she sighed angrily.

"How did you cope when you were traveling?" she asked, amused.

"I waited until I got to a phone, none of these 'conveniences.'"

Madison chuckled wondering how such a brilliant doctor could be so technologically inept.

"How is it possible that a general surgeon can be off every weekend?" Beth overheard and duly reported, to spread the gossip among the nursing staff.

"Well, you know *who* she is."

"That doesn't excuse it. It's not fair and she hasn't been here long enough that she should have such privileges. I heard that she wanted to breed maggots in one of the laboratories to debride wounds."

"I heard she did that on a patient already."

"Yeah, but we don't have the facilities. It's called debridement therapy and I guess someone was thinking what would happen if they evolved from maggots to actual flies and got in the duct work or something…."

"You know, you aren't making friends with some of the senior staff," Deanna was warned.

"I didn't come here to make friends. You asked me here when I expressed an interest to share my knowledge elsewhere. It's not my fault I'm ruffling feathers."

"Can't you at least try to get along?"

"If you haven't noticed, they aren't really trying either."

"Look, I agree with you about that painkiller tolerance case," the doctor argued with her.

"Did you hear about that already?" she laughed.

The patient had come in and been labeled drug-seeking. Deanna had disagreed. The patient had merely built up an immunity to the drugs. Since being labeled drug-seeking, they had been unable to handle the pain from their existing condition and this led to more hospitalization. Doctors had begun to refer him to substance abuse programs. Then he met Deanna, who not only listened *to* him, but worked *with* him. She explained to him that it wasn't his fault. "You've built up a tolerance for these," she indicated the prescriptions he had on file for pain. "As your body adjusts to them, you need more and more to get the desired effect. If you've been on them for years, you need five or ten times the amount you once did and that could kill you. Your liver, for one, would have trouble processing such copious amounts."

She went on, "Now, if you were addicted to them, you would be irrational about the need for these medications. You've been completely honest, something an addict would not be, to get out of pain. From what you told me, you never take it unless you have no choice and you aren't justifying the dosage because," she lifted her hands to make quotation marks in the air, "you had a 'hard day.' Instead, you take it because the pain has simply become intolerable."

"Let's wean you off all these," she indicated the many medications different doctors had prescribed in order to silence the patient's efforts to find a cure for his pain. "You will always be in pain. In the next couple of weeks, it's going to be bad as your body adjusts to not having these, but I'm going to give you this," she indicated the script she was writing. "I want you to take this, and this *only,* for the two weeks. Come see me after that and we will give you something that you can handle instead of this endless cycle."

He was so grateful for her insight and attempts to help alleviate the chronic pain he had been in since he hurt his back, that he would do anything she told him. The script was for a placebo, but he didn't need to know that. He needed to be free of the addictive elements of all the other prescriptions.

"Now, you can take an over the counter pain pill like acetaminophen or ibuprofen, but nothing else." She indicated all the other prescriptions, "Turn all these in and we'll dispose of them," she advised. Before she handed him the script, she held it back as he reached for it. "Promise?"

He would have agreed to anything, and she held the script until he brought in all the unused medication so they could dispose of them properly. He had offered to flush them down the toilet, but Deanna had pointed out that some of those pills would just float down and might end up in the ecosystem. They couldn't allow that.

"He was in pain and the doctors were just medicating him to shut him up," Deanna explained. She was answerable for her actions to the hospital after all. She just didn't have a high opinion of those who thought themselves better than her. Now, if they treated her as an equal, she never really had a conflict with them.

"Yes, but you are ruffling feathers," she was advised.

"Maybe the feathers need ruffling," she answered and went on with her work. No one could fault her there. She worked harder than most attending doctors—except weekends—she insisted on having those off, except for an occasional surgery if she was needed.

Deanna was enjoying seeing Madison. It was easy to be friends once again. They couldn't do it a lot as they both had home lives and frequently their work lives were insane. She didn't talk about her home life, but as she was adept at turning the conversations to Madison and her children, the redhead didn't notice at first.

Madison was very involved with her children's lives, as much as she possibly could be with her work schedule. Scott wasn't making it any easier and she wondered about going for full custody. He would be furious if she attempted that, but California was a no-fault state and the divorce itself had gone through easily. So far they agreed that the custody should be fifty-fifty, but they would live with Madison full-time with occasional overnighters at Scott's...especially now that he had a dog for them to take care of. Madison had been right. He regretted getting the beast that chewed up some of his nicest leather shoes.

"Get him a chew toy," she advised.

"Maybe you should take him?" he tried to weasel out of his responsibility. He regretted trying to show her up and then felt she had somehow manipulated him into getting the dog. He really wasn't suited to taking care of the dog, much less the growing children.

"Maybe you shouldn't have taken him in the first place," Madison pointed out. She would not be guilt-tripped into taking the dog. She would have loved having him, but she simply didn't have the time.

"He's not going to give up with that one, is he?" Deanna consoled when she heard the story.

"No," she shook her head. "He took the dog to show me up and is now regretting it. Let him wallow," she said bitterly.

"Was being married to him so bad then?"

"Not really. It was more like having another child that I had to take care of, and I didn't want that."

"What about the sex?" she teased, but she really did want to know.

"We aren't going there, okay?" she said mock-threatening. She knew Deanna was teasing, but then she wondered, was she really? They saw each other frequently now in the hospital, but was it by design or accidental? Deanna had been able to hide those first few weeks when she came on...no one ever did find out who sent Madison those exotic flowers, which she still had growing in her windows at home. They worked well together when they were put on the same surgery. Deanna was still as confident and efficient as ever. Madison could see why other doctors with more experience resented this brilliant woman. She was opinionated, knew her facts, and read voraciously to learn more. When they weren't schmoozing her, on her free time at the hospital she could frequently be found reading up on procedures and cases, researching against future cases. She'd been all over and seen and learned things they could only hope to achieve.

"That patient woke up during surgery," she continued on, complaining about the hospital and an incident the previous day. "It's called 'accidental awareness during general anesthesia.' When I became aware of it, I made the anesthesiologist aware of it. Good thing I was observing and not operating! That patient will probably end up with post-traumatic stress disorder," she said angrily, knowing she was right.

"Well, at least you caught it before too much damage occurred." she'd heard about the uproar that had happened in the surgery.

"Yeah, I probably could have been more diplomatic about it," she said in regret. Once the patient had been truly out, she'd let the incompetents know of her displeasure. She'd insisted on replacing the anesthesiologist mid-surgery and insulted not only the one she'd had, but the chief of surgery. "It just pisses me off when I'm trying to help and they doubt every friggin' word I tell them."

"I can see you won't stay beyond the six months you agreed to," Madison tried to fish for information. Deanna had told no one of her plans and Madison would miss her friendship. At least, that was what she was telling herself.

"You never know," Deanna said without making a commitment. She had more than one person wanting to know if she would stay on. She knew she was a troublemaker in an environment such as this, but she had brought in a lot of notable cases. Word of mouth meant the hospital got referrals and they liked that.

"I think you picked up a tape worm," Deanna told the woman.

"I did?" she sneered in disgust at the very thought.

"No, I meant your daughter," she shook her head at the obtuse woman.

"How is that possible?"

"Handling food that has been tainted…" she began and then named other ways the girl could have been losing the weight she had lost. She was rail thin, something she was thrilled about; however, she was not getting the nutrients she should have and was ill.

"But she looks so healthy…" the mother began, objecting.

"Is she really? She has lost a tremendous amount of weight very quickly. You say she doesn't exercise, so it has to be diet or something else. Does she take pills? You said no. Does she throw up her food? You said no. Let's test and…" she left off as the girl, listening, protested.

"Mom, I'm fine…let's go," she whined.

"We are going to get to the bottom of this, Tessa, if this is the last thing we do!" her mother repeated her earlier edict once again.

"And that's another thing we need…a stool sample," Deanna reminded her.

"I have one right here. You asked last time," she pointed out, pulling the small container from her enormous purse.

Deanna was amused, hoping that the container had been screwed tightly shut. She didn't need to run any more tests. The telltale signs of tape worms were in the stool sample. Some of it was still moving. As Deanna pointed this out to the young girl's mother who was grossed out by the whole thing, she heard the mother begin to berate her daughter.

"How in the world could you not notice those…those…things coming out of you?" she began with a huff.

"But, Mom, I was only supposed to…" she protested, trying to clam up about her knowledge of her 'mystery illness.' The one reason they had sought Deanna out was because of her specialty.

"Tessa…" Deanna began before her mother could. She turned the young girl on the chair so she was facing Deanna and couldn't see her mother even in her peripheral vision. She felt a one-on-one with the girl would be better than having mommy's approval, or in this case, disapproval. "Did you take something to get in this state?"

Tessa debated owning up to what she had done. After a long time, almost feeling her mother's dragon breath on her neck, she began. She didn't see the warning look Deanna had given the mother to keep her quiet, not an easy thing to accomplish. "Yes, I took a pill," she admitted.

"When?" she asked.

"Three months ago, when I went to a clinic in Mexico."

Deanna nodded. It confirmed what she was now thinking. "Weren't you supposed to take another pill a month or so after to kill it?" she asked, knowing there were 'weight loss' clinics in Mexico that gave out larvae that grew into tape worms.

"Yeah, I forgot," she admitted.

Deanna wanted to shake the privileged teen. She had everything—money, looks—and all she wanted was to be thin, just like the other girls. This was extreme and she hoped that the girl would be closely supervised in the future. "You know these things can kill you, right?" she asked kindly.

"Don't they just die…?" the teen asked naively.

Deanna shook her head. "Nope, they can grow to three feet in length." She let that sink in to the teen's young mind as she realized how long that really would be in her body. "If they break off, get into your brain, you'll be gorked," she said in the slang that the teen would understand.

"Really?" the teen asked in fear, her eyes widening to perfect round orbs.

Deanna nodded. "Yep, and once you're gorked, you know there's no coming back."

"Can you get this thing out of me?" she asked fearfully, finally realizing how gross it was.

Deanna couldn't let her off that easy. "You realize I have no idea how big it is?" she hedged, lying slightly. She could know with the right x-ray. The contrast would show how big the worm really was. "You put a worm in your healthy, young body. This could affect you for the rest of your life," she explained, putting the fear of God in the young idiot. At this age they never realized how fragile life was. Deanna had seen involuntarily cases of worms in a healthy body in third-world countries. She was incensed that this healthy young thing had done it deliberately…to lose weight.

"You can't get it out?" she asked and her tone was genuinely scared now.

Deanna realized she wouldn't listen to any other jibes she might see fit to give her. She also knew, with the mother listening, she might have gotten more than she intended. "I'll see what I have that can help you, but this is going to be a slow process." She didn't tell her that she would be given a killing agent and that the other pill the teen 'forgot' to take would have taken care of the organism. It would take days, possibly weeks, for all the pieces of the worm to leave her body through her fecal matter. She had a nurse fetch some praziquantel, also known as Biltricide, which would kill the tape worm inside her patient.

"You are going to have to wash your hands thoroughly after every time you go to the bathroom. If you get this on your hands, you can re-infect yourself or others," Deanna explained. Although it was rare, it could happen. "I want to see you in a month with another stool sample." Deanna gave the mother another container to put the fecal matter in. She watched as the teen drank the praziquantel down. It was not a good taste, at least not by her facial expression. "These things can get in your muscles and to the brain," she explained again to put the fear back in the teen. She was a bit too cocky, but her mom was listening and would probably give her hell. Deanna pulled the mom aside before the two of them left. "I would mention this to the other parents of anyone who went on that trip. Girls travel in packs, and if one of them is infected, you can bet there are others."

"I don't want anyone to know about this," she hissed, horrified at what *her* friends would say.

"Well, then you might be responsible for the disease continuing or maybe they will convince Tessa that this was a one-time deal and she should do it again. You need to stop it now," she advised. She was grateful her parents had kept her busy at this stage in her life in school and that she didn't have the social pressures her age group would have to lose weight, but then she had been a doctor at this teen's age. She knew she was a bit of a different story.

Deanna knew that the woman may or may not talk to the other parents, but she hoped she would. She did end up treating two other girls with praziquantel in the following week, but patient confidentiality kept her from asking if they knew Tessa. She was able to confirm that they too had been to Mexico. She rolled her eyes at the privileged teens and their stupidity.

"I think, Robby, you have Nosophobia," Deanna explained kindly.

"I'm not a hypochondriac?" he asked, relieved at her diagnosis.

Deanna nearly smiled as she explained. "To a degree, I'd say you are; however, if I were you, I'd get a new therapist as the one you've been seeing isn't getting to the root cause of your problem."

"But this Noso…" he began, grasping at the disease.

"It's a phobia, Robby. You have an abnormal fear of disease and that makes you a bit of a hypochondriac, a germaphobe even," she explained. "See a therapist for it, and if they can't help you, see another," she advised.

Sometimes, people like this just wanted a word for what they were feeling. Robby didn't care that he had a phobia, now he had a word for what it was. That was a huge relief and he promised to get help for it.

Deanna wasn't so sure he would, but it was a nice thought. She couldn't help them all, she could only try her best.

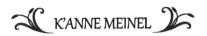

CHAPTER TWENTY-TWO

Madison laughed as Deanna shared her many stories. Her flair for the dramatic made them interesting and the common medical bond the two of them shared made it even better. When Madison related her take on some of the stories, after all they shared some of the same patients now and then, it wasn't quite as vibrant or exciting. They even shared surgery from time to time, she recalled the first time at this modern hospital.

Madison looked across the surgery table, amazed at the transformation. Deanna had removed her nose stud, her two sets of earrings, the stud in the upper part of her ear, as well as her necklace and of course, her family crest. She was professional and efficient, but she looked naked without all the jewelry. She wasn't quite as...overwhelming...or as intimidating. Even her high-tops had been replaced with the surgical stockings that everyone wore over their shoes, only Deanna was just wearing stockings. She'd be barefoot if she could, but she needed the warmth of her socks—these were still flamboyant and very gay, rainbow colors and vibrantly loud.

Madison didn't realize how often she had been seeing Deanna until someone mentioned something about seeing them out. She froze at the question and then dismissed it. They were friends after all, weren't they?

Deanna wouldn't classify it as that. She had tried to steer them down a path that might revive their previous relationship, but she wondered if they could. It had been a different time and place, and definitely so very long ago. She wasn't exactly sure how she felt about this grown-up Madison. Her memories were all about the youthful adult named Maddie. This responsible Madison with children conflicted with what she felt about the younger Maddie. She couldn't read Madison either. She wasn't sure Madison wanted anything more than friendship. She was willing to wait to find out, but her time at the hospital was coming to an end. She knew it and the hospital knew it....

As Madison listened to one of Deanna's many stories about patients and her experiences, she couldn't help but enjoy them. Deanna told them so well. She knew some of them, but never told Deanna when she repeated one because they were told slightly different each and every time. She sometimes wondered if Deanna were courting her. She appreciated getting out, but she worried that the doctor wanted more than she was willing to give. Did she want to go back to that kind of a relationship? She knew she admired Deanna—she had loved her—but could she be in a relationship openly with this woman? She had to wonder if she was just bouncing back from her divorce from Scott. Tom hadn't been a good transition date even if initially he had intrigued her. So going out with Deanna under the guise of friendship wasn't the 'next' which she had heard was always a bad date...Tom certainly qualified as that.

Madison had heard that Tom had hit on Deanna. She'd refused him of course, but then Deanna refused all dates, or so the gossip said. For some reason this pleased Madison and as she analyzed it she wondered if she took some perverse pleasure that the busy doctor only took time out for her. She'd made no play for her, hadn't even brought up that Madison had left her so long ago. That bothered her to a degree. She remembered leaving Mamadu quite clearly. The fear in the air about the camp being overrun was burned in her brain. Also her fear over leaving Deanna and never seeing her again. Ironically, she was driving Deanna's donated Rover in their attempt to escape. She remembered clearly that she had been crying. She knew that she had to go. She wanted to say something to her before she left, but she couldn't. She hadn't wanted a relationship with a woman, she wanted children, and she had wanted...Deanna. But the doctor had never told her that she loved her. Madison had convinced herself that Deanna did not love her and this had helped her to make the decision to not only leave, but to break up with her. It had made her last weeks in Mamadu horrible. Even arriving in Lamish after a harrowing trip back, avoiding lines of soldiers, skirmishes, and an actual war that was going on around them, she'd not stopped the tears from trickling down and fogging her vision. Those with her thought she was crying out of fear for what might happen to them, what could happen. Their comfort had been unwelcome and unnecessary, but she accepted it rather than explain she was crying for what she had left behind…the first person she had ever loved wholeheartedly.

Deanna had memories of that night too, that she didn't share; she never talked about it with anyone. They'd been so short-staffed and the casualties kept coming in. Seeing Maddie leave in her Rover. She couldn't convince Maddie to love her, to stay with her, to *not* leave her…she couldn't even get her to talk to her anymore…she had to let her go. She had work she could throw herself into. It had been never-ending and they needed her and her skills.

"You're friends with Doctor Kearney, aren't you? Can't you ask her?"

"What?" Madison looked up from the paperwork she was trying to process so she could move on to actual work, checking on patients. She hadn't been paying attention to the gossip around her, she had work to do.

"Doctor Kearney. You see her a lot, can't you ask her?"

Madison was confused and it showed clearly on her face. "Ask her what?"

"If she's staying?" Bonnie asked exasperatedly. She knew Madison didn't like to gossip, but she had hoped because of the friendship that the two shared, she would know.

"Staying where?" she was very confused and coming into the conversation midway wasn't helping.

"Here, at the hospital. They are saying she's been asked to stay, but that she isn't."

Madison quickly thought, *'Was the six months up?'* Deanna hadn't said if she was staying or not and Madison wouldn't tell even if she had. When asked what they spoke about, she usually mentioned that they had worked together in Africa and were friends from back then, but she didn't share the same kind of exciting stories that the doctor was known for. People had been surprised to find out that she had worked over there. She shrugged off Bonnie's questions and finished up her work so she could move on, but it didn't stop her mind from wondering.

Madison had watched Deanna. She showed the same care for patients that she had back in Mamadu. She'd heard the gossip already. Here in Los Angeles, it was thought odd how much time Deanna spent with her patients. Normally it was the nurses who did all the work, but Deanna was different. She got to know her patients, listened to them, and actually cared. A standard joke was that for every twenty-four hours of care, only five minutes was actually provided by the doctors, the rest was by the nurses. Deanna wasn't like that. If she had a patient who needed her, needed to express concerns, she was there, answering their questions, talking to them and alleviating their worries. She could be found playing with the children, bringing in balloons—reminiscent of what she did back in Mamadu. Madison wondered at that. For someone who didn't want to procreate, she really was good with children.

There was so much about Deanna that was a conflict of sorts, from stereotypes to just her personality…she was so different from the other doctors, from other women, from others…

"Hey, lady, whatcha doin'?" a voice called.

Madison was nearly in tears. Her minivan was refusing to start and she had no auto service to have it checked. She had been trying to start it for a good fifteen minutes and it was dead. The voice had her looking up, her eyes full of tears. It took a moment for them to clear.

"Hey, are you okay?" Deanna asked, concerned. She was looking in the driver's side of the vehicle, an umbrella keeping the rain off her nice clothes.

Madison realized how nicely Deanna was dressed, something she had noted the many times they had gone out to dinner. She was relieved at the sound of her voice for some reason. "I can't get this bucket of bolts going," she lamented, wondering if it was something serious that she wouldn't be able to afford to get fixed.

"Do you have Triple A?" she asked, concerned, ignoring the tears. If Madison wasn't going to mention them she wouldn't embarrass her by asking about them. She could hear the frustration in the redhead's voice.

Madison shook her head. She wanted to put her forehead back on the wheel and in an attempt to do something she turned the key again…and again, nothing.

"Well, there is nothing you can do in this," Deanna pointed out, indicating the rain. "Why don't I give you a ride and maybe tomorrow the weather will be nice and I can give you a jump-start?"

Madison looked up and realized that was sensible. She knew she was tired after a sixteen-hour shift. Her frustration over the car not starting really had nothing to do with her tears over her fatigue. The combination was sending her over the edge. She pulled the keys from the ignition and nodded, reaching for her purse and looking around the minivan for anything she shouldn't leave in it. She rolled up the window that had been ajar to let in air and clear the fog from the windows. She opened the door.

"Are your lights on?" Deanna gently asked.

"What? Why?" she was confused.

"Because if you left them on this morning because of the rain, I'll bet your battery is dead from that."

The sense of that comment had her checking and sure enough, the button was pulled out fully. She ruefully pushed it back in and wondered if the battery would regain enough of a charge to turn over tomorrow. She closed and locked the door behind her. Deanna had raised the umbrella high enough to cover them both.

"Come on, let's get out of this," she said and led Madison to her Rover in the next lot.

"Are you sure? I could get a cab…" she began, but she wasn't so sure she could afford one. A bus this late wasn't really a good idea in L.A.

"Come on…" Deanna encouraged her, taking her arm.

"But I'll still need my car…."

"I'll pick you up tomorrow and we can jump-start it, okay?" she promised.

Madison let herself be led to the much newer Rover and it wasn't until she was tucked inside that she realized how chivalrous Deanna had been. It was odd and she mentally began to realize how many times over the past months with their weekly dinners how often Deanna had held doors, even chairs for her, and she had accepted it without thinking.

Deanna had turned on her vehicle with a remote starter so the heater was already going full blast and their breath, which would normally have fogged up the cold windows, soon dissipated. The efficient heating system was already warming their legs and she turned it down slightly as the blower was too loud for chatting. "You'll have to give me directions," Deanna commented, looking over at Madison curiously, wondering what was on her mind.

Madison was thinking too hard. Was Deanna courting her? She woke up at Deanna's statement in order to direct her. She sat admiring the expensive Rover, knowing she would never be able to afford such a luxurious vehicle with her nurse's pay.

"You're very quiet," Deanna commented, wondering if she should turn on the radio to cover the silence. The windshield wipers were loud and the rain slapping at them was the only noise. "Are you okay? Rough day?" she asked, concerned. They'd never had any trouble keeping a conversation going.

Madison, in an attempt to keep her thoughts from being spoken out loud, grasped at that. "Yeah, rough day," she sighed, managing to sound tired even though she really wasn't. "You know how it is," she added.

"Yeah," Deanna sighed loudly in sympathy. "I do know." She had so much more to deal with, but she never belittled the nurses' contributions. She was very thoughtful of the staff who helped keep her patients clean and healthy. They were the ones who dealt with the vomit and bodily functions. The interns were supposed to contribute, but many times they were well aware of the fact that they would be doctors, and learned their arrogance early. Deanna never had. She could frequently be seen helping the nurses, or rather they willingly helped her, cleaning and administering to her patients. Those interns who worked with her were expected to do just as much and they appreciated her differently from the other doctors. Deanna also had to administer her family's company and that led to long nights. She insisted on having time to herself, which had led to some resentment when she had weekends off, but that was her own time and her own business. She didn't talk about that and many had wondered.

They chatted easily and were soon at Madison's little house. Deanna looked curiously at the WW2 bungalow, but didn't ask about it. "I'll pick you up tomorrow. Is 7:30 okay?" She glanced at the clock. It had taken them twenty minutes to drive from the hospital. That would get them to the hospital in the morning with time to spare. She wasn't due until ten, but that was okay. It would give her time to go over paperwork and she wanted to accommodate Madison.

"I don't have to be in until nine tomorrow. What time are you due?" she asked, concerned that she was imposing on her friend. Her hand was on the door handle, ready to make her escape.

"Oh, that's even better. I'll pick you up at 8:30?" she answered without answering fully.

"That's good, and thank you for the ride," she said politely as she got out into the rain.

"Here," Deanna insisted, handing her the umbrella.

"What about you?" she reluctantly took it and opened it above her to keep the downpour off.

"I have a garage," she admitted.

"Oh, then thank you again," she smiled, unknowingly causing Deanna to catch her breath. She wondered briefly where Deanna lived, she had never asked.

"See you in the morning," she dismissed and was rewarded with that same smile. The car door was shut, but Deanna rolled down the window using the button on her side as she watched Madison safely make her way to the front door. It wasn't until she saw her fumble with her keys, unlock the door, and go inside that she drove away.

Madison was very conscious of Deanna watching her go to the door. Their house wasn't in an unsafe neighborhood, but it had been a long time since anyone waited for her. It took forever to find the right key—she hadn't left the porch light on for herself and the kids wouldn't have thought of doing that for her—before she could insert it in the lock. She would have looked back, but didn't think she could see Deanna with the dark and the rain, so she went inside. She heard through the closed door as the vehicle drove off. Now she could allow her thoughts of Deanna to roam, but the children captured her attention so she'd have to wait until later.

"What's this?" she asked as the dog accompanied the children in greeting her. She liked the dog, but she didn't know why it was at her home.

"Dad had to go out of town and he said you wouldn't mind," Conor told her as he bent down to try and hold the exuberant pup who was greeting the head of the household.

"Oh he did, did he?" she answered, annoyed. He could have at least asked her.

"Yeah, we get him the whole week. Isn't it great?" Chloe asked as she too bent down to try and control the pup.

"Did he bring food or any of his toys?" she asked as she looked in at the mess in the living room…newspapers and the kids' toys were everywhere. She was certain the kids hadn't done that by themselves. She sighed, genuinely tired from a long day's work, and now to come home to this.

"No, but we can go buy some," Conor said confidently.

"No, we can't. The car wouldn't start and I have no way to get any," she told him, annoyed. She pushed the undisciplined pup down repeatedly. This really was becoming a bad situation.

"But what will he eat?" Chloe asked, worriedly.

"Call your father and tell him to bring something over," she told the child as she went to take off her coat. The pup started to chew on the umbrella she had turned upside down. "Don't let him do that, it's not mine!" she ordered the children, pulling it from the dog who thought she wanted to play a game and jumped at it, tearing the nylon. "Dammit!" she exclaimed, knowing she would have to replace it before she could return it to Deanna. "Keep that pup down!" she ordered Conor as she tried to hang the ripped umbrella out of the way of the jumping dog. She hung her coat over the wet and dripping umbrella, hoping out of sight would be out of mind for the dog. "You, call your father right now!" she pointed at Chloe. They could see she was becoming angry and quickly scurried to do her bidding.

Madison didn't need an untrained puppy in her organized, little house. She found two spots where he had left a present. She grabbed paper towels and cleaned it up.

"Daddy's on the phone," Chloe told her importantly and handed her the cordless.

"Scott? How dare you leave this pup of yours over here without asking me?" she started in on him.

"The kids said it would be fine and it saves me from having to dump it at a pet hotel. Do you know how expensive those things are?"

"You left it with no food and you didn't ask me. How would the kids know whether it could stay here or not? My house isn't puppy proof and he isn't even house-trained!" she was taking her fatigue out on him and didn't care. The kids were listening, wide-eyed and fearful.

"C'mon, just go pick up a bag of dog food, I have to get going…" he began whiningly.

"I have no car, mine died in the hospital parking lot," she informed him frostily. This was the same kind of shit she put up with in their marriage and she wasn't going to put up with it now. This lack of responsibility was so child-like and so typical of him. "You should have asked ME!"

"Well, can't you order it or something…?" he began, sensing her anger, but knowing she couldn't do much on the phone.

"You think I'm made of money or something?"

"I'll pay you back," he promised, and at that moment, he meant it.

"No you won't! You never do!"

"Look, I'm kind of in a hurry here…" he began, but she cut him off.

"I just got home from work. I don't have any food for this dog. You didn't ask ME if you could leave it! You better do something and NOW!" she ordered angrily.

"Or what? You gonna take it to the pound?" he countered just as angrily. She was always ordering him about. That was why he had divorced her…at least that was what he thought now.

"You really want to push that? You want me to tell our children that you want me to take the dog to the pound?" she said it aloud so that they would hear it. She knew they were listening and she was right on the button, they set up a squalling immediately.

"You can't do that, Mommy!" began Chloe, whining.

"Don't make him do that, Mommy!" Conor chimed in.

Scott could hear the whines and was just glad he wasn't there to put up with it. The children always got their way with him and he couldn't stand the noise. "Alright, alright, I'll get some food over there," he promised, wondering how it was going to interfere with his fishing trip plans. He knew asking the children to take the dog was the coward's way out, but he wanted to go. He didn't want to have to ask his ex-wife for anything and there was the real possibility that she would say no.

She waved the kids to silence with her hand. "You better have something here within an hour, Scott or I'll make the plans you just suggested," she threatened, knowing he would take the fall for the idea and not her. She also knew she would do no such thing. It wasn't the dog's fault he was a bad dog owner.

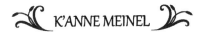

"Alright, I'll take care of it," he told her angrily and hung up on her. *"The bitch,"* he thought angrily as he looked up and made another phone call. *"Always ordering me about. Good thing I got rid of her."*

Madison finally got the dog contained in the kitchen on the linoleum. She used the children's old baby gate to keep him from the rest of the house. She had just had been thinking of getting rid of all the baby things last week and this would have gone too. Timing was everything. She cleaned up the living room, finding another accident of the dog's. She was about to make dinner for the children when the doorbell rang.

Scott had arranged to have groceries delivered and they gave her a fifty-pound bag of dog food. Why she needed such a large one, she had no idea as she signed for it. She wondered how long he intended for the dog to stay at her house? She knew it had probably cost him more than he had planned to arrange this, they probably had a minimum on the delivery, and she didn't feel one bit sorry for him.

The dog tore into the small bowl of food like it hadn't eaten in days. She was hard put to know where to put the rest of the big bag so the pup wouldn't be able to get into it. For now, she put it up on the counter, using her muscles to lift the heavy bag.

Next, she had to feed the kids and herself, but she hadn't had a chance to change her clothes from work. She sighed, wishing she had help tonight when she was so tired.

Deanna had headed across town in time to hit rush hour traffic. It took her almost an hour to get home, but she didn't mind giving Madison a lift, she enjoyed chatting with her and spending time. She was a little frustrated, unsure how to take their friendship to the next level and scared of suggesting more. She didn't want to lose the friendship she had so carefully cultivated with Madison. After all these years, how could she tell her she wanted what they had had back in Mamadu?

She hadn't intended to seek her out, in fact she had been genuinely surprised to find her at the hospital. She hadn't expected her there. In fact, she didn't know where to find Maddie MacGregor, even though she had looked when she got back to the States. Realizing that Maddie had moved on hadn't stopped her from thinking about her from time to time. Life and living it, realizing her responsibilities, Deanna had a lot of time that she couldn't or wouldn't use to think about what could have been. She realized a lot of the mistakes she had made back in Africa. She had few regrets, but she had wished many times over the years that she had simply told Maddie that she loved her. This Madison that she had come to know again was a challenge. She didn't seem to be any more willing to be Deanna's partner than Maddie had been ten years ago.

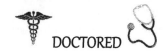

Deanna knew she was going to have to make some decisions and make them soon. She couldn't stay at the hospital, there was too much conflict there. She knew she could go back to Boston and run the family's pharmaceutical company, but she didn't want to. It was the reason she had set it up with the managers she had in place—competent people who could take care of it with minimal supervision. She knew the people she had to answer to, the investors, would prefer to have a board of directors and bloated paychecks in place, but as she owned the majority shares and it was her name on the door, she still pulled all the strings and they answered to her. As long as it was profitable, she felt they had no reason to complain. They just wanted it to be like every other company out there and she refused. She saw no reason to have people in jobs that weren't necessary. It worked fine the way her father and sister had run it, the only difference was that Deanna didn't sit and run it herself anymore…she had a managerial staff for that. She preferred to be the doctor she had trained to be.

That was why it wasn't working out at the hospital, they wanted to capitalize on the fact that the owner of Kearney Pharmaceuticals was working there. The notoriety alone would bring in world-class doctors to their facility. Deanna had thought to go back to being Doctor Cooper many times, but that name had died painfully ten years ago and she wouldn't be revived. It had been a necessary name at the time, but Deanna really was proud of the name Kearney and always had been. She wouldn't allow the hospital to use her anymore. The conflicts that had arisen already showed her that she needed to move on. Her only hesitation was Madison, now that she had found her.

To Deanna, Madison was 'the one that got away.' To find her after all this time was kismet, fate, she didn't know what, but she believed enough in the mystic side of medicine that she knew they had to have met again for some reason. She knew what she wanted, but she was still so unsure about her Maddie…

She drove her Rover up the driveway, the large steel gates closing automatically behind the vehicle. Turning around in the cobblestone drive, she backed into the garage easily. From the garage she effortlessly walked into the house, not worrying about the rain at all as she had mentioned to Madison. She checked the mail that the maid had left on the counter and most went into the recycling bin. The few bills she would take to the roll top desk in her office where a larger packet that came daily was waiting for her.

First, she put down her keys by the garage door along with taking off her jacket. She pushed a button on the microwave after seeing the note that read 'push me' left there by her housekeeper. She grinned at the simple message, so warm and cozy, and she laughed, grateful she had people to take care of her and to make her life easier. The large house was quiet, but the maid and the housekeeper had the night off. Deanna preferred the silence. Only on the weekend was the house in an uproar, and the maid and housekeeper spent the week cleaning up after her weekends. Right now, she was looking forward to the quiet evening of eating, going over Kearney Pharmaceuticals' paperwork, the computer, and perhaps catching something on the television. A nice, quiet, evening. She had thought of inviting Madison out, but without notice, that was a no-no because of her children. She wondered once again what Madison's husband had been like and then dismissed it. She wasn't with him anymore.

Slowly she ate the pot roast, carrots and potatoes…one of her favorite meals and Aura, her housekeeper, knew it. She had probably made the meal months ago, then portioned it out and defrosted it today for Deanna's evening meal. It was still fresh and delicious. It was also convenient because she could read her paperwork or the newspaper at the dinner table without any interruptions. She enjoyed it enormously. It was, however, lonely.

Tonight she was restless. She knew she was coming to the end of her time at the hospital. She already knew where she was going next. She'd taken weekend drives further up north on the coast to decide and find her next step. She'd even bought some real estate in anticipation of the next phase in her life; however, she hadn't discussed any of this with Madison. She'd like the redhead to join her, but they weren't at that point in their relationship and she wondered if Maddie—she kept thinking of her that way—knew she was being courted? She'd made no moves that would be misconstrued, but she'd made sure to see her daily at work, even if only in passing, and eaten out with her at least weekly, work allowing.

She paced through the large house, looking at the rich woodwork, the dust-free shelves that held first edition books she had brought out from the family library in Boston.

"Why don't you move home?" her mother had asked time and time again.

"California feels like home, Mom," she had answered.

"That house hasn't been lived in by anyone in years," she pointed out.

"I'll make it my home."

"You could work anywhere in the world…."

"Yes, but you didn't like it when I was in South America much less Africa."

"The less said about *that* place the better," she spat angrily, remembering when Deanna had been in Africa, she had stayed far too long, *far too long!*

"Okay, okay. I'm not going to argue with you about it."

"I do prefer you in the States," she conceded.

"I kinda like it too."

"But you could do your work in Boston," she pointed out again, an endless and persistent need to have her close.

"California suits me better."

"It's a woman, isn't it?"

Deanna had laughed. Her mother 'got it.' "Yes, Mom, there's a woman."

"Do I get to meet this one?"

"I don't know yet, Mom."

"Well, is she decent?"

"I only date decent ones."

"That woman in South America was totally indecent…" she began and then stopped herself. She knew if she antagonized Deanna again she would pick up and move back to the jungle…she'd never see her again.

"She healed me when I needed it, Mom," she pointed out quietly.

"Nothing but a savage!" she tried to spit out and then stopped herself. She was doing it again and she had promised herself if she got Deanna back she wouldn't do that. She had gotten her only remaining daughter back and whole again, if different. She'd been a mess after Africa and *that* woman; it was all that continent's fault that Deanna had been in the state she had been in when she got back to Boston. She'd only been able to keep her there for a year before she left for the Amazon, and that due to….

"Mom," Deanna said warningly, and that was enough to stop the rigid woman from mouthing off about Africa or the woman she knew had broken her daughter's heart. She didn't know the whole story and that was Deanna's fault. She couldn't share the whole story of everything that had happened there. The love she had found she had shared, but the implication that the woman had left her heartbroken had been blown out of proportion. Deanna had known she was emotionally immature when she had known Maddie back then and now was hoping to make up for it. It had, after all, been ten years. She wasn't the same woman she had been back then.

She thought about starting a fire in the large fireplace in the den. Her Kearney Pharmaceuticals work waited for her, both in the packet that she had read through over dinner, and now on the computer. Her phone went off and she struggled to answer it, the damn numbers and letters too small for her finger to punch correctly and she frequently made mistakes in answering it. Technology wasn't that important to her, she preferred field work. "Hello? Hello?" she finally answered, but she must have hung up on them. They would call back if it was important. Sighing at the way her life had gone, she finished her work without lighting the fire and headed upstairs to the massive bedroom that was her own, intent on a warm, hot bath.

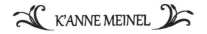

She walked into the Roman bathtub, big enough for two people to practically do laps. Filling it with water nearly to the rim, she felt decadent as she floated in it. It allowed her to fully relax and she let her thoughts wander. They frequently wandered to Madison and her desire for the redhead, something that had never waned. The thoughts turned sensual and her hand crept down her body, still basically girlish, with a small paunch of flesh below her belly button that came with age, and further down to her clit, where she rubbed as she remembered making love to Maddie back all those years ago. It didn't take long before she was able to cum, but it was hollow. Nothing like the feel of having someone else do this to her body, the feel of flesh against flesh, the sensuality of touch. She missed having someone in her life so bad that she had been tempted to date others, but, having found Maddie again, she couldn't imagine anyone else. She had to give it a good try and so far she was failing miserably. After months of eating out regularly, they were not beyond the 'friend' stage and she had no idea how to suggest it. She didn't know if she would lose Maddie if she did. Time was coming to a head though and she knew she couldn't waste any more of it. There was so much Maddie—she corrected herself mentally—Madison didn't know about Deanna and she wanted her to know it all.

She was abruptly brought out of her daydreams by her cat joining her in the tub, exuberantly splashing in the water that it loved so much. She shook her head as she sat up and laughed at its antics. For a cat to love water as much as this one did was unnatural, but he enjoyed it as much as a dog and played in it at every opportunity. She'd had to keep the pool locked against his attempts to get into the house where it was kept. The chlorine wasn't good for his skin and he was only allowed in the large pool when Deanna was in there entertaining. For now, he contented himself with sharing her baths. She'd tried to keep him out, but the scratching at the bottom of the door and the resulting damage held her hostage and it was easier for her to share her tub than to keep him out. He entertained her and she was just thankful she'd had some peace and quiet during dinner, which led her to speculate where he had been in the large house while she was eating and working. She'd have to take a walk around and make sure he hadn't damaged anything while she was at work. She knew her housekeeper and the maid cleaned up after her during the week anyway, but asking them to keep watch over the large cat was a little much. Deanna cleaned the cat pans herself, electric things that only required her to remove the hopper where the debris from this large cat was raked.

That night she went to sleep with his purrs echoing in her ear as she snuggled up to his tawny coat and threw a leg over his long body, imagining how much nicer it would be to sleep with a woman, but wondering if any woman would put up with the large cat. She didn't want just *any* woman. She wanted Madison back and in her bed.

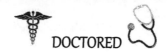

CHAPTER TWENTY-THREE

"Hey, I brought you hot chocolate and an Egg McMuffin. Didn't know if you'd had time for breakfast?" Deanna greeted her.

"Thanks so much for picking me up. Oh, God, that smells heavenly," she answered as she got in the Rover. It was overcast today and looked like more rain, but that's what happened twice a year in southern California. You got rain in November and February, and sometimes it lasted longer in the spring; however, it was cold! Madison got in and wrapped her hands around the hot chocolate. She knew that hot chocolate from Starbucks was very over-priced and something she never indulged in, but she didn't mind that Deanna had bought it for her. It smelled incredible and tasted even better. The Egg McMuffin was a bonus. She hadn't had more than a slice of toast this morning between cleaning up after the exuberant puppy who had pulled the fifty-pound bag of dog food off the counter and all over the kitchen, feeding the kids, and getting them off to school.

"Buckle up," Deanna warned, watching as Madison enjoyed the treats she had brought her. She thought nothing of bringing them either, she just thought of it as 'taking care' of her girlfriend, something she wished she could do more of as she fantasized about what it would be like if they were together permanently.

"Oh, yeah," she murmured, trying to buckle up one-handed as she juggled the hot chocolate and sandwich. Deanna laughed at her and grabbed the buckle she had in one hand and clicked it into place.

"You okay?" she asked, a familiar refrain.

"Wonderful," she said as she sank in the heated leather seat. She looked perky this morning after a night's sleep, but she wouldn't tell Deanna that the puppy had kept her up most of the night with its whining. She'd finally yelled at it in frustration and it had cowered, which made her feel like a real chump for taking her anger out on the defenseless, dimwitted dog. It had quieted and gone to sleep after she threw it a blanket to sleep on over the cold linoleum. She only hoped it would not tear apart her house during the day while she was at work and before the kids got home from school. She hated that they were latch-key kids, but they were old enough to take care of themselves for a few hours between the time that they got home from school and she got home from work.

"Anything going on today at work?" Deanna asked her to make conversation. She cursed herself for starting that inane type of conversation. They spoke mostly of work, rarely about what had happened the last ten years, and never about Africa. That was never discussed or the relationship that they had had there so long ago. Deanna knew more about what had happened to Madison since then and Madison never asked about Deanna. She'd learned to glean what she could from her stories.

They chatted on the twenty-minute ride back to the hospital and Deanna hopped out and tried the van which barely turned over, but was able to start. She was thrilled.

"Rev the engine a few times, maybe drive it around the lot," Deanna advised before she went to park her own vehicle in the doctors' lot.

Madison saw Deanna several times that day and was able to take some time out for teasing her once she got a good look at her.

Madison looked down at Deanna's rainbow laces and commented, "Nice laces. Do they glow in the dark?"

Deanna grinned as she looked down. "Thank you….um, I think they do," she answered, puzzled, trying to remember if they did glow or not. She started to laugh and Madison joined in.

"Hey, you know we go out once a week, and I appreciate it," she quickly added, seeing the look in Deanna's eye. "Why don't you come to my house sometime and I'll cook for you."

"You cook?"

"Of course I cook! I have to eat, don't I?" she began protesting before she realized Deanna *was* teasing.

"I'd love to come over. Just let me know what night so I can make arrangements," she promised, still smiling at having teased the redhead, who was now blushing.

"I'll let you know," she said dryly. She wasn't sure she shouldn't be angry over being teased about her cooking.

They finally set a date and Madison made sure it was for a time that was well after the destructive pup had left her home. She was nervous about the invite. After all, what would the well-disciplined doctor think of her children, her home, her cooking….

It wasn't to be for a while though, as Deanna repeatedly cancelled.

The first time they set a date, Deanna rushed up to her after surgery. "I'm sorry. I won't be able to make dinner tonight. I can't explain right now, but I've got to go."

Madison watched with a frown on her face as the doctor nearly ran off.

The second time they set a date, Madison was in the surgery that ran over and knew that it wasn't going to happen.

"Third time a charm?" Madison asked, to see if Deanna would really come over for dinner that evening.

"I am sorry about the cancellations," Deanna said honestly.

"Well, just means more for me and the kids," she answered dryly.

"Your kids are going to be there?" she tried to tease.

Knowing that Deanna had never wanted kids, Madison wasn't amused at the question. "Of course my children will be there. Where else would they be? Should I send them outside while you and I have dinner?" She sounded a bit prickly.

"Relax, I was just kidding," she tried to placate her.

Realizing she was overreacting, Madison shrugged it off. "Well, dinner is at seven. I gave you the address that first time. Do you still have it?" She'd completely forgotten the time that Deanna had dropped her off when it was raining and picked her up the next morning.

Deanna confirmed she still had the address and watched as the red-headed nurse huffed off. She grimaced as she realized she had pissed her off a bit.

CHAPTER TWENTY-FOUR

Deanna pulled up at the house, feeling pretty stressed out by the dinner. She wasn't sure if it was the actual dinner or meeting Madison's kids that was making her nervous.

She was dressed in a nice silk blouse, a blazer, designer jeans, and high-tops. Casual and elegant in a nice combination. She'd had to change at work, and while it wasn't much different than what she wore at work, she had wanted to look nice, to make a good impression. She nervously fluffed her hair to make it stand on end, a funky look she enjoyed. She twisted her nose ring in the mirror, making sure it was snug against the skin. She checked her appearance, was satisfied with her look, and taking a deep breath, she opened the car door. Grabbing the bouquet of flowers, this time yellow roses with a mix of carnations—something simple, elegant, and nothing to remind her of Africa—she headed to the front door to knock firmly.

"Chloe, would you answer the door?" Madison called from the kitchen where she was putting the last details on the dinner…something she had done a couple of times already for this meal. She couldn't believe that Deanna was here, actually *here*, for dinner and to meet her kids. She was actually worried about it.

"Got it," the little girl answered as she ran to the front door and opened it without asking who it was. She looked at the woman on the doorstep. Her mother had told her that an important doctor was coming to dinner. Instead she saw a woman with blonde, spikey hair, earrings, and a stud in her nose. She was wearing a nice jacket and had on cool high-tops with rainbow colored laces, and she was carrying a bouquet of flowers. "Can I help you?" she asked respectfully.

"Hello, you must be Chloe. I'm Doctor Kearney. Your mother invited me to dinner," she explained to the little girl. She looked to be about eight or nine, maybe a little younger Deanna thought, doing the math in her head.

"You're Doctor Kearney?" the girl asked incredulously. "You're a girl!" she stated unnecessarily.

Deanna laughed at that. She was used to stereotypes in the workplace, but to find one in a little girl was hilarious. "Yes, I am," she agreed with a smile. "Can't girls be doctors?"

"Girls are nurses," the girl stated without hesitation.

"Chloe? Who's at the door?" Madison called from the kitchen as she came around the corner to see what was taking so long. She had concluded it couldn't be Deanna since she wasn't in the house yet. She hadn't expected her daughter to confront her friend. "Deanna? What's going on?" she asked curious, the frown lines on her brow creasing.

"Your daughter informs me that girls can't be doctors, only nurses. I guess I shouldn't mention that there are male nurses then?" She suddenly remembered Shawn from Mamadu and looking at Madison's face, she wondered if she thought the same for some reason.

Madison was embarrassed at her daughter's assumption that Deanna couldn't be a doctor because she was a girl. She too, in that instant, remembered Shawn and Mamadu and looked up into Deanna's twinkling blue eyes. She was relieved that her friend was amused rather than insulted. "Come in, come in out of the cold," she encouraged as she reached the door and pulled Chloe to the side. "Doctors can be men or women," she told the little girl.

"Nuh uh, just like dogs are boys and cats are girls, doctors are boys and nurses are girls," she insisted before running off.

Deanna started laughing and Madison rolled her eyes. "Come on in and take off your coat," she encouraged, reaching out her hand for it, but Deanna handed her the flowers instead. "Why, thank you, these are beautiful," she said.

"How old is she?" Deanna asked as she took off her jacket.

"Chloe is eight," she told her as she hung up the jacket on the wall peg.

"Is this Conor?" she asked as a little boy peeked around his mother.

"Yes, this is Conor. He is seven," Madison confirmed proudly and tried to pull him around to greet their guest. "I guess they aren't used to strangers," she said exasperatedly as he finally escaped back into the living room and out of sight.

"It's okay, naturally they are shy," Deanna tried to cover.

"Come on into the kitchen, dinner is almost ready," Madison told her as she turned and, unable to help herself, buried her nose in the flowers.

"Can I help?"

"No, no, I got this," she told her as she reached above the stove for a vase to put the flowers in. She soon had them arranged and carried the vase to the table to set off her best silverware and place settings. She was very aware of Deanna watching her.

"So, what are we having?" Deanna asked to make conversation.

"I put on a roast and I have potatoes and carrots and…" she left off as Deanna began to giggle. "What's so funny?"

"Have I ever told you my favorite dinner?"

"No, why? Don't tell me you're a vegetarian…" she began and then, remembering all their meals, she knew that couldn't be true.

"No, I'm no vegetarian. My favorite is roast with carrots and potatoes," she grinned.

"Come on, you're just saying that to be polite."

"No, really, you can ask my housekeeper, she'll tell you."

"You have a housekeeper?"

Blushing, Deanna nodded as she answered. "Yeah, she kinda came with the house," she confessed.

"Of course she did," she answered as she easily lifted the roast from the pan and onto the serving platter. She expertly arranged the vegetables around the meat and poured the juices into a pan to make gravy.

Chloe came running in, forgetting for a moment that they had a guest and asked, "Is dinner ready, Mommy?"

"In a few minutes, darling. You and your brother go wash up for dinner, okay?"

Chloe took a good look at the female doctor and her eyes widened when she saw the shoes with rainbows in them. She quickly headed back out of the kitchen.

"Chloe?" Deanna asked, and the little girl stopped for a moment. "Could you show me where I could wash my hands?"

Fearful for a moment, the little girl nodded and then turned. Deanna grinned at Madison and followed the little girl out of the kitchen into a little powder room.

Madison grinned. If her children were too shy to accept Deanna, she'd find a way to communicate. She always did. She'd seen it happen at the hospital, she'd even seen it in Mamadu with the language barrier. Why hadn't she ever wanted children of her own? She was so good with them!

The dinner was delicious and while it was hard to carry on an adult conversation with two children at the table, Madison had been right. The children were charmed by Deanna. It was also difficult to see around the flower arrangement and finally Deanna got up, picked up the vase, and placed it on a side board so she could see into Madison's lovely eyes and carry on some of the conversation directly with her instead of around foliage.

"So you go on a boat?" Conor was saying, fascinated at something Deanna had explained to him.

"No, it's called a Waverunner by Sea-Doo. You sit down on it and it's like your own little boat. You and your mom should come and try it out some weekend," she offered.

Conor looked at Madison and with pleading eyes asked, "Could we do that sometime, Mommy?"

"We'll see, Conor. You finish your dinner for now," she answered and he took that to be a 'yes' because he wanted it to be one. She looked up at Deanna's amused eyes and shook her head laughingly.

"Can I ride too?" Chloe asked, looking earnestly up at the doctor she was now in awe of.

"You have to ride with an adult, but the Waverunners are big enough for two, even three passengers."

"Wow, cool," Chloe responded, no longer shy. "Do you wear those shoes at the hospital?"

Deanna looked down at her shoes, surprised at the question and not remembering which ones she was wearing. She smiled as she answered, "Yes, yes I do."

"They let you?" she confirmed.

"Yes, they do," she nodded, wondering what other stereotypes this kid was hatching and sort of surprised that Madison's children would have them. She had glanced at the pictures around the dining room and saw none of them were of a man and she wondered at Madison's ex-husband. Who he was, what he was like, who the children looked like?

"Finished?" Madison asked as she scooped up the last of her potatoes that were filled with gravy.

"Let me help you get that," Deanna offered.

"No, no, you are our guest. I'll get that," Madison insisted, and copying her mother, Chloe began to help clear away the dishes from the table.

"How come you don't have to help?" Deanna asked Conor who sat there waiting.

"Mommy didn't say I had to help."

"Oh," Deanna answered, wondering if this bit of sexism came from the ex-husband or from Deanna herself. "Maybe you could help, show what a man you are," she mumbled, almost to herself, hoping the little boy would take the hint…he didn't. He just sat there watching as his mother and sister cleared the table. Deanna felt awkward not helping and finally began pulling the dishes to her side of the table to make it easier for Madison and Chloe to clear it.

"Here we go," Madison called bringing out slices of cake for them all.

"Does mine have extra frosting?" Conor asked greedily.

"Mine does," Chloe assured him. "I got a corner!"

"Mommy!" he started to whine at her teasing.

"I helped, I should get more," Chloe defended herself.

"Children, we have a guest!" Madison hissed, turning red.

Deanna pretended she hadn't heard, but she waited until Madison was seated before she started on her own piece. She didn't say anything other than, "This is delicious," before subsiding in silence and observing the family together.

After Chloe's hissed admonishment, it was amazingly quiet at the table as the children dug into their own slices of cake. Finally, Deanna couldn't stand it anymore. "So your mom tells me you have a dog. What kind is it?"

"Daddy got us a dog," Conor said proudly.

"Yeah?" Deanna turned her full attention on the boy. "What kind is it?"

He shrugged and continued demolishing his cake. She wondered how much got in his mouth since a considerable amount was around the edges. She looked up at Madison and smiled.

"It's a flea-bitten varmint," Chloe announced proudly.

"It is?" Deanna pretended amazement and she was amused. Obviously the child was repeating something she had heard an adult say at some point.

The little girl, a duplicate of her mother, nodded solemnly. "His name is Fluffy."

"That's amazing. Did your mother ever tell you about the time that we got a dog to raise a litter of kittens?" she asked the little girl.

Chloe's eyes went round as she looked to see if Deanna was teasing her. At her earnest look and nod, she turned to her mother. "Nuh uh, a dog can't raise kittens!" she insisted.

Madison looked at Deanna in surprise. She'd forgotten about that incident. She turned to her daughter. "It's true. The kitten's mother died and Doctor Coo…Kearney," she said, correcting herself, "delivered the babies and they had to nurse. So we put them with a dog that had babies and she raised them." She thought the children too young to hear about nursing and such.

"Did they bark?" Conor wanted to know.

"No, but they grew as big as the dog," Deanna told him.

"Cats aren't as big as a dog," he insisted.

"Some are. What about a lion or a tiger?" she asked him.

He thought for a moment and then nodded, warming to her.

They chatted about cats and dogs through the rest of dessert, and much to Madison's amazement, Conor took his and Deanna's plates into the kitchen for her. Deanna grinned and followed into the kitchen.

"Okay, you two. Get ready for bed," Madison told them as she loaded the dishwasher and Deanna looked on.

"Aww, Mom," they both protested.

"Nuh uh, march!" she insisted. She'd had a late dinner for Deanna's sake, but the children did have school in the morning. "I'll be in to check on you in a minute."

Both kids scampered off to change for bed and Deanna looked on as Madison easily filled the appliance.

"You were a big hit," Madison said as she filled the door compartment with soap.

"Yeah, you think so?"

"Oh yeah, they answered you and asked questions. Believe me, that's a hit," she smiled as she closed up the dishwasher and set it.

"Well, it's all a matter of finding their interests."

"Well that flea-bitten varmint is theirs." She lowered her voice, "God, I can't stand that dog. If he would just get it trained," she lamented.

"Let me guess, he bought it and now doesn't want to take care of it?"

"Got it in one. He was trying to outdo me and now he wants me to take it. Like I have the time."

"I hear you. I'd have a zoo if I had the time, but I only have a cat."

"You have a cat?" she asked surprised.

"Yes, his name is Spot."

Laughter bubbled up in Madison's throat at the name. "Let me get this straight, you have a cat and you named him Spot?"

Deanna nodded as though it made perfect sense. "Yes, I have a cat and named him Spot," she repeated back to her laughing friend. "If you met him, you would understand."

"When do you have time for a cat?"

"Oh, I've had time for him for a while, although he's still pretty much a kitten. He makes time for me. He adores me."

"I'd love to see this cat of yours," she laughed at the image of Deanna sitting with a docile cat on her lap. She remembered her with the wild cats in the village. The combination had her eyes warming and she found herself remembering her feelings for Deanna from so long ago. She still wondered at their returned friendship. Was there more there that she wasn't picking up on?

"Well, I guess I should be going," Deanna said as the laughter wound down. She didn't want to overstay her welcome.

"Oh, do you have to? I was hoping you could stay a little while, but if you have to work tomorrow...."

"Actually, I have a three-day weekend," she said. "I can stay a little while."

"Mommy, we're ready," a little voice said from down the hall.

"The living room is through there," Madison said nodding towards the room. "I can bring coffee...."

"How about hot chocolate? Coffee will keep me up."

"Hot chocolate it is, but don't let the kids know or they'll want some," she answered quietly as she walked by Deanna.

Deanna resisted the urge to reach out and catch Madison in her arms. As it was, it was a near thing as she caught the scent of perfume coming from the redhead's body, a scent that was uniquely Maddie. Deanna closed her eyes for a moment and corrected herself...it was Madison now.

"So who's this doctor you've been seeing?" Scott asked the next time he dropped off the kids after a day of having them.

"Doctor I'm seeing?" Madison frowned, trying to figure out who he meant.

"Yeah, the kids keep talking about a Doctor Karney or something. Who is he?"

Laughter bubbled up at his assumption as well as the incorrect name. "Doctor Kearney, and she's an old friend."

"I never heard you talk about her," he griped. She was always correcting him. He put the kids' backpacks down in the hall.

"That's because I knew her back before I met you."

"And you are friends again?" he asked, confused.

"She started working here a few months ago," she simplified. He didn't need to know any more than that.

"She eats here regularly now?"

Shrugging as though she didn't care too much so that he wouldn't realize how important Deanna was becoming to her, she answered, "Oh that's an exaggeration, she's only been over a couple of times." She also didn't mention how many times they had been out to restaurants over the past months.

He seemed relieved that the doctor was a woman. He wouldn't have thought of a romantic interest there. He probably just figured that Deanna was a new friend, or that was what Madison was hoping. She was relieved when he dropped the subject and they began to talk about parenting things.

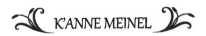

CHAPTER TWENTY-FIVE

"You know your kids are going to be angry that they missed this," Deanna teased as she picked up Madison in her Rover one Saturday morning.

"Well, Scott got tickets to the Dodgers' game and wanted them this weekend. I couldn't disappoint them by having them make a choice," she told her friend, but secretly she was thrilled to have this time alone with Deanna. The kids liked her a lot and were all over her whenever they had dinner at Madison's house. She'd become Dr. D to them.

"Well, I hope you enjoy this," she said as she put the last bag of Madison's in the backseat of the Rover.

"I've been looking forward to it," Madison confessed with a smile. She had slathered herself with sunblock in anticipation of a day of sun with Deanna. She'd smiled ever since she saw the blonde pull up in front of her house with a trailer behind the SUV carrying the two Waverunners. She was right, the kids were going to be very upset that they missed this. She hadn't even mentioned it to them once she knew of the conflict of schedules. She justified it that they were spending time with their father. She had the weekend to herself, and Deanna to herself.

"This is going to be so much fun," Deanna responded with a smile as she got in and carefully pulled away from the curb.

"Yes, it is," Madison agreed.

They chatted easily on their way down to the lake. It had been recommended by one of the other doctors at the hospital and they had gotten up early enough that by the time they got to Puddingstone Lake the sun would be nice and hot. Madison had packed them a cooler full of sandwiches and chips, and Deanna had a cooler full of ice, sodas, juices, and even a beer or two. They had planned for a full day of fun in the sun.

After paying her launch fee, Deanna slowly backed the trailer with the two Waverunners down the boat ramp. Once it was deep enough to offload them, she put on the parking brake and opened her door. Madison opened hers and followed. Together they removed the covers and ties to each of the Waverunners and Deanna slowly let the cable out until each was floating free of the trailer.

"Let me move this one over there and I'll come back for that one," she told Madison as she put on a vest.

"Do you want me to do anything?"

"Not until I get the second one off, then you can go park the SUV and trailer…somewhere in the shade if you can?"

"You trust me to drive that thing?"

"You can, can't you?"

"Sure, but it's an expensive setup…."

"I trust you," she smiled from behind her sunglasses. She walked out wearing diving socks and pulled herself up on the first Waverunner. She pulled the key attached to the spiral plastic chain on her wrist and tried to start the Waverunner. She had to prime it a second time before it started with a roar. Slowly and carefully, she drove it to the side of the ramp before tying it off, hopping off, and returning for the second.

"That looks like so much fun," thought Madison as she watched how easy Deanna made it look.

Once the second one was started and Deanna was putt-putting away to the side with it, Madison hopped in the driver's seat and slowly pulled up the ramp into a parking spot. She was lucky, the angle of the trees was such that it was in the shade. She began to close the sun roof, the windows, and to lock up the SUV.

"Everything okay?" Deanna said at her window and Madison jumped. She'd been so careful about locking everything up, she hadn't noticed the blonde walking up. "You okay?" she asked with a laugh, seeing the redhead jump.

"You're gonna give me a heart attack," she told her, her hand splayed against her chest.

"Well, good thing I'm a doctor then," she said with a grin. Deanna helped her make sure everything was locked up. She handed Madison a vest to put on over her swimsuit and t-shirt. They were both wearing shorts. "Do you have something for your feet?" Deanna asked.

"I couldn't find those socks you suggested," she didn't mention how expensive the ones she had found were. She simply couldn't justify putting that into her budget this last week.

Deanna wasn't fooled. "I brought an old pair of mine, just in case. They may be a bit large on you, but they grip well." She handed her a set of booties that Madison slipped on. They felt funny, the neoprene trying to act like a second skin.

"You got sunblock?" Madison asked as she showed the spray she'd used on her arms and legs. She was so much paler than Deanna.

"I used something at home, but I'm sure we will need more," she answered and allowed Madison to spray her down as she turned. "Let's leave the rest of this stuff in the car until we need it." She put her car keys, her license, and some cash in a neat little canister that could be put around her neck and would float if it was tossed off or came off. She had small floats attached to the spiral key chain for the Waverunners too. "Come on, we'll use the same one until you feel confident enough to use one on your own."

Madison gulped. She hadn't anticipated sharing one of those things. She envisioned her arms around the blonde's waist and then in the same instance envisioned Deanna's arms around her. Neither prospect upset her and she could feel her heart beating hard in her chest.

Deanna, not realizing why Madison was being reluctant, spoke up, "Come on, it's as easy as driving a car, and twice as much fun." She seemed oblivious to how Madison was feeling, but she wasn't. She had seen how sexy Madison looked in her swimsuit. It was darker than the t-shirt she was wearing over it and she hoped at some point Madison would remove the t-shirt, and maybe the shorts, so she could enjoy the view of the swimsuit. Meanwhile, she would have to be patient.

Deanna showed Madison the basic safety features of the Waverunner. The keys were attached to her wrist on the plastic spiral key chain so that if she, as the driver, were thrown from the boat, it would turn the Waverunner off. These Waverunners would turn in a circle, so you could swim to the back and pull yourself up on it, even in deep water.

"You do know how to swim, right?" Deanna asked, teasing her.

"Of course I do!" she returned, mock-indignant.

"Well, I never saw you swim in Africa. How could I know?"

"Just be glad there are no crocodiles to feed you to here!"

Deanna joined in on the laugh. They had found talking about Africa a lot easier since the first meal they had shared at Madison's. They still hadn't spoken about why Madison had left or what happened after she left, but they were making progress, sharing stories about it now and then with the children.

Deanna started up the Waverunner and Madison got on behind her. She found that there were handles on the vest that could pop out and she could hold instead of wrapping her hands around Deanna's torso like she had envisioned. She was slightly disappointed, but the fun of their first lap around the lake soon soothed any problems that could have come up. Deanna took it easy so that Madison could feel how the waves chopped at the hull of the runner and how it affected driving. She slowed as she came back to the boat ramp so they could change places and Madison could drive.

"This is such fun!" Madison called over her shoulder as she now drove carefully back out. Deanna had warned her to take it slow until they got out beyond a certain point that was marked by buoys. They didn't need anyone to yell at them for hot-dogging it.

"Let 'er rip," Deanna yelled back as she hung onto the handles on either side of Madison's vest.

"Are you sure?"

"Can you handle it?"

Madison rose to the challenge as she opened up the throttle. It felt different as she sped up and she could feel how easy it would be to lose control. As she began to take a turn, she pulled a little too quickly and the Waverunner flung them both sideways and off its seat. They both went into the air, her wrist connection to the key was released, the machine turned off, and by the time they were in the water it was turning in a circle back towards them. They both came up sputtering.

"Oh, my gosh, that was great. Are you okay?" Madison called as she looked to see a smiling Deanna.

"That was funny," she responded as she began to swim towards the circling machine to get to the back of the seat. Madison followed, using clean, strong strokes as she swam. Together they arrived at the machine, which had stopped after its first circle and was floating in the lake. The waves had caught up to them and made climbing on the back of the machine hard. One by one they pulled themselves up onto it, breathing hard at their exertions. "Wow, that's a workout," Deanna commented as they both finally got back on.

"I thought I was in shape," Madison commented as she too was panting.

"You're in great shape," Deanna said before she could stop herself and then blushed.

Madison turned away, but not before a smile lit up her face at the unintended compliment. She carefully pulled the connector at her wrist, the Slinky-like wristband holding it there. She connected the key once again and started up the machine like she had seen Deanna do. It started like a charm.

"Head back to the landing. I want to race you on these things," Deanna called in her ear.

Madison was still smiling as she dropped Deanna off.

"You hungry or thirsty yet?"

"No. You?"

"A little thirsty, but I can wait a few rounds. I want you to see what these things can do!"

They spent the next couple of hours going round and round on the course laid out on the lake. There were buoys sticking up to show where they could drive. A couple said 'no wake', so if they went over toward those, they could not be racing or revving up their boats. They stayed away from those since speed was what they wanted at the moment. They stopped for lunch and put more gas and oil in the fuel tanks. Deanna kept a couple of extra plastic gas cans filled with the specially mixed fuel for just that purpose. They filled both tanks, but only after they ate a lunch of sandwiches, juice, and water to stay hydrated. It was amazing how much water they needed out in the hot sun despite being on the water.

"I'm taking this off," Madison stated when they returned from filling the tanks with the empty gas cans.

Deanna got her wish as Madison removed her t-shirt and shorts and left them to dry out on the trailer. Deanna followed suit, but didn't see Madison's expression at her toned body. "Do you have any more of that sunblock? We should probably use some more."

"Yeah, um, yeah," she agreed and turned away to grab some.

They raced some more, sending admiring glances each other's way as they spun around and enjoyed cavorting on the water. Finally, the course became a little boring and Deanna suggested they take it slow and explore the rest of the lake. Also, they could chat easier as they putt-putted along and looked at the lake houses along the pretty shore.

"How about that one?" Madison pointed to one particularly nice house. They'd been playing 'what if' about the different houses and if they owned one.

"I like that one, that gray stone is beautiful. Look at that boathouse over there," she pointed. It was all in rich woods and couldn't possibly be that old, it looked too pristine, and it hadn't faded or weathered.

It was as they were coming round after going as far down as they could that they were attacked. It came out of nowhere. Neither of them had noticed, but they had been watched and targeted. The huge bird came at them viciously and with the intent to kill.

"Holy shit!" Deanna yelled, having gotten clipped by a wing in the head. "Look out!" she called to Madison.

The beaks of the two swans were just as deadly and just intent on them.

"Take off! Get out of here!" Deanna called to Madison when she saw that the birds were swans. She knew they could be lethal. Their wing spans alone were like seven feet. She'd heard of them attacking and killing full-grown men in the past. They both sped off, the birds hitting them twice more on the Waverunners themselves before they got far enough away.

"What the hell was that about?" Madison asked, wiping away a bit of blood trickling down the side of her face.

"Are you hurt?"

"A little. He clipped me good. Damn, what the hell?" she asked as she felt the pain of the small wound.

"Let me see that," Deanna ordered and pulled up alongside Madison. They both cut the motors and floated there, looking furtively back to where they had been attacked for any signs of the deadly birds. The cut was superficial.

"Why would they attack us like that?" Madison wondered as she gulped at the nearness of Deanna. She looked so muscular in the form-fitting swimsuit. Her eyes had looked so intently at the wound. It was all she could do not to reach out and touch.

"We probably got too close to their nest or something," Deanna told her. She wasn't unaffected by their nearness. It was tempting to kiss the spot to make it better. She'd gotten a good view down Madison's swimsuit too. Her breasts were definitely bigger for having had two children.

"Wow, they certainly knew how to organize that attack."

"We never saw it coming," Deanna grinned. "Are you okay? Do you want to call it a day?"

"Hell, no! I'm not going to let some swan ruin my day of fun in the sun!"

"Atta girl!"

They spent another hour doing the course, racing each other. Deanna got thrown once more when she didn't pay attention, but to be fair, Madison had distracted her, in more ways than one, by standing up and revving her engine. Deanna had done a somersault over the water before falling into the lake and coming up sputtering. She had needed the swim back to her machine to cool off anyway.

They were finally so tired out from all the fresh air and sun that they drove the machines back and Deanna backed the trailer onto the ramp and into the water. This time, Madison drove one onto the trailer while Deanna used the lift to pull it tightly on board and clamp it down. By then Madison had driven the other one over and it was ready to be tied down. Madison fetched the covers and they both covered up the machines for the ride back to town.

"Wow, that was a fun day!" Deanna commented as she carefully pulled up the ramp and away from the lake.

"The kids are going to be so jealous."

"We can come back."

"Soon I hope! That was so much fun."

"Did you want to stop and eat somewhere?"

"Like this?" Madison looked down at her t-shirt covered swimsuit, which had clung to her immediately.

Deanna had noticed the cling and didn't mind at all. It clung in all the right places. "Well, we'll probably be dry by the time we get back into L.A."

"I'm not hungry yet. How about you?"

"Not yet, and I know once I eat, I'll get sleepy." She yawned for effect. After all that sun and exercise, she was already a bit tired and she still had to drive.

"Do you want something to drink? I can reach," she offered as she wiggled up on the seat and reached in the back.

Deanna didn't answer right away. She had been treated to the sight of Madison's curvy derriere in the swimsuit bottom, practically in her face. It was a good thing she had to concentrate on her driving across the parking lot. She could imagine if that had happened on the road, they would have crashed. "Yeah, I'll take an apple juice and a water," she was finally able to squeak out.

Madison was aware her backside was exposed, she only wished she had really planned it. She was wondering what Deanna might be thinking about it. She almost wished she could ask her as she came back to the front seat with two waters and two apple juices. She quickly shimmied into her seat belt before they got on the road.

"All set?" Deanna asked to cover up for her momentary lapse.

"All set," Madison agreed.

Deanna set out after checking everything one more time. She even stopped the SUV to check the trailer, the covers, and the ties. She slipped off her booties and slipped on sandals to drive in.

"Do you want these back?" Madison asked, rolling off the booties she had been wearing. She wiggled her pruney toes appreciatively.

"Eventually," Deanna answered and threw her own in the backseat next to the vests they had stowed there.

They slowly made their way back to Los Angeles and away from Puddingstone Lake. They vowed to return sometime soon, the kids would demand it. "Hey, they have hot tubs up here. Doesn't that sound wonderful under the stars?" Madison pointed at the sign.

"I have a hot tub at my house," Deanna mentioned before she could think.

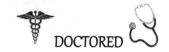

"You'll have to show me some time," Madison answered before she could think.

The drive was a little quieter after that, each lost in the meaning of what they had said and what it could mean, neither asking the other. Finally, an uneasy conversation started over a billboard they saw, distracting them both from their thoughts.

"Do you want to come in and eat something?" Madison offered when they got to her place.

"No, thank you. I think the sun kept me from really being hungry. I just want to go home and sleep," Deanna grouched in a teasing way.

"I think I got more sun than you did!" she answered back, showing off her reddish skin. They had both gotten sunburned, but not too badly thanks to the sunblock.

"You put some lotion on that, young lady," the doctor teased as she put the last of Madison's things on her porch for her.

"Do you have someone to help you with all that?" she indicated the trailer and the Waverunners as well as the cooler and other things in the back of the Rover.

"Yeah, but I like to do things myself," Deanna said with a self-deprecating grin.

"Thank you for a really wonderful day out," the redhead told her appreciatively. She really wanted to kiss the blonde, but didn't know if that would be appropriate. They were, after all, just friends. Was she reading too much into this?

"I had a good time too. Now we know what to do for when we take the kids," she smiled. She was glad that Madison couldn't see her eyes boring into her, hungering for the body under that t-shirt and swimsuit. "I'll call you tomorrow to see how you're faring," she promised as she began to back away.

"Drive safe," she called as she watched her walk towards the Rover and Waverunners. Deanna went around to the driver's side and quickly got in. Waving madly, she slowly drove away from the curb.

Madison waved until Deanna was out of sight. Almost like a kid who didn't want their best friend to leave. It was more than that…she knew it was more. She wasn't sure how to *make* it more though. Sighing, she began to take her things inside.

Deanna was wondering if she should say something. She didn't want to ruin what they had. She'd had so much fun, but she wanted more…she needed more. She had so much more to share with Madison when she was ready. It was going to be hard to share with her; she hadn't told her everything.

CHAPTER TWENTY-SIX

"Are you going to the party for the opening of the new children's wing?" Deanna asked Madison as she looked over the chart on an operation they had just finished.

"Uh, I'm sure I'm not invited," Madison laughed as she waited for any further directions from the doctor.

Deanna looked up. "Why wouldn't you be invited? You're a member of this hospital."

"You don't see the class distinctions around here, do you? Nurses are good for scutt work, for dating, or for boinking, but they aren't on an equal level with the doctors, much less the surgeons."

Deanna looked at her as though she had sprouted antennae. "What are you talking about?"

"Remember when you were an intern and the doctors treated you like a servant?" Madison waited until Deanna nodded. It took a moment, after all Deanna was a teen when she was an intern. "That's how they treat nurses around here…all the time."

"I don't do…" she began defensively.

"No, you don't, but many do," she was quick to reassure.

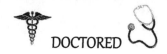

"So, are you going to go?" she dismissed the unpleasant part of the conversation they had just had.

"I don't think so. There is no point and it's too expensive to get an invitation…" she began and then was interrupted by Deanna.

"Look, I have to go. Let's just say it was a mandatory suggestion," she sighed. "I'd kinda like someone there I can laugh with and make fun of the other doctors with," she lowered her voice and they shared a girlish giggle.

"What? As your date?" she asked, flippantly, her heart beating hard from the implication and her audacity.

Deanna frowned, imagining what it might do to Madison's stellar reputation as a trauma nurse. "No, as my friend," she clarified.

Madison felt a bit disappointed, but didn't let it show. "I don't know if I have anything to wear and then I have to get a babysitter…" she began. The kids had been disappointed to find out about the excursion on the Waverunners and had been acting up, asking when Deanna was coming over again and when they got to go.

"C'mon, those are just excuses. I'll pay for the damn tickets and I'll pick you up. All you have to do is put on somethin' purty," she changed her voice to sound like a redneck and the two of them shared a laugh.

"Okay, okay, I'll go," she promised, and then immediately regretted it. She'd have to find a nice dress and she didn't own one. She wanted to look nice *for the party*, at least that was what she told herself. She almost convinced herself she would be dressing up for the party.

The night of the gala for the new children's wing at the hospital, as they were calling it, Deanna dressed carefully. She'd hired a small limo to drive them; she didn't want to worry about drinking and driving. The kids were kind of put out that they couldn't go, Madison confessed, but they were looking forward to seeing the two friends dressed up.

Conor opened the door and did his best to try and whistle at the vision of loveliness on their doorstep. "Wow, Doctor D, is that really you?" he asked in an awed voice. Even he could tell that she had made quite an effort to clean up. Normally dressed in nice blouses and designer jeans, the rainbow high-tops were long gone and the high heels she was wearing replaced them. A bit of leg showed through the slit in her gown and the color of the satin nearly matched her blue eyes. Her hair was spiked up, but it looked hip and stylish. The jewelry she was wearing showed off the expanse of neck, emphasizing her blonde beauty. She was expertly made up, emphasizing her blue eyes, eye liner hiding the missing eye lashes. The lipstick she wore made her lips look full and very kissable.

"Yep, Conor, it's me. Is your mom ready?" Deanna smiled. The bright red of her lips was a startling contrast to her white teeth.

"Um, yeah, she's still in her room," he told her and Deanna walked into the house as Madison was coming out. They both stopped to stare. Neither had seen the other *this* dressed up.

"Wow," Deanna breathed as Madison said the same.

Madison was dressed in a stunning green dress that came down to her knees. It sparkled with silver material in the pattern. With Madison's red hair worn down instead of the usual ponytail, it really showed off her Irish heritage beautifully. Her skin, still holding a tan from their weekend out, made her look stunning.

"Are you ready for this thing?" Deanna finally found her voice as she smiled her appreciation.

"Just got to get my purse," Madison answered as she stared at the stunning blonde in her hallway.

"I think you should take us," Chloe insisted as she saw how nice her mother and Doctor D looked.

Deanna looked down at the little girl looking on wistfully and understood. She smiled at the young girl and said, "This is an adults-only party. Someday we should have a dress up party, shouldn't we?"

"Oh, can we?"

"Well, maybe, someday. When is your next birthday?"

"Last month," she stated. Deanna looked up in hurtful alarm at Madison, who shook her head.

"You mean six months ago?" Madison corrected the little girl.

"Um, yeah."

Just then a teenaged girl arrived. "Here's Stacy to watch you two tonight," Madison announced as she smiled at the girl hesitating on the doorstep.

The two children and the teen were soon watching TV, talking about the popcorn Madison had announced they could make, and the pizza that was due to be delivered. The two adults slipped outside.

"You look wonderful," Deanna mentioned as they walked to the limousine.

"You look pretty good yourself," Madison admired and meant every word of it.

They arrived at the hotel that was holding the reception. There hadn't been enough room at the hospital with all the invitations. The steps up to and into the ballroom were carpeted in red for the guests. There were round tables everywhere and a large dance floor. In back of it all was a long table where the directors of the hospital sat with their spouses. In one corner was a covered twenty-foot picture displayed so that everyone in the room would be able to see it when it was time. They'd hung it within five feet of the ceiling and had lights trained on it. Below it and also covered, was a table containing brochures and pamphlets.

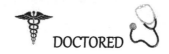

It wasn't long before the room was full of laughing and talking people. It got quite loud until one of the directors stood up and made a speech. That many people couldn't remain absolutely quiet though, and you could hear discreet conversation and people moving about. Four different directors made speeches of varying lengths. The ballroom had beautiful pressed wallpaper lining the thirty-foot-high walls with wooden panels separating each section of the wall and creating a very definite French look. It was really quite beautiful with the chandeliers glistening.

Finally, the fourth director sat down and they were served. Deanna and Madison had roast chicken with asparagus and new potatoes seasoned with garlic. They were served champagne in long flutes, but both women made sure to eat before having any of the champagne. They didn't want to get sick this evening.

Harold, one of the leading board members, gave everyone a good forty-five minutes to eat and when he saw enough people had finished and were milling about, he got up to give his speech. He kept it fairly short, thanking all the correct people and noting how their contributions had affected LA Medical Center and allowed them to build the new children's wing with its beautiful new entrance. He told everyone that they were fortunate to acquire the talents of a world-renowned portrait artist who had painted them a lovely portrait for the entrance. He introduced Joan Woods.

Fortunately, Joan had finished her meal and done repairs to her make-up. Harold had mentioned that he wanted her to say a few words before the unveiling. She stood up and headed to the podium in the center of the long table. It seemed to take forever to walk that distance. Every eye in the room was on her, hundreds of them. She was well-fortified with an excellent meal and two flutes of champagne. She hadn't written a speech, but she felt well-prepared. Finally, she reached the podium.

"Ladies and gentlemen, I would like to thank the kind directors of this hospital and in particular, Mr. Waterman, for the opportunity to create this portrait for your hospital. It wasn't difficult...you might say I was inspired. As you will see its beauty and realize how special it is, you will understand how perfect it is for this new wing. In fact, I'd like to donate the money I was paid to make this beautiful portrait to the children's wing." She hesitated a moment to let the applause die down before continuing, "Without a long speech to further keep you from enjoying this gala, I give you Grace, Hope, Charity, Wisdom, and Compassion." So saying, she flung her arm out and the waiters pulled the ropes holding the drapery from the portrait.

There was a collective gasp and then applause began. It rose in volume as people began to stand and give Joan an ovation. She had changed the final painting and it wasn't just one woman, Grace, in the picture. She had painted children around the bottom of it and it looked like the silhouette ghost angel was looking down on them with the title words across the painting in script on three levels. She stepped down from the podium and began to return to her seat, but was stopped by the directors and their wives. She shook dozens of hands, was told over and over how beautiful it was, how generous her donation. Mr. Waterman made his way to her and gave her a hearty kiss on the cheek, telling her how happy she had made him and the board. He told her the donation wasn't necessary, but she insisted. She finally explained that she would make it back in prints as, per their contract, she had the copyright.

People took this as an opportunity to socialize. Many people made their way to the portrait to view it up close and to pick up the matching brochure that was on the table below it. It had a copy of the portrait on the front and information about the gala inside. In small print on the back, Joan's Malibu studio was listed for people to obtain prints of the work. The orchestra began tuning up.

Harold began introducing Joan to people from the hospital. Department by department, he introduced people she couldn't hope to remember. It was amazing how many people he knew. She must have been with him an hour when he took her to another table and began introducing them. "This is Doctor Kearney of Kearney Pharmaceuticals," he made it sound like her pedigree was so very important. Deanna was not amused. All night long people had been snubbing Madison when they realized she was 'just a nurse' and she had become angry about it. While many did not recognize her from the hospital, as Deanna's friend they assumed she was the doctor's date. Deanna didn't mind, and Madison hadn't thought much about it until she overheard a few catty remarks.

"Of course she would bring a woman."

"Well, I think showing off that you're a lesbian is outrageous."

"Who is that she is with?"

"They don't dare offend her, Kearney Pharmaceuticals and all."

"What's wrong?" Deanna finally asked her when she saw that Madison looked particularly angry.

"Do you realize people think I'm your date?"

"No, I didn't think they would. A few people came as friends. There are some," she indicated the artist they were celebrating, Joan Woods, "that are clearly lesbian."

"Well, I am not," she hissed.

"Okay, so go dance with some of the men," Deanna shrugged. Inside she was angry. Not only at whatever people had said that had upset

Madison, but that Madison was upset over the lesbian aspect of it. She herself wandered away to get a drink.

Madison realized she had just insulted Deanna and was sorry for it. She found some of the nurses and other technicians she worked with at the hospital and managed to have a good time, but she was aware, very aware, of where Deanna was during the rest of the evening. All of the members of the board were sucking up to her and the blonde was attempting to be charming to them and not offend any of them. When Madison went to look for Deanna to see if she was ready to leave, she accidentally overheard a conversation she was sure she was not supposed to hear.

"No, I'm sorry. My time is up in a few weeks and I'll be winding down my caseload accordingly."

"You're sure we can't entice you into staying on longer?" Harold almost pleaded.

"Look, I agreed to the six months and I gave you the six months. You've got to admit I've ruffled a few feathers. I think it's time I move on."

"Well, ruffled feathers can be soothed…."

"I am ready to move on to my next challenge."

"Are you going back to the Amazon?" he asked, intrigued.

Madison, listening in, was bumped right then and didn't hear Deanna's answer. The bump put her right in the blonde's line of vision.

"Hey there, are you about ready to go?" Deanna asked her, forestalling her own inquiry.

"Yes, any time you are."

"Well Harold, I'm going to call it a night," she turned and offered her hand to the older gentleman.

"I thank you for coming tonight. It's been very interesting, don't you think?" he indicated the unveiling of Joan Wood's latest creation for their lobby.

"In many ways," Deanna murmured, but she wasn't looking at the artwork, she was looking at the attractive redhead who caught her look and blushed. "Shall we go?" she asked, innocently. She would have taken Madison's elbow, but decided against it as they walked along. Deanna, more than Madison, kept having to say good night or goodbye to people as she went.

Madison wondered if people were paying Deanna attention because she was a doctor or because she was a Kearney. For some reason, she didn't notice that they sent her admiring glances too. Whether they noticed her because she was with the brilliant doctor or because of her own good Irish looks, she wasn't aware. She just wanted to leave after all those hours.

Finding their limo, they both quickly got inside. Deanna let out a big sigh of relief. "Glad that's over," she commented with a little smile. She had decided that she would have to let Madison do what she wanted. It was apparent she only wanted to be friends and the good doctor would have to be content with that. She'd known pursuing her again that this might be the outcome, and while she was disappointed, she hadn't been sure she would win.

"It was beautiful seeing everyone dressed up, but it isn't so very different from the hospital itself," Madison stated.

"How do you mean?"

"They all still gossip," she said with a tone that clearly indicated she was sick of it.

"Yes, people will be people," Deanna agreed, unwilling to argue with her. "I did have some intelligent conversations. It just gets tiring when all they want to talk about is donations and doing this and that." She shook her head.

"Doesn't Kearney Pharmaceuticals donate a lot to causes like that?" she indicated the gala they were pulling away from.

"Yes, in fact we give millions to things like that. I prefer getting by on my own merits though."

"Like the Cooper-Aloe project?"

Deanna nodded. "Yes, things like that. But I earned my degree and I want to use it. They wouldn't let me use it there if they had their way. They just want to show me off like a poodle or something."

"Well, that's coming to an end," Madison said and couldn't help the bitterness that crept into her voice.

"What do you know of that?" Deanna asked, an elegant eyebrow rose in question.

"I overheard you and that board member. You said you are leaving in a few weeks."

Deanna nodded. "Yes, that's true."

"You don't think you might have mentioned that to your *good friend*." She used hand gestures to make quotation marks around how she had introduced Madison several times that evening.

"I was hoping to talk to you about that…" Deanna began.

"When? Before or after you left?"

Deanna chuckled, amused, seeing Madison had no reason to be angry. "Before. I wanted to…."

"Look, you just came back into my life, my *children's* life, and now you're going to go?" she asked angrily.

"No, I was going to offer…."

"Because if that's how you're going to be, I don't want you in my life!" She couldn't help it. She was hurt, she was angry, but mostly she was angry with herself. She should have been proud to be associated with Deanna Kearney, even introduced her as her good friend. Instead she had swatted that down, declared that she was not a lesbian, and now Deanna was leaving…probably to go back to South America and that witch doctor she had fallen in love with so long ago. It was better that Madison put an end to this before she got hurt, before her children got hurt.

"What?" Deanna asked, confused. She had been about to offer Madison a job, but had been cut off twice now. She didn't understand her unreasonable anger.

"Look, I have children to look out for now. If you don't understand that because you have never wanted that in your life," she shot at her low, her hurt from ten years ago coming back up, "…you shouldn't have let our friendship get this far!"

"Let our friendship get this far?" She was puzzled. "What the heck are you talking about?"

"If you weren't going to stay…" she began, but she wanted to cry and she didn't know why.

"It was always going to be temporary. I only agreed to six months," she answered, still puzzled at Madison's anger over the situation.

"But I let my children get to know you and I thought…" she stopped herself from saying what she had nearly revealed.

"Madison," Deanna began gently, wanting to take the woman into her arms, "what did you think?"

Madison didn't want to say, but in the darkness of the back of the limo, her anger propelled her onward, it was that or cry about the situation. "I thought, perhaps, you were courting me," she sniffed as she fought the tears that wanted to burst out.

"I was," Deanna answered simply. She reached for the light so that she could see Madison and her expression…to show the redhead that she was sincere.

As the flick of the light transformed the back of the limo from the dark anonymity to a bright reveal, Madison wanted to hide her face. Tears were already forming in her eyes. At the simple admission that Deanna was indeed courting her, she opened her eyes wide. "You were?" she asked in wonderment.

The blonde doctor nodded her head. "Once I realized you were at the hospital I had hoped we could resume our friendship. I never stopped thinking of you," she confessed. Finally, they were talking about it.

"You didn't?" she looked on with amazement.

Deanna shook her head. "You always haunted me. I wanted to stop you from leaving that day, but it was so dangerous. I wanted you out of that danger." She then admitted something she hadn't told anyone. "I should have gone with you."

Something about the tone stayed with Madison, something wasn't being said. She tucked that away to address later. "I don't think it would have worked then. I'd convinced myself you'd just wanted a fling because you never told me that you loved me."

That fitted some of the puzzle pieces into place for Deanna. She'd suspected as much over the years. Her lack of being able to express herself verbally back then had cost her. "If I had told you, would you have stayed with me?" she asked now.

Madison looked at the blonde, those amazing blue eyes making her want to kiss the doctor. "I don't know. I was so afraid of what people thought or would think."

"And now?"

Madison started to blush as she realized she hadn't acted much differently tonight. "I guess I'm still afraid."

"Madison…Maddie," she whispered as she leaned in, "I love you. I've always loved you," she said before she gently kissed the redhead.

Madison closed her eyes. The lips were still as soft as she remembered, the feelings they engendered the same. Hearing that Deanna had loved her made her melt and she went with those feelings. Her own arms snaked around the blonde, holding her in place so she could return the kisses. They started so gently and quickly became heated.

Deanna couldn't pull Madison close enough. She found herself hiking Madison's dress up high on her thighs so the redhead could straddle the blonde on the back seat of the limo. "Mmm, mmm," she moaned into the kisses as Deanna caressed her exposed legs. Deanna arched and their centers ground slightly together. Deanna tipped her from her lap onto the seat of the limo and lay on top of her.

Madison loved the feel of Deanna's weight on her, her fingers clasped the doctor's buttocks to her as she ravished her lips, her tongue probing deeply to fence with the blonde's. She gentled the kiss by sucking on the tongue offered to her.

"God, I want you," Deanna admitted.

"Take me home," Madison breathed. All these months had built up to this. She had thought of making love to Deanna time and time again. She knew, despite her fears, that she wanted to be with her.

"You want to go home?" she queried, confused again.

"Take me to *your* home," she clarified, her hand reaching for Deanna's to press between her legs. "You've started something and I need you to finish it," she whispered.

"Just a moment," she gulped as she closed her eyes, feeling the heat beneath the palm of her hand. She sat up and made sure her dress was in place before pushing the button to lower the wall that separated the front from the back. "Could you take us to my house?" she asked the driver. At his nod, she pushed the button again to raise the separator. She looked down again at Madison, her Maddie, in her arms and looking up at her with lust-filled eyes. "Are you sure?" she asked gently.

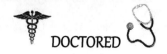

"Yes, take me," she answered and leaned up to pull Deanna's head down to kiss her.

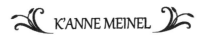

CHAPTER TWENTY-SEVEN

Madison woke and could tell it was early. The sun was trying to come in the large windows, but it was the angle of the sun that told her it was still early. For a moment she was disoriented as she looked around the huge room she was in. As she looked at the bed hangings, she panicked for a moment. Had she gone home with someone…then she remembered. She was in Deanna's home. She was in Deanna's bed. She looked around at the four-poster. It was amazing how the rich maple finish matched the walls of the bedroom. It was obviously an old piece, as was everything she could see in the room, all antiques. She looked around in the light of the early morning and could see the apparent affluence. She hadn't really noticed the night before, but then, she'd had other things on her mind.

Deanna had been so tender to her, so loving. Madison had practically ripped her dress off in her haste to be naked with her. She'd dreamed of this. She'd finally admitted to fantasizing about the good doctor all these years. Deanna was very physically fit, with a little paunch that surprised Madison as she caressed the body, almost a middle-age paunch. She didn't dwell on it long as her fingers touched and caressed and probed in response to Deanna's own caresses and touches. She could only think about getting closer, to feel her against her own skin, to love her…love. Deanna had admitted to loving her!

Madison sat up in the luxurious bed. What was she going to do? Did she love Deanna again? Yes, she admitted that to herself, she'd always loved her. It was only her own foolishness that had torn them apart so long ago. She could admit that too, since she was being honest with herself. Having Deanna back in her life was wonderful. That a brilliant, beautiful, and accomplished woman such as Deanna Kearney could love her simply amazed Madison. She looked around the room again…such opulence. There was even a chandelier in the bedroom! How fancy! Could she get used to this? She realized then she was thinking about a future with Deanna.

Could she openly live with a woman? What would her friends say? What would her coworkers say? She'd lose their respect! She knew what Scott would say. She knew what her mother would say. Her children adored Deanna though. Wasn't she allowed to have some happiness in her life? Could Deanna make her happy? That was an easy yes, she could. Madison knew she wasn't interested in Deanna's money, not in the least. She loved the woman, the amazing and dazzling woman that was Deanna Kearney.

"Oh, God, Kearney Pharmaceuticals," she moaned to herself. Anyone in their right mind would think she was a gold digger. She hadn't known that Deanna was a Kearney when she originally fell in love with her though. She had thought she was a Cooper. That hadn't bothered her in the least ten, almost eleven years ago. It shouldn't bother her now.

She did admit that people and what they thought still bothered her. Could she get over that? It was what she had allowed to break them up so long ago. She hadn't been strong enough to go against what people would think if they found out two women were in love. Was she stronger now? Times had changed. Wasn't it more acceptable nowadays? Was she looking for justification?

Her thoughts were interrupted as the door to the master bedroom was opened. "Mom?" a voice called. In walked a young boy who looked curiously at Madison who was hiding her nudity in the sheets. "Oh, pardon me," he excused himself. "I'm looking for my mother."

"Your mother?" Madison asked, curious, studying his mullato features. She began to realize who his mother must be when Deanna walked in the room.

"Roman, Aura has breakfast for you downstairs," she said firmly as she sidestepped the young man.

"I'm sorry for my intrusion, ma'am," he said courteously with a little bow as he left the room, closing the door behind him.

Deanna turned, carrying a tray with coffee, juice, and two plates on it. She began to chew on her lip as she came closer to the bed, walking around a large chest at the foot of it.

"Is that your son?" Madison asked the obvious question as she looked at Deanna carefully. She was already dressed for the day in slacks and what looked like a silk blouse.

Deanna set the tray down on the bed. Bowing her head slightly, she nodded. "Yes, I named him Roman."

"You've been married?" she asked surprised. They hadn't talked about anything like that and she knew she would have remembered if they had. She wondered how old the boy was, he seemed so…mature.

Deanna shook her head as she looked up slightly. "Do you want some breakfast?" she asked instead.

"I'm curious…" Madison began, but Deanna cut her off.

"Could we talk about it after breakfast? I'm starved."

Madison nodded and reached for the coffee, only it wasn't coffee, it was hot chocolate. It brought back instant memories of Africa and Mamadu.

The breakfast was painfully quiet. Instead of loving it was awkward, and they both picked at the plates of eggs and bacon Deanna had brought up. Madison caught Deanna absentmindedly pulling on her eyebrow a couple of times. The last time, she brought her hand up and said, "Don't."

Deanna looked at her, then at the hand touching her own, and she stopped immediately. She shrugged in an almost ashamed manner.

"We're not making much headway here are we?" she finally asked, indicating the breakfast.

Madison had to agree with her. "I need to get dressed."

"I brought you some clothes. I thought you wouldn't want to wear the dress home."

Madison was pleased with the thought and then gasped, "My children…I never said I was going to stay out all night!"

"I called your babysitter and explained we had car trouble and you would be spending the night at my house. I said that you would be home in the morning. It's only 7:30," she pointed out.

"Car trouble? In a limo?"

Deanna shrugged. "It was the best I could come up with. I didn't want her, or them, to worry."

Madison was grateful for that and pushed aside the plate of food she had barely eaten and went to get out of the bed. It was then she realized how naked she was. "Um," she began.

Deanna realized her dilemma immediately. She grabbed her robe from the foot of the bed and shoved it Madison's way before turning with the tray and giving her some privacy. She put the tray on a table in the room and by the time she turned back Madison had entered her bathroom and closed the door. She sighed. She had awoken with so many hopes and dreams. To have Madison back in her bed had been a big break. She had imagined they would talk everything out this morning.

When Madison returned to the bedroom, the bed was already made, the tray gone and Deanna was sitting in a rocking chair in the large bedroom. She looked up as the redhead came out of the bathroom. "We should talk," she said, indicating another chair that looked comfortable.

"I should get home," Madison answered, feeling uneasy and sensing she wasn't going to like this.

"This won't take long," the doctor answered, feeling hurt.

Madison sensed the hurt in Deanna and wondered at it. She took a deep breath and asked, "So, your son, is he adopted?"

Deanna shook her head. "No, he's nine and he's all mine."

Madison frowned at her, putting the numbers together and coming up with… "Then you got pregnant…"

"I was raped, Maddie," she said quietly. She pushed Madison back in her chair when she would have gotten up to comfort her. "You need to hear this." She looked at the redhead with fearful eyes. "Roman knows the circumstances of his birth," she added, "just not all the details. I'd prefer it that way."

Madison waited where she was, held at first by Deanna's touch, and now by the pain she saw in her beautiful blue eyes.

"After you and the others left, we were a mobile medical clinic. We were on the run for a very long time. We were always under the threat of being overrun by guerillas fighting in the area. They decided we should pull out and evacuate. It was too late though and they captured us. Dr. Burton was killed defending me and my honor, of all things. Dr. Wilson was tortured and he is now in a clinic in Switzerland as a patient…permanently. They didn't let us go, but we managed to escape a week later. I found out I was pregnant three months later when I was trying to work in the Amazon. I had to get out of Africa, away from the memories...." She looked at Madison searchingly. "I couldn't get rid of the persistent flu-like symptoms that I had. I couldn't believe my eyes at the results of the blood test I took. I prayed I'd miscarry, but it wasn't to be. Against all the odds and sickness so great I should have died." At this, Madison again tried to rise, but Deanna held her arms down on the arms of the chair as she leaned in to tell her the story.

"Did you want to die?" Madison asked softly, the hurt she was seeing in Deanna's eyes was real.

Deanna nodded. "I'd lost you and then with what happened…" her voice broke. The tears in her eyes welled up. She swallowed and lifted the back of her hand to wipe at the tears.

"Shhh, don't cry, don't cry…If you don't want to finish it's okay," she tried to tell her, tried to take her in her arms and comfort her.

Shaking her head, the blonde refused. "No, I want you to know," she swallowed. Finding reserves of strength, she continued. "I stayed for a while in South America…."

"With her?" Madison asked, feeling jealous and unable to control it. She'd always felt it though, that woman had inspired love in Deanna long before Madison had met her.

Deanna looked at Madison through the tears, seeing all the insecurities that had plagued her. Swallowing back the last of her own anxieties over this relationship, she bravely continued on. "Yes, she nursed me back to health. I stayed there until Roman was a little boy, until my mother insisted I come home. I lied a little to you about coming home first, my father and sister died only a few years ago, not ten like I said. With my father and sister gone, they needed me to organize the foundation. She also wanted to meet her grandson. My sister's kids are spoiled, elitist brats. They are simply waiting for their trust funds to kick in. Little do they know that I am in charge of them. They tried to make my life hell when I stayed with my mother. They were cruel to Roman until I moved out. I couldn't stay, I was restless." She let Madison go and got up to pace.

"We had so much to work out and I didn't have to stay. They wanted a board of directors…I didn't want to give up my family's autonomy. I wanted to go back to the jungles, but how could I do that to Roman? I didn't want to do that to *her* again. She'd saved my sanity when I might have done something foolish, and for what? My virtue?"

"Did you consider suicide?" Madison gasped, realizing she could have lost Deanna and never have known.

Deanna paused in her pacing and looked at Madison. "That, and worse," she confessed.

"What is worse?" she wondered, but didn't realize that she had spoken until the blonde answered her.

"There are freedom fighters and I wanted to kill the bastards who did that to me. I don't even know who my son's father was because of what they did. I couldn't let anyone touch me for so long…" she sobbed.

This time Madison didn't wait, she got up and pulled Deanna into her arms. She would never have guessed. This confidant and intense woman had been so strong for so long, she hadn't ever thought she had weak moments. "It's understandable you wanted them to pay for what they did…" she began.

"I don't think you understand," Deanna pushed her back to hold her at arm's length. "A doctor saves lives, she doesn't take them. I was thinking of things I could do to them, to all of them. It would have hurt a lot of innocents too, but I didn't care. I was half a world away and I was thinking chemical warfare!"

Madison was startled by the vehemence she saw in Deanna's eyes. The blue had turned almost a crystal white. She was angry and hurt and oh so vulnerable at the moment. "But you didn't," she said softly.

"Only because they wouldn't let me leave. They made me work, made me use my skills until my mind returned to me and I realized I would never be able to find the man who was responsible, the men who did..." her voice broke again.

Madison wondered briefly what exactly they had done to her and then dismissed it. It didn't matter. What mattered was that Deanna was here now, she was better, and she hoped she had left that in the past. "You have Roman. Are you ashamed of him?"

"Of Roman?" she asked incredulous. "Of course not. He's my joy!" she said proudly. "He isn't a child protégée, thank goodness," she added as an afterthought. "But he is smart in his own way and proud to be a Kearney. He doesn't want to be a doctor," she laughed. "He says it's too time-consuming. He wants to be a businessman and run Kearney Pharmaceuticals someday. The Foundation, he says, is in good hands until he is old enough and experienced enough to take it on." She smiled as she repeated his words. "Not bad for a nine-year-old, eh?"

"No, not bad at all," Madison smiled back at her. She had a flash of her own children, wondering if she didn't push them enough.

"Well, that's the story I kept from you," Deanna finished with a big sniff as she wiped her leaking eyes on her sleeve and her runny nose on the back of her wrist. "Oh, excuse me," she said as she ran to the bathroom, leaving the door open to grab a tissue and blow her nose. She washed her hands up to her elbows to get rid of the snot, shaking her head at herself. She, of all people, should know better. She grabbed a washcloth and wiped her eyes, removing the last vestiges of her makeup from them. She looked into the mirror. She could see where she was missing spots of eyelashes and eyebrows, and sighed. The stress had been getting to her recently. She needed to get out of that hospital, it was getting to her.

"Are you okay?" Madison asked from the doorway where she was watching her.

"I'm fine," Deanna answered, knowing there were so many meanings to that phrase and she'd heard them all from her patients over the years. She herself had been 'fine' many times over the years. She took a deep breath, centering herself, and released it slowly, expelling the bad karma she had invoked with her memories. She did this several times until she felt her normal self. When she had her equilibrium back, she looked up once again at Madison and asked, "Do you want to go?"

Madison nodded. She had watched Deanna pull herself together amazingly well. It only strengthened her awe of this woman. After going through God only knew how much, she had come out the other side. People thought her blessed for her brilliant mind, but this, this was the real Deanna Kearney. She still thought of her as Doctor Cooper, but she wasn't. She hadn't been that young and carefree woman for a long time.

They left the bedroom hand in hand. Madison looked at Deanna frequently, hoping to convey her sympathy, her pride, and that she was there for her if she wanted to discuss any more with her. She wouldn't pry, she'd never repeat it, but she did have questions.

"Hey, Mom, are we…?" the boy came to a skidding halt on the socks he was wearing in the large foyer at the bottom of the enormous staircase they were descending.

Madison didn't remember the stairs from the previous night, but then she'd been fogged up about a lot of things, caught up in a lust that only Deanna could assuage.

"Roman, I'd like you to meet a friend of mine." She pulled Madison forward to her side, proudly. "Madison this is my son, Roman…Roman Kearney. Roman, this is Madison…" she began, but he excitedly interrupted her.

"MacGregor? This is the Maddie of your stories?" he asked with obvious joy on his face.

Madison looked surprised and turned to Deanna. Deanna just smiled and nodded at her son. "Yes, Roman, this is the Maddie of my stories," she confirmed gently. "It's rude to interrupt though. She prefers to be called Madison now."

"My apologies, Ms. MacGregor," the boy said formally, back to the well-mannered kid she had met in the bedroom. Remembering she had been nude under those covers in the bedroom, she blushed slightly as she nodded.

"My mom speaks of you often when she tells me about Africa and her time in Mamadu," he continued almost as formally.

There was a loud crash in one of the rooms off the foyer where they were standing and Deanna suddenly asked, "Where is Spot?"

The boy looked guilty. "We were playing and I forgot," he began and quickly left on slippery socks to see what the cat had gotten into.

Deanna tried hard not to laugh and failed, a slight snort came out and Madison looked at her in surprise. The boy obviously delighted her. There was no hint of the sad tale she had told her up in the bedroom, no hint of the anxiety or utter desolation she had indulged in, however briefly. "Come on, I better get you home before you see my cat and run away in terror." She tugged at the hand she was holding and Madison realized that the boy hadn't even noticed they had been holding hands, or if he had, he had accepted it.

"Why, what's wrong with your cat?" she asked as she was led to the front door, but Deanna wouldn't tell her, she would only smile. "Is it okay to leave your son alone while you…?"

"I have a housekeeper," Deanna reminded and led her, not to the front door as Madison had assumed, but to a set of stairs that led down to a built-in garage. There was room for six cars, but there were only two—the Rover that Madison was familiar with and a Volvo station wagon, plus the two Waverunners they had so much fun on the other weekend. Other than that, the large garage was strangely empty. Deanna made sure to tuck Madison in the SUV, even pulling the seat belt across to securely fasten it, stealing a kiss in the process. "All tucked in?" she asked with a grin.

Madison was bemused. She'd learned more about Deanna in the last few hours than she had in the months they had chatted. She couldn't recall one time where she had asked Deanna direct questions about her past or what she had done in the last ten years, much less what had happened in Africa after she had left. She felt very selfish about that and ashamed. She should have asked, taken an interest. She should have known long before this morning what had happened. As a result, she was fairly quiet on the ride home. It wasn't until they'd pulled up in front of her house that she realized Deanna had held her hand the entire drive home. As she went to pull it away, Deanna pulled back and looked at her.

"Are you disgusted?" she asked quietly as she pulled off her sunglasses.

"Disgusted?" she asked, confused. "With what?"

"With what I told you this morning." The blue was completely back in her eyes and they were looking earnestly into Madison's own green eyes.

"Of course not," she answered. Something was lacking, a bit of conviction perhaps and Deanna pounced on it.

"But…?"

"But nothing…" she began, but those blue eyes probed and held her. "I should have asked sooner about what happened to you. I feel ashamed that I never did. How selfish of me. I could have…."

"Changed nothing that happened to me," she finished for her. "Eventually I would have to tell you about my past. I've told you and now we don't have to talk about it again, okay?"

"No, we don't have to talk about it, but I would love to hear more about your son. You never said…."

"That's because Roman is the only true innocent in this. I could have left Africa when you did. Instead, I convinced myself that I was indispensable, that I couldn't possibly get hurt. A man was killed because of me. Not a man I liked, perhaps, but in the end, he was chivalrous. Another man lost his mind with what they did to him. I was lucky to get him out, but maybe it would have been better if he had died. That boy is the only true innocent here. I aim to make sure he knows how much I love him and how much I need him in my life. I will never let anything happen to him if I can prevent it."

Madison was fascinated with how impassioned Deanna had become. She looked like a fierce mother protector and she had never even considered that this woman could or would be one. She smiled. "It's obvious you love him dearly. Is that why you always wanted weekends off?" she guessed.

Deanna nodded. "That's when he comes home from his school in Santa Barbara. He is in a private school up there, protected from his cousins and the media that follows the Kearney's. I want no gossip to reach him if I can help it."

"What…what does he know of his father?"

"As much as I do," Deanna shrugged. "He knows that his father was not a very nice man and that in the heat of battle people do things they shouldn't. He knows he was a soldier and that I don't know his name. How can I tell him I don't know which man he was?" she asked sadly, but quickly centered herself and released the negativity. "He knows that I love him dearly and would do anything for him."

Madison smiled. "We should introduce my kids to him someday soon, okay?"

"That sounds like a fine idea. Maybe we should take the Waverunners out again?"

"Oh, God, that was so much fun," Madison remembered. "They were so jealous."

"I imagine so, but I loved spending so much time alone with you, *just you*," she finished huskily.

Madison realized then that Deanna was very adept at hiding her emotions. Until last night she had no idea that this woman had ever loved her. To find out that she had loved her way back in Africa and still loved her, soothed any hurt she had. She leaned in to kiss her.

Just then the passenger side front door opened. "What the hell are you doing?" a voice raged at Madison. "You leave *my* children alone with a babysitter overnight, what? So you can whore your way with a…" he looked past her and realized she was with a woman, "…a WOMAN? You are with a woman? What are you now, a dyke?" he roared.

"Scott!" she gasped. "No, it's not like that, it's…" she tried to protest, but he wasn't listening as he berated her. He grabbed her arm and tried to drag her from the Rover. The seat belt caught and she began to fall to the ground from the two counter-pressures.

Deanna was out the driver's side of the Rover in an instant and ran around the front of the vehicle. She pulled at Scott, yelling, "Let her go! You're hurting her! Let her go!"

Scott was enraged and backhanded Deanna, not really realizing she was pulling at his arm. It unbalanced him and the swat he meant towards her instead smacked across her face and nose. She instantly started to bleed down the silk of her blouse as she fell to the ground.

"SCOTT! You've hurt her!" Madison screamed as she released her seat belt and hopped out to go to Deanna, bending down to look at her.

He was furious and went after Madison. She lifted an arm to hold him back, but his leg kick went under it and hit her in the ribs, knocking her to the ground and making her lose her breath. He aimed at the downed Deanna next.

A neighbor tackled him, but not before he got in one good kick at the fallen blonde. He fought the man who had grabbed him, but by then another neighbor joined in, having been drawn by the shouts. He never even heard the yells of his children at what he had done. Finally, the police were there and Scott was in handcuffs. An ambulance was called and they checked both Deanna and Madison for cuts and bruises. Deanna had a bad bloody nose and would have a bad bruise where he kicked her, but she refused to go the hospital. Madison too would have a bad bruise, but that was all. She was shaking in reaction and Deanna tried to hold her. Madison, embarrassed by the public display, instead took her children in her arms.

"Do you wish to file charges?" Deanna was asked after the police had all their statements. Deanna hesitated only a moment before nodding. Scott was taken away in the back of the police car, still yelling things like "Dyke" at his ex-wife and Deanna.

"Deanna, you can't do that," Madison tried to argue.

Deanna couldn't be budged. "He attacked me and worse, he attacked you. You are willing to let him get away with that?"

"Deanna, he is the father of my children," she tried to plead, but there was no swaying the blonde. Finally, unable to talk to her, Madison shepherded her children into the house, away from the prying eyes of her neighbors and the gossip that had already started. She looked back once at the blonde. Deanna watched her go and couldn't say a thing.

CHAPTER TWENTY-EIGHT

Madison arrived at the hospital a little late the next day. She had had to go and get her injury looked at as she was having a hard time breathing. As he had been wearing work boots, the bruising and subsequent swelling from the kick were nasty looking and causing her discomfort. The doctor had ordered x-rays and while she was okay, it would take time for it all to go away. She was put on limited work detail.

Madison looked for Doctor Kearney, but was hit with a very large dose of gossip when she arrived. Apparently Deanna had a broken nose and a cracked rib and everyone was talking about it since she wouldn't say how she had gotten it. Madison made sure her own bruise was not visible and protected it from jostling with her arm. Her supervisor, while annoyed that her work was limited, seemed to buy the excuse that she had taken a fall. She didn't put two and two together and for that Madison was grateful.

Madison didn't see Deanna for several days and when she did she saw that her face was very bruised from the break to her nose. She wasn't seeing any patients like that and spent a lot of time catching up on paperwork in her office.

"Can I see you?" Madison hesitated at the door she had just knocked on.

Deanna looked up and nodded. "Close the door behind you," she told her.

Madison closed the door and walked across the small office to the chair across from Deanna. "May I sit down?" she asked politely and at Deanna's nod she sat. Swallowing, feeling a lump in her throat, she asked, "What are you going to do about Scott?"

"What do you think I'm going to do?" she asked thoughtfully, her head turning slightly to the side as she studied Madison.

Madison already knew that his bail was set too high for him to get out. She was considering taking out a second mortgage to pay for it, but that was taking time. "He doesn't deserve to stay in jail."

"I beg to differ. He attacked you, then he attacked me." She waited to see what Madison would respond.

"He didn't mean to hit you…" she began defensively. He had acted out, childishly perhaps, but he'd been incensed.

"My ribs would beg to differ."

Madison noticed that Deanna was sitting very straight in her chair. If her own ribs were any indication, she could only imagine how much hurt the blonde was feeling. At least her ribs weren't cracked, just badly bruised, with a clear imprint of the shoe he was wearing on them. "He was just upset," she answered lamely.

"I got pretty upset when I saw him try to drag you from the car."

"Well, we were kissing."

"We were about to kiss. We were just talking..." she clarified the point. It was obvious she was sticking to the exact part of the story she told the police. Scott had 'thought' they were about to kiss, but they hadn't.

"Deanna, please. Scott isn't a bad guy. He's just like a child and he was upset."

"Me too."

"We can't afford the bail…."

"Why should you even worry about his bail?" she asked angrily, her eyebrows, which had noticeable gaps in them, beetling together.

Madison didn't know why she focused in on Deanna's eyebrows, but she did. Deanna must have been very upset if she was pulling out the hairs. "He was my husband…."

"*Was*, key word," she pointed out. "He attacked you. He attacked me."

"He was upset…" she repeated.

"He had no right."

"Deanna, he's really sorry…."

"I'm sorry too. He's going to have to pay for what he did to me, for what he did to you."

"I'm not pressing charges."

"I am."

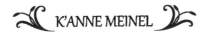

Madison sat back gingerly in the chair, her own bruised ribs hurting in the effort to try to convince Deanna to drop the charges. It was clear she was hurt and angry. "I guess we have nothing more to talk about then, do we?"

Deanna carefully schooled her features so that the hurt and anger she felt didn't spill out. "I guess we don't," she answered sadly.

"You won't change your mind? You won't let him off with a warning this time?" She had to try once more, for her children's sake.

"Why? So he can get upset again someday and hurt someone else?"

"It was an accident. He didn't mean to break your nose," she repeated exactly what he had told her when she visited him to talk about the bail. He had pleaded with her to find a way to pay it. He had talked fearfully of what he had experienced in jail so far. She'd talked to some very unscrupulous bail bondsmen since then. Their fees were outrageous and she couldn't afford them.

"I'm sure he didn't. You and I were merely talking and I gave you a ride home. I still don't understand why he went ballistic."

"He put two and two together…."

"…And what, came up with five?"

"I told him that I was in love with you," she tried harder.

Deanna realized what Madison was trying to do. "Was he like that during your marriage? Jealous? Possessive? ...Abusive?"

Madison shook her head immediately. "He had no reason to be. I never even looked at another man while we were married."

"How about another woman?" she asked pointedly.

Madison had been looking down, now she looked up into Deanna's blue eyes. "I suppressed those feelings. They were inappropriate…."

"To whom? You? Him? Your family? Or anyone else who might gossip about a woman loving another woman?" She saw the knowing look appear in Madison's eyes. "Yes, I realize how much people gossip around here. I know how much a part of that you are, to a degree. No, I don't think you gossip, but I know it bothers you if there is any part of any indiscretions aired. Your divorce, the reasons for it. What if they find out you and I were lovers? That we hooked up the other night?" She saw the look in the redhead's eyes change to genuine fear. "I won't say anything. I thought we were friends. I thought we were *more* than friends," she finished sadly.

"We are friends. We are...."

"What? Friends with benefits?" Deanna was angry. She had finally told Madison she loved her. She had realized her mistakes of a decade before. She had fully disclosed what had happened to her. She'd been honest and open, and hurt and betrayed, all in a matter of a few short hours. Her life right now was not what she had envisioned.

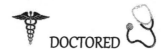

"No, it wasn't like that! I loved you," at the look of hurt in Deanna's eye she amended that statement, "I love you."

"You have a funny way of showing it."

"What? I should let my husband," she slipped, "*ex*-husband rot in jail because you want him to be punished for a mistake he made? Are you sure you aren't taking it out on him because he knew me intimately?"

"Yeah, that's why, Madison. He's seen you naked so I want him to go to jail for that," she said sarcastically. Her hand started to come up to her eyebrow and her fingertips started rubbing along the hairs that were left.

"Stop that," Madison said automatically, seeing the gesture.

Deanna almost smiled, but remembered their conversation. "He has to realize you don't belong to him anymore. He doesn't have the right to get angry like that. You have the right to date anyone you wish."

"Yes, I think he realizes that now. He was hurt. He lashed out like the child he is. It's why I divorced him, I got tired of his childish behavior."

"I'm sorry, Madison, I won't drop the assault charges," she said with finality.

"I'm sorry too, Deanna," she answered sadly and got up to leave.

"Madison, I don't want to lose you," she tried one more time to get the redhead to see reason.

"You already have," she said quietly as she left the office.

Madison couldn't afford the second mortgage on her home. The interest rate alone would kill her and the rate the bail bondsmen offered her wasn't much better. She knew Scott would be good for it, but she also knew that he expected her to take care of it for him. She couldn't. She just couldn't put her children's home in jeopardy. He pleaded with her, he guilt-tripped her. After what she had told him about her love for Deanna, he really laid it on thick. She finally stopped visiting him since she couldn't help him. She heard that he lost his job since he was stuck in jail until the court date. She also found out there had been several other incidents, that was the reason his bail was set so high. She had thought the bail was set so high because Deanna was a Kearney, because of her prestige and connections. She felt bad for that, for thinking that about Deanna. It was all just such a horrible situation.

The day of the trial, Madison took off from work. Her bruises had faded and she had avoided Deanna around the hospital like the plague. Because of her status, she had been able to avoid being put on Doctor Kearney's surgical service. She reassigned her own nurses time and again when she was. She wouldn't talk to Deanna and it seemed the doctor felt the same. Her facial bruises slowly faded, Madison saw, as she surreptitiously watched from afar.

Madison wasn't surprised when Scott was levied a rather large fine. He would serve no further jail time and was let off for time served. The judge, however, warned him that his vicious temper would do him no good and he was ordered to seek counseling for it as part of his probation. Another expense that he couldn't afford now that he didn't have a job.

"It's all that bitch's fault," he hissed at Madison as they left the courtroom. "What the hell do you see in her other than a large checkbook?"

"I don't see her, Scott and I'd appreciate it if you would keep what I told you quiet."

"It's all her fault," he repeated. "She didn't have to pursue this."

"Yes, Scott, she did."

Deanna hadn't appeared in court. The judge took the statement from the police and from her lawyers. High-powered and very expensive lawyers appeared on her behalf. Her x-rays and the damages to her person were taken into account. That, along with his past behaviors had determined his fate.

"What do you mean? I barely hit her?" he reasoned outside of the courtroom.

"You kicked her. You cracked her ribs," she countered. "You kicked me!" She was looking at him as though for the first time. He had behaved like a petulant child who hadn't gotten his way.

"You know I didn't mean it," he tried to contend. They'd had this same conversation many times.

"Yes, Scott, I know you think you didn't mean it. I do think you need help. I'm glad you have to see someone about that temper of yours."

"How the hell am I going to afford that? I no longer have health insurance now that I lost my job!"

"Well, I guess you are going to have to get a new job first thing then."

Sarcastically, he answered, "Yeah, with this on my record, that's going to be easy."

"You did this to yourself," she pointed out.

"That bitch did it to me," he nodded towards the hired suits that had just left the courtroom.

"No, Scott, you did it. You should have stopped. Nothing happened," she was grateful she hadn't told him that she had slept with Deanna, his rage would have been something to behold. She regretted telling him anything at all about Deanna. She now realized the childish behavior he had exhibited in all the years she had known him. While endearing at first, he had never developed into the adult he should have been.

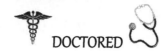

"Do you really want it known that you're in love with a dyke?" he asked meanly, with a hint of a threat in his tone as he hissed the question.

"What do you mean?" she asked warily as she began to back away from him.

He grabbed her arm to hold her in place. "I mean you better find a way to help me pay for that fine or I'm going to start telling your friends exactly what you told me." He changed his voice to mock a woman's. "I loved Deanna in Africa, Scott. I've fallen back in love with her." His voice returned to normal, with a threatening overtone as he continued, "How do you think that will look? Do you really think people will let you keep the kids when I get through with you?"

"I told you that in confidence," she hissed back, horrified that he would use it against her. This was blackmail. He knew very well that gossip around the hospital was prevalent. She'd never live it down. Threatening the kids though, that was the last straw!

"Yeah? Then you better help me pay for this fine or I'll talk to Bonnie or Beth or social services…" he let the menace hang in the air.

"You okay, ma'am?" a police officer had noticed Scott's hand on her arm and the expression on her face.

Scott let go immediately and stood up straight. Madison staggered back, showing she had been trying to get away.

"No, officer, I'm not," she said and saw the surprised look in Scott's face. "He was just threatening me. Blackmailing me actually, over the fine he just received in that court," she nodded towards the courtroom they had just exited.

"I was just kidd–" Scott began defensively, but the officer wasn't buying it. He immediately signaled to someone and before Scott knew it, he was in handcuffs again and being read his Miranda rights. "You can't do this…it's all a misunderstanding," he tried to say, but no one was listening to him and Madison stood back, letting it happen.

Madison went down to the police station and gave her statement. She explained fully how he had threatened her and was trying to blackmail her into paying off his fine. This, added to the fact that he had just appeared in court, led to another arrest. Madison, upset at what she had done, left the police station shaking.

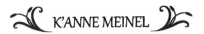

CHAPTER TWENTY-NINE

Madison tried to find Deanna to apologize. She'd realized that the doctor had been right and she had possibly thrown away any hope of a relationship with her. She also realized she didn't care anymore what her coworkers and friends might think about her being in love with a woman. That was drilled home when she phoned her mother to catch up and confessed to having Scott arrested. Her mother had been horrified to realize what she had done, hadn't listened to any of Madison's objections or attempts to explain, and had completely sided with the *man* in her life, even though they were divorced. Madison had almost confessed that she was in love with a woman out of sheer pettiness, but knew that it wasn't the time. Her mother was traumatized enough over Scott's imprisonment and her involvement in it. Catholic guilt was heaped on her shoulders.

Madison realized she had allowed her own fears over what others might think to rule her life. She had walked away from the only woman, the only person, she had ever truly loved. To find out after all these years that Deanna had loved her too, despite everything, she should have been happy and over the moon in love with her. Instead, she was trying to find her to apologize and had started to wonder if she was avoiding the redhead.

"Hey, have you seen Doctor Kearney?" she asked at the nurses' station on four.

"Oh, she's down in the E.R. today causing trouble," Bonnie grinned. People loved the courteous doctor, but there were a few, and those were usually doctors, who didn't because she told it like it was. She was honest, straightforward, and usually more knowledgeable than they were. They resented her for it and let it be known.

Madison grinned knowingly, but didn't comment. "Thanks," she answered instead and headed for the stairwell.

"You think something is going on with those two?" Beth asked as Bonnie and she watched Madison walk away.

"C'mon, Madison was married to Scott. Remember?" she scoffed.

"I heard Scott is in jail," Alyson commented as she walked up with a chart.

"He is?" the other two said together.

Alyson looked up, surprised, as though they should already know about it. "Yeah, he broke Doctor Kearney's nose. Didn't you know?" Inside she was thrilled to be the one to tell them and spread the tale. Kudos to her.

"No," Bonnie gasped.

"Do you think it was over Madison?" Beth speculated.

And so the gossip mill continued at the hospital, getting more fanciful with each telling, until there was very little truth in it.

"Dr. Kearney, may I have a word with you?" Madison asked politely when she found Deanna attending to a woman.

"Just a moment," she dismissed absentmindedly as she discussed things with her patient.

"No, I didn't say it was the Guinea worm. You get that by drinking from stagnant ponds or bodies of water that may contain water fleas. Those bugs carry the larvae and when ingested, infect the host. The larvae will grow and develop inside the host's body. After a year the female worms will start to crawl out of your skin."

"So I have a Guinea worm?" the woman asked as her son looked on fascinated at what the doctor had just told them. She was better than Google.

"Ma'am, that's why I asked the questions after your son said you'd developed a fever, swelling, and localized pain after a worm came out of your skin. Again, have you been anywhere that you may have drunk the local water that might not have been clean?" she asked patiently.

Madison nearly smiled. So often patients would check on the web before they came to be treated. The odds of this woman having a Guinea worm were pretty far-fetched but, since Deanna was an infectious disease specialist, she'd been called.

It turned out the woman did have worms, not Guinea worms, but worms nonetheless. They were working their way out of her skin slowly, a few millimeters at a time, and the only way to get rid of these was to pull them out.

"We'll start you on antibiotics, but if this is a Guinea worm infection, there is no known cure or treatment. All we can do is keep pulling them out as they appear," Dr. Kearney explained.

The woman was impressed with Dr. Kearney's manner and knowledge, and promised to come into the walk-in clinic daily to have the worm, or any others that might appear, pulled out of her skin. Madison swallowed hard at the idea, but being in the medical field she had seen worse.

Once Deanna was done with her patient and had given her directions to the waiting nurse, she turned to Madison. "Was there something you wanted?" she asked professionally.

"Yes I needed to ap–" she began, but just then the alarms at the entrance of the Emergency Room went off as a young man charged in.

"Where is he?" he shouted, brandishing an automatic rifle. "Where is he?" he screamed as several people backed away.

Deanna froze where she was standing at the end of her patient's bed. The boy was not full grown, but he was wearing gang clothing, a bandana around his forehead, and holding the gun as though he knew how to use it. Madison stared as a security guard jumped him, knocking him to the floor.

Several people jumped on him as he struggled with the guard. The gun went off into the ceiling, the loud report of it echoing in the Emergency Room, creating panic with the personnel and patients. Deanna stood frozen where she was as she watched the drama unfold. Madison looked at her curiously, wondering why she didn't react. Several people struggled with the boy until someone injected him with something and he soon slumped underneath the pile.

"Get him handcuffed," one of the attendings called. They soon had the young man in handcuffs, in a bed, and the gun was confiscated. The clip held twenty rounds. That news made several people shudder.

It was only when the young man was in a bed and the curtains drawn that Madison noticed Deanna react. She seemed to grab the end of her patient's gurney to steady herself, before drawing a deep breath and walking away.

"Dr. Kearney? Deanna?" Madison called, but was certain Deanna never heard her as she stepped into an elevator and the doors shut. The next day Madison heard through the grapevine that Dr. Kearney had quit on the spot and emptied her office. The hospital was all atwitter.

CHAPTER THIRTY

"Hello, may I speak to Doctor Kearney?" Madison asked formally at the gate. She'd had the devil's own time trying to remember the way to Deanna's home in this exclusive community. She'd driven down the wrong road more than once and she knew that the suspicious glances her old minivan was getting in a community full of expensive vehicles might result in the police being called. Still, she persevered and finally she recognized the gates and pulled up to the box and pressed the button.

"Who is calling?"

"My name is Madison M–MacGregor," she stuttered, almost giving her married name.

"One moment please," the disembodied voice came through the speaker box. Madison waited there, hoping her van wouldn't overheat as it idled. Finally, almost majestically, the gates began to open inward. "You can go in now," the voice came back to say.

"Thank you," Madison called over the noise of her van before putting it into gear and starting up the drive. She'd noticed the grounds the other day as they left, but had not really thought about it at that moment. She'd been too caught up in being with Deanna and realizing that they were in love, the shock of what the blonde had told her, and meeting her son.

Madison drove up the fairly long driveway, which curved through manicured lawns and into a large circle in front of the mansion. That night so many weeks ago, she hadn't noticed the house. She'd been wrapped in Deanna's arms, ready to be taken she'd wanted her so badly, heatedly making out in the back of the limousine together. She didn't even recall going up the sweeping staircase to that magnificent bedroom. She certainly remembered making sweet love to the attractive blonde. It had been very mutual, the desire to please, the desire to touch, the…desire. She couldn't kiss her enough. She wanted her skin against the blonde's, she'd almost wanted to crawl inside of her to get close enough. It had been sweet, time and time again, as they assuaged their pent-up need ten years in the making.

Parking the van, she looked up at the imposing wood doors, the same maple color she had noticed inside. They were beautiful and now she noticed the crest on them, carved and impressive. As she cut the engine and got out to approach them, they were opened.

"Hi," said the nine-year-old boy who recognized her. "You're Mrs. MacGregor, Maddie, right?"

"Ms," she said, automatically correcting him.

"Oh, sorry," he answered. "My mom is out back," he told her courteously. "If you would come this way?"

Madison had to wonder at the impeccable good manners that the young man displayed. Were they born with that or was it taught? Her own children, only slightly younger than this boy, weren't nearly this polite.

She looked about curiously as he led her through the foyer and past the staircase to a part of the house she hadn't seen when she'd been there last, through what was obviously a morning room to a patio and down some stairs. As she noticed Deanna lying next to a pool, she also saw an incredible sight reminiscent of Africa. Running across the lawns that swept up to the pool doors was a large cat, a caracal that she had last seen so long ago. This one was full-grown and running at full speed towards the woman they were approaching. Just before they got there, Madison stopped momentarily to watch as it dove on the woman on the chair.

"Ooof," the woman let out as the full weight of the animal fell on her. "Spot!" she gasped when she got some breath back. "Jeezus, couldn't you warn me?" she looked up as her son's shadow fell on her.

"He got you good," he started laughing like any other normal boy would.

"Yeah, he got me good," she grinned as she turned the huge cat onto its back to pet it. It was obviously pleased with itself as it started purring loudly. Madison could hear it from where she was standing and observing. It looked up at her with its odd eyes, the tufts of its ears making it look like a lynx of some sort. It stopped purring abruptly as it realized it didn't know her. Madison froze as it got up off the woman and came over to smell her.

"It's okay, he's still a kitten," Deanna told her, seeing Madison's stance.

"A kitten?" she squeaked out.

"Yeah, they take time to mature."

The cat, deciding she was harmless, rubbed against her a little, not realizing its size, and actually moved her slightly before something else distracted it and it went bounding off after a leaf. The boy ran off after the cat.

"That is Spot," Deanna announced, amused.

"Spot? Yeah, I can see why you call him that," Madison returned, sarcastically.

Deanna grinned up and indicated a chair. "Well, he's a lot of contradictions."

"As are you," Madison agreed as she sat down primly.

"So, what's up?"

"I was wondering if I could talk you into coming back to the hospital," she began.

"The hospital sent *you?*"

The redhead shook her head. "No, I came on my own."

"Well, they can't pay me enough to come back. Besides, the contract is up this week and I'm opting out."

"Because of the incident in the E.R.?"

Deanna nodded. "Yes, that, and I'd already decided to open my own clinic up in Santa Barbara."

"You're opening your own clinic?"

The blonde nodded again as she squinted through her glasses. "Yeah, I've been thinking about this for a while and I think it would be best if I did things my way in my own clinic. That way, people can come to me to be taught or for my skills. I can do what I want, the way I want it."

"Wow, that's quite an undertaking."

"Yeah, I'd been looking for a place and found it about three months ago. It's taken that long to get it in shape and get the licensing I have in mind from the State of California. Fortunately, this is a progressive state and they allow for the different," she indicated the cat that was now wrestling, claws sheathed, with the little boy. "I found a house a couple weeks ago."

"You're moving up there?" Her heart began to sink. That meant she was going and wouldn't be back. Well, Madison could visit. Santa Barbara wasn't that far from Los Angeles.

Deanna nodded again, her eyes, invisible from the redhead, watching her reactions carefully. "Yes, it's time to stop living on the family's name and make my own," she indicated the grand house and grounds. She smiled, knowing it didn't mean anything as she had made her own name with the Cooper-Aloe formula as well as her own innate skills. "The house is beautiful. Roman and I are going up tomorrow when I return him to school to take a look at it. You want to come along?"

Madison wanted that more than she could say, but she tried to be cool about it. "I'd have to bring the kids and now that we have their dog..." she stopped talking.

"Well the kids are certainly welcome, but is the dog potty trained?"

"Mostly," she replied with a defeated voice. Since Scott's incarceration she'd had the full responsibility for the beast.

"Well, I'll just leave this beast," she said as the cat returned and climbed into her lap like he belonged there, "home with Aura." She started hugging the large cat, but it took off to run with the boy who ran by. "Nice huggling you, Spot," she laughed.

"Huggling?" Madison teased as she watched the large cat run off like something from National Geographic.

"Well, he is hard to hug and I love cuddling with him, so it became huggling."

"*That* makes sense," she laughed.

"So what brings you out to the Chateau?" she joined in the laugh.

"The Chateau?"

"Yeah, Dad bought a chateau here in Southern California and the name stuck," she indicated the large mansion.

"Gawd, this is beautiful," she breathed, looking around at the manicured lawns. The boy was wrestling again with the large cat, giggling. "He really gets a workout," she commented.

"Spot is so playful. He's better than a dog somedays."

"How do you feel about dogs?"

"I love them, but I still think yours should stay home tomorrow," she grinned.

"I'll get a kennel," she promised and then worried about the additional expense. Without Scott working, and in jail for who knew how long, she had no child support to help her make ends meet.

"What were you just thinking?" the astute blonde asked, watching carefully.

Sighing, Madison decided to level with her. "I had Scott arrested again after court the other day."

"What?" Deanna sat up, surprised. Her lawyers had told her his penalties, but she hadn't heard this tidbit.

"Yeah, he was grabbing me and trying to blackmail me into paying his fines. He wanted me to take out a second mortgage on the house or he was going to spread rumors about us. He wanted the kids involved with social services too."

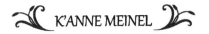

"He what?" Deanna suddenly sounded angry, almost ominous.

"Yeah, and when he wouldn't let my arm go at the courthouse, a cop asked if I was okay and I said no. Scott was surprised that I told them exactly what he was try to do. I was too," she confessed.

"Why did you?"

"I'd had enough, and when he threatened the kids," she shook her head sadly. "I'd put up with his childish behavior for years. It's why I divorced him. I was done raising a big child along with the other two. I loved him, I thought, but…" she left off.

"But what?" Deanna asked softly.

"I didn't realize what love was until I saw you again," she looked up briefly as she said it, starting to cry.

"We had a few things to work out you know," she said equally as soft and made no move to comfort the redhead.

It was a tense few minutes as Madison tried to get her emotions under control. Watching the boy with the large cat helped distract her and allowed her to take deep breaths. Finally, she nodded and swallowed, wiping her nose on her sleeve. Sniffling one more time, she asked, "Do you want to try again?"

"We shall see," Deanna answered without committing.

"I do need to apologize. You were right about him," she put in, hoping to sway her.

Deanna shrugged and looked out at her son and cat.

CHAPTER THIRTY-ONE

"So, we're going where?" Conor asked for what must have been the fourth time.

"Santa Barbara," Madison answered patiently as she packed a lunch for them all. Deanna had offered to take them out, but Madison wanted to contribute something to this trip. There was no way she could compete with what Deanna had so she wanted to do this.

She had stayed a couple of hours watching the blonde interact with her son and the cat who had proved to be just an overgrown softie. He was playful like any kitten and tired just as easily, falling asleep leaning again Madison who was learning all his favorite scratch spots. When he began to purr it was a deep rumbling and then he must have forgotten he was purring as he started to drool. Deanna had laughed as Madison jumped up and away from the amount of drool coming out of the big cat. He'd looked up sleepily at her wondering why she had woken him, his expression clearly said, "What?"

"He purrs backwards," Deanna told her.

"He what?" she asked, confused.

Deanna started laughing. "I think he forgets he is purring and the saliva starts leaking out…he purrs backwards." She made it sound like a perfectly plausible explanation for his drooling.

"Is that a real thing?"

Deanna was giggling as she shook her head and Roman joined in at the joke they had just played on the trusting redhead. Madison grabbed a pillow and threw it at the both of them, which led to a pillow fight. Spot wanted nothing to do with it and left the humans to this disgraceful display of behavior that didn't befit his dignity. It didn't stop him from grabbing a pillow, hugging it close, and starting to kick at it. Deanna had to grab the pillow to keep it from being ripped to shreds by his back feet.

"So she has a lion?" Chloe asked, almost fearfully. They had heard Madison's story about visiting Deanna's home.

"No, it's a Caracal," she corrected gently as she finished up the sandwiches and added chips to the large bag of picnic lunch she had packed. She wondered briefly if she should add drinks, but didn't have a way to keep them cool, and then she heard the honk of a horn outside the house.

"They're here," Conor called from where he looked out the front window. He recognized Deanna's Rover. "There's a boy with her," he said importantly.

"That's Roman, Dr. D's son," Madison said casually.

"She's got a son?" Chloe asked and then ran to look too.

Madison finished packing the lunch, adding water bottles, and then lugged the zippered bag to the front door just as the doorbell rang. Fluffy sprang into action immediately, barking furiously at the 'invading hordes' in *his* home.

Nothing would shut him up until they answered the door so Madison put down the bag and opened the door. "Hello," she said over the barking dog who stopped to look at the people on the doorstep. He eyed them distrustfully.

"Hello," Deanna said brightly and Roman parroted her. "Are you all ready to go?" she asked as she eyed the dog too.

"Yep, just have to grab my purse. I made us sandwiches," she indicated the bag then scooped it out from under the interested dog's inquiring nose.

"Here, I'll take that," Roman offered immediately. Then he noticed the two younger kids eyeing him, almost as much as the dog had.

Deanna noticed their mutual interest. "Roman, I'd like you to meet my children. This is Chloe and Conor. Kids, this is Roman, Dr. D's son."

In typical kid fashion, all the kids nodded shyly at each other and then pretended not to really see each other, glancing back and forth.

"Do we need anything else?" Deanna asked helpfully.

"I have to put Fluffy on a leash," Madison added and went to the table in the hall.

"Why don't you kids put that in the back of the Rover and get in the back seats—you all decide where you're going to sit," Deanna ordered them and Roman turned, carrying the bag, followed by the other two eager kids.

"Wait, grab jackets," Madison warned them and both grabbed them off the couch where she had lain them earlier in preparation for the trip.

"Do you have a jacket?" Deanna asked helpfully.

"Oh, I forgot," Madison said and put the leash on the dog as he lunged to follow the children. She handed the leash to Deanna and opened the hall closet to get her own jacket. Madison was surprised when Deanna helped her put it on one-handed. She wasn't used to being helped, even Scott hadn't done that. She smiled bashfully. Grabbing her purse, she reached for the leash.

"I take it we're taking the dog? No kennel?"

"I couldn't afford one," she admitted sheepishly and attached the leash to the dog's collar.

"I've got him," Deanna said helpfully, accepting the situation with no question, and pulled the eager dog to her side saying, "Heel," very firmly and authoritatively. The dog looked up, surprised, as though he had never heard anyone give him a command before. Strangely, he only pulled slightly on the leash as she pulled back once again and repeated the command. She patted him on the head when he listened, not completely, but enough that she praised him with a "Good boy."

Roman was in the far back of the Rover with Conor. Deanna put Fluffy on a seat next to Chloe and Madison got in the front passenger seat.

"Are we ready? Everyone in seat belts?" Deanna called to the kids.

"Fluffy isn't in one," Chloe teased.

"Well, tell Fluffy that he should get in one," she teased back as she started the car and looked at Madison with a smile. "We're off, vroom, vroom," she said and Roman called from the backseat.

"You have to put it in gear, Mom."

"Oh, that's what's wrong," she teased and put it in drive and carefully pulled away from the curb.

As they pulled out, Madison began to remember the long drives from Mamadu to Lamish in another Rover a long time ago. She was amazed that the kids had started chatting, oblivious to the adults in the front seats. "Do you want some music?" Deanna asked cordially.

"That would be nice," she answered and was surprised to hear a symphony start playing when Deanna turned on the music. She quickly turned it off and turned to a local rock and roll station with current hits to listen to as they made their way to the 405 freeway heading north. They all enjoyed the music and Madison was surprised her kids even knew some of the songs. Roman encouraged them to sing along and the adults joined in. Madison wasn't surprised that Deanna could sing. It wasn't particularly pleasant, a bit off-key, but she could sing and didn't hesitate to do so. They all enjoyed themselves as they turned from the 405 to the 101 and headed west towards the coast.

With traffic, it took well over an hour to get up to Santa Barbara. Roman pointed out things to the younger kids since he made this trip weekly, and Madison listened, learning more about Deanna than she had known. "Yeah, my school is up here, so when Mom moves up here I don't have to stay in the dorms anymore. It's fun though. There are lots of kids from all over that live there," he told Chloe and Conor.

"Mom, how come we don't go to a school where we would stay overnight?" Conor asked.

"Oh, that's a very special school. You'd miss me, wouldn't you?" she teased.

"Do you miss your mom?" Conor asked Roman.

"All the time, but it's better now that we live on this coast," he said importantly.

"Where else did you live?" Chloe asked as she turned in her seat to talk to the older boy. Her hand was resting on a happy Fluffy who was panting and trying unsuccessfully to put his nose out a window.

"We lived in Boston for a while, but my cousins were mean. Before that, we lived in South America for a while."

"South America? Where's that?" Conor asked.

"It's south of here, dummy," Chloe said disdainfully.

"Chloe," Madison warned. "Mind your manners."

"It's a whole continent," Roman explained. "We lived in the jungle with my mom's friends."

"In the jungle?" the boy was wide-eyed.

Madison found it fascinating how accepting of the lifestyle the boy was. He had no idea how special and different it was. Her children were fascinated by this biracial child that had done so much and done such diverse and unique things. She was relieved that they hadn't said anything about the difference in skin color that he had from blonde-haired and blue-eyed Deanna. They accepted him completely and easily. She envied that in the children. She glanced back at Roman and smiled. He really was a good-looking young man and she hoped his manners would rub off on her own children. She had studied him yesterday and decided his physical features were very similar to Deanna's.

"There's Ventura," he said, pointing at the beach they were passing on the 101 heading north now. "I've seen dolphins out there."

"Have you ever petted a dolphin?" Chloe asked seriously, she had a penchant for those animals.

"Nope, have you?"

"Nope."

The conversation continued and Madison realized Deanna was smiling and nodding along as the kids exchanged information. The radio was low enough that their voices carried in the SUV.

When she got to Santa Barbara, she turned into the hills and wound around until she came to a set of gates not that much different from the house she had in Los Angeles. She pushed a code into the security box and the gate began to swing inward. She waited until it was completely open before she drove in. The driveway went up a rather steep hill and at the top was a one-story house that spread out over the hilltop. They drove around to the back of the house and parked in the driveway in front of a four car garage that went into the hill itself. The rock around the outside looked like it had been quarried from the hill and it lined the driveway like cobblestones and also lined the sides of the garage and up the sides of the house.

"Cool," Conor breathed and his exclamation was echoed by Chloe.

"Is this the house you found, Mom?" Roman asked unnecessarily.

"No, I thought we'd just start going to strangers' houses and see what we find," she teased and then turned back to grin at the boy who laughed at her sarcasm. "Come on, you kids. Let's go check out my new house."

They all got out of the car including Fluffy, who immediately started sniffling the foliage around the house and lifting his leg. "Is he fixed?" Deanna asked Madison.

"I have no idea, good question," she answered, wondering if Scott had taken care of that or if she would have to.

"You have the keys?" Roman asked his mother as they climbed out of the vehicle.

"Yep, right here," she patted her pocket as she waited for the dog to stop peeing and then pulled him over. "Come on F–Fluffy," she said, the name seeming to stick in her throat for a moment. She looked at Madison and pulled down her sunglasses so she could see her roll her eyes.

Madison laughed and held out her hand for the leash as Deanna pulled the keys out of her hand and unlocked a door to the right of the garage. Inside you could go into the large bays of the garage to the left or up a flight of steps into the main part of the house. They began to climb the steps and Deanna had to unlock another door. Inside was a very large kitchen with marble countertops of pearl gray color that were absolutely stunning. The wood of the cabinets was a cherry color that was lighter than most cherry wood and the inlaid designs were obviously hand-hewn. The top cabinets were all glass with a reflective mirror inside. Once the lights were on, it lit up the kitchen beautifully, showing its warmth. The ceiling was of copper that made the cherry wood look even paler. The kitchen led to a dining room and on the other side, beyond a wall, was a large living area with a big screen television already attached to the wall.

"The last owner had nowhere to go with that," Deanna indicated the sixty-inch television.

"Oh, cool," the younger kids breathed.

"Oh, look at that," Madison marveled, for beyond the living room was a patio area with an in-ground swimming pool, which was dug into the side of the hill and glass on one side to make it an eternity pool.

"Beautiful, isn't it?"

"Mom, can we go swimming?" Conor asked excitedly as he saw the pool.

"Well," Madison didn't know what to say, they weren't invited here to swim.

"Let's look around a bit more, eh, champ?" Deanna smiled down at his enthusiasm.

At the front of the house to the right of the front doors was a room that could be considered a library, but was obviously a warm den with a fireplace and bookshelves lining all of the walls. The light in the room was incredible and enhanced by strategically-placed skylights.

"Wow, this is incredible," Madison marveled.

"Isn't this great?" Deanna asked her with a smile. "I can't wait to order some books," she enthused.

"Why don't you take some from the library at the house?" Roman asked her.

"I will, but some should remain there," she answered with a smile as she ruffled his hair. It wasn't completely straight like her own, but her ruffling had it sticking on end and he ducked as he smiled.

"Where are the bedrooms?" Chloe asked.

"Across over there," Deanna pointed to a hallway beyond the kitchen and to the left of the front door. They all walked across stone floors that were of the same stone used on the outside of the house, but polished to a high sheen. A hall began beyond the kitchen area with a powder room, a laundry room, and four bedrooms off of it. Each bedroom had its own bathroom. The master bedroom was twice the size of any of the smaller bedrooms with a luxurious bathroom.

"That's a lot of bathrooms to clean," Deanna commented.

"Yeah, I'll have to interview someone to come in and take care of that for me. I wonder if they might want to work at cleaning the clinic too," she murmured as she showed off the bathroom with a sunken tub and a steam shower that was big enough for four people.

"That might be a lot to ask of one person," Madison pointed out. "Why do you need this much room?" she asked over the children, who were discussing the rooms and what should be in them.

"I'll show you why," and with that she opened the windows in the bathroom where blinds had hidden the view. The hill they were on gave them a fine view of the Pacific Ocean. Later, as she showed them around the outside of the house, Deanna found they could sit on the patio that led up to the front door and the view was incredible—the Pacific Ocean in front of them and the mountains of Santa Barbara rising behind them, the white of the stones that were visible almost looked like snow. "I'm going to have to hire gardeners. The owners apparently fired the previous gardeners for some reason," Deanna confided, looking at the overly long grass.

Fluffy started barking at something in the overgrown foliage and Madison pulled him back. "I don't want to know what he might have found," she stated to Deanna. They watched as the children ran back and forth across the lawn, the hill no problem for their young legs. "That will work up an appetite."

"Are you hungry?"

"I could eat," she teased. It had been several hours since they had breakfast.

"Why don't we go down by the pier and grab…" Deanna began.

"I packed a lunch, remember?"

"Oh yeah, sorry."

"We could probably use something to drink besides the water that I brought."

They gathered up the children and locked the house behind them as they made their way out the garage door again. Deanna showed them a large room under the house off the garage that could only be a rec room, but contained nothing but indoor-outdoor carpeting at the moment.

"That TV should be down here," Madison commented.

"I agree, good idea. It's really too big for the living room and the furniture I have in mind."

"This indoor-outdoor carpet, do you think it's a good idea?" They continued talking decorating ideas as they got back into the SUV, the children discussed the merits of different playground equipment, and the dog just wanted to go back and figure out what he had found in the jungle back there.

"Who's hungry?" Deanna asked as she drove down to the pier and parked. Taking the chorus of "MEs" as a good sign, she grabbed the bag of sandwiches and carried it while Madison managed Fluffy. "Roman, could you buy yourself and the others sodas and get me a juice?" She turned to Madison. "What would you like?"

After choosing juice, Madison looked out at the brilliance of the ocean and nearly had her arms yanked out of their sockets as Fluffy tried to chase seagulls. "God, this dog is going to be the death of me," she stated exasperatedly and watched the children run off to get everyone drinks.

"He just needs training," Deanna commented in return. "Let's grab that table," she pointed to a set of tables the city had laid out on the sand. The children should be able to find them on their return, but Deanna made sure to sit herself facing away from the ocean to keep an eye out for them.

"What's the clinic like?"

Deanna smiled as she began to describe how homey it was. She had six examination rooms and she had an option on the other side of the building, which was exactly like her own. "The way they set up the medical facilities, it's like a duplex. I'll have a lab finally," she breathed, remembering how they had flipped at some of her more outlandish ideas in L.A. She told some of the plans she had in place, how much equipment had already been delivered, and how much was set up. "The surgery is top notch and I've had some of the most advanced equipment brought in."

"Who's setting it up?" Madison asked casually.

"My staff and some of the companies I contracted with who manufacture…" she continued on, oblivious of Madison as she gushed about the new clinic.

The children returned and their conversations turned back to the house, Roman's school, and the ocean behind them. "Can we go swimming?" Conor asked again.

"You didn't bring your swimsuit," Deanna pointed out. In fact, it was too chilly with the ocean breeze, but she didn't want to point that out, not yet.

"Maybe next time, Squirt," Deanna smiled as she answered him and took a big bite of the ham sandwich she had been offered. "Mmmm, Doritos," she turned her smile to Madison, showing orange teeth from the chips.

"Gross," Madison teased, indicating her teeth with a gesture.

"What? You don't want a kiss?" Deanna murmured playfully as she took another bite of a chip.

"Oooh, gross," Conor overheard her. "Women don't kiss," he stated.

"Sure they do," Roman countered.

"Nuh uh, men kiss women," Chloe argued.

"Not my mom," he argued back.

"That's enough," Deanna cut it off before it escalated. "I'll say this…some men kiss men, some men kiss women, and some women," she indicated herself, "kiss women."

"You do?" Chloe asked wide-eyed.

Deanna glanced at Madison who had frozen mid-bite, not sure how to contribute to this uncomfortable conversation. "Yes, Chloe, I do," she said quietly, not elaborating. Children didn't always need details.

"I saw a man kiss a man at school," Conor suddenly spoke up.

"You did?" Madison gulped.

"Yeah, Sam Ryan's got two dads," he answered as though it was no big deal.

Deanna decided to challenge him. "But it isn't okay for two women to kiss? It's okay for two men?"

He thought about it as he chewed on a corn chip and then sipped his soda. "I guess it's okay if they love each other."

Deanna smiled and nodded encouragingly, but didn't say anymore. She caught a glance of Madison and was pleased at the surprise she saw on her face. She grinned to herself at how eye-opening the day had been.

They spent the afternoon playing on the beach, tiring out both the kids and the dog.

"I'm sorry we didn't get to see the clinic," Madison stated sincerely.

"There will be another time, and Roman does have to get back to school," she said as she drove him back up into the hills on different roads.

"Is this a good school?"

"Yes, they have students from all over the world, diplomats even. He can learn up to five languages and go to a prep school nearby."

"Wow, you have it all figured out."

Deanna nodded. "I had to," she said quietly. The kids didn't hear them, they were discussing their afternoon and the school and still bringing up the relative merits of playground equipment they had decided the house needed.

"Hey, I'll see you next weekend," Deanna said affectionately as she hugged Roman goodbye.

"Yep, I'll call you before bed," he promised with a smile. Turning to take a step to the SUV he held out his hand to Madison. "It was a pleasure to spend the day with you, Ms. MacGregor," he said formally.

"Thank you, Roman. I had a very nice time with you this weekend," she answered, including the previous day as she had gotten to know him.

"See you, Roman!" Conor called to him excitedly.

"Bye, Roman!" Chloe called with a smile and waved.

"See ya," he said with a big smile and grabbed his bag to put on his shoulder. "Bye, Mom," he said and headed into the large building. It was a three story edifice of white stone that stretched out on both sides of the main entrance. One side was for younger students: living quarters in the upper stories and classrooms below. The other side was all classrooms for older students with another building in the rear for living quarters. A large field behind the school was used for the various sports taught to their students—from European football, or soccer as it was called here, to lacrosse and other activities. It was truly a multi-cultural school.

"You pick him up every weekend and take him back?" Madison asked as Deanna got back in and buckled up.

"No, I don't always have the time. We have a car service that picks him up on Friday nights and usually takes him back on Sunday night. That way he can spend the weekend at home with me."

"That's why you insisted on weekends off," she verified.

"Yep, I insisted." She drove away from the school expertly and down out of the hills to Highway 101, heading south towards Ventura.

"I can see why you want to locate your clinic up here, it's beautiful."

"Yes, I am negotiating with a hospice type service where people can be taken care of long term, but not terminal patients. That way I can attend to them on site. That's why I kept the option open on the other half of the clinic as I grow."

They talked about it a bit with interruptions from the now sleepy children becoming rarer and rarer as they drove.

"I think we tired them out," Deanna commented as she pointed with her thumb to the back seat where two little children and a dog were snoring happily.

"All that sun and air, it was magical," Madison enthused. She too was feeling the effects and was sleepy, but she'd very much enjoyed the day talking with Deanna and seeing how well their children got along. She was disappointed that they didn't talk about anything personal, about their future, and she hoped to rectify that, perhaps when the children weren't around.

"Are you hungry? Do you want dinner? I kinda feel like a steak," she mentioned as they passed a Sizzler restaurant.

"We'll have to wake them," she indicated the children in the back seat.

"What if we left them and the dog inside?" Deanna joked.

"Could you imagine," Madison giggled.

They shared a laugh.

"Why don't you take us home? I'll put that tired doggie in the kitchen and I could make…" she began, but Deanna interrupted.

"You don't have to cook, and I said I wanted a steak. How about we take that Fluffy Fluffer…" she joked at the dog's name, "…home and we all go out to eat?"

"You don't have to…."

"But I want to…."

They went back and forth for a while until Madison agreed to Deanna's plan. Madison felt leaving the dog for a few hours would be okay, it wasn't really any different from when she had to go to work. The dog woke up the crabby, tired children as Madison tried to get him out of the back seat, but when she explained that Deanna was taking them out to eat they perked up happily. Eating out didn't happen very often and it was usually a drive-thru at one of the fast food restaurants. Hearing they were going to the Sizzler thrilled them; they had never been.

"Never?" Deanna teased as they set off to find one nearby.

"Nope," Chloe confirmed and then turned to Deanna, "We haven't, have we?"

"Nope," she parroted her daughter's tone.

They had a lovely dinner at the Sizzler, where they specialized in steaks and seafood. The adults had delicious meals. There was also a large buffet of fruits, vegetables, and desserts to choose from. Madison would only let the children put as much on their plates as they could eat. Anything they put on it, they *had* to eat, she told them. As a result, they tried many things and got a delicious treat of ice cream for dessert. They were stuffed and very sleepy after that full meal. Deanna had to help Madison carry them from her SUV.

"I think they will sleep well," she teased as Madison struggled to unlock her front door.

"I think I will too," she mumbled as she got the door open.

"Oh, you don't want to go out dancing tonight?"

"I have to work in the morning. I rarely get the whole weekend off," she explained.

"I was wondering about that," she admitted.

Madison led her to the children's rooms and by the time she had Chloe dressed and ready for bed, Deanna had Conor stripped. He was in his underwear and she was struggling to put pajamas on the poor, tired, little boy.

"Leave him as he is," Madison whispered.

"Are you sure? I almost got this," she answered back in the same whisper. She was struggling to get the relaxed child's arms through his nightshirt.

"Yeah, leave him for this one night."

Deanna tucked him in tight and leaned down to give him a peck on the cheek. He was a sweet boy and she'd seen the bit of hero worship he had for her own son. She gazed at him for a moment before she followed Madison out of the room. She glanced back at the second twin bed where the little girl lay sleeping. "Chloe okay?" she whispered, hearing the dog trying to get out of the children's gate in the kitchen.

"She's flat out. Today was awesome."

"I enjoyed it too," she sighed mightily, stretching her back. "I'm going to be busy furnishing the house and the rest of the clinic in the coming weeks," she confided.

"It sounds daunting and yet exciting," Madison admitted. "Can I interest you in some hot chocolate?"

"Sounds wonderful," she answered, not willing to call it a night and knowing there was more they could talk about…there was always more. They never seemed to run out of things to talk about.

Madison soon had two steaming mugs of hot chocolate before them as they discussed the various stores that Deanna would shop in for furniture. "Can't you just see a cherry wood desk in that library?"

"I think maple would look better in there. You have all that cherry in the kitchen," she gave her opinion. It went on and on and when the clock struck midnight they both jumped, not realizing the time.

"I better get going, I don't have to work tomorrow, but you do," Deanna said regretfully. She didn't want to go home. She wanted to be invited to stay over, but they had yet to resolve many things.

Sighing deeply, Madison had to agree. She had to be up in six hours and it wasn't enough, she was a firm eight-hour sleeper. She slowly walked Deanna to the front door. Deanna turned and they shared a peck, but nothing like the passion of the past. Madison worried about that the whole night through as she tossed and turned. Deanna wondered if perhaps they were just not meant to be; it was always such a struggle.

Over the coming weeks they never saw each other. They tried to talk on the phone, but with their schedules, it was nearly impossible. Deanna showed time and again that she was technologically inept as she hung up on Madison repeatedly with her cell phone. Sometimes it was impossible to get through, and then to have their conversations cut off mid-sentence was frustrating. Texting was rare with Deanna's technologically-challenged world, although she did *try*.

Madison wondered why Deanna hadn't asked her to join her in Santa Barbara, or at least invited them up again. Deanna wondered why Madison hadn't asked to work with her up in Santa Barbara; she hadn't indicated she would ever leave Los Angeles.

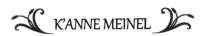

CHAPTER THIRTY-TWO

The sign was professionally made, with a hand reaching out to pet a cat inside a big circle with a slash through it. Below it read:

Notice regarding the cat: We are aware that the cat is frequently in the clinic and we do all we can to remove it, but it comes back at every opportunity. Please do not touch the cat. If you touch it, you do so at your OWN RISK.

Madison looked at it and read it twice to be sure what it said. She glanced around the lobby and saw a big gray cat washing itself on one of the chairs. Under the professionally made sign someone had written in handwritten letters, "If you are allergic, *stay out*." She laughed at the incongruity of it and made her way up to the counter.

"I'd like to see Doctor Cooper?"

"Who?" asked the receptionist behind the glass. She looked curiously at the redhead.

Madison realized her mistake immediately and wondered at the slip of the lip. "I'm sorry. Doctor Kearney, please?"

"Do you have an appointment?" she asked, almost by rote. It was obvious she asked the question all the time.

"No, I don't. If she has a minute, could you tell her Madison MacGregor is here?

"MacGregor?" she asked to confirm and at Madison's nod, she indicated a chair in the waiting room. "I'll ask."

Madison looked around, wondering if she should sit anywhere near the cat who was now looking at her suspiciously, probably wondering if she was here to remove it. She decided to sit on the other side of the waiting room. She looked at the décor before she sat down.

One of the posters read:
Deadliest animals:
Shark 10 people killed per year
Lion 100 people killed per year
Elephant 100 people killed per year
Hippopotamus 500 people killed per year
Crocodile 1,000 people killed per year
Tapeworm 2,000 people killed per year
Dog 40,000 people killed per year *Rabies
Snake 50,000 people killed per year
Roundworm (intestinal parasites) 60,000 people killed per year
Human 474,000 people killed per year
Mosquito 725,000 people killed per year
What can we do for you today?

Madison laughed at that. Those facts were rather alarming. With Deanna being an infectious disease specialist and allowing for alternative forms of healing, she wondered at the patients the clinic was fielding. She knew from the phone calls they had exchanged that she was already quite busy. She'd hired a professional marketing company and they'd made up brochures and even had cute little commercials airing, advertising the clinic and alternative medicine. Deanna was well on her way and she'd already hired two more doctors who agreed with her style of doctoring. They already had plans to have the other side of the duplex turned into an extension of the clinic.

"Madison?" a familiar voice was calling to her from the doorway.

"Hello, Deanna. I figured I should get up here on my first available day while the kids were still in school." She spread her hands to show she was holding nothing, gesturing wide. "And here I am!"

"Yes, you are. Come on," she gestured her inside to the inner sanctum of the clinic. "I wish you had told me you were coming so I could have made more time…."

"Well, I'll observe if nothing else," Madison told her.

Deanna was really pleased to see Madison. The weeks had stretched out and she couldn't believe how busy they were. It was exactly as she had envisioned. She explained what each room was for. It was a far cry from the casual conversation they'd had about the clinic before she opened. She now used many of the techniques she had wanted to try in L.A., but had been hung up by bureaucracy. Things like maggot debridement therapy were not sneered at here. She also had bee sting therapy, which helped arthritis sufferers immensely.

"People actually come in here to get stung by bees?" Madison asked, surprised.

"You'd be amazed how healthy it is to receive bee venom. It's especially helpful with rheumatoid arthritis, swollen joints, and a host of other ailments. There is a theory it can prevent adjuvant arthritis, but that needs more research before a paper can be written on it," she enthused. "It helps enormously when your body produces those chemicals in response to the venom. Of course, we have to watch out for patients who could go into anaphylactic shock from the stings. A good background check and careful observation is a must."

"Ah, Doctor Lee," she introduced the doctor to her *friend*, Madison. "I'm still learning so much from him," she explained when they were out of earshot. "He has an amazing set of books on alternative healing and medicine from China that his father translated from Putonghua or Mandarin into French," she explained. "He is now translating that into English. It's amazing!"

"So, anyone losing weight with larvae here?" she teased and saw Deanna look a bit angry.

"No, we won't be practicing irresponsible medicine here," she assured her.

Madison was very impressed with the clinic. Alternative medicine, often thought of as weird or extreme in the face of modern medicines, really did have merits and she was sold on it herself. Too often patients relied on modern technology and medicine, to the point that it defeated its original purpose. She'd like to work in this environment and wondered how to broach the subject to Deanna.

Deanna had a patient and gave Madison a doctor's coat to make her look 'official' to the patient. Deanna introduced her as a visiting colleague and the patient was satisfied with that explanation for her presence.

Madison observed how professional, caring, and knowledgeable Deanna was and she thought about how often she had observed that in her friend. From Mamadu, Africa to Los Angeles, California, she'd always been the same thorough doctor that Madison had admired. In addition to that, she was a good friend and lover. Madison had thought about that night so many times since it happened, she wondered if she was going over it again and again to memorize it.

After seeing three patients, Deanna took off her sterile gloves for the last time and said, "What say you we play hooky the rest of the afternoon?"

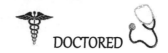

"What about your patients? I can only stay until three. I have to get home and there is bound to be traffic," she cautioned.

"I have only one consult that, fortunately, canceled and my paperwork can wait until tomorrow. Come on, let me tell my staff then you and I take off."

In short order Deanna was ready to go and they headed out in her Rover. "I'm going to have to trade this thing in soon if I continue to put so many miles on it," she said as she caressed the dashboard.

"I hear you. I'm always crossing my fingers that the van will start," Madison tried to relate, but knew that she couldn't really compare a ten-year-old minivan to a fairly new Rover that probably cost ten times what her van did.

"How about I show you how the house is coming together after all these weeks?" Deanna asked.

"Sounds good," Madison replied with a smile. She had heard about the shopping expeditions, the returns, the pieces that just didn't work out, and some of the lovely finds that Deanna got to brag about. She lived vicariously through their phone calls about Deanna's purchases. She was also envious to a degree as she had to watch every dime. She wasn't kidding about the van.

The house was lovely. The pieces showed Deanna's good taste. She hadn't just lived in the Los Angeles home because it was part of her family's properties. She had been raised in luxurious surroundings and the pieces she had chosen were warm and rich and expensive.

"Get off there," she shooed Spot from one of the leather couches where he was laying. He just looked at her as though daring her to make him get off. She did too, shoving him to the floor. "You have your own cat tree," she told him and he just blinked at her sleepily in reply.

Madison laughed at the cat tree when she saw it. It was over six feet in height and obviously made for smaller cats. It looked like a real tree with limbs and colored foliage. Still, it was sturdy, about eighteen inches around, and the cat could climb it as its sides were made up of carpeting. Later, she saw him lying on the uppermost branch of the tree. Deanna had an identical cat tree outside by the pool under the overhang for him, explaining how much he enjoyed being outside.

"He caught a rabbit on the property the other day. I think their days are numbered around here."

"Do you worry that he might get out or get away?"

"I have him micro-chipped and I have a permit from the State of California. The property is fenced and gated, so I have done all I can," she shrugged, knowing that having a semi-wild animal as a pet was a responsibility and one she enjoyed.

"Oh, this is lovely," Madison said when she saw Roman's room. He had a bunk bed with a desk and a computer under it. Posters on the wall had everything from planets to the latest bands. The boy had eclectic tastes.

"He seems to like it," Deanna replied as she looked around at the clean room.

"Do you have a housekeeper here?"

"Yeah, she comes in three times a week," Deanna admitted. "I don't have time for some things," she sighed at her frailties, something she had come to grips with a long time ago—she couldn't do everything. "I love having Roman here every night."

She showed Madison the master bedroom, which had a lovely four-poster bed not much different than the one in L.A., just different hangings.

"You bought all of this new?" Deanna asked to make conversation, feeling suddenly nervous. They were in the house alone, the housekeeper was obviously not here, and Roman was at school.

Deanna could almost sense Madison's nervousness…it was a palpable thing. She'd made sure she brushed by her a couple of times as she showed her the house and the changes they had made: from the removal and replacement of the sixty-inch television screen to the furniture in the den. "Is something wrong?" she asked, hiding the smile that threatened to break.

"I…I…don't know what you're talking about," Madison answered as she turned to leave the room, but Deanna was standing firmly in her way.

"Why did you come up to Santa Barbara today, Madison?" she asked huskily, longing to take the redhead into her arms, but not willing to make her any more uncomfortable than she obviously was.

"T…to…see you, of course. It's been weeks," she stuttered out. She was trying not to look at Deanna, but she couldn't help it. She was lovely. She'd recently gotten a haircut and her hair was standing on end. She looked so cool standing there, holding her captive without even trying.

"Is that all?"

"I've missed seeing you at the hospital. I've *missed* you."

"I'm here now," she stated the obvious.

"And I'm here too," she admitted. She was hoping that Deanna would take her in her arms, and yet was scared that if she did they would make love. She couldn't for the life of her make the first move.

Deanna couldn't taunt her anymore and reached to take Madison in her strong arms. "I've missed you too," she said huskily before her mouth descended on Madison's. Lovingly, she kissed her. Gently, insistently, she coaxed Madison's mouth open so she could plunge her tongue inside. Her fingers rose to gently caress along Madison's face, the tips skimming along her jaw as she kissed her heatedly. Her fingers raked into her red hair as she cupped the back of her head to hold her in place so she could have her way with her lips.

"Mmm, mmm," Madison moaned into Deanna's mouth. "Oh, my gawd," she breathed when she pulled back slightly to murmur against the blonde's lips. "I want you," she said before she returned to kissing her passionately.

Deanna slowly walked them towards the large, empty bed, and when Madison's legs hit the edge, she gently lowered her onto it, her body covering the redhead completely as her fingers began to look for the edge of her shirt. Fingers encountered taut skin and the redhead murmured appreciatively. The fingers slid under the shirt, raising it as they searched for and found Madison's bra and plunged inside, cupping her breast and immediately teasing the peak. Deanna pressed down mons to mons, frustrated already that there were pants and jeans between flesh.

Madison pulled Deanna tightly against her body, allowing her to maneuver her to the bed, loving the feel of Deanna's body on top of her own. She groaned aloud when she ground suggestively against her and reached between them to slip her hand into Deanna's pants, finding her gushing into her palm. "Oh, my God," she gasped.

Deanna removed her hands from Madison to pull at her own clothes, removing them quickly, her blue eyes holding the green eyes captive as she stripped. She then started on Madison's clothes. First the shirt…she couldn't resist plunging her face between the mounds of flesh that constituted her bosom. She inhaled Madison's scent, then another more pervasive smell tickled her nostrils and she quickly unbuttoned the redhead's jeans and yanked them down. She could see the panties that she wore were soused by the scent she was seeking. She leaned her nose in and inhaled, sighing deeply and lovingly. She yanked the panties down, pleased to see those red hairs that led to her charms. She reached out with her tongue to taste.

"Wait, wait," Madison gasped, trying to yank off her pants and panties that were around her knees, but her shoes were still on. Feeling Deanna's tongue on her clit was nearly her undoing as she arched up.

Reluctantly, Deanna pulled back, seeing Madison struggle to slip off first one, then the other sports shoe, yanking on the socks almost violently as she then pulled off the jeans and the panties completely. "Now?" she asked, cocking an eyebrow as she smiled and then plunged between her lover's legs, putting those legs over her shoulders so she could indulge to her heart's content.

"Oh, my God," Madison gasped as it was so quick, so violent and yet,,,so needed. She ground her center into Deanna's mouth, reaching down to hold the blonde's head in place. The short blonde hairs stuck up between her fingers as she pulled her closer, if that was possible. "Ungh,

ungh," she grunted passionately. She fell back after a moment, her back arching as the first of the waves struck her body. She bucked and convulsed as she came over and over again.

Deanna licked at each and every fold she could reach, her fingers plunging as her thumb rubbed. She felt the passion rising in the redhead, her groaning was matched by the humming that Deanna performed against her lover. More liquid shot out of Madison and splashed across Deanna's chest. She felt the redhead tensing and then her body began to spasm, nearly hitting her sensitive nose that had recently healed. She pulled back to protect it and watched the most glorious sight as Madison began to convulse in orgasm. First one, and then another…it was beautiful to watch and she had a huge smile on her face at what she had caused. She slowly rose up from her kneeling position over the side of the bed, letting Madison's legs fall from her shoulders, and covering her now cooling body with her own, but now Madison clasped her around her middle using her legs. Madison rolled them until she was on top, reaching down and plunging her fingers inside a surprised Deanna.

"Ohhh," she gasped at the sensation. Madison grasped Deanna's breast with her lips and began laving attention on the very erect nipple with her tongue. The combination sent bolts of pleasure through her belly button and straight down to her clit. It didn't take long for her to begin to feel the tingling that signaled she was coming, and when it hit her, she rode the wave enthusiastically, spasming against the redhead who held onto her as she convulsed. Deanna bit at her own lips, feeling the blood tingling back slowly into her lips and her toes. She'd been surprised by the intensity and speed of her orgasms. Slowly, she came down from the incredible high. She was so pleased, but when she finally opened her eyes, she saw Madison crying silently. She hadn't even been aware of it.

"What's wrong?" she asked.

"I'm so happy," she replied and tried to hide her face.

"If you're happy, why are you crying?"

"I don't know. Maybe I'm afraid of what will happen between us," she confessed.

From an incredible and intense high to this. Deanna could feel the anger begin inside of her. Slowly, she got up and gathered her clothes. She glanced at a surprised Madison and said, "Get dressed."

"Are you angry at me?"

"My housekeeper and son are due home soon," she answered as she turned her back to draw on her clothes. She nearly ripped her expensive and very sexy underwear in her haste to get dressed. It wasn't until she saw in her peripheral vision that Madison was completely dressed, running her fingers sexily through her long red hair, that she turned around on her. "I'll take you to your van," she said coldly and left the bedroom, not even considering that Madison wouldn't follow her.

Madison was in shock and followed along automatically. She got into the SUV and didn't say a word. She twisted her hands over and over as she thought about what to say or to do. It wasn't until they were back at the clinic that she woke up from her daze. "Are you angry with me?" she asked stupidly.

CHAPTER THIRTY-THREE

"**W**hat do you want from me, Madison?" she asked angrily. "I've tried to give you time to adjust. I've tried to romance you, to let you get to know me again. I don't want to be your fuck buddy," she cringed at the crudity of that statement. "I don't want to be friends with benefits. I want *you*," she tried to lean forward and take Madison's hands in her own, but the redhead turned slightly away, almost in shame. "I want to have you live with me, to make a family. I have a nice home, I have the practice I wanted, but then I ask myself, what do *you* want?" she finished gently, the anger dissolving

Madison looked up, surprised at the question. No one had asked her what she wanted in a very long time. The only act of independence she could remember was going to Africa, and she had paid for that defiance in various ways for years. First with her mother and her guilt trips, and then the knowledge that she had loved Deanna and not taken advantage of what she offered back then. She thought with Deanna back in the picture they could be friends, just friends, but Deanna wanted more. Madison wanted…she wasn't sure what she wanted. She wanted Deanna, but she also didn't want people to know, to judge, to gossip….

"I can't continue to do this Madison. You know how I feel," she tilted her blonde head so Madison was forced to look at her. "I finally could admit to loving you," she said softly. "I can't live with the pain of not having you around every day. I can't live in the closet," she saw Madison start at that; she'd hit a nerve. "I am out. Everyone knows I'm out. If you can't live with that, with being with me, then let me go…for both our sakes," she pleaded, tears in her blue eyes.

Madison looked back and forth between those eyes, judging, analyzing what she had just said. Deanna was right, it wasn't fair. Her indecision had cost them…so much time, so much love. Did she love Deanna enough to let her go? Did she want that?

"Go home, Madison," Deanna said gently and reached to take her hand, despite her attempts to avoid it. "You know what I want. You know I want you, I want your kids, I want a family. I want to provide for you, to replace that dilapidated old van, to take you to places when we vacation. I want…you," she finished quietly. "But you have to decide what you want. Do you want to give up everything in L.A. and move here to be with me? Do you want people knowing that you are in a relationship with a woman? Can you live with that? Can you love me through the good and the bad?" Her voice changed slightly as she continued, "Through sickness and in health, until death parts us?" She smiled at her paraphrasing, but she stopped it there as she saw the tears in Madison's eyes begin again. "You have to let me know…soon?"

Madison couldn't speak. Her throat had swollen and she just nodded. She reached up to wipe the tears with her free hand. She squeezed the other hand holding hers, hoping to convey that she would think about it, make a decision. She swallowed a couple of times before she was able to speak at all, then in a small voice she squeaked, "I have to go."

Deanna nodded in agreement. "I hope to talk to you about this soon." With that, she let go of Madison's hand and watched her get into her minivan and start it up. She wasn't reassured when Madison didn't even look back.

CHAPTER THIRTY-FOUR

Madison did think about it, the *whole* ride home. She had to be careful to concentrate on the drive, but she did think about the whole situation. She'd not been very brave her whole life. The whole Irish-Catholic guilt trips growing up, being expected to marry and produce more children. She'd revolted by becoming a nurse and having the audacity to go off to Africa. She'd paid for that over and over again. She'd done what was expected, married, produced children…but was that enough? When was it 'her' turn? When was it time for Madison to have a life, one she really wanted? But what did she want? She thought back to Madison in her twenties, the one that was scared about life and yet willing to travel all the way to Africa to help others, to get experience. She'd gotten so much more than she had expected. She'd never considered being with a woman. Finding Deanna had at first intrigued her, fascinated her, and then the curiosity of wondering what it would be like to be with her. Falling in love had never occurred to her. Finding that love had been such a precious gift. She hadn't known what to do with it when she realized Deanna didn't say she loved her too. She didn't realize that Deanna showed her love, she expressed it in the little things. That Maddie of long ago was gone…but was she really? Why couldn't Maddie, or the more grown up Madison, make a decision about what she wanted?

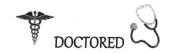

Deanna was offering her the world. Yes, she was enormously wealthy and could give both Madison and her children things she couldn't hope to have, but that wasn't the attraction, not in the least. It was the security of knowing that she loved and was loved that appealed. She knew she loved Deanna. She was sure of Deanna's love for her now. She understood a lot more now.

Intellectually, she knew she shouldn't take into account what others would think of her and her decisions. If she missed this chance, let Deanna go as she asked, she'd be giving up a part of herself she hadn't known was smothering for so long. She was happy with Deanna in her life. She'd felt so good these last months since Deanna came back into her life. Could she openly admit that she loved a woman and was going to make a life with her?

She thought about the lovemaking they had just committed. It was so different from the night of the gala. The night of the gala had been exhausting, but a coming together that was ten years delayed. She'd wanted Deanna more than she could remember ever wanting anyone. Not just sex, that was the difference from today and that night. Today wasn't really lovemaking, it was more about the raw, sensual sex, and she'd needed that too. She hadn't intended to have sex with Deanna when she came up to Santa Barbara. She'd just wanted to see her after all these weeks—to touch her, to be with her. She fed her soul. They had so much in common. They were very compatible. Not just the medical stuff, but even seeing what she bought for the house, her new and beautiful house. They were things she would have loved to have bought with Deanna, had she been here. None of the choices were anything she would have objected to.

Her thoughts returned to the sex. The night of the gala was so sensual, but on a different level. Deanna had been so loving, so caring of what Madison had been feeling…taking care of the redhead's needs first as she wanted it so badly, so urgently. And then taking them further, slowly and intricately…like a dance that wasn't going to end as she made love to her over and over again. It had been exhausting and invigorating. Each of them fell asleep in the other's arms, satisfied…finally. Madison admitted she wanted that too. The lovemaking, the easy affection, the attention. She wanted the whole package and that was what Deanna was offering.

She found herself daydreaming about making love to Deanna, about things she still wanted to try…things she thought too naughty to mention. That distraction nearly ran her off the road and she caught herself before she got in an accident.

As she approached her home, she realized it wasn't a hard decision. She would just have to be brave, ignore the gossips, and go forward with her choices. Whether they were good or bad, they were her choices, Deanna had made that very clear. She smiled as she drove into her driveway, the van seeming extra loud as she turned it off and listened to the silence around her.

"Hey, Mom," Conor called as she entered the house.

"Hey, Mom," Chloe echoed and got up from the cartoons she was watching to give her mother a hug. "Grandma called," she told her with her arms wrapped around her waist.

"Yeah? What'd she want?" she smiled, looking down at the little girl. She could see the potential young lady already sprouting in this young girl-child.

"She wondered if you were at work, were we home alone, and what we were doing? She wants you to call," she told her importantly.

"Grandma said we should come for a visit and see our cousins," Conor put in as he wrinkled his nose at that. His cousins were loud and boisterous and there were so many of them he never remembered all their names.

Madison mentally rolled her eyes. She knew what that meant. Her mother wanted her to come back east so she could verbally chastise her in person for getting a divorce, for not having more children, and for not following the more traditional role of housewife and mother. The fact that her children were home alone, watching television, without a mother supervising, probably had sent her into a tither. The fact that they were only home alone for an hour didn't enter into it. They were alone and all sorts of things could go wrong with that. Madison agreed. It didn't escape her notice that if she accepted Deanna's offer there would be a housekeeper around for the days when they couldn't get home before the children. She sighed and smiled at the kids as she left them to the television and coloring they were doing to make a phone call.

"Hello, Mom. Chloe said you wanted me to call?"

"What are you thinking, leaving those two wee children on their own out there in Los Angeles? I heard on the news there were gang shootings just last week!"

Madison didn't dare tell her about the gun in the E.R. several weeks ago. "Mom, Los Angeles is as safe as any other big city. I live in a safe neighborhood. The kids were home alone for not even an hour."

"When you were little, do you recall me ever leaving you home alone for one moment?" she asked.

Madison was picturing her mother like a chattering mother wren, all fluffed up and pecking at her. "I know, Mom," she sighed, knowing nothing she was going to say would convince her otherwise. She was tired from the long drive home and all that she had on her mind.

"And you don't even have a father figure there for them to come home to," she continued. "You should come back here to the old neighborhood. I know several young men who would be pleased to…"

"Mom, I'm not looking to get married again. I'm happy the way things are," she tried to tell her, but knew it was falling on deaf ears. A happy woman was married and having children. It didn't matter if she was compatible with her mate, she was only happy if she procreated. Mentally, Madison shook her head.

"Why I never heard such rubbish…" she began and continued on for five minutes before Madison finally had enough.

"Was there something specific you wanted, Mom? I'm kind of tired here. I've had a long day."

"What were you doing?" she finally thought to ask.

Madison debated about telling her the truth, the whole truth, but knew in her small world that this would be a shock that she might not be able to weather. She wasn't ready to admit it on some levels herself although she'd given herself a good talking to on the way home. "I visited a friend…" she began, but her mother interrupted her.

"You are off visiting friends when you should be home waiting for your children to get home from school…" she began, but Madison, finally tired of being berated her whole life, snapped.

"No, Mother, I wasn't just off visiting friends. I was visiting my girlfriend and she has made me a very interesting proposition. I've got a lot to decide and I'll let you know when I have made those decisions. Until then I would appreciate it if you'd stop yelling at me all the time."

There was silence for a moment as her mother digested being chastised in return. This didn't have a precedence. She was used to getting her own way her entire life. Her children obeyed her, although this one had given her trouble from time to time. "You watch how you talk to me, missy. You should be careful how you use that word 'girlfriend' in this day and age. People might think…."

"Mom," she interrupted angrily, "I don't care what people might think," and she realized for the first time in a long time, she didn't care. She wasn't going to allow anyone, even her mother, to bully her into feeling ashamed of calling Deanna her girlfriend. She savored that word in her brain for a moment. If she wanted it, Deanna could be her girlfriend or more….

"W–why…" her mother began huffily.

"Look, Mom, it's my life. I'm the one paying my bills, I'm the one raising my kids. It's my life," she stressed. "How I choose to live it is no one's business," she stated and finally, finally things began to click into place as she realized the truth of her words.

"Well, I never…" the words trailed off as Madison interrupted once more.

"Well, maybe you should." She was feeling good, but she no longer wished to argue with her mother. She wasn't ready to antagonize her further and she also wasn't ready to shock her…not yet, not today. "Look, Mom, I'm tired. It was a long drive and I have things to do including getting dinner ready for the kids. I should go."

"Well," she huffed again. "It's about time you put those children first and…."

"I'll call you next week, Mother," she said as though she actually meant it and hung up mid-harangue. She stared at the phone realizing how satisfying it had been to get in the last word with her mother. She also loved the fact that hanging up on her with the phone was so much more satisfying than what could be accomplished with a cell phone. It must be the physical sensation of slamming down the phone that did it. While it hadn't been pleasant, it had been long overdue. She felt herself becoming stronger by the moment as she realized it was all up to her. It was her decision. She looked around the kitchen and, hearing the kids still in the living room, headed for it.

"Hey, you guys, I have an idea I'd like to discuss with you and I want you to listen. Turn off the TV," she told Chloe who looked at her with some trepidation.

"Did we do something wrong, Mommy?" Chloe asked.

"No, baby, I just have something I wish to discuss with you two."

"What?" Conor asked, sitting up from the paper he was drawing on.

"What do you two think about the idea of moving to Santa Barbara and living with Dr. D and Roman?"

"Really?" Chloe breathed, her eyes wide.

"We'd have to change schools?" Conor asked, realizing a lot more of the social implications than his sister at the moment. He'd lose all his friends.

Madison nodded. "Deanna asked me today and I thought I'd ask you two what you think?" She knew it didn't really matter what these two small children thought. It was her decision, but it was at that moment that she realized her mind was already made up, she was just looking for the push.

It was Conor who realized what she might not be saying quicker than his sister. "Would we be like Sam Ryan?"

"Who?" Madison asked, blinking her confusion and wondering what this person had to do with anything.

"You know, he's the one with two dads. Would we have two moms?" He waited patiently for her answer as Chloe turned to look from one to the other.

Considering keeping it a secret a moment longer, Madison made up her mind. Nodding, she answered her son. "Yes, it would be like that. Would you like Dr. D to be your other mom?" She held her breath waiting for their answer. Her look encompassed both children.

Chloe asked, "Would you sleep in the same room?"

Madison hesitated, not wishing to tell them too much, but at the same time realizing that these two little urchins' opinions were the only ones that really mattered at the moment. No one, not her friends, not her family—especially her mother—mattered more. What happened between her and Deanna was personal, private, and wholly their own business, but without going into too much detail she could be honest with her children. "Yes, I love her," then unable to help herself she asked, "Is that okay?"

"Would we get to live in that house we saw? The one without any furniture?"

Madison nearly laughed aloud at her relief. Children had different priorities than who she slept with. "Yes, but it has furniture now. Deanna bought some," she confirmed with a smile.

"Would I get my own room or would I share with Roman?" Conor asked and from his tone Madison couldn't tell which way he wanted it.

"Well, if we do this, I think we would have to ask Dr. D and certainly consult with Roman," she answered carefully.

"Can we bring Fluffy?" Chloe worried.

Madison hadn't considered that. Scott had avoided her since he got out on probation again, this time with harsher restrictions. He hadn't picked up the dog and Madison had to assume that he wasn't going to. "I'm sure we can…" she began, but she realized she still had a lot to consider.

"Doesn't Dr. D have a cat? Won't he mind?" Conor worried, still thinking about whether he had to share a room or not.

Madison hadn't thought of Spot in all this. She crossed her fingers as she answered, "I'm sure they will adjust."

For the kids, it was settled. Madison was amazed at how easy it was for them. She waited until they were fed and in bed to call Deanna.

"Hello?" she answered the cell phone, seeing Madison's picture come up on the screen's caller I.D. She'd had some help with that since she was lucky to even be able to answer it. She hung up on a lot of people using the thing and was relieved to use a conventional phone instead.

"Yes," Madison said simply with a grin.

"Yes?" Deanna was confused. She'd worried all afternoon and evening since she watched Madison drive away, she couldn't help but make comparisons to her leaving in Mamadu so long ago. This time, at least she wasn't getting out of the way of a war, but there was Los Angeles traffic and that could be like a war…a million things could have happened. She had thought of texting Madison—she was learning to do that better these days—but hadn't wanted to put any more pressure on the redhead than she already had. The ultimatum had weighed heavily on her soul all afternoon long. Had she gone too far by issuing it? She'd been distracted and Roman had noticed when he got home from school and ate dinner with her. She was a bit too quiet and he'd asked her repeatedly if something was wrong.

"I'll move up there," she clarified, the joy in her voice was obvious.

"You will?" she asked, incredulous, and then to be sure, pinching herself to make sure she wasn't dreaming. The pain told her this wasn't a daydream.

Madison nodded as though Deanna could see her. "Yes, I am going to put in my two weeks' notice at the hospital tomorrow and I'm going to call a realtor too."

Deanna blinked. This couldn't be true…It was too good to be true.

At the silence, Madison got a little nervous. "Is that okay?" Had she assumed too much?

"Absolutely! Do we have to wait two weeks to see each other? Have you said anything to the kids?" She began to get excited as her mind began to race with ideas.

Madison smiled again at the enthusiasm she could hear in Deanna's voice. "We better not wait that long. I might explode," she told her.

"Explode?" she wondered at the phrasing.

Her voice lowered with longing. "I want you," she whispered. She knew the kids were asleep, but still.

"I can't wait to see you again," she admitted happily as her mind raced with plans.

"Um, the kids brought up an interesting point or two," she mentioned.

Feeling a bit of trepidation, she asked anyway, "Like what?" She was sure they could work out any glitch, she was still excited.

"Fluffy and Spot need to meet," she smiled as she said it, the names seeming incongruous to her at the moment. How unoriginal they were.

Deanna rolled her eyes as she laid back on the couch. She wished she had a phone cord to twirl through her fingers, instead she reached up and began to touch her fingertips to her eyebrows and then her eyelashes in a gesture of comfort. "I'm sure they'll be fine," she began and then thought better of it, "or they'll adjust."

"Your cat is as big as my dog," the redhead pointed out.

"But he's just a big kitten," she tried to defend him.

"Where was he today?" she wondered.

"Somehow he got locked in the rec room. I didn't find him until Roman got home." She was loving this, talking about simple things. She was so happy she could burst…explode.

"That leads me to another problem that the kids mentioned."

"Oh?" she hoped it was as simple as the last.

"Are the boys going to share a room or…?"

Deanna thought for only a second before answering, "There is room for everyone to have their own."

"You don't want to have a guest room or an office?"

"I have the den, and we can put a pullout bed in there or in the rec room for any guests. The kids should have their own space."

Madison was loving how easy this was sounding. She felt a tiny curl of fear in her stomach, but pushed it down, blaming it on nerves. She wouldn't allow any doubts to ruin how happy she was. She could hear the joy in Deanna's voice too.

"You, of course, will share my room…I'll make room in my dresser," she teased and then got serious. "Are your children ready for that?" she worried.

"Actually I was asked about that…" she teased, smiling as she did so.

"What'd they ask?" she worried…kids could be tricky. They either were clueless or could put a real monkey wrench in the works.

Madison told her and they shared a laugh at how easy they accepted things.

"Hurray for Sam Ryan and his two dads!" Deanna put in.

She then went on to tell her what her mother had said.

"Is that going to be hard?"

"Yes, but you know what?"

"What?" she asked quickly, looking to deal with any problems before they became insurmountable.

"It's time I faced up to my fears—the gossip, whatever—and did things that make me happy. I realized that today…you make me happy," she told her shyly.

"Thank you," she answered simply, humbled by the declaration. Trying to lighten up the mood she asked, "When is your next two days off?"

"I actually have two half days and then two whole days off before I work two weeks solid. Two of the nurses are pregnant and out on maternity leave at the same time. It's screwing up the schedule. They won't be happy when I give my two weeks' notice."

"Do you want to give them more?" She didn't want to hear a yes to that question, but she had to be fair.

Madison was already shaking her head. "No, I want to be with you, Deanna. I've cost us both with my indecision and worries. I can't wait to begin our life together."

"Why don't you pack your van with whatever you want to start moving and bring it up with you? We'll start putting things away piece by piece and then move you up here completely when you are ready. Do you want to wait until you sell the house?"

"What about the kids' school? If I come up on my days off, they are in school this week."

"Well, they will have to miss some, won't they? Besides, we need to get them enrolled up here."

"I don't know if I can afford…" she began.

"Babe, I was serious about taking care of you."

"I don't want to be kept…"

"You won't. You make me happy. You make me complete. You're bringing your family, *our* family, to make it complete. Believe me when I say I want to do this."

Madison still had some concerns, but thought she should enjoy what she had without ruining it before it began. It was happening so fast, but she was excited about it. They discussed things for a while before the long drive and the stress of the day caught up with her. She was yawning so much she had to get off the phone. They reluctantly hung up the phone, promising to text or call first thing in the morning.

CHAPTER THIRTY-FIVE

Madison was riding high as she went into work. The van had trouble starting that morning, but even with that annoyance she was in a great mood. Bonnie commented on it, but she just told her she'd had a great day off. Speculation began by ten in the morning that she had a new boyfriend. Madison didn't tell anyone and wouldn't speak of it, but she'd made an appointment with her supervisor and gave her two weeks' notice.

"We'll miss you around here. You've done excellent work," she was told. Madison could tell she wanted to know why she was quitting, but couldn't ask and was hoping that she'd volunteer the information. She held her tongue.

On her lunch break, she called a realtor whose signs she'd seen in the neighborhood. She wanted to list her own small house and made arrangements to meet him after work for a tour of the house, and possibly to sign a contract to sell the place. She also texted Deanna on her breaks, being careful to only do it when no one was around to see the smile on her face. She felt radiant and, for the first time in a long time, she admitted to herself that she was happy.

That night, she met the kids at the house. She got home from work before them due to the half day off. She would only be working one week of the two solid weeks she was supposed to, and her supervisor wasn't very happy about that. Still, she understood Madison was moving on, even if she didn't know where, what, or who to. Out of guilt, loyalty, she didn't know what, Madison agreed to the two solid weeks.

"Let's pick up this place," she sighed as she saw the mess the dog had made in the kitchen with the newspaper. She wondered if the dog just did it out of boredom and reminded herself to pick up chew toys at the store. Scott hadn't brought any of the dog's toys over and had only taken the kids a few times since he got out. She explained to the kids about selling the house and they got to work with gusto. It was fairly presentable before the realtor got there.

The man who showed up was a pleasant person and very personable. Madison thought he must have to be, being in the real estate business. She was surprised that property values had gone up and she might get a decent price for the place. She'd no longer have a mortgage and she was grateful Scott hadn't talked her into taking out that second mortgage as it would have worked against her now. Still, she was sad to see the place go as she signed the papers to put it on the market. The realtor agreed to have a sign up the next day and to put it onto the computer as soon as they took some pictures. Since she had a half day off the next day too, he would come over right after she got off work; it would work out well for them both. She'd just shown him out of the house and gone to tell the excited kids when the doorbell rang again. She thought the realtor had forgotten something and answered the door with a smile. That faded immediately when she saw Scott on the doorstep.

"That your new boyfriend leaving?" he pointed with his thumb at the new Cadillac that had just driven away. "Got money, does he?"

"No, that is not my boyfriend," she explained and then resented that she had to explain at all. Who she had over at her house was none of Scott's business. "What do you want?"

"I came to see my kids. Isn't that obvious?" he asked with a tone and tried to enter the house.

"I thought we agreed you were going to call before coming over?" she asked.

"Well, I forgot. And here he is," he said as the dog spotted him and came leaping through the living room, his tail going wildly, knocking things off low tables. He quickly got down so he could roughhouse with the shaggy beast.

Madison saw the mess the dog was making again and sighed wearily. She didn't know what was worse: the kids, the dog, or Scott.

"Daddy!" Chloe called when she spotted Scott crouching down to greet the dog.

"Daddy!" Conor echoed as he heard his sister and came running.

Looking over the heads of the kids, Scott was surprised to see the anger in Madison's eyes. She pointed at the dog and raised a questioning eyebrow. He quickly looked away, but not before she saw the guilty look on his face. She knew then he had taken advantage of her. He was going to leave the dog with her so he didn't have the responsibility anymore.

"How about we go out for an ice cream?" he asked to a chorus of 'yes' from the children.

"I'm sorry, we haven't eaten dinner yet and it's not convenient," Madison told him icily. She also wanted to caution the children against telling him anything about their plans…not yet, not now. She didn't need the headache that would cause and she hadn't thought about how to tell him yet.

"Well, missing dinner won't hurt this one time," he said jovially, always the good guy, always the cool dad.

"No, Scott. They aren't going." She hated having to be the bad guy, but he had done this throughout their marriage and she wasn't going to be tricked or taken advantage of. "You really should have called before coming over. We already have plans."

"What plans?" he asked, getting annoyed with her.

"That's really none of your concern. You should have called first," she told him again.

"They're my kids too and I'd like to take them out," he told her ominously.

"Of course. Please call first and we can discuss it when it's convenient." If she was agreeable, he had nothing to argue about.

"What? I can't take them out now?"

She shook her head. "No, I told you, we already have plans."

"But I wanted…" he began, but she cut him off. She could see the kids wanted to chime in and she didn't want that. They might say something she would regret. She'd slightly shaken her head at Chloe and Scott saw that. He was getting angrier, thinking there was some secret they might be keeping from him.

"I understand that," she said kindly, not raising her voice, "but you didn't call and we were just about to go out."

"We were?" Conor put in.

"See? He didn't know about it. You're making this up. Or are you going out with the boyfriend?" he pointed with his thumb again, to where the Cadillac had disappeared.

"That was not my boyfriend and it is none of your business what we are doing," she was trying not to let the anger she was feeling come to the surface. If she lost it, he would win.

"Well, I want…" he began again.

"Scott," she said firmly, "it's not convenient. You'll have them in a few days per our agreement, but I really have to go. If you'll excuse me?" she said, holding the door.

He wasn't that obtuse and got the hint. He wasn't happy about it. He'd wanted to try to talk to her about helping him with his fines once again. He'd gotten another job, but it didn't pay as much as his previous job. Sighing deeply, he got up from his crouched position, slipped the dog off his lap, and ruffled Conor's hair. "Sorry, big guy. Mommy won't let you go this time, but we'll make it up another time, okay?" he told him, firmly putting the blame on Madison.

Madison was ready to take him on, but not tonight, not now. She buried her anger deep as she let him out of the house. She leaned against the door with a sigh of relief.

"Where are we going?" Conor asked.

"What?" she turned her head to look down.

"You said we were going out to Daddy."

Knowing she'd been caught in a lie, she thought quickly. "We have to go out and get boxes if we are going to start packing to move."

Both kids got excited and ran to get their jackets. They were soon off to the store to see what boxes they could scavenge. That evening they began sorting things. By the time she was home from work after her second half day off, the sign was up in their yard offering the house for sale, and they had filled the minivan with as much as it would hold and still leave room for them all to ride. Deanna was expecting them and despite the late evening traffic they were sure to encounter, Madison set out. The van sputtered a few times and she worried about it making all the way up to Santa Barbara. The start and stop traffic of the 405 didn't help things and the 101 was just as bad. When they got to Ventura it sputtered out. She was hard put to pull it to the side of the highway with no power steering. She tried to start it a couple of times, but it wouldn't and she started to cry. It was late, it was dark, and she was tired and stressed. She called Deanna to explain and within an hour a flatbed truck was there to pick up the van. Deanna arrived too, to gather her in her arms and comfort her.

"Come on, you guys. Let's get home," she told them cheerfully as she ushered them into the Rover.

On the front seat was a cup holder with three strawberry sundaes sporting whipped cream and a cherry on top. Deanna grinned. "I thought after all that," she pointed back at the tow truck that had just finished pulling the van onto the bed and tying it down, "you could use a little lift."

Madison, despite the kids that had climbed into the back seat with the dog, leaned over and gave her a peck on the lips. "Thank you," she said with complete relief. She felt much better.

"Oooo," Chloe said, but the two adults ignored her. She'd get used to it.

They handed out the sundaes and Deanna waited until the flatbed truck with the van started up and got back on the highway before starting the Rover and following.

"What do you think is wrong with it?" she nodded to the van on the flatbed as they passed it. He was to deliver it to the house in Santa Barbara so they could offload the stuff inside.

"I don't know. It's been acting up more and more lately."

"Just getting old?"

"No idea. I think sometimes it's where I buy my gas."

"I've heard of that happening. Maybe it's time to get a new one?"

"I can't afford that…" the redhead began, but Deanna just sent her a look that was barely visible in the oncoming lights and they let it go.

They unpacked the van the next day after Roman went to school. He'd shared his bedroom with Conor after all and they tucked Chloe in on the couch. After both kids had met Spot and gotten over their initial fears—realizing he was just an overly large cat with the mentality of a kitten—they all settled down. The only problem was Fluffy, who growled every time the large cat came near. Spot could only respond in the same way. Fluffy spent the night locked in with the boys so they could acclimate him to his new home and housemate in the morning. It was just too late at night to worry about cat and dog fights.

"This is my room?" Chloe asked with awe as they began to bring the things they had packed into the house.

"Yes. Let's leave everything of yours in the middle of the room so we can choose a new paint color." Deanna suggested.

"Me too?" Conor asked, not to be left out.

"You too, buddy," she promised. "Think about what colors you want while we get this unpacked," she grabbed another box from the van.

Between the four of them and the housekeeper that Deanna introduced as Vera, they got it unpacked in record time. "The dealership will be sending a flatbed," Deanna told Vera as they got in the Rover to go shopping. Deanna insisted that they had to get furniture for each of the rooms as well as paint and, of course, register for school to start in a couple of weeks.

CHAPTER THIRTY-SIX

Madison was thrilled to wake up in Deanna's arms, in her house, knowing her children were under the same roof with her and they were going to move here permanently. She smiled up at the blonde who had woken before her and was gazing down at her.

"You know you have a freckle there," she pointed at one on the redhead's cheek.

"Where?" she smiled, causing her cheekbones to rise and move the freckle.

"There," she said huskily as she leaned in and kissed it.

"Where?" she repeated throatily.

"There," she answered and kissed another spot.

"Where?" she gasped out, enjoying the sensation.

"There," it became a game of trying to find them, and then Deanna started tickling until Madison started giggling and then shrieking. All too soon it came to an end as the children charged into the room, the dog following along for good measure.

"What's going on?" Chloe asked, alarmed, not used to seeing her mother sleeping with anyone, not since her father had left.

Both adults, out of consideration for Madison's long night, fatigue, and children in the house, were wearing sweats and dressed fairly modestly. They were laughing from their wrestling match.

"Did you know your mother is ticklish?" Deanna asked, playfully.

"No. Is she?" Conor said in delight and went to dive on the bed. Roman and Chloe jumped on the large bed too and soon the dog joined them. Only when the cat decided to come in did the dog begin to growl.

"No, Fluffy," Deanna ordered firmly.

"He's afraid of that big cat," Conor told her and Deanna wondered if the boy was too.

"Spot's just a big ole softie," Roman told him.

"Fluffy just needs to learn his place here. He's the new guy and he's welcome, but Spot was here first so they will both have to adjust," Deanna told the kids and exchanged a look with Madison that said more than the youngsters realized. They would all have adjustments to make.

"Who is hungry?" Madison asked the room at large, just to get them all out of the bed.

A chorus of "me" met her question and the kids started scrambling.

"Roman, you still have to get ready for school," Deanna called before the boy could leave the room completely.

"Aww, Mom. I thought I could stay home today and help," he tried to wheedle. Conor looked on hopefully.

"Absolutely not. Don't you have a homework assignment due today for history?" she asked.

"Oh, yeah, I forgot," he said dejectedly as he turned to go into his room.

"Is it done?" she called before he could shut the door.

"Yes," he answered and closed the door.

"Now what are we going to do with these two?" Madison asked, looking at the dog and cat eyeing each other warily. She was certain in a fight the big cat would win.

"As I said, they are going to have to work it out. They'll adjust," Deanna told her and pounced on the redhead, bearing her to the bed as she began to kiss her again and again…because she could.

"Uggh, Mom!" Chloe said from the door. She was carrying the clothes she had worn the previous day.

Deanna sat up immediately and Madison sat up behind her, looking guilty at being caught. "What can we do for you?" she asked to hide her embarrassment. Deanna was right, they were going to have a lot of adjusting to do with kids and pets.

"What should I wear?" the fastidious little girl asked.

"If that isn't too dirty, wear it again and we will unpack your suitcase later for something clean," her mother instructed her.

Chloe turned with a heavy sigh as though the adults were just too much and made her way to the powder room to change. The dog followed her.

Deanna turned back to Madison, her eyes were sparkling happily. "I don't suppose we have time for…?"

"A quickie?" Madison finished for her, her own eyes sparkling in barely held glee. She laughed. "There will be time for that later."

"Promise?" Deanna growled as she leaned her forehead against Madison's.

"Promise," she kissed her, then just as it was turning interesting the cat jumped on the bed to get some attention. Sighing, Madison got up and out of the bed to get dressed while Deanna wrestled a little with the cat.

"So, paint first or furniture?" Deanna asked.

Both children answered, "Paint," as Madison answered, "Furniture." They exchanged looks and laughed joyfully. Madison was taking some well-deserved time off while Deanna was here to help her move in.

"I think we should get the furniture first so we know that the paint we buy will match," Madison was quick to add to forestall the children from arguing.

Deanna drove them to an outlet store and they spent time checking out beds, the kids bouncing on the mattresses as Madison tried unsuccessfully to stop them. Deanna had a lot more success as she explained that if everyone did that the store wouldn't be able to sell the furniture that got wrecked.

"For someone who didn't want children, you sure get along with them well," Madison said as they walked along looking for bedroom sets together. Deanna had gone to hold her hand, but understood when Madison avoided it. She pretended it didn't hurt, but Madison had seen the look and was trying to work up the courage to be that public. After all, she had said yes.

By the time they had lunch at a small café, they'd chosen Conor's bedroom set, but been unable to find one that Chloe liked. It was like a treasure hunt. She wanted something like a princess would have, but at the same time the tomboy in her didn't want anything so girly.

"How about," Deanna began as she took a bite of her sandwich and then a sip of her soda to wash it down, "we get something similar to what Roman has, but in white? That way you can put princess stickers on the wood and later, when you outgrow them, you can peel them off?"

Madison could have kissed her for coming up with a solution to the little girl's difficult problem. She smiled widely to show her appreciation, her eyes sparkling with promises as Chloe embraced the idea. The problem had been that the little girl had never had a room of her own or a choice in her furniture. She'd accepted what was in the past, and the choices she now faced were a bit overwhelming.

"I like Roman's furniture too," Conor began.

Deanna headed off a possible problem there by saying, "Yeah, his is cool, but I like yours for the chest of drawers and the hidden door." She took another bite of her sandwich, looking innocent as she began to chew. She waited.

"What hidden door?" the boy asked, suddenly enthused again for the furniture they had picked out for him.

Deanna pulled out the brochure of the bedroom set they had bought along with the receipt…an amount that Madison had wanted to question, but the blonde never even blinked at. She showed him on the bedroom set diagram. The hidden door was something he had obviously missed.

"Ohhh, maybe I should get…" Chloe began, sounding a little envious.

Deanna looked at the little girl and shrugged. "You should have said, but I don't think it comes in white, and of course we have to find those stickers…."

The little girl debated for a moment, "Couldn't we paint the wood?"

Deanna nearly smiled as Madison's eyes went wide. The price of these sets and the girl wanted to slap paint on the wood? She waited a moment before answering, swallowing another bite of her sandwich. "Well, then your bedroom wouldn't be as nice for a princess who wants to play at being in a tree house now and then."

That settled the matter for Chloe. She wanted her own set after that, and two hours later they found it at another store. It was perfect for what Deanna had suggested, or at least the little girl thought it was.

"How did you do that?" Madison asked. She had finally worked up the nerve to hold Deanna's hand…first in the Rover in front of the children, and then in the actual stores. No one knew them up here. She would start with small steps here and continue on; it would become easier. Few, if any, really noticed. They were after the women's money, not to judge them or their values.

"I was a young girl once too," Deanna answered quietly. She'd gotten a call from the dealership. The van was fixed and ready. She didn't tell Madison how much it had cost. They were heading there now.

"Did you have a bedroom set like that?" she was curious what kind of child she had been. After all, she'd been in high school at such an early age.

"No, my parents didn't have time for frills like that, but I wanted one sometimes. Other times I was worried about advanced chemistry," she admitted with a rueful little grin.

"You had sugar and water in the gas tank, ma'am," the mechanic informed Madison.

"I what?" she asked, alarmed.

"Now, sugar alone won't do anything. It's an old wives' tale that it will gum up the engine," he forestalled her as she obviously had heard that one. "If it got in the engine your fuel filter would catch it; however, with the water added too that needed some work, so we dropped the gas tank and cleaned it out. You're lucky you caught it right away 'cause it could damage your engine," he explained.

"How in the world did that get in there?" the redhead asked, bewildered.

"Oh, kids do pranks like that all the time," he assured her. "I'm sure that's what happened, although...with the amount," he sounded a bit puzzled, as though he too was wondering if it was kids and a prank.

She was relieved it wasn't something more expensive. "How much do I owe you?" she asked.

"It's all taken care of," he said, holding up his hands as she reached into her purse for her checkbook. Glancing at Deanna who was looking up at the ceiling, Madison realized she had already taken care of it.

"Thank you," she said and squeezed Deanna's hand.

Smiling at the redhead, she was pleased she could help. They went to leave, but the mechanic stopped her again. "We also gave it a full tune up and changed the oil and air filter," he quickly told her. "If you have any other problems, let me know."

She thanked him and wondered when the oil had last been changed. She was a little embarrassed to realize she couldn't remember and was grateful that Deanna had taken care of that for her.

"Do you want to head down to your house tonight so we can pack up another load in the morning?" Deanna asked. "I'm sure Roman won't mind missing one day of school. In fact, I'm sure he'll love it."

"Are you sure? The traffic will be horrendous this time of day."

"Let's pick up Roman's clothes at the house and go. In fact, why don't you go on ahead and I'll catch up?"

"We're taking two cars?"

"Yeah, that way we can pack them both up completely. We'll have movers take the heavy stuff. That way, you can pack all the little things that you don't want broken."

"I can't afford movers..." she began and then caught herself as Deanna grinned. "Okay, okay, we'll go on ahead."

"I'll call you on the cell when we are on our way," Deanna promised as she leaned in to give her a peck on the lips.

"Ugh, Mom," Conor said as they arrived at the Rover.

"Get used to it, bucko. I love your mom and I'm going to do a lot of that," Deanna teased him. "You guys want to ride back to Los Angeles with me or with your mom? I have to go pick up Roman."

"You," they chorused and Deanna turned to Madison, laughing. "I guess I got the kids."

"I guess you do. I should feel rejected, shouldn't I? Betrayed at least?" she laughed too as she collected a couple of things from the dash, including her sunglasses, and transferred them to the van which was waiting nearby.

"I'm just the current flavor of the month," Deanna assured her as she stood by.

Madison turned with the things in her hand and shook her head. "Not just the month," she responded huskily as she leaned in for another kiss. "I'll see you at the house in Los Angeles. Don't be long, but don't speed either," she warned.

"I won't," she promised and teasingly slapped her on her rear, which caused Madison to start in surprise and turn back with a glare, which turned to laughter that they both shared.

Deanna watched as Madison started up the now smooth-running minivan and put it in gear. She didn't get into the Rover until the redhead began to drive out of the dealer's parking lot.

"Ready to go, guys?" she called to the two in the back seat.

"Ready," they said in unison.

"I just want to pop home and pick up some clothes for Roman for tonight and tomorrow," she told them as she headed home.

In quick time, she had a bag packed for Roman, grabbed all the kids' toothbrushes, and they were on their way to Roman's school to pick him up. He was delightfully surprised at their plan.

"I thought you said I couldn't miss school?" he asked suspiciously.

"Plans change," Deanna answered with a grin. She handed him a snack pack and then reached in the bag where she had two more for the kids in the back seat. The three kids chatted easily as she headed down the 101 towards Ventura, hoping she wasn't too far behind Deanna.

CHAPTER THIRTY-SEVEN

Madison didn't like making the drive back down to Los Angeles alone. It was too reminiscent of the other day. Was it really only a few days ago she'd been given an ultimatum and made the choice to change her whole life? She was so happy. She loved Deanna and today had been so much fun. She was tired though, and the traffic didn't help things. Not having the children with her was odd, but she knew they were safe with the doctor. She smiled. She had wound up with a doctor, wouldn't her mother be proud? Then she sobered. No, her mother wouldn't be proud when she found out she had chosen to live with a woman, doctor or not.

When she got to the house, she started dinner. She knew everyone would be hungry when they got there. She had warned Deanna not to stop and pick up any food. She was going to cook for them and it would be ready by the time they arrived. She didn't want to talk on the phone when they were both driving so their conversation was short. She smiled. Her lover, her partner, her girlfriend was coming home with the kids. What an odd thing to say, and yet it made her heart happy.

Since she had some time alone before the kids got there with Deanna, she quickly packed some things. There were some adult toys that she didn't want them to see. She had hoped to talk to Deanna about the toys.

She hadn't tried them yet and wondered if the blonde would be intrigued, offended, or amused. She hoped she'd be interested in trying them out. She'd bought them intending to try them herself, but felt foolish. Now, she eagerly anticipated talking to Deanna about them. She just didn't want her to see them yet, and she especially did not want the children to see them! She got them buried deep in a box and started packing clothes from her dressers, wondering what she was going to do with her furniture, when she heard someone knock on the door. Deanna must have flown down that freeway! She'd told her not to speed! She'd had no idea how close she was behind her.

Opening the door with a, "Hey, darling…" her voice died off as she saw Scott on the doorstep.

"Hi, darling," he repeated back sarcastically, looking at her angrily. His suspicions that she had a new boyfriend in her life were confirmed with that one declaration.

Madison looked down at herself to see if she had gotten dirty from packing, but could see nothing. Glancing back up, she asked, "What are you doing here? What did I tell you about calling first?"

"I want to see my kids," he said crossly. "What is with that sign?" he pointed with his thumb at the sign that was planted firmly in her yard.

"I'm selling the house," she told him stupidly, as though it should be obvious.

That wasn't quite what he meant and they both knew it. "Why?" he asked suspiciously. After all the wrangling in the divorce that she had done to get it, she was selling it now? The argument was that the children needed a home and it was logical for her to have the house since they would be living with her most of the time. He'd been relieved that he didn't have the responsibility to pay the mortgage anymore and had gladly signed it over to her.

"Because I'm moving."

"And you didn't think to inform me?"

"It's none of your business…" she began, only to be cut off.

"It is my business when I need to know where my kids are. Speaking of which, why aren't they home?" he asked.

"What? Are you watching the house?" she asked, her own anger surfacing.

"Yeah, I am, as it seems I can't trust you!"

"What the hell are you talking about? I just put the house on the market yesterday," she told him. "You saw the real estate agent driving away."

"That the guy with the Caddy?" he asked, calming himself down now that he had the information he wanted.

She nodded and crossed her arms, trying to calm her own anger.

"Where are the kids?"

"With friends," she hedged, justifying in her mind that Deanna and Roman *were* friends…a technicality. "I told you, call first and we can make arrangements. They're still coming over this weekend, right?" she asked to distract him. She'd have to talk to the kids about what they could discuss with him, but she would have to tell him about her move and living arrangements soon. She just didn't want to discuss it now with him in a mood like this. She wondered if there was a reason for the increased moodiness, beyond his being arrested. Was he taking something? She was in the medical field, she would be able to tell, wouldn't she? She knew the answer to that last question before she even finished forming it. Some people hid drug and alcohol use better than others.

He looked at her suspiciously, then satisfied with the information he'd gotten out of her, he turned to leave. Just then he saw the Rover pull up in front of the house with the kids inside. "Now, who is this?" he asked aloud and then got angry once again when he saw the woman who had caused all his troubles.

Deanna sped up when she saw the man standing on the lawn outside Madison's house. She recognized him and quickly put the car in park, turned it off, and hopped out. "Stay in the car," she ordered the kids in a tone that would normally assure she was obeyed.

"You!" he said and pointed a finger at her accusingly.

"Scott," Madison said in a warning voice.

"I want no trouble," Deanna said, her hands going wide to show she had nothing but her keys in them.

"You caused nothing *but* trouble," he answered loudly. He glanced at his kids and saw their fearful looks, which angered him further.

"Look, just be on your way and I'll…" she began, but he started walking towards her rapidly.

"You'll do nothing," he ordered her. "You be on *your* way."

"Hey, I got no beef with you," she tried, but he started poking at her.

"Scott, stop," Madison tried pulling at his arm. He shook her off as though she was nothing but a fly.

"Look, dude, you need to calm down," Deanna tried again.

"You need to stay away from my kids and my wife," he began. The kids got out of the car and started towards them.

"She is not your wife," Deanna backed up as he kept poking her in the chest to emphasize his words.

"Scott, you need to stop," Madison tried again, beginning to cry as she pulled at his other arm.

"And you need to go back in the house," he turned on her and then looked at the cowering kids. The third one drew his attention for a moment and then he focused on his own. "Get in the house," he snarled at them and they ran, the third kid looking at Deanna, who flicked her head towards the house before he too followed them.

Deanna took advantage of Scott's momentary distraction to pull her cell phone from her pocket. She may be technologically inept, but she knew how to dial 911 for an emergency.

"What are you doing?" he turned back to her with a snarl.

"I don't think you are aware, but the last time we had an altercation an order of protection was issued. You are now in violation of that order."

Fed up with being arrested and now facing the threat of it once again, he became furious. "Who the hell do you think you are?" he practically spat in her face.

"Scott, please," Madison tried again, the tears pouring down her face. She had never felt so helpless in all her life, watching this drama unfold.

"Scott, please," he mimicked condescendingly. "What, have you hooked up with this dyke?" he snarled.

Deanna answered him, at the same time speaking very clearly so that those listening on the phone could hear her: "I'm Doctor Deanna Kearney and I'm at," she looked up and gave the exact address from Madison's house. "I've got an order of protection and you, sir, are violating it." She figured even if he managed to get the phone from her, the information was recorded. Police would soon be on their way.

"Why, you bitch," he snarled trying to get the phone from her, but she pulled her arm out of his reach. He lunged for it, nearly knocking her to the ground.

"Scott, please don't! Leave her alone," Madison pleaded.

They didn't have to wait for the police. The neighbors who had helped once before were there again. "Look, mister, you've been warned before," one of them told Scott as he came running up. "Leave the ladies alone," he advised.

Scott had a new person to focus on and he turned to the man. "This is none," he pointed at the man's chest, poking him now, "of your business!"

"I'm making it my business," he bluffed as he saw over Scott's shoulder that the other neighbor had come running out.

"Yeah?" Scott responded belligerently. "You and what army?"

Deanna nearly rolled her eyes at the corny line. She was more concerned about Madison who she could see just beyond Scott. The tears concerned her, and the worry she saw on her face.

"I'll be happy to help," the second neighbor volunteered and Scott turned to see who else had arrived to stick their nose in his business. "This doesn't concern either of you! That's my wife!" he said, pointing at Madison angrily.

"Ex-wife," both Deanna and Madison said at the same time and exchanged a look. At any other time that would have been funny. At this moment though, it angered Scott and he turned on Deanna again.

"You stay out of this, you dyke!" he roared, poking her in the chest again painfully and causing her to back up against the Rover.

"Well, aren't we a cup of sugar all wrapped up in cellophane?" she asked mockingly. She smiled for added effect.

Madison tried to signal to the blonde not to antagonize him further. She saw the fist he was making and wasn't surprised when he swung.

The two neighbors saw the fist, but too late, and both were too far away to stop it.

Deanna saw the fist too. As he balled his hand into a fist and struck out at her, she ducked. He hit the hood of the Rover…*hard!* Deanna clearly heard the crack of bones breaking as he began to howl.

"You bitch! You bitch! You see what you made me do?"

She stepped aside and said, "You did it to yourself." She crossed her arms and stood there nonchalantly; she'd heard the sirens. He hadn't heard them over his yells and probably his pounding blood pressure. She was sure the pain was making him a bit upset too.

"I'm going to fucking kill you, bitch," he roared again and as he lunged, both neighbors held him back. One of them unknowingly hit his busted knuckles causing him to roar again in pain. "I'll kill you! I'll kill you!" he screamed just as a police car came up and parked.

The police clearly heard his threat. Deanna pulled the order of protection from her purse and the police took statements from everyone. Next they put a now irate and irrational Scott in the back of their patrol car. He tried to kick out the protection screen and then the windows.

"You may wish to stop by the hospital and have that fist taken care of. He's broken several knuckles," she advised.

"Thank you, Doctor Kearney," one of the officers said to her.

Deanna watched as they drove away and then she turned to Madison. During her statement, Deanna had put her arm around the distraught woman. She hadn't shrugged her off, but now she wondered if they were back at square one. The last time she had her ex-husband arrested…. "Are you okay?" she asked quietly, hoping to take her in her arms again.

Madison nodded and, surprising Deanna, put her arms around her. "Take me inside and hold me," she ordered. Deanna was happy to oblige.

They had a quiet, if late dinner, and the kids went to bed. The adults lay in Madison's bed just holding each other. "Have I screwed things up again?" Deanna finally had to ask. The redhead had been too quiet for too long and she was getting nervous.

Madison turned around and looked at her in the light of the lamp next to her bed. "I'm sorry, I've been thinking," she confessed.

Deanna didn't know why, but she tensed up. "Care to share?"

"I'm going to have to file for full custody and an order of protection of my own," she said sadly.

"Do you want some help with that?" she asked gently, holding her tight.

Madison nodded; she had no idea how to do all that. "Do you know a good lawyer?"

Deanna pulled back and her blue eyes were bright in the light. "Are you serious? I'm a Kearney!" she said proudly.

The redhead realized how silly that must have sounded. Of course Deanna knew a good lawyer! She probably had a fleet of them. They shared a laugh at Deanna's indignant statement. "We better get some sleep if we are going to pack up tomorrow," she said as she laid her head on Deanna's shoulder…because she could.

Deanna gently laid the two of them back down on the bed. It wasn't until she was sure Madison was asleep that she extricated herself from the redhead's grasp. She tiptoed in and checked on the kids, glad she had left the dog up in Santa Barbara. She returned to the bed to curl around Madison protectively.

It was then that Madison stopped pretending to be asleep and smiling, actually went to sleep.

The next day they filled both the vehicles until all that was left was the bulky furniture. "I don't want all this," Madison told Deanna. "Some of it just won't go with your nice stuff," she confessed.

"You take what you want. Anything you want, we will make it fit. Otherwise, we'll donate it to a charity. Someone can use it and benefit from it. Or you can have a garage sale and keep the spending money," she advised.

"Well, the realtor said it would sell better if it was furnished, so for now I'm going to leave it. There are a couple of pieces that I like," she reconsidered now that she knew Deanna was all for it.

They were about to leave when a nice Lexus pulled up to the house. Deanna walked casually, but protectively, in front of Madison. The kids were already in the Rover. She signaled them to stay there. "Can I help you, gentlemen?" she asked as they got out of the nice car.

"Are you Ms. Kearney?" one of them, an older gentleman, asked respectfully.

"Yes, I'm Doctor Kearney," she corrected him. It happened all the time and she was used to it.

"Sorry. Of course, I knew that," he apologized. "I'm Walt Whitman, your lawyer, not the writer," he introduced himself and Madison was taken back to Africa, to a time when Doctor Burton had introduced himself in a similar fashion. "Hi, I'm Richard Burton, not to be confused with the famous Richard Burton, but *Doctor* Burton, and I run this little outpost of iniquity."

"Ah yes, Feiock referred you," she answered, holding out her hand.

"This is my associate and another of your attorneys, Lance Buchard," he introduced the other man.

"How do you do?" Deanna murmured as she shook his hand too. She turned to Madison and gestured her forward. "This is my partner, Madison MacGregor," she said proudly and smiled at being able to use that term.

"How do you do, Ms. MacGregor?" Mr. Whitman said cordially as he shook her hand. "I'm very happy to make your acquaintance. You are one of the reasons I am here."

"I am?" she asked, confused.

"Yes, darling. I made a call to my lawyer, Mr. Feiock, and told him what was going on here yesterday with Scott. I asked him to handle it for you," Deanna confessed. She had forgotten the phone call she made first thing that morning to one of her lawyers in Boston. With all the packing they had done that day, she hadn't found time alone with Deanna to tell her, but she had promised to help her so she didn't feel out of line. She turned back to the two lawyers. Judging by their suits, they had cost her over three hundred dollars an hour. She didn't care. "What did you find, gentlemen?" She took Madison's hand in her own and tugged her forward so they were standing side by side for this information.

"Well, Scott has really landed himself in some hot water. Not only breaking your order of protection," he nodded towards Deanna who nodded back, encouraging him to continue, "but he broke four of his five knuckles on your car." He barely concealed a laugh, turning it into a cough before continuing. "He confessed he had been spiking your van's gas tank. Did you notice any problems with it?" he asked.

"He put sugar and water in my gas tank?!" Madison gasped angrily.

The older man nodded sympathetically. "Yes, he thought if you needed him that you might come back to him."

"Why, that rat, I'll..." she began irately.

"Well, ma'am, whatever you decide to do, it's going to have to wait," he interrupted gently.

"Why? What else?" she asked.

"With the violations of his parole and the orders against him, he's going to stay in jail and he will go to prison for a while," he informed her.

Madison gasped, feeling sympathetic towards the man who was the father of her children. Then, remembering his rage, she asked, "Is he on drugs?"

The man shook his head, "Why, I don't know. Was I supposed to ask about that?" he looked at Deanna, wondering if he had screwed up. Kearney Pharmaceuticals was a powerful client. He didn't want to offend.

"No, we didn't think to ask that," Deanna assured him. She saw Mr. Buchard relax behind the older man.

"Well, we got the order of protection. He will not be able to come near you when he gets out...all supervised visits," he handed her some paperwork with her name on it. The judge had granted these fairly quickly after realizing who the firm representing Madison MacGregor was. Plus, with all the violations against the state, it was obvious to him that Scott was unfit as a parent. He had no problem signing off on what they asked. "I would suggest, ma'am, that you get a post office box in Santa Barbara and have all mail routed through there so that he doesn't know where the children are."

Madison was dazed. She realized she hadn't known Scott at all. He'd gotten so violent, so angry. She glanced at the children hanging out the windows of the Rover, unable to hear the adults, and worried about them. Then glancing at Deanna, whose blue eyes were looking at her worriedly, she realized she was safe. Once the house was sold, he wouldn't know where they were. "How long will he be in prison?" she asked.

"Well, for now he's in jail awaiting sentencing, and that will take time. Finally speaking up, Mr. Buchard told her, "They didn't grant him bail. We will, of course, monitor it for you and let you know if we hear anything." He too, knew that Kearney Pharmaceuticals was an important client. And since she was now Doctor Kearney's partner, Madison was important to them too. He wondered if they would handle the prenuptial agreement if it came to that. He glanced between the two women, wondering at their relationship.

"Thank you," she said quietly. She was quite overwhelmed with how respectful they were being to her and how much they had accomplished. She had thought that she and Deanna would go find a lawyer and sign some papers at the courthouse. She thought they would have to wait weeks or even months to find out if she got sole custody. She expected they would have to appear before a judge, get home visits at least. She glanced at Deanna and realized what a powerful woman she was moving in with.

"I thank you, gentlemen, for coming out and telling us in person," Deanna said formally.

"Anytime, Doctor Kearney," Mr. Whitman assured her. "If you need anything else, here is my card," he handed her one from his suit pocket.

"Here is my card, Ms. MacGregor," Mr. Buchard handed Madison one of his. "If you have any questions or need any advice, please feel free to call."

The women thanked them and the two men got back in the Lexus. Deanna looked at Madison and asked, "Are you okay?"

"Whew, that's some customer service," she tried to joke. She also realized that neither of these men had judged them or their relationship. They just took care of business for them. She was strangely relieved.

Deanna smiled. She was used to that kind of service. She knew it was a privilege of wealth, but she didn't utilize the favors it could incur or let that wealth corrupt her in any way. "Are you okay to drive?"

Madison looked up from the embossed card she was caressing. "Yep, I'm ready. I am hating that drive already!" she said in an attempt to cheer up. The news the men had brought her was kind of overwhelming and depressing. She looked at the papers she was holding and reminded herself to put them in her purse so she had them on her at all times.

"We can stay in the house and drive up tomorrow," the blonde offered.

"No, we can't. I have to work tomorrow," Madison reminded her.

"Are you driving down in the morning?" she asked, alarmed that she had forgotten.

"Well, the kids have to finish the next couple of days of school down here until I finish my two weeks' notice. I thought we'd stay here and come up after that," she looked up to see if that was okay with Deanna.

"Gosh, I'd forgotten. I guess I thought with this," she indicated the two packed vehicles, brimming with material wealth, "that we were set. I forgot how fast this all happened."

"Are you okay?" Madison turned the question back on the doctor.

Deanna smiled. "I can get through this…if that drive doesn't kill me first!" she joked. It really wasn't a bad drive, beautiful actually, but the bumper to bumper traffic that frequently came up in that section of Los Angeles was wearying. "Come on, let's get this show on the road!"

They each got in their vehicles. The van took three tries before it started properly. "I thought they fixed this," Madison murmured, annoyed, as she headed out. She wondered if Scott had somehow gotten into the gas tank again and vowed to buy a locking gas cap. The kids had chosen to ride in the Rover again, which really gave them more room in the van to lay the seats flat and pack things in it.

"I thought they fixed that," Deanna murmured thoughtfully, watching Madison try to start the old minivan.

Once Madison pulled out, Deanna put her Rover in gear and followed her to the freeway. Once again they took the 405 north to the 101 west and then north up to Santa Barbara. The traffic wasn't bad until they got on the interchange to the 101. Deanna pulled up alongside Madison and rolled down her window. She yelled, "Hey, lady!" and waited for Madison to roll down her own window. She laughed as the older van had cranks instead of a button to roll the window down. "Hey, lady!" she called once it was down. Deanna smiled. "Going our way?" she asked.

Madison couldn't say what she wanted with the children laughing and looking at her from the Rover. She just laughed, nodded, and held up her thumb as though she were hitchhiking. She heard Deanna turn up the radio and the kids joining in singing some song. She laughed, enjoying their antics. The traffic was so slow they were neck to neck, until a break had Deanna pulling ahead and Madison following her the rest of the way up to Santa Barbara.

"Oh, do we HAVE to empty these?" Madison whined playfully as they pulled up to the house on the hill.

"How about we put it all in the garage and you sort it as you put away?" Deanna asked to be helpful.

"We'd still have to climb those stairs with the boxes and stuff," she answered.

Deanna had stopped in front of the garage. "Follow me," she called and put the Rover in reverse.

Puzzled, Madison followed her as she pulled back down the driveway and up onto the lawn to the front door of the house. She realized what Deanna was doing…avoiding those stairs to the garage. Even one flight of stairs was one flight too many with all the boxes of household items, toys, and the few smaller pieces of furniture they had been able to fit into the two vehicles.

The cat and the dog greeted them all. They had come to some sort of uneasy alliance in the absence of their humans—they weren't growling at each other anymore. As their humans brought in box after box and put them down to be sorted later, they had plenty to sniff and smell over.

It was quite late when they finally all got to sleep. Madison's butt was dragging in the early morning light as she got the kids up and into the van for the drive down to Los Angeles. She promised they could go back to sleep on the drive down and she would buy them McDonalds before school, but only if they cooperated now in getting up and getting dressed.

"You don't have to get up for hours. Stay in bed," she ordered Deanna, who didn't listen to her and got up to see her off.

"You take care of yourself and roll down the windows if you get sleepy!" she advised as she kissed Madison goodbye. She didn't like the forced separation, but there was nothing else they could do as Madison finished her time at work.

CHAPTER THIRTY-EIGHT

Madison walked into the hospital and found it was rife with gossip. She hated it as soon as she heard it. People wanted to know why she was leaving, where she was going, if she had gotten a new job. Mostly they wanted information they could share with others. She didn't say much other than yes, it was true…she had put in her notice and she was leaving. Other than that, she had nothing to say.

"I saw a for sale sign in front of your house?" Beth asked, fishing for information.

"Yes, I put it up for sale the other day," she admitted.

"Where are you moving to?"

"I already moved," she said, distracted, as she finished up some paperwork and moved away.

"But where...?" she began to ask, but Madison had walked away.

In the operating room it wasn't much different. "I hear we are going to lose you here shortly?" Dr. Traff commented as they worked on an appendix.

"Yes, I gave notice," she answered, getting the forceps ready before he could ask for them.

"Forceps," he ordered a moment later and she put them in the palm of his hand with a satisfying thwump.

Questions like that continued, but Madison wouldn't share. Working her time rotation was proving exhausting. She spent her evenings talking to Deanna on the phone. It was odd, the house had so much removed from it that it echoed. During the day, the various realtors took people through, but there was very little left except furniture and some bedding. They had a few clothes to change into, but the majority of things were already up in Santa Barbara at their new home.

"That damn van won't start again," she bitched one night, completely exasperated by the whole thing. "I thought that mechanic said he'd fixed it!"

"Well, he fixed the things he found wrong and he did a tune up, but that doesn't mean he found why it won't start," Deanna pointed out. She too felt ornery. She wanted them to be together and this time apart was already wearing on her.

"Oh, I'm not blaming him. I know Scott did something," she sighed, exasperated, as she leaned back on her bed. "I'll have one of the neighbors jump-start it."

"I wish I could be there to help you," Deanna stated, feeling as though she had let Madison down.

"I wish you were here to jump me too," she said, but her voice had changed to a seductive one.

"You bad girl, you," she laughed.

"Well, you could you know…" she offered.

"Don't start." For some reason, Deanna was reluctant to have phone sex. With the kids there, and knowing the noise echoed, she felt uncomfortable with the idea.

"C'mon, I miss you…" Madison teased.

"You will see me next week," she responded firmly. She was adamant. She wasn't going to have phone sex. She tried to change the subject. "I talked to my mother today."

"Oh, really. How did that go?" They had both spoken about how to tell their mothers about their living arrangements. Madison was avoiding her mother's calls, which had gone from weekly to daily. She justified it by thinking she was too busy…her mother had a knack for calling when she was working anyway. It was too easy to listen to her messages and then delete them from her voice mail. They were all accusing, berating, or downright hostile. Apparently Scott's parents had contacted Madison's. She didn't want to hear it anymore. Her siblings had started in too. She was going to have to fess up soon enough and she wasn't ready for that.

"Well, she knew about you from Africa," she began.

"What? What did you tell her?" She was horrified, thinking how her own mother might react when she found out…and she would find out eventually about her relationship with a woman.

"Remember, she has known I was gay for a long time," she soothed Madison's ruffled feathers.

Madison relaxed. That's right, Deanna had known when she was *much* younger. She always did do things young. "Well, what had you told her?"

"She knew I was in love with you. She actually pointed out that I rarely told people that I loved them, herself included. Roman helped me with that."

"Wait, what?"

Deanna smiled, realizing she was confusing the redhead. Her mind was jumping ahead, talking in shorthand. "Okay, she helped me realize that was probably one of the reasons you didn't stay…that I couldn't express myself back then. When I had Roman, he helped me learn to express my feelings, to say the words aloud easier. I haven't had any problem since then."

"Ahhh. Okay, I get it now. So what did you tell your mother today?"

"I told her I'd met someone. She told me she knew, that I'd been different on our phone calls in the last few months, so she could tell. That is one sharp, old bird," she laughed.

Madison joined in on the laugh. She'd compared her mother to a ruffled wren on more than one occasion.

"Then I told her you were moving in with me. She told me she knew that too. We have an attorney in common, and while he didn't share the particulars of what I called him about, he mentioned that I had a partner now and we were moving in together." She sighed. It seemed that parents knew everything. She spent a lot of time staying ahead of Roman and knew that well. It was only now that she appreciated her own mother and what she had put her through as a child. She'd been so far advanced, that must have been frightening.

"Did you tell her I was the same woman as the one in Africa?" Madison waited with baited breath.

"Yes, and after a few choice words, she asked what had changed. I told her that we'd both grown, we were adults now, and that I loved you dearly."

"What was her response?" Madison asked, hoping it was something good. She wanted to tell her mother too, but she was certain it wouldn't be as good as this story. She could hear the genuine affection Deanna had for her mother in her voice. Her heart warmed at hearing that Deanna loved her dearly, that she could so easily tell her mother these things.

"She congratulated me and then asked when she could meet you. She also wanted to know if we were going to have more children. She wants to meet and probably spoil your two."

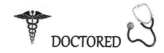

"You already spoil them," Madison smiled. She was almost intimidated by the idea of meeting the mother of this amazing woman she loved so much.

"I haven't yet begun to spoil them," she defended herself. "By the way, the furniture arrived."

"Well, don't set it up until I get there."

"Oh, too late."

"But we wanted to paint, or did you forget?"

"What do you think I did after you left? I had to keep myself busy somehow." She was laughing, but also telling the truth. The house had reeked of fresh paint for days and keeping the animals out of the rooms had been a hassle. She was certain Spot was learning how to turn the latches on doors. It wouldn't surprise her. He was that smart, and he was teaching Fluffy some bad habits. He was also keeping Fluffy in line on some levels. The two of them would probably gang up on their humans when they were all together.

"So the rooms are painted and the furniture is all in?" she asked excitedly. She was looking forward to seeing them.

"Yep, and I found some stickers, but I didn't put them on Chloe's bed, that's her job. Besides, I thought we could shop for some more."

"Isn't Roman getting a bit jealous about all this attention you give them and all the things you are buying for my kids?"

"He's not like that. I think he is the least material kid I have ever known. Maybe it was the few years we spent in the jungle, but he's great," she bragged. "I like him…I'll keep him," she teased.

"That's too funny. Babe, I hate to cut this off, but I'm so tired…" she said as she yawned. These late night chats were so warm and cozy, but she was looking forward to when they could be in person. She wanted to start their life together.

"Yeah, me too. Good night, baby. I love you," she said in a seductive tone.

"Oh sure, start that NOW," she teased and then, "I love you too…Good night."

Neither of them wanted to hang up the phone. It was like being teenagers all over again, although Deanna had never had this. She loved every moment of it. Finally, they both realized they had to work the next day and hung up the phone.

'I got an offer,' Madison texted Deanna excitedly.

'On the house?'

'No, on the kids…lol…yes, silly, on the house.'

'Is it a decent one?'

'I think so. It's five over asking.'

'Maybe you should see if they up the offering?'

Madison laughed at the mistype. Deanna had been doing so much better at texting these days, but still made some funny mistakes. *'Maybe,'* she texted back.

The last two days, Madison was so busy she was unable to take phone calls, especially at work. The delay almost cost her another offer that came in. It was even better than the first one and she accepted, contingent on the first bidders being advised that a counter offer was in the offing. A small bidding war went on while she was finishing her last shift at the hospital. The staff gave her a nice cake and a going away present, and by the time she had finished working her last day at the hospital, she had also sold her house. She was excited. As she turned in her identification and went to leave the hospital for the last time, Bonnie called to her.

"Telephone," she pointed at the blinking line.

"Don't you know? I no longer work here," she called back.

"Is that what you want me to tell them?" She still wondered where Madison was going, but no one had gotten it out of her. The speculation was rampant.

"Yep! Goodbye! Goodbye!" she called to those who saw her leaving. She was so happy she felt like she was floating. Tonight was the last night in her house. The realtor was coming by for her to sign the final papers now that it was sold. She couldn't believe it had sold in a little over two weeks, but apparently the market was hot. She wondered if she would have gotten more if she had held out a little longer, but she was anxious to get out and get home to Deanna. She missed her far too much and only the thought that she would be in her arms tomorrow kept her going. She'd been counting the days and now mere hours separated them.

Once home, she went through the empty cupboards, closets, and checked things for the umpteenth time, looking for things that weren't there anymore, hadn't been there for weeks. She couldn't help but impulsively check again and again, certain she would forget something and leave it behind. But after two weeks, she knew there wasn't anything left. It was all moved out; they had been thorough. She and the children would spend one last night in this tiny house before they moved into the bigger house in Santa Barbara. If they needed to visit Los Angeles and stay over, the Kearney home—the Chateau—would be available to them.

Madison sometimes felt overwhelmed by everything and it hadn't even started yet.

The children were home when she got there and she told them about the sale. They were happy even if they didn't quite comprehend it. They were looking forward to seeing their dog, Dr. D, and Roman…in that order. Even Spot was on their list of things they were looking forward to. They also wanted to try out the pool in their new home. Their needs were a lot simpler than Madison's.

There was a knock on the door and Madison went to let the realtor in. "Hello," he greeted her. "Ready to sign a few hundred times?" he teased.

"Ready and willing. Is it always that frantic?"

"Well, when they bid like that and they want the place that much, yeah," he smiled. No, it didn't happen like that, not often, but he was happy that it had sold so quickly. There were rumors that an altercation happened in this neighborhood not that long ago and the police were called. He didn't want such rumors to hurt his sales of homes in this area. He had her documents all ready for her—a yellow arrow next to where she had to sign, which was removed after every signature was taken care of. He explained what each and every section meant and why she was signing. She'd had an inspection—the inspector went through one day while she was at work—and the buyers had signed off on their own inspection. Everything was in order and the money would be in escrow. Within a few weeks the house would transfer over. "Well, that's it," he said with a smile as the kids started acting up. He was relieved to get out before they interrupted his work. "Thank you very much," he shook her hand, and after a few more words they parted. He put the documents in his briefcase and left.

"Ms. MacGregor?" a voice startled her as she let the realtor out.

"Yes, I'm Ms. MacGregor," she confirmed, wondering who the young man was on her doorstep.

"I have a package for you," he told her. "Would you sign here, please?" He held out a clipboard and pointed at a line.

With a puzzled frown, Madison signed and then he handed her a manila envelope that bulged oddly. "What is this?" she murmured, opening it. Out slid a set of car keys and the title to a vehicle. She looked up at the young man who stood there smiling.

"We parked it right there," he said, pointing to a brand new minivan. "If you want, I can help you transfer your things over to your new van?" he offered.

"What? Transfer…?" she was dazed.

He smiled, hoping she was understanding him. He could see she was stunned. "That van there," he said slowly, "is your new van…and if you wish to dispose of your old van…I can help you transfer your things over.

I also have a check here if you care to sign over the title of your old vehicle to me. A Doctor Kearney," he consulted his clipboard, "arranged it, if you are okay with it?" he asked, worriedly, but he was confident she would be. Who turned down a free minivan?

"Doctor Kearney what?" she asked dumbly as it all began to penetrate and then hit her all at once. Deanna had purchased her a new van! Why that sneaky…she smiled. "Why, yes, you can help me move my things over. And yes, I would like to see that check you have there," she told him. She didn't care how much it was. She would have donated it to a church otherwise and now she didn't have to. Deanna was taking care of her and her family. She turned back into the house. "Kids, come out here," she called.

"What is it?" they both asked as they came to the door.

"Doctor D bought us a new van and we need to move our things over from the old van," she told them excitedly. They immediately caught the excitement and began to run towards the new van to look at it.

Between the delivery guy, the kids, and Madison, they soon had the few things she kept in the van put away in the new one. He checked under the seats, under the mats, in the glove compartment, and even behind the sun visors for anything they might have left. He handed her a check after she handed him a signed registration paper. She was excited about the new van and couldn't wait to call Deanna and share her excitement. Then she got an idea.

"Kids," she called and they came over once they finished climbing over the seats and the backs of everything.

"Fluffy is going to love that thing," Chloe promised.

"So is your mom," Madison teased. "Do you think you can help me move a few pieces of furniture?" she asked.

"Why?" Conor asked.

"I thought if we could move it ourselves, pick up our clothes, and clean out the fridge, we could leave for Santa Barbara tonight and surprise Dr. D and Roman. I kind of miss them."

"Me too," Chloe agreed wholeheartedly.

"Me too," Conor echoed his sister.

Between the three of them they loaded the few pieces that Madison couldn't bear to part with: a table her grandmother had given her, a whatnot that fit in a corner, which she could already imagine in the den of the new house, and a few other pieces. Next they loaded their suitcases and the last of the food and they were packed. She took one more look through the empty cabinets and closets, stripped the beds, and they were ready to go. Madison left her keys on the counter in the kitchen, ready for the new owners. The realtors had keys too so she wouldn't be needing them anymore. She was ready to try out her new van. She plugged her phone into the outlet in the car…how handy and how modern! She hadn't called Deanna yet; she was hoping she was working late so she could surprise her.

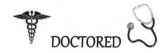

They had just gotten on the 101 heading for Ventura and had hit their first traffic pileup when the phone rang. Thinking it was Deanna, Madison picked it up without looking at the caller I.D. "Hello?" she said in a chirpy voice, feeling good.

"About time you answered that durn thing," her mother's voice came through the line.

Madison nearly groaned aloud. She should have known her mother wouldn't give up trying to reach her.

"Hello, Mother," she said formally.

"Where have you been? I've been trying to reach you. Your brother and sister have tried too! I even called that hospital today and they told me you no longer work there! What is going on out there? Have you lost your mind? Are Scott's parents right that you had him arrested again?"

Madison thought about hanging up, she really did; however, that might not stop her mother. She had to berate her; it was in her nature. She also thought of letting her yell until she lost steam, but neither option was going to work. Her mother expected answers, so Madison waited until she paused long enough to take a breath and then started answering the many questions being thrown at her.

"I've been busy working. I've just come off nearly a two-week stint. I know you've been trying to reach me, I got the phone messages, but I was working and couldn't return the calls…with the time difference it was impossible. Yes, I know they were calling too," she answered, in reference to her siblings. "I just didn't have time to call back. And yes, I quit my job at the hospital. I have a better job in a private clinic. I've sold my house and I'm moving up to Santa Barbara." She knew that would get back to Scott's parents and to Scott himself. She hadn't bothered to contact him—she had attorneys who handled such stuff for her now.

"Is it true what Scott says, that you're involved with some dyke doctor out there?" she asked in a horrified, gossipy manner.

After everything Madison had overcome to escape the gossip at the hospital, the way she had allowed what people thought to imprison her for so long, she wasn't going to let her mother talk that way about anyone…and especially not Deanna. She loved Deanna and wasn't going to stand for it. "How dare you?" she barked back, her voice rising. The kids were using the new headsets that had come with the van and couldn't hear her. They were in the back seat watching a movie that had been on the seat for them. Deanna had thought of everything. A screen flipped down and they were absorbed in watching the DVD.

"Deanna is the most generous woman I have ever met and if you are going to talk that way about her, you and I have NOTHING to say to each other," she threatened.

"Don't you talk to me like that, young lady," she started, trying to keep Madison in her place.

"I'm a middle-aged woman, Mother. When you can talk to me with respect, and realize I am an adult making adult choices, then you can talk to me. Until then, we have nothing to say," she said angrily in return. She refused to be cowed.

"But…but…she's a woman," she gasped.

"She's also a world-respected doctor," she countered with a laugh, knowing her mother might someday grasp that, maybe even brag about it. "I love her, and until you accept that, I want nothing to do with you. I don't wish to be contacted by any of you if that's the attitude you are going to have. Until you talk to me in a tone that isn't accusing or criticizing of me, I don't wish to speak with you or anyone in the family."

"But we're your family…" she began. Her tone was changing. She wasn't used to being spoken to in this manner.

"I made my own family, Mother. You choose to believe Scott's parents rather than hear the truth from your own daughter? Are you aware he attacked me? Are you aware he attacked others? His temper is his downfall and he can no longer see his own children without supervision. He did this…*he did*…not me…and not Doctor Kearney. He is responsible for his own actions and I *refuse* to take the rap for him. I'm raising my children and I refuse to raise him too!"

She was on a roll. Many of these things had built up over the years. She had always been accepting of the status quo, but she wasn't willing to take it anymore.

"I'm an adult. When you and the family learn to accept that, then we can talk. Until then, don't call me again. I'm starting my new life with my new family and your bigotry and attitude aren't welcome!" With that, she hung up the phone. Her heart was beating hard. She could hear her pulse in her ears. She glanced back in the child mirror, attached below the rearview mirror, and saw both kids were still watching the movie. She was glad they weren't aware of the conversation that had just taken place.

She rolled down the window a little, pressing a button instead of using a hand crank. That was a luxury she hadn't expected to ever have. She tried to forget the awful conversation she had just had with her mother and just enjoy her new van. She felt positively decadent in it. The new car smell was prevalent and it was so clean. She was determined to see it stay that way for as long as she could, but with children and a dog it might be hard. She saw in the children's mirror that Conor had put his feet up against her seat. Her arm snaked around behind her and she batted his feet to the floor. He looked up, startled, and sat up so his feet weren't an issue anymore. She wondered if he thought she had eyes in the back of her head since he hadn't noticed the mirror. She laughed to herself.

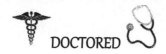

She pressed in the code to their gate. Their gate…that reality felt so odd. She had never lived behind a gate, but this was a nice community they were living in and it felt wonderful as the gate swung slowly open. Deanna told her she had gotten remote openers for the gate and one was waiting for her at the house. She was smiling as she drove up their drive and parked in front of the garage. She looked up at the house, eagerly anticipating seeing Deanna again.

The garage door swung open before she or the kids could get to it.

"Madison," Deanna gasped as she opened her arms and the redhead walked right into them. They hugged, hard, as they rocked there. "You are a sight for sore eyes," she told her as tears streamed out of her blue eyes. She cupped both sides of Madison's face as she kissed her fervently. "I have missed you so much!" she told her.

"I love you! I couldn't wait one more minute," she told her as she hugged her back, hard. "I love you," she whispered against the blonde's lips.

Deanna looked over Madison's shoulder. "You got the van," she said joyfully.

"You sneak, you," Madison teased.

"I told you," she said quietly. "I want to take care of you. We needed a van for all these ruffians," she indicated the two children who were waiting to greet her, and spying Roman, she pulled all three kids in for a group hug. "I missed you guys!" she told them exuberantly.

"Can we use the pool this time?" Conor asked as he squirmed to get away.

"Yes, and you can use anything in our house you want, but you have to ask an adult first so that we know what you are doing, okay?" She got him to promise. "Guess what," she asked as she let them all go, her question directed at Madison's kids.

"What?" they asked together.

"Your bedrooms are ready and waiting for you," she whispered, as though telling them a big secret.

"Really?" Chloe squealed.

"Can we go, Mom?" Conor nearly shouted.

"Go on. We can empty the van tomorrow," she told them, smiling at their exuberance. She had her arm around Deanna and they watched together, smiling, as the three children took off up the stairs.

"What do you have in this van of yours?" Deanna teased her.

"*Our* van has some furniture and some groceries," she told her and leaned in for a kiss, unable to get enough of them. She found such comfort in them. She'd missed her so much.

Deanna hugged Madison so tight to her body she lifted her up, squeezing her mercilessly.

"Wait, wait," she gasped. "I can't breathe."

Deanna laughed exuberantly, turning around and around with Madison in her arms. "Oh, God, I love you! You're here! You're here!" she said excitedly, almost like the three little kids who had just gone inside.

"I couldn't wait any longer…not one more night," she confessed as Deanna lowered her back to the ground to kiss her soundly.

"Come on. Let's get the groceries and go into the house."

Together, they took the few bags of groceries—the last of the things from the kitchen in the house in L.A.—and put them away in their new kitchen. Madison couldn't stop smiling as she bumped into Deanna time and time again in the kitchen, learning where things went. "I hope your housekeeper won't mind me cooking now and then."

Deanna came up behind her, put her arms around her from behind, and nuzzled her ear. "*Our* housekeeper won't mind," she assured her.

"Mmm," the redhead leaned back in her lover's arms. "I'm looking forward to it."

"I'm looking forward to other things," Deanna whispered in her ear. "I found an interesting box," she confessed.

Madison turned around in Deanna's arms. "Did you go through my things?"

"I started to put away your clothes for you, but I stopped after I found that one box. I'm sorry, I didn't mean to…,"

The redhead was embarrassed and the red of her skin clashed horribly with the red of her hair. She looked down, but then was brave enough to look up again. "What did you think of them?" she asked in reference to the adult toys. She looked down again immediately.

"I'm looking forward to experimenting with them," Deanna told her honestly, putting her fingers under Madison's stubborn little chin and raising it for a kiss. They continued until a noise in one of the bedrooms had them pulling apart, panting slightly. "I suppose we should see what they are up to," Deanna said regretfully, wishing at the moment that neither of them had children.

Deanna took Madison's hand and led her to the two bedrooms they had chosen for Chloe and Conor's bedrooms. The rooms looked amazing…perfect pictures of a child's room. This was exactly what Madison had always wanted for them and had never been able to provide. "Oh, the painting looks wonderful," she exclaimed. The furniture was perfect too and the kids were bouncing all over it in Conor's room. "Stop that," she ordered, seeing Conor trying to launch himself off the bunk and Chloe climbing up after him.

"Hey, you heard your mother," Deanna told him, a little more sternly. "We had an agreement if we bought you a bunk bed, remember?" she reminded him.

He had forgotten and nodded. He sat down on the mattress and Chloe returned to the floor.

"I love my bedroom too," she told Deanna. "Mommy, did you see it?"

"Yes, I did and it's lovely. You are going to have to place those stickers carefully," she told her with a smile.

"I've changed my mind. I don't want to ruin the white," the little girl told her now that she had seen her very own bed in her very own bedroom.

Madison was thrilled with that announcement. "What are you going to do with all those stickers?"

"Maybe I'll get a sticker album. I could ask Santa for one for Christmas." They both knew she didn't believe in Santa, but played along anyway.

"That's a good idea, and who knows, your new friends might have ideas about them too," Deanna put in.

"What new friends?" she asked, surprised.

"Aren't you going to make new friends at school?"

"Oh, yeah, I forgot."

Deanna laughed as she put her hand on the young girl's head and pulled her in for a one-handed hug.

"Well, it's late and we had a very long day. Wash up and let's get ready for bed," Madison announced.

"Awww, Mom," Conor complained.

"And you, make that bed. I had the sheets on there and not pulled off the edges," Deanna added.

"That's no fair," Conor complained again.

"What's not fair?"

"You two, ganging up on us!"

Deanna and Madison exchanged a look and started to laugh as they nodded. "Yep, that sounds about right," Madison said as she pointed at the bathroom. "March!" she ordered.

Once the children were tucked into their new beds and Roman was in his 'old' room, the two women snuggled in their own bed. Madison was telling Deanna about her day: from the cake, to signing the papers on the house, to the van showing up and packing up one final time, and finally to her mother's call.

She started crying as she remembered the horrible things her mother had said to her and her own anger over it.

Deanna was thrilled that she had stood up for herself. "Shhh, baby, shhh. It's all right. She'll come around. She won't be able to help herself. She's just surprised and thought she could bully you again. She knows better now. Shhh," she comforted her. She tried to kiss her, but sensed that making love wasn't what Madison was in the mood for. She wanted her so bad, but she was willing to wait. They had the rest of their lives together for that.

Slowly, Madison stopped crying and was able to snuggle into Deanna's arms…because she wanted to…and because she could. "Thank you," she said sleepily, exhausted from the very full day of work and the long drive.

"For what?" Deanna pulled back to ask.

"For everything. For loving me enough to wait for me. For teaching me that I always had this strength in me. For taking care of me," she said gratefully.

"I love you. No thanks are necessary. Always be honest with me, love me, and that is all I will ever need."

Slowly, talking things over and relaxing, they both fell asleep as the cat figured out how to open the latch handle on the door and snuck into the bedroom to join them. The dog soon followed. They woke up, unable to move, with the two animals trying to take over the bed.

"Psst," Deanna woke first and tried to wake Madison. She poked her with her finger. She would have tried with a toe, but there was a cat in the way. "Psst," she called and was rewarded with a sleepy, green eye opening to the bright sunlight.

"Mmmm?" she asked inquiringly.

"We seem to have company," she rasped in a sleepy morning voice.

Madison leaned up and looked down at the animals sprawled on their bed. She looked at Deanna and knew she couldn't be happier. She was home, this was part of her family, and she was happy. This was her happily ever after. It wasn't an ending…it was a beginning. She couldn't wait for it to begin. She leaned over. The dog squeaked as her body leaned on him and she kissed her partner good morning. "I love you."

THE END BEGINNING

If you have enjoyed *DOCTORED* you'll look forward to a sample of K'Anne Meinel's splendid and unforgettable novel:

LAWYERED

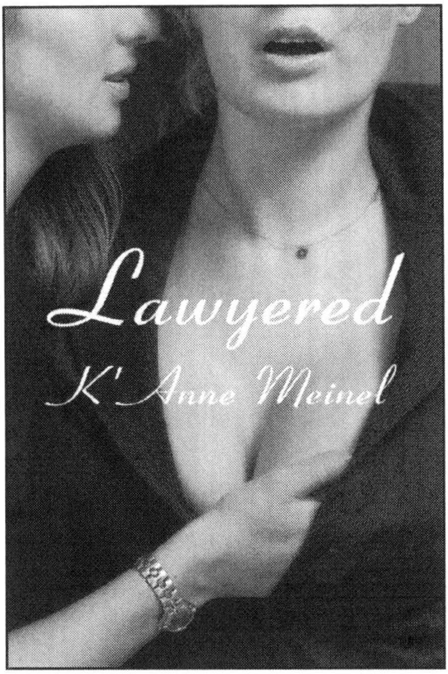

CHAPTER ONE

The view from her window wasn't that impressive as she looked at the dismal aged and gray buildings outside on an equally dismal and gray day in New York, but at least she had a window and a view. Not all associates had a window, most were in inner offices but she was a senior associate, a lawyer of counsel if you will, and it was part of her perks. She looked out her window a long time, lost in thought even though she knew she should be getting to the pile of briefs on her desk. Instead she daydreamed about the incredible offer she had just received. She had known it was coming, she knew she deserved it, but at the moment wasn't sure if she should be insulted.

Nia Toyomoto worked for one of the most prestigious law firms in Manhattan. It wasn't a small thing to be an associate at Chase-Dunham. It wasn't a small thing to be a lawyer of counsel either. To be offered a partnership though was something that Nia had worked towards for years.

Everyone knew she was on the fast track, everyone knew that she deserved it, but at this moment, she wasn't sure. When Stewart Dunham had scheduled this morning's meeting she had assumed it was for a personal update on certain cases that she was handling for him, for others, and with others. Although she had eventually expected the offer, the stipulations had surprised her. She didn't realize her personal life would be part of the offer. Not that she had anything to hide but being a partner at Chase-Dunham required a certain panache that Nia simply didn't have at this time. Stewart had kindly pointed out that they needed her to 'spruce' herself up, to become a bit more social. It was not a matter of her talents as a world class attorney, no, that was *why* they wanted her to be a partner. It was a matter of smoozing with the right people, having parties, attending the elite of the elite. Her reputation was such that she fit in but her appearance left a little to be desired. She was all business. They wanted her as a partner but they also wanted her to use every means at her disposal to get them new clients. Not that she hadn't drawn them in the past with her incredible expertise but being a partner meant that she would represent the firm on levels that she hadn't thus far. Her talents alone wouldn't sell the firm.

Nia sighed. She wasn't one to get ahead on her looks. She was overly tall for the average woman at 5'10" and this for someone of Asian descent was almost unheard of. Not that you could tell she was Asian except for the certain narrowing of her eyes that gave her a feline like appearance. Her father was pure Asian, a former executive from Japan, he had fallen in love with a German-American woman who Nia had inherited most of her looks from. The clunky black glasses she wore hid the slightly exotic Asian tilt of her eyes. Her smooth round face v'd becomingly, but with her straight dark brown nearly black hair with occasional reddish tints that she held severely back in a bun, she gave herself a no nonsense appearance. She had never cared for her looks. She wasn't like other women. Her nails were cut short, purely functional; no polish had ever graced them. Her long legs were encased in nylons and this only because she was fairly pale in appearance and the style was to have a semblance of tan. She had business suits but these too were merely functional. She owned six or seven that she interchanged to provide variety but these were of lessor quality and again, she just hadn't cared. Now they were making her care, in fact making it a condition of her partnership.

The suggestion and not too subtly that her partnership hinged on her doing a makeover, buying better clothes, and a better place to live was ludicrous. But Nia knew that the good ole boy network could find other reasons to deny her this plum chance. She also knew at thirty that she would be one of the youngest partners in Manhattan. She also knew she deserved it. She had worked hard all her life for this very thing.

She had graduated high school in three and a half years and would have graduated in three but for the moron that was the principal at the time thought her too young at sixteen to graduate her junior year. She had to wait until she was seventeen and graduated halfway through her senior year. It wasn't that her grades hadn't warranted an early graduation, no, she had always been effortlessly at the top of her class but this was an age where he felt her social abilities would be hindered by not graduating with her peers. Nia didn't have a lot of friends and those who really knew her knew she was destined for great things. Graduating early would only expedite those goals she had set for herself. Once she graduated from high school she had gone straight to college. Attending Wellesley College, she had sailed through in three years before enrolling in Harvard Law School for her graduate work. If she could have done it in one year she would have but had done it in the normal three years before graduating at the top of her class. An offer from Wall Street and Chase-Dunham had been the culmination of her dream. She'd had other offers of course, many from those she had worked for in summer internships, but Wall Street and Chase-Dunham's reputation was such she knew that was where she wanted to be. For her to be an associate there had guaranteed her future, something she didn't really think about in the broad spectrum of life, instead she wanted very specific things in life and now this partnership was part of that dream.

To hold it up because she wasn't properly garbed or social or looked right for the part angered her but when she thought about it practically she understood. She was perfect for the job and she knew she would eventually capitulate but it didn't set well with her that it was mandated by the men in this firm. Then she thought of how few partners over the years had been women, especially on Wall Street much less in Manhattan.

She thought for a long time about what other goals she had set for herself and realized that at thirty she had achieved most of them. She had gotten into Wellesley on a scholarship and paid for extras through the little her mother sent her after Papa's death. Papa had died after he knew his only child had graduated from high school and his life insurance had paid off their home but left very little for frivolous living, her mother had pinched every penny. Going to an Ivy League School had never been in doubt but paying for it had been. It was expensive to be so highly educated. Nia had taken that seriously. Never had she thought about any other school after Wellesley but Harvard. It had not been a dream but a serious plan that had only been in doubt due to a lack of funds. Nia had graduated in due time with debts so high that they boggled the mind. The job that she had expected from her high grades, internships, and moral standards had come through and she had begun to pay off those debts through her frugalness.

She lived in a studio apartment that was so small she couldn't swing a cat for hitting everything. Her mother had passed away and Nia had sold everything of value including the house that they owned except for nine boxes of 'trinkets,' paying off her student loans and using the little left to buy stocks to help fund her IRA and for security later in life. Her salary was such that she could move to a larger apartment and in fact she had enough now to buy a very nice place but she had no one she wanted to show her postage stamp apartment to, no one really saw it other than one or two close friends, she didn't need a larger one, until now. Her frugal living though would pay off now. She had the funds to do what they wanted and with style but her innate sense of fair play almost balked at the idea of changing her lifestyle, her appearance, her everything for a promotion. It was sexist and discriminatory and they would get away with it unless she refused to play, did she want to give up everything she had worked for to stand on the moral high ground? She could sue, theoretically. What they were asking *was* illegal but did she really want to be known as the lawyer who sued their own firm over her looks? That would certainly create waves in the legal community and also insure that she wouldn't get another job with any other firm in New York, much less Manhattan, *ever*.

A knock on her door had her spinning around in her leather chair and looking up surprised as Stewart Dunham stuck his head in the door. "You busy?" he inquired with a smile. Stewart Dunham was a spare man of fifty five who had inherited the firm of Chase-Dunham through the expedient manner of marrying Elliott Chase's daughter. They had worked together through some lean years and had expanded it exponentially from their partnership. When Elliott Chase had passed away, Stewart Dunham had been one of the first on Wall Street to hire women and bring in clientele that had appreciated his foresight. The people he hired were excellent; he had an eye for talent and had picked Nia Toyomoto himself. She had worked a summer internship up in Boston for a friends firm and he had raved over her insight, her brilliance, and her enthusiasm. He had watched and learned as she participated in the debate team up at Harvard. An Alumni himself, he had availed himself of her records and been suitably impressed. He had romanced her into coming to work with his firm right out of college and had never regretted it. Her work was consistently superior and she deserved every promotion they had ever given her. His other partners had been worried that they were giving the youngster too much too soon but he knew she could handle it. She had been only twenty three when she graduated Harvard but had within one year won them an impossible case. The lawyer of record had to drop out at the last minute for cause and she had picked up the slack despite her lack of experience and with very little supervision had won and the senior partners had been suitably impressed. Her record since then had been equally impressive. If she just didn't look so...frumpy. From her horn rimmed square glasses to her unattractive and severe bun of hair she screamed 'old maid' and he knew some of the clients wouldn't want to work with a partner that made them feel like she was their grandmother. He had often wondered if she were a dyke but she gave no appearance of that either. She didn't date men, she didn't date women, she didn't date that he knew of. She was kind of uni-sex and that didn't set well with the partners. Many insisted that if she represented the firm she needed to take advantage of her feminity and had complained about her lack thereof for years, now they insisted on this change or no, they didn't want her as a partner.

She smiled kindly and this changed her austere appearance, without really answering the CEO of Chase-Dunham she asked instead, "What can I do for you Mr. Dunham?"

"Would you come with me for a moment?" he gestured outside her office.

Nia rose up and walked immediately over to her small office door. Stewart held the door for her and she walked out before him. He indicated the elevator and she assumed they were going up to the Senior Partner's level to the private offices of the CEO which were on a floor above the associates and counselor levels. They stood as equals as they waited for the elevator. Nia's own height was only an inch or two below Stewarts. He thought she would be even more impressive once she realized her full potential, it had to be her decision though, and she could still turn them down, although they both knew she would be foolish to do so. Stewart was risking, big time, that she wouldn't take offense to what they had shoved down her throat in their offer. Instead he hoped, and gambled, that she would grasp it with both hands and prove the nay-sayers wrong, very wrong. He had always seen the potential of this woman from her days at Harvard, he still saw potential, if his daughters had shown any inkling of the talent of this young woman he would like to think they would be as good as she. His son had gone in a totally different direction and become an accountant. He had been very disappointed but survived the blow to his ego.

Stewart led, not to the CEO offices but to a corner office at the opposite end of the building. Nia hadn't really been to these offices since she had very little business with some of these partners and almost none with the senior partners except when they needed a consult on a case they were handling. They walked into a nice little office that would suit any executive secretary or assistant as people now called them. Through this empty and rather plain office they walked into an immense corner office that had not one but two banks of floor to ceiling windows. The room was absolutely bare of furniture. Stewart led her to the windows and they stood looking out at the impressive Manhattan skyline as Nia wondered why she had been brought here. They hadn't spoken the entire ride up in the elevator or really since they had left her office.

"I thought perhaps you might need a little something to make the offer even more worthwhile," Stewart began.

"Mr. Dunham, I assure you..." Nia began but stopped when he held up his hand.

"Please, if you accept this position you will have to begin calling me Stewart. This isn't a standard partner agreement we have offered you, Nia. This office is just one of the perks. You will have to choose a car that we will pay for. You will have to choose an apartment that we will make sure your mortgage is handled through our banking contacts and the payments reasonable. You will have six weeks paid vacation. The perks you might pass up from refusing are more than you realize."

Nia looked at him incredulously. They hadn't even discussed the perks of her partnership agreement. This office? It was incredible. She glanced around and for some reason the sun began to shine through the impressive windows. She could already picture the office with deep cherry wood furniture making it a warm and professional one. She could even put in an electric fireplace she thought barely controlling the grin that threatened at her thought. A car? What was wrong with her little Fiat? She realized though that she would be a fool to pass it up but she had played her cards too well for too long to show them to this master player. She nodded coldly as she considered her options which she really knew were few. She could quit but that would be self-defeating, besides she loved her job. She could refuse and remain an associate but it would never be the same, they would treat her as though she had insulted them. She could sue but then she would never again work in Manhattan and who wanted to hang out their own shingle with *that* on their resume? She could accept and have a make-over. She needed to think about it but she had already told this man and his partner's that very thing when they made their initial offer.

"Here is one more thing for you to think about," Stewart finished with. Nia looked at him expectantly. "We are waiving your buy in, your bonus' will be deferred for the first three years but you do not have to come up with the normal buy in amount. Based on your performance and what we anticipate you bringing into the firm in the future we have decided that this will be enough for your buy in."

Nia was incredulous, this offer, this incredible deal was worth possibly a million dollars or more!

~End Sample~

About the Author

K'Anne Meinel is the BEST SELLING author of LAWYERED, REPRESENTED, and SAPPHIC SURFER as well as several other books including her first SHIPS which was written in 2003 over the course of two weeks. She then played with it for several years before publishing it as an e-book and then was approached to publish it in book form. After that it was published on other sites as an e-book. In the meantime, she published some 50 short stories, novellas, and novels of various genres. Originally from Wisconsin many of her stories have taken on locations from and around the state. A gypsy at heart she has lived in many locations and plans to continue doing that. Videos of several of her books are available on You Tube outlining some of the locations of her books and telling a little bit more…giving the readers insight into her mind as she created these wonderful stories.

~ *Because a publisher should stand behind their authors*~

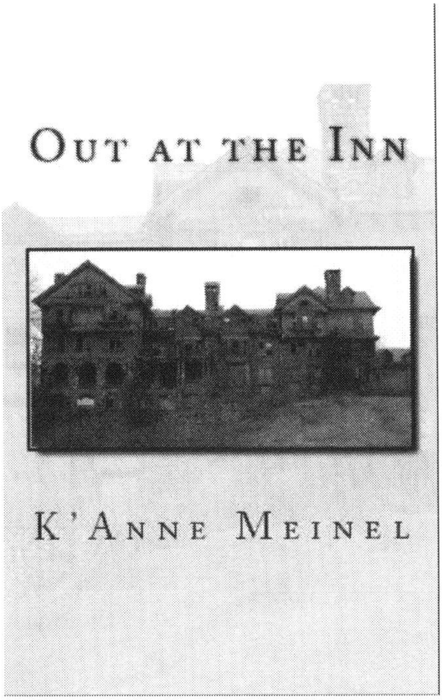

Among the majestic shoreline of the Central Coast of California lies a secret…Leah Van Heusen finds a hidden staircase….

The ancient house she finds among the overgrown foliage is amazing…and eerie, most wouldn't even step a foot closer, but she is intrigued and feels drawn to the old mansion….

Leah finds more than she bargains for after seeking out the owner and purchasing the entire estate for a dollar. As she starts to restore it, she finds out who her real friends are, she also finds out who her family really is…What's a few ghosts between friends?

Between repairs, upgrades, and finding out the houses secrets, Leah has her hands full. Finding out her sexuality and dating is the least of her worries. As her beloved dream of an Inn becomes reality she finds it suddenly in jeopardy, who will kill for it or the immense fortune that she has found?

www.shadoepublishing.com

Shadoe Publishing ~ *Because a publisher should stand behind their authors*~

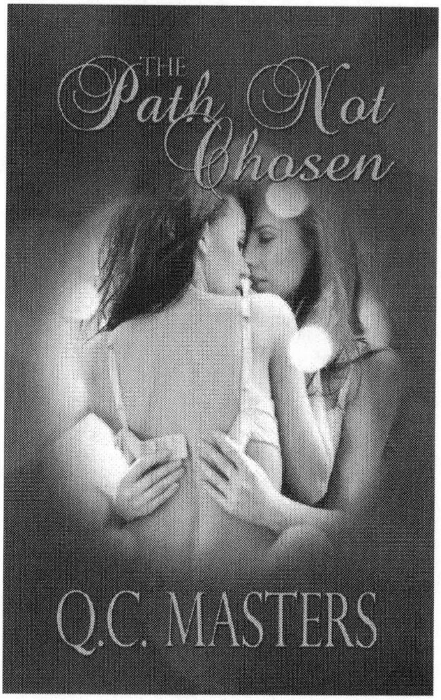

What do you do when you meet someone who changes everything you know about love and passion?

Paige Harlow is a good girl. She's always known where she was going in life: top grades, an ivy league school, a medical degree, regular church attendance, and a happy marriage to a man. So falling in love with her gorgeous roommate and best friend Alyssa Torres is no small crisis. Alyssa is chasing demons of her own, a medical condition that makes her an outcast and a family dysfunctional to the point of disintegration make her a questionable choice for any stable relationship. But Paige's heart is no longer her own. She must now battle the prejudices of her family, friends, and church and come to peace with her new sexuality before she can hope to win the affections of the woman of her dreams. But will love be enough?

www.shadoepublishing.com

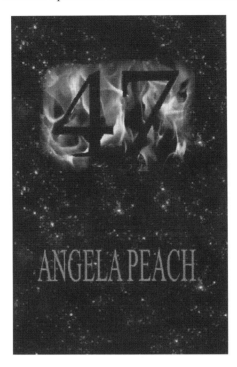

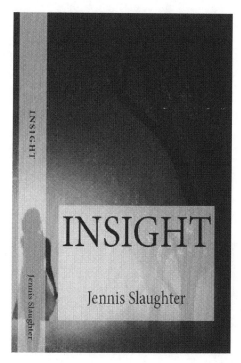

~ *Because a publisher should stand behind their authors*~

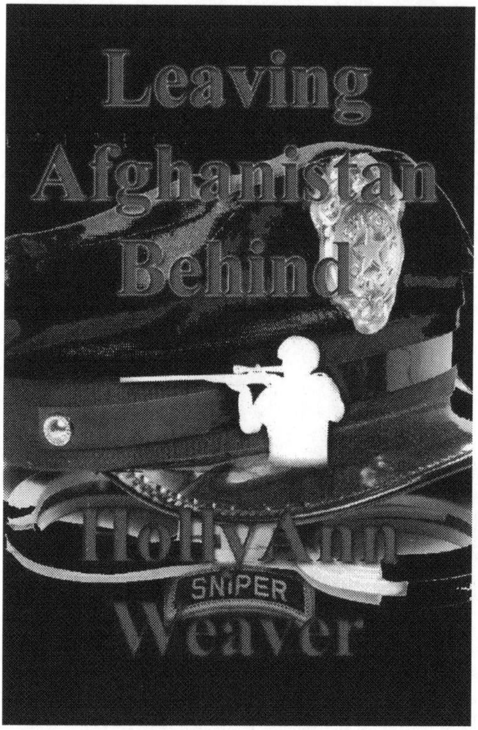

Amelia Gittens had the credit of being the first and only woman thus far in the United States military of being a sniper in combat, made possible by being in the Military Police unit of the crack 10th Mountain Infantry Division. After retirement she joins the City of New York Police Department, and suddenly finds herself involved in a suspect shooting incident which soon encroaches upon her entire life. In order to protect her therapist who has been targeted as a revenge killing, Amelia takes on the responsibility as if she was still in the Army, treating it as a tactical maneuver.

www.shadoepublishing.com

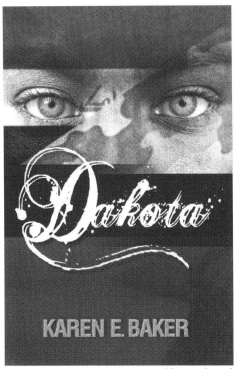

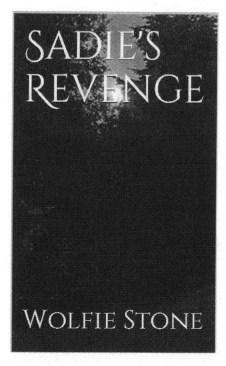

56703519R10177

Made in the USA
Charleston, SC
26 May 2016